Martin Conisby's Vengeance

MARTIN CONISBY'S
VENGEANCE

MARTIN CONISBY'
VENGEANCE

BY
'JEFFERY FARNOL

BOSTON
LITTLE, BROWN, AND COMPANY
1921

TO
MY DEAR AUNTS

MRS. MARRIOTT
AND
MISS JEFFERY
"AUNTIE KIE"

I DEDICATE THIS BOOK

CONTENTS

v

Contents

MARTIN CONISBY'S VENGEANCE

CHAPTER I

How My Solitude Came to an End

"Justice, O God, upon mine enemy. For the pain I suffer, may I see him suffer; for the anguish that is mine, so may I watch his agony! Thou art a just God, so, God of Justice, give to me vengeance!"

And having spoken this, which had been my prayer for three weary years, I composed myself to slumber. But even so, I started up broad awake and my every nerve a-tingle, only to see the moonlight flooding my solitude and nought to hear save the rustle of the soft night wind beyond the open door of the cave that was my habitation and the far-off, never-ceasing murmur that was the voice of those great waters that hemmed me in,—a desolate ocean where no ships ever sailed, a trackless waste that stretched away to the infinite blue.

Crouched upon my bed I fell vaguely a-wondering what should have roused me, hearkening to the distant roar of the surf that seemed to me now plaintive and despairing, now full of an ominous menace that banished gentle sleep.

Thereupon I must needs bethink me how often I had waked thus during my long and weary sojourn on this lonely island; how many times I had leapt from slumber, fancying I heard a sound of oars or voices hailing cheerily beyond the reef, or again (and this most often and bitterest phantasy of all) a voice, soft and low yet with a wondrous sweet and vital ring, the which as I knew must needs sound within my dreams henceforth,—a voice out of the past that called upon my name:

"Martin—Oh, Martin!"

And this a voice that came to me in the blazing heat of tropic day, in the cool of eve, in the calm serenity of night, a voice calling, calling infinite pitiful and sweet, yet mocking me with my loneliness.

"Martin, dear love! Oh, Martin!"

"Joan!" I whispered and reached out yearning arms to the empty air. "Damaris—beloved!"

Beyond the open door I heard the sighing of the wind and the roar of the surf, soft with distance, infinite plaintive and despairing. Then, because sleep was not for me, I arose and came groping within my inner cave where stood a coffer and, lifting the lid, drew forth that I sought and went and sat me on my bed where the moon made a glory. And sitting there, I unfolded this my treasure that was no more than a woman's gown and fell to smoothing its folds with reverent hand; very tattered it was and worn by much hard usage, its bravery all tarnished and faded, yet for me it seemed yet to compass something of the vivid grace and beauty of that loved and vanished presence.

Almost three years of solitude, of deluding hopes and black despair, almost three years, forgotten alike of God and man. So that I had surely run mad but for the labour of my days and the secret hope I cherished even yet that some day (soon or late) I should see again that loved form, hear again the sweet, vital ring of that voice whereof I had dreamed so long.

Almost three years, forgotten alike of God and man.

And so albeit I prayed no more (since I had proved prayers vain) hope yet lived within me and every day, night and morn, I would climb that high hill the which I had named the Hill of Blessed Hope, to strain my eyes across the desolation of waters for some sign which should tell me my time of waiting was accomplished.

Now as I sat thus, lost in bitter thought, I rose to my feet, letting fall the gown to lie all neglected, for borne to me on the gentle wind came a sound there was no mistaking, the sharp report of a musket.

For a moment I stood utterly still while the shot yet rang and re-echoed in my ears and felt all at once such an ecstasy of joy that I came nigh swooning and needs must prop myself against the rocky wall; then, the faintness passing, I came hasting and breathless where I might look seaward and beheld this:

Hard beyond the reef (her yards braced slovenly aback) a ship. Betwixt this vessel and the reef a boat rowed furiously, and upon the reef itself a man fled shorewards marvellous fleet and nimble. Presently from his pursuers in the boat came a red flash and the report of a musquetoon followed by divers others, whereat the poor fugitive sped but the faster and came running to that strip of white beach that beareth the name Deliverance. There he faltered, pausing a moment to glance wildly this way and that, then (as Fortune willed) turned and sped my way. Then I, standing forth where he might behold me in the moon's radiance, hailed and beckoned him, at the which he checked again, then (as reassured by my looks and gesture) came leaping up that path which led from the beach. Thus as he drew nearer I saw he was very young, indeed a mere stripling. From him I glanced towards his pursuers (they being already upon the reef) and counted nine of them running hitherward and the moon aglint on the weapons they bore. Thereupon I hasted to my cave and brought thence my six muskets, the which I laid ready to hand.

And presently comes this poor fugitive, all panting and distressed with his exertions, and who (clambering over that rampire I had builded long ago to my defence) fell at my feet and lay there speechless, drawing his breath in great, sobbing gasps. But his pursuers had seen and came on amain with mighty halloo, and though (judging by what I could see of them at the distance) they were a wild, unlovely company, yet to me, so long bereft of all human fellowship, their hoarse shouts and cries were infinitely welcome and I determined to make them the means of my release, more especially as it seemed by their speech that some of them were Englishmen. To this end I waited until they were close, then, taking up my nearest piece, I levelled wide of them and fired. Startled by the sudden roar they incontinent scattered, betaking them to such cover as they might. Then I (yet kneeling behind my rampire) hailed them in mighty kindly fashion.

"Halt, friends!" cries I. "Here is harm for no man that meaneth none. Nay, rather do I give ye joyous welcome in especial such of you as be English, for I am an Englishman and very solitary."

But now (and even as I spake them thus gently) I espied the fugitive on his knees, saw him whip up one of my muskets (all in a moment) and fire or ever I might stay him. The shot was answered by a cry and out from the underbrush a man reeled, clasping his hurt and so fell and lay a-groaning. At this his comrades let fly their shot in answer and made off forthwith. Deserted thus, the wounded man scrambled to hands and knees and began to creep painfully after his fellows, beseeching their aid and cursing them by turns. Hearing a shrill laugh, I turned to see the fugitive reach for and level another of my weapons at this wounded wretch, but, leaping on him as he gave fire,

I knocked up the muzzle of the piece so that the bullet soared harmlessly into the air. Uttering a strange, passionate cry, the fugitive sprang back and snatching out an evil-looking knife, made at me, and all so incredibly quick that it was all I could do to parry the blow; then, or ever he might strike again, I caught that murderous arm, and, for all his slenderness and seeming youth, a mighty desperate tussle we made of it ere I contrived to twist the weapon from his grasp and fling him panting to the sward, where I pinned him beneath my foot. Then as I reached for the knife where it had fallen, he cried out to me in his shrill, strangely clear voice, and with sudden, fierce hands wrenched apart the laces and fine linens at his breast:

"Stay!" cried he. "Don't kill me—you cannot!"

Now looking down on him where he lay gasping and writhing beneath my foot, I started back all in a moment, back until I was stayed by the rampire, for I saw that here was no man but a young and comely woman.

CHAPTER II

My Troubles Begin

Whiles I yet stood, knife in hand, staring at her and mute for wonder, she pulled off the close-fitting seaman's bonnet she wore and scowling up at me shook down the abundant tresses of her hair.

"Beast!" said she. "Oh, beast—you hurt me!"

"Who are you?" I questioned.

"One that doth hate you!" Here she took a silver comb from her pocket and fell to smoothing her hair; and as she sat thus cross-legged upon the grass, I saw that the snowy linen at throat and bosom was spotted with great gouts of blood.

"Are ye wounded?" quoth I, pointing to these ugly stains.

"Bah! 'Tis none of mine, fool! 'Tis the blood of Cestiforo!"

"Who is he?"

"The captain of yon ship."

"How cometh his blood on you?"

" 'Twas when I killed him."

"You—killed him?"

"Aye—he wearied me. So do all my lovers, soon or late."

Now as I looked on this woman, the strange, sullen beauty of her (despite her masculine apparel) as she sat thus combing her long hair and foul with a dead man's blood, I bethought me of the wild tales I had heard of female dæmons, succubi and the like, so that I felt my flesh chill and therewith a great disgust and loathing of her, insomuch that, not abiding the sight of her, I turned away and thus beheld a thing the which filled me with sudden, great dismay: for there, her sails spread to the fitful wind, I saw the ship standing out to sea, bearing with her all my hopes of escape from this hated island. Thus stood I, watching deliverance fade on my sight, until the ship was no more than a speck upon the moon-bright waters and all other thoughts 'whelmed and lost in raging despair. And now I was roused by a question sudden and imperious:

"Who are you?"

" 'Tis no matter."

"How came you here?"

" 'Tis no matter for that, either."

"Are you alone?"

"Aye!"

"Then wherefore trouble to shave your beard?"

" 'Tis a whim."

"Are you alone?"

"I was."

"And I would you were again."

"So do I."

"You are Englishman—yes?"

"I am."

"My mother was English—a poor thing that spent her days weeping and died of her tears when I was small—ah, very small, on this island."

"Here?" quoth I, staring.

"Twenty and one years agone!" said she, combing away at her glossy hair. "My mother was English like you, but my father was a noble gentleman of Spain and Governor of Santa Catalina, Don Esteban da Silva y Montreale, and killed by Tressady—Black Tressady——"

"What, Roger Tressady—o' the Hook?"

"True, Señor Englishman," said she softly and

glancing up at me through her hair; "he hath a hook
very sharp and bright, in place of his left hand. You
know him? He is your friend—yes?"

"I know him for a cursed pirate and murderer!"

"*Moi aussi, mon ami!*" said she, fixing me with her
great eyes. "I am pirate, yes—and have used dagger
and pistol ere to-day and shall again."

"And wear a woman's shape!"

"Ha—yes, yes!" cried she, gnashing her teeth.
"And there's my curse—I am woman and therefore do
hate all women. But my soul is a man's so do I use
all men to my purpose, snare them by my woman's arts
and make of 'em my slaves. See you; there is none
of all my lovers but doth obey me, and so do I rule,
with ships and men at my command and fearing no
man——"

"And yet," said I, interrupting, "you came fleeing
hither to save your life from yonder rabblement."

"Tush—these were mostly drunken rogues that knew
me not, 'listed but late from a prize we took and burned.
I shall watch them die yet! Soon shall come Belvedere
in the *Happy Despatch* to my relief, or Rodriquez of
the *Vengeance* or Rory or Sol—one or other or all shall
come a-seeking me, soon or late. Meantime, I bide
here and 'tis well you stayed me from killing you, for
though I love not Englishmen, I love solitude less,
so are you safe from me so long as we be solitary.
Ah—you smile because you are fool and know me not
yet! Ah, ah—mayhap you shall grow wiser anon.
But now," said she, rising and putting away her comb,
"bring me where I may eat, for I am famished with
hunger."

"Also you are very foul of blood!" said I.

"Yes," says she soft-voiced, and glancing from me
to her stained finery and back again. "Yes. And is
this so great a matter?"

"To-night you murdered a man!"

"I killed him—yes. Cestiforo—he was drunk. And was this so great a matter?"

"And you—a woman!" said I, marvelling.

"Aye, to my sorrow!" said she, gnashing white teeth. "Yet am I strong as a man and bolder than most."

"God preserve me from such!" quoth I fervently.

"You—you?" cried she. "What thing are you that seeming man must blench at a little blood? Are you yourself so innocent, you that know Tressady o' the Hook?"

"Howbeit I am no murderer, woman."

"Ah—bah!" cried she, with flick of scornful fingers. "Enough of words, Master Innocent. Bring me where I may eat and bed me till morning."

Thereupon (and mighty unwilling) I brought her into the cave and lighting two candles of my own contriving, I set before her such viands as I had, together with bread I had newly baked, and with no word of thanks this strange, fierce creature fell to eating with a voracity methought very disgusting.

Now the more I saw of her the more grew my disgust and the end of it was I determined to put the whole length of the island betwixt us and that at once. To this end I began collecting such articles as I should want, as my light hatchet, sword, pistols, etc. I was buckling on my belt when her voice arrested me, albeit she spoke me very sweetly and soft:

"You go now to your woman—your light of love—yes?"

"There is no woman but yourself," said I, frowning.

"Liar! Then what of this?" and she pointed slender finger; then I saw that tattered garment lying where I had dropped it and this woman spurning it with her foot. So I stooped forthwith, and snatching it from her desecrating touch, folded it across my arm, whereat she fell to sudden laughter very ill to bear.

"Ah—ah!" said she, softer than before and most hatefully a-smiling, " 'tis for her sake your chin goeth bare and smooth—yes? She is over-nice in the matter of——"

"I tell you she is gone!" said I in fury.

"Gone—gone, is she? And you alone here, longing but for her return, through weeks and months and years waiting for her to come back to you; is not this the truth of it, yes?" Now I, knowing this for very truth, could but scowl, finding no word to say, whiles this creature nodded and flashed white teeth in her hateful smile. "You loved this woman," said she, "do love her; dead or living, rotting bones or another's delight, you do love her yet, poor, miserable fool!"

All unheeding, I folded the garment with reverent hands while she taunted me thus, until, seeing me nothing moved, she fell to rank vileness, bespattering that pure memory with tongue so shamelessly foul that I (losing all patience) turned on her at last; but in this moment she was on her feet and snatching my sword made therewith a furious pass at me, the which I contrived to parry and, catching the blade in this beloved garment, I wrenched the weapon from her. Then, pinning her in fierce grip and despite her furious struggles and writhing, I belaboured her soundly with the flat of the blade, she meanwhile swearing and cursing at me in Spanish and English as vilely as ever I had done in all my days, until her voice broke and she choked upon a great sob. Thereupon I flung her across my bed and taking such things as I needed, strode out of the cave and so left her.

But scarce was I without the cave than she came following after me; and truly never was greater change, for in place of snarling dæmon here was tender maid all tearful sighs, gentle-eyed and with clasped hands reached out to me in supplication and (despite her male attire) all woman.

Perceiving the which, I turned my back upon her and hasted away all the faster.

So here was I, that had grieved in my solitude and yearned amain for human fellowship, heartily wishing myself alone again and full of a new apprehension, viz: That my island being so small I might chance to find the avoidance of this evil creature a matter of some difficulty, even though I abandoned my caves and furniture to her use and sought me another habitation.

Now as I went I fell to uneasy speculation regarding this woman, her fierce, wild beauty, her shameless tongue, her proud and passionate temper, her reckless furies; and bethinking me of all the manifest evil of her, I felt again that chill of the flesh, that indefinable disgust, insomuch that (the moon being bright and full) I must glance back, more than once, half-dreading to see her creeping on my heels.

Having traversed Deliverance Sands I came into that cleft or defile, 'twixt bush-girt, steepy cliffs, called Skeleton Cove, where I had builded me a forge with bellows of goatskin. Here, too, I had set up an anvil (the which had come ashore in a wreck, together with divers other tools) and a bench for my carpentry. The roof of this smithy backed upon a cavern wherein I stored my tools, timber and various odds and ends.

This place, then, I determined should be my habitation henceforth, there being a little rill of sweet water adjacent and the cave itself dry and roomy and so shut in by precipitous cliffs that any who might come to my disturbance must come only in the one direction.

And now, as I judged, there being yet some hours to sunrise, I made myself as comfortable as might be and having laid by sword and belt and set my pistols within easy reach, I laid down and composed myself to slumber. But this I could by no means compass,

being fretted of distressful thought and made vain and
bitter repining for this ship that had come and sailed,
leaving me a captive still, prisoned on this hateful
island with this wild creature that methought more
dæmon than woman. And seeing myself thus mocked
of Fortune (in my blind folly) I fell to reviling the
God that made me. Howbeit sleep overtook me at
last, but an evil slumber haunted by visions of this
woman, her beauty fouled and bloody, who sought out
my destruction where I lay powerless to resist her will.
Low she bent above me, her dusky hair a cloud that
choked me, and through this cloud the glitter of her
eyes, red lips that curled back from snapping teeth,
fingers clawed to rend and tear; then as I gazed in
horror, these eyes grew soft and languorous, these
vivid lips trembled to wistful smile, these cruel hands
clasped, soft-clinging, and drew me near and ever
nearer towards that smiling, tender mouth, until I
waked in a panic to behold the dawn and against the
sun's growing splendour the woman standing and holding my pistols levelled at me as I lay.

Now I do think there is no hale man, howsoever
desperate and careless of life, but who, faced with sudden, violent death, will not of instinct blench and find
himself mighty unready to take the leap into that dark
unknown whose dread doth fright us one and all; howbeit thus was it with me, for now as I stared from the
pistol muzzle to the merciless eyes behind them, I, that
had hitherto esteemed death no hardship, lay there in
dumb and sweating panic, and, knowing myself afraid,
scorned and hated myself therefor.

"Ah—ah!" said she softly but with flash of white
teeth. "Will ye cower then, you beater of women?
Down to your knees—down and sue pardon of me!"
But now, stung by her words and the quaking of my
coward flesh, I found voice.

"Shoot, wanton!" said I. "Shoot, lest I beat you

again for the vile, shameless thing you are." At this she flinched and her fierce eyes wavered; then she laughed loud and shrill:

"Will ye die then? Yes? Will ye die?"

"Aye," I nodded. "So I may be quit of you."

"Hath dying then no fears for you—no?"

" 'Tis overpast!" quoth I.

"Liar!" said she. "Wipe the craven sweat from you! You beat me, and for this you should die, but though you fear death you shall live to fear me more.—aye, you shall live awhile—take your life!"

So saying, she tossed the pistols down beside me and laughed.

"When I wish to kill and be done with you, my steel shall take you in your sleep, or you shall die by poison; there be many roots and berries hereabout, Indian poisons I wot of. So your life is mine to take whensoever I will."

"How if I kill you first?"

"Ah, bah!" said she, snapping her fingers. "Try an you will—but I know men and you are not the killing sort. I've faced death too oft to fear it, or the likes of you. There lie your pistols, fool; take 'em and shoot me if you will!"

Thereupon I stooped and catching up the pistols tossed them behind me.

"And now," said I, rising, "leave me—begone lest I thrash you again for the evil child you are."

"Child?" says she, staring as one vastly amazed, "child—and to me, fool, to me? All along the Main my name is known and feared."

"So now will I whip you," quoth I, "had others done as much ere this, you had been a little less evil, perchance." And I reached down a coil of small cord where it hung with divers other odds and ends. For a moment she watched me, scowling and fierce-eyed, then as I approached her with the cords in my hands, she turned on her heel with a swirl of her embroidered coat-skirts and strode away, mighty proud and disdainful.

When she was clean gone I gathered me brush and driftwood, and striking flint and steel soon had a fire going and set about cooking certain strips of dried goat's flesh for my breakfast. · Whiles this was a-doing I was startled by a sudden clatter upon the cliff above and down comes a great boulder, narrowly missing me but scattering my breakfast and the embers of my fire broadcast. I was yet surveying the ruin (dolefully enough, for I was mighty hungry) when hearing a shrill laugh I glanced up to find her peering down at me from above. Meeting my frowning look she laughed again, and snapping her fingers at me, vanished 'mid the bushes.

Spoiled thus of my breakfast I was necessitated to stay my hunger with such viands as I had by me. Now as I sat eating thus and in very ill humour, my wandering gaze lighted by chance on the shattered remains of a boat that lay high and dry where the last great storm had cast it. At one time I had hoped that I might make this a means to escape from the island and had laboured to repair and make it seaworthy but, finding this beyond my skill, had abandoned the attempt; for indeed (as I say) it was wofully bilged and broken. Moreover, at the back of my mind had always lurked a vague hope that some day, soon or late, she that was ever in my dreams, she that had been my love, my Damaris, might yet in her sweet mercy come a-seeking me. Wherefore, as I have before told, it had become my daily custom, morn and eve, to climb that high land that I called the Hill of Blessed Hope, that I might watch for my lady's coming.

But to-day, since Fate had set me in company with this evil creature, instead of my noble lady, I came to a sudden and fixed resolution, viz: That I would

waste not another hour in vain dreams and idle expectations but would use all my wit and every endeavour to get quit of the island so soon as might be.
Filled with this determination I rose and, coming to
the boat, began to examine it.

And I saw this: it was very stout-built but its planks
wofully shrunk with the sun, and though much stove
forward, more especially to larboard, yet its main timbers looked sound enough. Then, too, it lay none so
far from high-water mark and despite its size and
bulk I thought that by digging a channel I might
bring water sufficient to float it, could I but make good
the breakage and caulk the gaping seams.

The longer I looked the more hopeful I grew and
the end of it was I hasted to bring such tools as I
needed and forthwith set to work. All the morning,
and despite the sun, I laboured upon this wrecked boat,
stripping off her cracked and splintered timbers and
mightily pleased to find her framework so much less
damaged than I had dared hope, insomuch that I presently fell a-whistling; but coming on three ribs badly
sprung I became immediately dejected. Howbeit I
had all the wood I could wish as planks, bulkheads and
the like, all driven ashore from wrecked vessels, with
bolts and nuts a-plenty; thus as I worked I presently
fell a-whistling again.

Suddenly, I was aware of the woman watching me,
and glancing at her as she leaned cross-legged against
an adjacent boulder, she seemed no woman but a pert
and handsome lad rather. Her thick hair, very dark
and glossy, fell in curls to her shoulders like a modish
wig, her coat was of fine blue velvet adorned with silver
lace, her cravat and ruffles looked new-washed like her
silk stockings, and on her slender feet were a pair of
dainty, buckled shoes; all this I noticed as she lolled,
watching me with her sombre gaze.

"What would you with the wreck, fool?" she demanded, whereupon I immediately betook me to my whistling.

"You do grow merry!" said she, frowning, whiles I whistled the louder.   And when she would have spoken further, I fell to hammering lustily, drowning her voice thereby.

"Will you not speak with me then—no?" she questioned, when at last I paused.   But I heeding her no whit, she began swearing at me and I to hammering again.

"Curst fool!" cried she at last, "I spit on you!" The which she did and so swaggered away and I whistling merrier than ever.

CHAPTER III

How I Heard a Song That I Knew

I was early at work next morning, since now my mind was firm-set on quitting the island at all hazards, thereby winning free of this woman once and for all. To this end I laboured heartily, sparing myself no pains and heedless of sweat and sun-glare, very joyous to see my work go forward apace; and ere the sun was very high my boat lay stripped of all the splintered timbers on the larboard side. My next care was to choose me such planks from my store of driftwood as by reason of shape and thickness should be best adapted to my purpose. And great plenty of wrought wood had I and of all sorts, it having long been my wont to collect the best of such as drove ashore and store it within those caves that opened on Deliverance Beach. Thus, after no great search, I had discovered all such planking as I needed and forthwith began to convey it down to the boat.

In the which labour the woman met me (I staggering under a load of my planks) and strutted along beside me, vastly supercilious and sneering.

"Hold!" cried she. "He sweateth, he panteth purple o' the gills! And wherefore, to what end?"

"To win free of two things do weary me."

"Ah—ah? And these?"

"This island and yourself."

"So! Do I then weary you, good Master Innocence?"

"Mightily!"

"Ah—bah! 'Tis because you be fool and no man!"

"Mayhap," said I, taking up my hammer, "howbeit I do know this island for a prison and you for an evil thing——"

"Ah!" sighed she softly. "I have had men hanged for saying less!"

"So would I be quit of you as soon as may be," said I, fitting my first timber in place whiles she watched me, mighty disdainful.

"So you would mend the boat, *amigo mio*, and sail away from the island and me—yes?"

"God knoweth it!"

"Mayhap He doth, but what o' me? Think ye I shall suffer you to leave me here alone and destitute, fool?"

"The which is to be seen!" said I; and having measured my plank and sawed it to proper length I began to rivet it to the frame, making such din with my hammer that she, unable to make herself heard, presently strode away in a fury, to my great content.

But, in a little back she cometh, and on her hip that bejewelled Spanish rapier that had once been part of Black Bartlemy's treasure (as hath been told) and which (having my own stout cut-and-thrust) I had not troubled to bring away from the cave.

Whipping out the long blade then, she makes with it various passes in the air, very supple and dexterous, and would have me fight with her then and there.

"So-ho, fool!" cried she, brandishing her weapon. "You have a sword, I mind—go fetch it and I will teach ye punto riverso, the stoccato, the imbrocato, and let you some o' your sluggish, English blood. Go fetch the sword, I bid ye."

But I nothing heeding, she forthwith pricked me into

the arm, whereon I caught up a sizable timber to my
defence but found it avail me no whit against her skill
and nimbleness, for thrice her blade leapt and thrice
I flinched to the sharp bite of her steel, until, goaded
thus and what with her devilish mockery and my own
helplessness, I fell to raging anger and hauled my timber full at her, the which, chancing to catch her upon
an elbow, she let fall her sword and, clasping her hurt,
fell suddenly a-weeping. Yet, even so, betwixt her
sobs and moans she cursed and reviled me shamefully
and so at last took herself off, sobbing wofully.

This put me to no little perturbation and distress
lest I had harmed her more than I had meant, insomuch that I was greatly minded to follow her and see
if this were so indeed. But in the end I went back to
my boat and laboured amain, for it seemed to me the
sooner I was quit of her fellowship the better, lest she
goad me into maiming or slaying her outright.

Thus worked I (and despite the noon's heat) until
the sun began to decline and I was parched with thirst.
But now, as I fitted the last of my timbers into place,
the board slipped my nerveless grasp and, despite the
heat, a sudden chill swept over me as borne upon the
stilly air came a voice, soft and rich and sweet, uplifted in song and the words these:

"There be two at the fore
At the main hang three more
Dead men that swing all in a row
Here's fine, dainty meat
For the fishes to eat,
Black Bartlemy—Bartlemy, ho!"

Awhile I leaned there against the boat, remembering how and with whom I had last heard this song,
then wheeling about I caught my breath and stared
as one that sees at last a long-desired, oft-prayed-for
vision: for there, pacing demurely along the beach
towards me, her body's shapely loveliness offset by em-

broidered gown, her dark and glossy ringlets caught up by jewelled comb, I thought to behold again the beloved shape of her I had lost well-nigh three weary years agone.

"Damaris!" I whispered, "Oh, loved woman of my dreams!" And I took a long stride towards her, then stopped and bowed my head, suddenly faint and heart-sick, for now I saw here was no more than this woman who had fled me a while ago with curses on her tongue. Here she stood all wistful-eyed and tricked out in one of those fine gowns from Black Bartlemy's secret store the which had once been my dear lady's delight.

Now in her hands she bore a pipkin brimful of goat's milk.

"I prithee, sir," said she softly, "tell now—shall there be room for me in your boat?"

"Never in this world!"

"You were wiser to seek my love than my hate——"

"I seek neither!"

"Being a fool, yes. But the sun is hot and you will be a thirsty fool——"

"Where learned you that evil song?"

"In Tortuga when I was a child. But come, drink, *amigo mio*, drink an you will——"

"Whence had you that gown?"

"Ah—ah, you love me better thus, yes? Why, 'tis a pretty gown truly, though out o' the fashion. But, will you not drink?"

Now, as I have told, I was parched with thirst and the spring some way off, so taking the pipkin I drained it at a draught and muttering my thanks, handed it back to her. Then I got me to my labour again, yet very conscious of her as she sat to watch, so that more than once I missed my stroke and my fingers seemed strangely awkward. And after she had sat thus silent a great while, she spoke:

"You be mighty diligent, and to no purpose."

"How mean you?"

"I mean this boat of yours snall never sail except I sail in her."

"Which is yet to prove!" said I, feeling the air exceeding close and stifling.

"Regard now, Master Innocence," said she, holding up one hand and ticking off these several items on her fingers as she spoke: "You have crossed me once. You have beat me once. You have refused me honourable fight. You have hurt me with vile club. And now you would leave me here alone to perish——"

"All true save the last," quoth I, finding my breath with strange difficulty, "for though alone you need not perish, for I will show you where—where you— shall find abundance—of food—and——" But here I stopped and gasped as an intolerable pain shot through me.

"Ah—ah!" said she, leaning forward to stare at me keen-eyed. "And doth it begin to work—yes? Doth it begin so soon?"

"Woman," I cried, as my pains increased, "what mean you now? Why d'ye stare on me so? God help me, what have you done——"

"The milk, fool!" said she, smiling.

"Ha—what devil's brew—poison——"

"I warned you but, being fool, you nothing heeded —no!"

Now hereupon I went aside and, dreading to die thus miserably, thrust a finger down my throat and was direly sick; thereafter, not abiding the sun's intolerable heat, I crawled into the shade of a rock and lay there as it were in a black mist and myself all clammy with a horrible, cold sweat. And presently in my anguish, feeling c hand shake me, I lifted swooning eyes to find this woman bending above me.

"How now," said she, "wilt crave mercy of me and live?"

"Devil!" I gasped. "Let me die and be done with
you!"

At this she laughed and stooped low and lower until
her hair came upon my face and I might look into the
glowing deeps of her eyes; and then her arms were
about me, very strong and compelling.

"Look—look into my eyes, deep—deep!" she commanded. "Now—ha—speak me your name!"

"Martin," I gasped in my agony.

"Mar—tin," said she slowly. "I will call you Martino. Look now, Martino, have you not seen me long—
long ere this?"

"No!" I groaned. "God forbid!"

"And yet we have met, Martino, in this world or another, or mayhap in the world of dreams. But we
have met—somewhere, at some time, and in that time
I grasped you thus in my arms and stared down thus
into your eyes and in that hour I, having killed you,
watched you die, and fain would have won you back
to life and me, for you were a man,—ah, yes, a man
in those dim days. But now—ah, bah! You are but
poor fool cozened into swallowing a harmless drug;
to-morrow you shall be your sluggish self. Now sleep,
but know this—I may slay you whenso I will! Ah,
ah—'tis better to win my love than my hate." So
she loosed me and stood a while looking down on me,
then motioned with imperious hand: "Sleep, fool—
sleep!" she commanded and frowning, turned away.
And as she went I heard her singing of that vile song
again ere I sank into unconsciousness:

> "There are two at the fore
> At the main hang three more
> Dead men that swing all of a row——"

CHAPTER IV

How I Laboured to My Salvation

I FOUND myself still somewhat qualmish next morning but, none the less, got me to labour on the boat and, her damage being now made good on her larboard side, so far as her timbering went, I proceeded to make her seams as water-tight as I could. This I did by means of the fibre of those great nuts that grew plenteously here and there on the island, mixed with the gum of a certain tree in place of pitch, ramming my gummed fibre into every joint and crevice of the boat's structure so that what with this and the swelling of her timbers when launched I doubted not she would prove sufficiently staunch and seaworthy. She was a stout-built craft some sixteen feet in length; and indeed a poor enough thing she might have seemed to any but myself, her weather-beaten timbers shrunken and warped by the sun's immoderate heats, but to me she had become as it were a sign and symbol of freedom. She lay upon her starboard beam half full of sand, and it now became my object to turn her that I might come at this under side, wherefore I fell to work with mattock and spade to free her of the sand wherein (as I say) she lay half-buried. This done I hove and strained until the sweat poured from me yet found it impossible to move her, strive how I would. Hereupon, and after some painful thought, I took to digging away the sand, undermining her thus until she lay so nicely balanced it needed but a push and the cumbrous structure, rolling gently over, lay in the necessary posture, viz: with her starboard beam accessible from gunwale to keel. And mightily heartened was I thus to discover her damage hereabouts so much less than I had dared hope.

So I got me to work with saw, hammer and rivets and wrought so diligently (staying but to snatch a mouthful of food) that as the sun westered, my boat was well-nigh finished. Straightening my aching back I stood to examine my handiwork and though of necessity somewhat rough yet was it strong and secure; and altogether a very excellent piece of work I thought it, and mightily yearned I for that hour when I should feel this little vessel, that had been nought but a shattered ruin, once more riding the seas in triumph.

But now and all at once, my soaring hopes were dashed, for though the boat might be seaworthy, here she lay, high and dry, a good twelve yards from the tide.

Now seeing I might not bring my boat to the sea, I began to scheme how best I should bring the sea to her. I was yet pondering this matter, chin in hand, when a shadow fell athwart me and starting, I glanced up to find this woman beside me, who, heeding me no whit, walks about and about the boat, viewing my work narrowly.

"If you can launch her she should sail well enough, going large and none so ill on a bowline, by her looks. 'Tis true seat-boat—yes. Are you a sailor—can ye navigate, ha?"

"Not I."

" 'Tis very well, for I am, indeed, and can set ye course by dead reckoning an need be. Your work is likely enough, though had you butted your timbers it had been better—so and so!" And in this I saw she was right enough, and my work seemed more clumsy now than I had thought.

"I'm no shipwright," said I.

"And here's sure proof of it!" quoth she.

"Mayhap 'twill serve once her timbers be swelled."

"Aye, she may float, Martino, so long as the sea prove kind and the wind gentle; aye, she should carry us both over to the Main handsomely, yes——"

"Never!" quoth I, mighty determined.

"How then—will ye deny me yet, fool? Wherefore would ye leave me here, curst Englishman?"

"Lest you goad me into slaying you for the evil thing you are."

"What evil have I wrought you?"

"You would have poisoned me but yesterday——"

"Yet to-day are you strong and hearty, fool."

And indeed, now I came to think of it, I felt myself as hale and well as ever in all my life. "Tush—a fico!" says she with an evil gesture. " 'Twas but an Indian herb, fool, and good 'gainst colic and calenture. Now wherefore will ye be quit o' me?"

"Because I had rather die solitary than live in your fellowship——"

"Dolt! Clod! Worm!" cried she 'twixt gnashing teeth, and then all in a moment she was gazing down at me soft and gentle-eyed, red lips up-curving and smooth cheek dimpling to a smile:

"Ah, Mar-tin," sighs she languorously, "see how you do vex me! And I am foolish to suffer such as you to anger me, but needs must I vex you a little in quittance, yes."

At this I did but shrug my shoulders and turned to study again the problem—how to set about launching my boat.

"Art a something skilful carpenter, eh, Martino," said she in a while; " 'twas you made the table and chairs and beds in the caves up yonder, eh, Martino?"

"Aye."

"And these the tools you made 'em with, eh, Martino?" and she pointed where they lay beside the boat.

"Nay," quoth I, speaking on impulse, being yet busied with my problem, "I had nought but my hatchet then and chisels of iron."

"Your hatchet—this?" she questioned, taking it up.

"Aye!" I nodded. "The hatchet was the first tool I found after we were cast destitute on this island."

"Ah—ah—then she was with you when you found it—the woman that wore this gown before me, eh, Martino?"

"Aye—and what then?"

"This!" cried she and wheeling the hatchet strong-armed, she sent it spinning far out to sea or ever I might stay her.

Now, beholding the last of this good hatchet that had oft known my dear lady's touch, that had beside been, as it were, a weapon to our defence and a means to our comfort, seeing myself (as I say) now bereft of it thus wantonly, I sprang to my feet, uttering a cry of mingled grief and rage. But she, skipping nimbly out of reach, caught up one of my pistols where she had hid it behind a rock and stood regarding me with her hateful smile.

"Ah, ah!" says she, mocking, "do I then vex you a little, *amigo mio?* So is it very well. Ha, scowl, fool Martino, scowl and grind your teeth; 'tis joy to me and shall never bring back your little axe."

At this, seeing grief and anger alike unavailing, I sat me down by the boat and sinking my head in my hands, strove to settle my mind to this problem of launching; but this I might by no means do, since here was this devilish creature perched upon an adjacent rock to plague me still.

"How now, Martino?" she questioned. "What troubleth your sluggish brain now?" And then, as she had read my very thought: "Is't your boat—to bring her afloat? Ah—bah! 'tis simple matter! Here she lies and yonder the sea! Well, dig you a pit about the boat as deep as may be, bank the sand about your pit as high as may be. Then cut you a channel to high-water mark and beyond, so with the first tide, wind-driven, the sea shall fill your channel, pour into your pit, brimming it full and your banks being higher than your boat she shall swim and be drawn seaward on the backwash. So, here's the way on't. And so must you sweat and dig and labour, and I joy to watch—Ah, yes, for you shall sweat, dig and labour in vain, except you swear me I shall sail with you." So saying, she drops me a mocking courtsey and away she goes.

She gone and night being at hand, I set aside two or three stout spars should serve me as masts, yards, etc., together with rope and cordage for tackle and therewith two pair of oars; which done, I got me to my cave and, having supped, to bed.

Early next morning I set myself to draw a circle about my boat and mark out a channel thence to the sea (even as she had suggested) since I could hit upon no better way. This done, I fell to with spade and mattock but found this a matter of great labour since the sand, being very dry and loose hereabouts, was constantly shifting and running back upon me.

And presently, as I strove thus painfully, cometh my tormentor to plague me anew (albeit the morning was so young) she very gay and debonnaire in her 'broidered gown.

"Ha!" said she, seating herself hard by. "The sun is new-risen, yet you do sweat wofully, the which I do joy to see. So-ho, then, labour and sweat, my pretty man: it shall be all vain, aha—vain and to no purpose."

But finding I heeded her no more than buzzing fly, she changed her tune, viewing me tender-eyed and sighing soft:

"Am I not better as a woman, eh, Martino?" asked

she, spreading out her petticoats. "Aye, to be sure your eyes do tell me so, scowl and mutter as you will. See now, Martino, I have lived here three days and in all this woful weary time hast never asked my name, which is strange, unless dost know it already, for 'tis famous hereabouts and all along the Main; indeed 'tis none so wonderful you should know it——"

"I don't!" said I. "Nor wish to!"

"Then I will tell you—'tis Joan!" Hereupon I dropped my spade and she, seeing how I stared upon her, burst into a peal of laughter. "Ah, ah!" cried she. "Here is pretty, soft name and should fit me as well as another. Why must you stare so fool-like; here is no witchcraft, for in the caves yonder 'Joan' meeteth me at every turn; 'tis carven on walls, on chairs, on table, together with 'Damaris' and many woful, lovesick mottoes beside."

Now I, knowing this for truth, turned my back and ground my teeth in impotent anger, whiles this woman mocked me with her laughter.

"Damaris—Joan!" said she. "At first methought these two women, but now do I know Joan is Damaris and Damaris Joan and you a poor, lovelorn fool. But as for me—I am Joanna——"

Now at this I turned and looked at her.

"Joanna?" said I, wondering.

"Ah, you have heard it—this name, before—yes?"

"Aye, in a song."

"Oh, verily!" said she and forthwith began singing in her deep, rich voice:

> "There's a fine Spanish dame
> And Joanna's her name
> Shall follow wherever you go——"

"Aha, and mark this, Martino:

> "Till your black heart shall feel
> Your own cursed steel
> Black Bartlemy—Bartlemy, ho!"

"But this was my mother——"

"Ha—she that stabbed and killed the pirate Bartlemy ere he slew her? But she was a Spanish lady."

"Nay, she was English, and lieth buried hereabouts, 'tis said; howbeit, she died here whiles I was with the Indians. They found me, very small and helpless, in the ruins of a burned town and took me away into the mountains and, being Indians, used me kindly and well. Then came white men, twenty and two, and, being Christians, slew the Indians and used me evilly and were cruel, save only one; twenty and two they were and all dead long ago, each and every, save only one. Aha, Martino, for the evil men have made me endure, I have ever been excellent well avenged! For I am Joanna that some call 'Culebra' and some 'Gad-fly' and some 'Fighting Jo.' And indeed there be few men can match me at swordplay and as for musket and pistol—watch now, Martino, the macaw yonder!" She pointed to a bird that stood preening itself on a rock at no little distance and, catching up the pistol, levelled and fired; and in place of the bird was nought but a splash of blood and a few poor, gaudy feathers stirring lazily in the gentle wind.

"See," cried she, with a little, soft laugh, "am I not a goodly *camarado* for any brave fellow, yes?"

"Truly," said I, turning away, "I think your breeches do become you best——"

"Liar!" she cried. "You know I am handsomer thus! Your eyes ha' told me so already. And look ye, I can be as soft and tender, as meek and helpless as any puling woman of 'em all, when I will. And if I hate fiercely, so is my love—ha, d'ye blench, fool, d'ye shrink; you thing shaped like a man, must ye cringe at the word 'love'?"

"Aye!" said I, over my shoulder. "On your lips 'tis desecration!"

"Desecration—desecration?" quoth she, staring on me great-eyed and biting at her scarlet nether lip. "Ha, dare ye say it, dog?" And crying thus, she hurled the pistol at me with aim so true that I staggered and came nigh falling. Stung by the blow I turned on her in a fury, but she leapt to her feet and showed me my own knife glittering in her fist.

"Ah, bah—back to your labour, slave!" she mocked.

"Have done, woman!" I cried. "Have done, or by the living God, you will goad me into slaying you yet——"

"Tush!" said she, "I am used to outfacing men, but you—ha, you should be fed on pap and suckets, you that are no man! 'Tis small wonder you lost your Joan—Damaris; 'tis no wonder she fled away and left you——"

Now at this (and nothing heeding her knife) I sprang at her and she, letting fall the knife, leapt towards me; and then I had her, felt her all soft and palpitant in my furious grip, heard a quivering sigh, saw her head sway back across my arm and she drooping in my embrace, helpless and a-swoon. And holding her thus 'prisoned and crushed against me, I could not but be conscious of all the tender, languorous beauty of her ere I hasted to lay her upon the sand. My arms were yet about her (and I upon my knees) when her bosom heaved to sudden, tremulous sigh and opening her eyes, she smiled up at me.

"Ah, Martino," sighed she softly, "do not these petticoats become me vastly well, yes?" And reaching up, she set her arms about me. "Am I not better than dream-woman, I that men have died for—I, Joanna?"

Now hereupon I shivered and loosing her hold rose to my feet and stood with head averted that I might not behold her. Presently she arose also and coming where lay the knife, took it up and stood turning it this way and that.

"Mar-tin," said she in her soft, dreamy speech, "you are mightily strong and—mightily gentle, and I do think we shall make a man of you yet!"

So saying, she turned and went away, the knife glittering in her hand. As for me I cast myself down and with no thought or will to labour now, for it seemed that my strength was gone from me.

CHAPTER V

TELLETH HOW ALL MY TRAVAIL CAME TO NOUGHT

THAT night, the moon being at the full and I very wakeful, I lay harassed of a thousand fretting thoughts, and each and every of this woman Joanna; and turning on my sleepless couch I cursed that hour the which had set her in my company.

Yet, even so, I must needs bethink me of all the supple warmth of her as she lay in my arms, of the velvety touch of her cheek that had by chance brushed my hand. Hereupon I would strive to turn my thoughts upon the labours of to-morrow only to find myself recalling the sound of her voice, now deep and soft and infinite sweet, now harsh and shrill and hatefully shrewish; or her golden-brown eyes, thick-lashed and marvellous quick in their changes from sleepy languor to flaming malevolence.

Thus lay I, haunted of her memory and all the sudden, bewildering changes of her moods until at last I started up, and coming to the entrance of my cave, saw her standing without and the moon bright on her face.

"Art wakeful too, Martino?" asked she softly. " 'Tis the moon belike, or the heat of the night." Here she came a slow pace nearer; and her eyes were sweet and languorous and on her vivid mouth a smile infinite alluring. Slowly she drew near, thralling me as it were with the wonder of her look that I had neither power nor will to move or speak. Confident of her-

self and assured in her beauty she reached out her
hands to me, her long lashes swept down, veiling her
eyes; but, even then, I had seen their flash of triumph,
and in that moment, bursting the spell that bound
me, I turned from her.

"Go—leave me!" said I, finding my voice at last.
"Here is no place for you!" And I stood thereafter
with head averted, dreading her sighs and tears; instead (and to my unutterable relief) she brake out
into a storm of sea-oaths, beslavering me with vile
abuse and bitter curses. Now, hearkening to this lewd
tirade, I marvelled I should ever have feared and
trembled because of the womanhood of creature so
coarse and unsexed. Thus she continued alternately
mocking at and reviling me until she must needs pause
for lack of breath; then I turned to look at her and
stood amazed to behold that passionate head bowed
upon her hands.

"Aye, I weep," she sobbed. "I weep because I am
woman, after all, but in my heart I hate you and with
my soul I despise you, for you are but a mock man,
—the blood in your veins skim milk! Ah, by God,
there is more of vigorous life in my little finger than
in all your great, heavy, clod-like carcase. Oh,
shame!" Here she lifted her head to scowl on me and
I, not enduring her look, glanced otherwhere. "Ha
—rot me!" cried she, wagging scornful finger. "Rot
me but you are afraid of me—afraid, yes!"

"True!" said I. "So will I win free of you so soon
as I may——"

"Free of me?" cried she, and throwing herself on
the sands, sat crouched there, her head upon her knees
and sobbing miserably. "So you will abandon me
then?" said she at last.

"Aye."

"Even though I—vow myself your slave?"

"I want no slave."

"Even though I beseech you on my knees?"

" 'Twere vain, I sail hence alone."

"You were wiser to seek my love than my hate."

"But I was ever a fool."

"Aye, verily!" she cried passionately. "So do you yearn ever for your light-o'-love, for your vanished Joan—your Damaris that left you——"

"Now I pray you go!" said I.

"I wonder," sighed she, never stirring, "I wonder why I do not kill you? I hate you—despise you and yet——"

Slowly she got to her feet and moved away with dragging step but paused anon and spake again with head a-droop:

"Living or dead, you shall not leave the island except I go with you!" Then she went her way and something in her attitude methought infinitely desolate.

Left alone, I stood awhile in gloomy thought, but rousing presently, I betook me into my cave, and lying down, fell at last to uneasy slumber. But waking suddenly, I started up on elbow full of an indefinable fear, and glancing without the cave, I saw a strange thing, for sand and rock and bush-girt cliff had on an unfamiliar aspect, the which I was wholly unable to account for; rocks and trees and flowering vines shone throbbing upon my vision with a palpitant glow that came and went, the like of which I had never seen before.

Then, all at once, I was up and running along Skeleton Cove, filled with a dreadful apprehension, and coming out upon Deliverance Beach, stood quaking like one smitten with a palsy; for there, lapped about in writhing flame and crackling sparks, was all that remained of my boat, and crouched upon the sands, watching me by the light of this fire, was she who called herself Joanna.

And now, perceiving all the wanton cruelty of this

thing, a cold and merciless rage took me and staring on this woman as she stared on me, I began to creep towards her.

I warned you, fool, I warned you!" cried she, never moving. " 'Tis a brave fire I've made and burns well. And now you shall kill me an you will—but your boat is lost to you for ever, and so is—your Damaris!"

Now at sound of this loved name I stopped and stood a great while staring at the fire, then suddenly I cast myself on my knees, and lifting up my eyes to the stars already paling to dawn, I prayed God to keep me from the sin of murder.

When at last I rose to my feet, Joanna was gone.

The sun was high-risen when I came again, slow and heavy-footed, to behold what the fire had left of my boat; a heap of ashes, a few fragments of charred timber. And this the sorry end of all my fond hopes, my vain schemes, my sweat and labour.

And as I gazed, in place of my raging fury of last night was a hopeless despondency and a great bitterness against that perverse fate that seemed to mock my every endeavour.

As I stood thus deject and bitterly cast down, I heard the step of this woman Joanna and presently she cometh beside me.

"You will be hating me for this, hating me—yes?" she questioned; then, finding me all regardless of her, she plucked me by the sleeve. "Ah—and will you not speak to me?" cried she. Turning from her, I began to pace aimlessly along beside the lagoon but she, overtaking, halted suddenly in my path. "Your boat would have leaked and swamped with you, Martino!" said she, but heeding her no whit I turned and plodded back again, and she ever beside me. "I tell you the cursed thing would ha' gone to pieces at the first gust of wind!" she cried. But I paced on with neither word nor look until, finding me thus blind and deaf to her, she cursed me bitterly and so left me alone and I, following a haphazard course, presently found myself in a grove of palmetto trees and sat me down in this pleasant shade where I might behold the sea, that boundless, that impassable barrier. But in a while, espying the woman coming thitherwards, I rose and tramped on again with no thought but to save myself from her companionship.

All the morning then I rambled aimlessly to and fro, keeping ever amid the woods and thickets, staying my hunger with such fruit as I fell in with, as grapes and plantains; or sitting listlessly, my hands idle before me, I stared out across these empty, sun-smitten waters, until, dazzled by their glare, I would rise and wander on again, my mind ever and always troubled of a great perplexity, namely: How might I (having regard to the devilish nature of this woman Joanna) keep myself from slaying her in some fit of madness, thereby staining my soul with her murder.

So came I at last to my habitation in Skeleton Cove and chancing to espy my great powderhorn where it hung, I reached it down and going without the cave, scattered its contents broadcast, this being all the powder I had brought hither.

It being now late noon and very hot, I cast myself down in the shade of a rock, and lying there, I presently came to the following resolution, viz: To shun the woman Joanna's company henceforth as well as I might; moreover (and let her haunt me how she would) to heed her neither by word or look, bearing all her scorns and revilings patiently, making no answer, and enduring all her tyranny to the uttermost. All of which fine conceits were but the most arrant folly and quickly brought to nothing, as you shall hear. For even now as I sat with these high-flown notions buzzing in my head, I started to her sudden call:

"Martino—Martino!"

Glancing up, I beheld her poised upon the rocks
above me and a noose of small cord in her hand. As
I watched, she began to whirl this around her head,
fast and faster, then, uttering a shrill, strange cry,
she let fly the noose the which, leaping through the
air, took me suddenly about the throat and she, pulling on it, had me half-strangled all in a moment. Then
as, choking, I loosed this devilish noose from me (and
or ever I could rise) she came running and casting
herself down before me, clasped my feet and laid her
head upon them.

"Martino!" she cried, "Oh man, beat me an you will,
trample on me, kill me; only heed me—heed me a
little!"

Now seeing her thus miserably abject and humbled,
I grew abashed also and fain would have loosed me
from her clasp but she held me only the faster; and
thus, my hand coming upon her head, she caught that
hand and kissed it passionately, wetting it with her
tears.

"Oh, Martino," said she, wofully a-sobbing, "I do
know at last wherefore—I may not kill you. 'Tis
because I love you. I was fool not to guess it ere this,
but—I have never loved man ere now. Aye, I love
you—I, Joanna, that never loved before, do love you,
Martino——"

"What of your many lovers?"

"I loved no one of them all. 'Tis you ha' learned
me——"

"Nay, this is no love——"

"Aye, but it is—in very truth. Think you I do
not know it? I cannot sleep, I cannot eat—except
you love me I must die, yes. Ah, Martino, be merciful!" she pleaded. "For thee I will be all woman
henceforth, soft and tender and very gentle—thine always! Oh, be merciful——"

"No," I cried, "not this! Be rather your other

self, curse me, revile me, fetch the sword and fight with
me——"

"Fight thee—ah, no, no! The time for this is
passed away. And if I did grieve thee 'twas but that
I might cherish and comfort thee—for thou art mine
and I thine henceforth—to death and beyond! Look,
Martino! See how I do love thee!"

And now her arms were about me, soft and strong,
and beholding all the pleading beauty of her, the tender allure of her eyes, the quiver of her scarlet mouth
and all her compelling loveliness, I stooped to her embrace; but even so, chancing to lift my gaze seaward,
I broke the clasp of these twining arms and rose suddenly to my feet. For there, her rag of sail spread
to the light-breathing air, was a boat standing in for
the island.

CHAPTER VI

How I Succoured One Don Federigo, a Gentleman of Spain

I was out upon the reef, waving my arms like any madman and shouting to the vague figure huddled in the stern sheets. As the boat drew nearer, I discovered this figure to be a man in Spanish half-armour, and the head of this man was bowed meekly upon steel-clad breast like one overcome with great weariness. But presently as I watched he looked up, like one awaking from sleep, and gestured feebly with his arm, whiles I, beholding here the means to my deliverance, babbled prayers of thankfulness to God.

After some while, the boat being within hail, I began to call out to this solitary voyager (for companion had he none, it seemed) how he must steer to avoid the rocks and shoals. At last, the boat being come near enough and the sea very smooth, I waded out and, watching my chance, clambered aboard over the bows and came, all dripping, eager to welcome this heaven-sent stranger and thus beheld the boat very foul of blood and him pale and hollow-cheeked, his eyes dim and sunken; moreover his rich armour was battered and dinted, whiles about one leg was knotted a bloody scarf.

"Señor," said I, in my best Spanish, "a lonely man giveth you right hearty greeting!"

"I thank you, sir," he answered and in very excellent English, "though I do much fear you shall abide

solitary, for as I do think I am a-dying. Could you
—bring me—water——"

The words ended in a sigh and his head drooped so
that I feared he was already gone. But, finding he
yet breathed, I made haste to lower the sail and,
shipping oars, paddled towards that opening in
the reef that gave upon the lagoon. Being opposite
this narrow channel I felt the boat caught by some tide
and current and swept forward ever more rapidly, insomuch that I unshipped the oars and hasting into
the bow, caught up a stout spar wherewith to fend
us off from the rocks. Yet more than once, despite
all my exertions, we came near striking ere, having
passed through this perilous gut, we floated into the
placid waters of the lagoon beyond.

Very soon I had beached the boat as securely as I
might on that spit of sand opposite Skeleton Cove,
and finding the Spaniard yet a-swoon I lifted him,
albeit with much ado, and setting him across my shoulder, bore him thus into the cool shade of the cave.
There I laid him down beside the little rill to bathe his
head and wrists with the sweet water and moisten his
parched lips. At this he revived somewhat and, lifting his head, eagerly drank so much as I would allow,
his sunken eyes uplift to mine in an ecstasy.

"Young sir," said he in stronger voice, "for your
kind charity and this good water may the Saints re-
quite thee. 'Tis three nights and two days since I
drank——"

A shadow fell betwixt us and looking up I beheld
Joanna. Now in one hand she grasped the Spaniard's
sword she had stolen out of his boat and her other
hand was hid behind her, wherefore I watched her narrowly, as she stood gazing down at this wounded man;
and at first she scowled at him, but slowly her look
changed and I saw her vivid lips curl in her baleful
smile.

"Oh," said she very softly, "Oh, marvel of marvels! Oh, wonder of wonders, even and in very truth it is Don Federigo de Rosalva y Maldonada, wafted hither by wind and tide to Joanna and judgment. Oh, most wonderful!"

Now hereupon this poor wounded wretch lifted himself to peer up into her smiling face with hanging jaw, like one amazed beyond all speech, whiles she, slim and shapely in her 'broidered gown, nodded her handsome head. "Verily," quoth she, " 'tis the hanging, bloody governor of Nombre de Dios come to Justice! I pray you, Señor, how many of our company ha' you strung aloft since last we met?"

Here, though with much painful ado, the Don got to his feet and made her a prodigious fine bow.

"The Señorita Joanna honours me by her notice," said he. "I should have doubtless known her at once but for her change of habit. And I am happy to inform the Señorita I have been so fortunate as to take and hang no less than five and twenty of her pirate fellowship since last I had the gratification of meeting her."

"Ha, you lie!" cried she passionately. "You lie!"

"They swing in their chains along the mole outside Nombre de Dios to witness for my truth, Señorita. And now," said he, propping himself against the rock behind him, "it is my turn to die, as I think? Well, strike, lady—here, above my gorget——"

"Die then!" cried she and whipped a pistol from behind her, but as she levelled I struck up the weapon and it exploded harmless in the air. Uttering a scream of bitter rage, she thrust with the sword, but I put up the stroke (thereby taking a gash in the arm) and gripping the rapier by the guards I twisted it from her hold. And now she turned on me in a very frenzy:

"Kill me then!" she panted, striving to impale herself on the sword in my hand. "If this man is to come betwixt us now, kill me in mercy and free me from this hateful woman's flesh——" But here, spying my arm bloody, she forgot her anger all in a moment. "Are ye hurt?" said she. "Are ye hurt and all to save this miserable fool!" And suddenly (or ever I might prevent) she caught my arm, kissing the wound, heedless of the blood that bedabbled her cheek in horrid fashion.

"Oh, Martino," said she, leaning 'gainst a rock when at last I broke from her, "you are mine now and always, as you were in other times long since forgot. In those days your blood was on my lips, I mind, and your kisses also ere you died. Mine you are to death, aye, and through death to life again—mine. And to-day is to-day and death not for you or me—yet awhile!"

When she was gone I turned to find this wounded man upon his knees, his head bowed above a little gold crucifix between his hands.

"Sir, what would you?" I questioned, struck by his expression, when at last he looked up.

"I make my peace with God, Señor, since I am soon to die——"

"Nay, sir, I do trust your hardships are ended——"

"Shall be, Señor, to-day, to-morrow, the day after?" said he, smiling faintly and shrugging his shoulders. "A sudden shot, steel i' the back—'tis better than death by famine in an open boat. You, Señor, have saved me alive yet a little, doubtless for your own ends, but my death walketh yonder as I know, death in form shapely and fair-seeming, yet sure and unpitying, none the less."

"Ha, d'ye mean yon woman?" I questioned.

"The Señorita Joanna—verily, Señor."

"Never think it!" quoth I. "'Tis wild, fierce creature, yet is she but a woman and young——"

Now hereupon this wounded man lifted weary head to stare on me, his eyes very bright and keen.

"Señor," says he, "either you do mock me, or you nothing know this woman. But I do know her well and too well. Señor, I have warred with and been prisoner to you English, I have fought Indians, I have campaigned again buccaneers and pirates these many years, but never have I encountered foe so desperate, so bold and cunning as this Señorita Joanna. She is the very soul of evil; the goddess of every pirate rogue in the Indies; 'tis she is their genius, their inspiration, her word their law. 'Tis she is ever foremost in their most desperate ploys, first in attack, last in retreat, fearless always—I have known her turn rout into victory. But two short months ago she vowed my destruction, and I with my thousands at command besides divers ships well armed and manned; to-day I am a woful fugitive, broken in fortune, fleeing for my life, and, Señor, Fate has brought me, through shipwreck and famine all these weary miles, into the grasp of her slender, cruel hands. Thus and thus do I know myself for dead man and shall die, howsoever I must, as becometh me."

His keen eyes lost their fire, his head drooped, and looking down on him as he lay huddled against the rock, I did not doubt but that much of this was no more than the raving of his disordered fancy.

So I set my arm about this poor gentleman and brought him into my habitation, where I loosed off his chafing armour and set myself to feed and cherish him, bathing the hurt in his leg, the which I found very angry and inflamed. This done I bade him be of good comfort and yield himself to slumber. But this he could no way accomplish, being restless and fevered and his mind harping continually on the strange fate had set him thus in Joanna's power and the sure belief that he must die, soon or late, at her hands.

"For look now, Señor," said he, "and observe my strange destiny. Scarce two months since I set out in a well-found galleon, I and three hundred chosen men, to hunt down and destroy this very woman—her and her evil company. One of their ships we fell in with, which ship, after long and sharp debate, we sunk. But it coming on to blow and our own vessels being much shattered by their shot, we sprung a leak, the which gaining on us, we were forced to take to our boats; but the wind increased and we were soon scattered. On the third day, having endured divers perils, we made the land, I with Pedro Valdez my chief captain and ten others and, being short of water, they went ashore one and all, leaving me wounded in the boat. And I lying there was suddenly aware of great uproar within the thickets ashore, and thereafter the screams and cries of my companions as they died. Then cometh Pedro Valdez running, crying out the Indians were on us, that all was lost and himself sore wounded. Nevertheless he contrived to thrust off the boat and I to aid him aboard. That night he died and the wind drove me whither it would; wherefore, having committed Pedro Valdez his body to the deep, I resigned myself to the will of God. And God hath brought me hither, Señor, and set me in the power of the Señorita Joanna that is my bitter foe; so am I like to die sudden and soon. But, Señor, for your kindness to me, pray receive a broken man's gratitude and dying blessing. Sir, I am ever a Maldonada of Castile and we do never forget!" There he reached out to grasp my hand. "Thus, Señor, should this be my last night of life, the which is very like, know that my gratitude is of the nature that dieth not."

"Sir," said I, his hand in mine and the night deepening about us, "I am a very solitary man and you came into my life like a very angel of God (an there be such) when I stood in direst need, for I was sick

of my loneliness and in my hunger for companionship
very nigh to great and shameful folly. Mayhap,
whiles you grow back to strength and health, I will
tell you my story, but this night you shall sleep safe
—so rest you secure."

CHAPTER VII

I Am Determined on My Vengeance, and My Reasons Therefor

I found this Spanish gentleman very patient in his sickness and ever of a grave and chivalrous courtesy, insomuch that as our fellowship lengthened so grew my regard for him. He was, beside, a man of deep learning and excellent judgment and his conversation and conduct a growing delight to me.

And indeed to such poor wretch as I that had been forced by my bitter wrongs to company with all manner of rogues and fellows of the baser sort, this Don Federigo (and all unknowing) served but to show me how very far I had sunk from what I might have been. And knowing myself thus degenerate I grieved mightily therefore and determined henceforth to meet Fortune's buffets more as became my condition, with a steadfast and patient serenity, even as this gentleman of Spain.

It was at this time he recounted, in his courtly English, something of the woes he and his had suffered these many years at the hands of these roving adventurers, these buccaneers and pirates whose names were a terror all along the Main. He told of the horrid cruelties of Lollonois, of the bloody Montbars called the "Exterminator," of the cold, merciless ferocity of Black Bartlemy and of such lesser rouges as Morgan, Tressady, Belvedere and others of whom I had never heard.

"There was my son, young sir," said he in his calm, dispassionate voice, "scarce eighteen turned, and my daughter—both taken by this pirate Belvedere when he captured the *Margarita* carrack scarce three years since. My son they tortured to death because he was my son, and my daughter, my sweet Dolores—well, she is dead also, I pray the Mother of Mercies. Truly I have suffered very much, yet there be others, alas! I might tell you of our goodly towns burned or held to extortionate ransom, of our women ravished, our children butchered, our men tormented, our defence-less merchant ships destroyed and their crews with them, but my list is long, young sir, and would out-last your kind patience."

"And what o' vengeance?" I demanded, marvelling at the calm serenity of his look.

"Vengeance, young sir? Nay, surely, 'tis an empty thing. For may vengeance bring back the beloved dead? Can it rebuild our desolate towns, or cure any of a broken heart?"

"Yet you hang these same rogues?"

"Truly, Señor, as speedily as may be, as I would crush a snake. Yet who would seek vengeance on a worm?"

"Yet do I seek vengeance!" cried I, upstarting to my feet. "Vengeance for my wasted years, vengeance on him hath been the ruin of my house, on him that, forcing me to endure anguish of mind and shame of body, hath made of me the poor, outcast wretch I am. Ha—'tis vengeance I do live for!"

"Then do you live to a vain end, young sir! For vengeance is an emptiness and he that seeketh it wast-eth himself."

"Now tell me, Don Federigo," I questioned, "seek you not the life of this Belvedere that slew your son?"

" 'Tis my prayer to see him die, Señor, yet do I live to other, and I pray to nobler purpose——"

"Why, then," quoth I fiercely, "so is it my prayer to watch my enemy die and I do live to none other purpose——"

"Spoke like true, bully lad, Martino!" cried a voice, and glancing about, I espied Joanna leaning in the opening to the cave. She was clad in her male attire as I had seen her first, save that by her side she bore the bejewelled Spanish rapier. Thus lolled she, smiling on me half-contemptuous, hand poised lightly on the hilt of her sword, all graceful insolence.

"Eye for eye, Martino," said she, nodding. "Tooth for tooth, blood for blood: 'tis a good law and just, yes! How say you, Señor Don Federigo; you agree —no?"

With an effort Don Federigo got to his feet and, folding his cloak about his spare form, made her a prodigious deep obeisance.

" 'Tis a law ancient of days, Señorita," said he.

"And your health improves, Señor, I hope— yes?"

"The Señorita is vastly gracious! Thanks to Don Martino I mend apace. Oh, yes, and shall soon be strong enough to die decorously, I trust, and in such fashion as the Señorita shall choose."

"Aha, Señor," said she, with flash of white teeth, " 'tis an everlasting joy to me that I also am of noble Spanish blood. Some day when justice hath been done, and you are no more, I will have a stone raised up to mark where lie the bones of a great Spanish gentleman. As for thee, my poor Martino, that babblest o' vengeance, 'tis not for thee nor ever can be—thou that art only English, cold—cold—a very clod! Oh, verily there is more life, more fire and passion in a small, dead fish than in all thy great, slow body! And now, pray charge me my pistols; you have all the powder here." I shook my head. "Fool," said she, "I mean not to shoot you, and as for Don Federigo, since death

is but his due, a bullet were kinder—so charge now
these my pistols."

"I have no powder," said I.

"Liar!"

"I cast it into the sea lest I be tempted to shoot
you."

Now at this she must needs burst out a-laughing.

"Oh, Englishman!" cried she. "Oh, sluggard soul
—how like, how very like thee, Martino!" Then,
laughing yet, she turned and left me to stare after her
in frowning wonderment.

This night after supper, sitting in the light of the
fire and finding the Don very wakeful, I was moved (at
his solicitation) to tell him my history; the which
I will here recapitulate as briefly as I may.

"I was born, sir, in Kent in England exactly thirty
years ago, and being the last of my family 'tis very
sure that family shall become a name soon to be forgotten——"

"But you, Señor, so young——"

"But ancient in suffering, sir."

"Oh, young sir, but what of love; 'tis a magic——"

"A dream!" quoth I. "A dream sweet beyond
words! But I am done with idle dreaming, henceforth. I come then of one of two families long at
feud, a bloody strife that had endured for generations
and which ended in my father being falsely accused by
his more powerful enemy and thrown into prison where
he speedily perished. Then I, scarce more than lad,
was trepanned aboard ship, carried across seas and
sold a slave into the plantations. And, mark me, sir,
all this the doing of our hereditary enemy who, thus
triumphant, dreamed he had ended the feud once and
for all. Sir, I need not weary you with my sufferings
as a planter's slave, to labour always 'neath the lash,
to live or die as my master willed. Suffice it I broke
free at last and, though well-nigh famished, made my

way to the coast. But here my travail ended in despair, for I was recaptured and being known for runaway slave, was chained to an oar aboard the great *Esmeralda* galleas where such poor rogues had their miserable lives whipped out of them. And here my sufferings (since it seemed I could not die) grew wellnigh beyond me to endure. But from this hell of shame and anguish I cried unceasing upon God for justice and vengeance on mine enemy that had plunged me from life and all that maketh it worthy into this living death. And God answered me in this, for upon a day the *Esmeralda* was shattered and sunk by an English ship and I, delivered after five bitter years of agony, came back to my native land. But friends had I none, nor home, since the house wherein I was born and all else had been seized by my enemy and he a power at Court. Him sought I therefore to his destruction, since (as it seemed to me) God had brought me out of my tribulation to be His instrument of long-delayed vengeance. So, friendless and destitute, came I at last to that house had been ours for generations and there learned that my hopes and labour were vain indeed, since this man I was come to destroy had himself been captured and cast a prisoner in that very place whence I had so lately escaped!"

Here the memory of this disappointment waxing in me anew, I must needs pause in my narration, whereupon my companion spake in his soft, dispassionate voice:

"Thus surely God hath answered your many prayers, young sir!"

"And how so?" cried I. "Of what avail that this man lie pent in dungeon or sweating in chains and I not there to see his agony? I must behold him suffer as I suffered, hear his groans, see his tears—I that do grieve a father untimely dead, I that have endured at this man's will a thousand shames and torment beyond telling! Thus, sir," I continued, "learning that his daughter was fitting out a ship to his relief I (by aid of the master of the ship) did steal myself aboard and sailed back again, back to discover this my enemy. But on the voyage mutiny broke out, headed by that evil rogue, Tressady. Then was I tricked and cast adrift in an open boat by Adam Penfeather, the master——"

"Penfeather, young sir, Adam Penfeather! Truly there was one I do mind greatly famous once among the buccaneers of Tortuga."

"This man, then, this Penfeather casts me adrift (having struck me unconscious first) that I might secure to him certain treasure that lay hid on this island, a vast treasure of jewels called 'Black Bartlemy's treasure.' "

"I have heard mention of it, Señor."

"Here then steered I, perforce, and, storm-tossed, was cast here, I and—my comrade——"

"Comrade, Señor?"

"Indeed, sir. For with me in the boat was a woman and she the daughter of my enemy. And here, being destitute of all things, we laboured together to our common need and surely, aye, surely, never had man braver comrade or sweeter companion. She taught me many things and amongst them how to love her, and loving, to honour and respect her for her pure and noble womanhood. Upon a time, to save herself from certain evil men driven hither by tempest she leapt into a lake that lieth in the midst of this island, being carried some distance by a current, came in this marvellous fashion on the secret of Black Bartlemy's hidden treasure. But I, thinking her surely dead, fought these rogues, slaying one and driving his fellow back to sea and, being wounded, fell sick, dreaming my dear lady beside me again, hale and full of life; and waking at last from my fears, found this the very truth. In the following days I forgot all my prayers and the great oath of vengeance I had sworn, by reason of my love for this my sweet comrade. But then came the pirate Tressady and his fellows seeking the treasure, and after him, Penfeather, which last, being a very desperate, cunning man, took Tressady by a wile and would have hanged him with his comrade Mings, but for my lady. These rogues turned I adrift in one of the boats to live or die as God should appoint. And now (my vengeance all forgot) there grew in me a passionate hope to have found me peace at last and happiness in my dear lady's love, and wedded to her, sail back to England and home. But such great happiness was not for me, it seemed. I was falsely accused of murder and (unable to prove my innocence) I chose rather to abide here solitary than endure her doubting of me, or bring shame or sorrow on one so greatly loved. Thus, sir, here have I existed a solitary man ever since."

"And the Señorita Joanna, young sir?"

When I had told him of her coming and the strange manner of it, Don Federigo lay silent a good while, gazing into the fire.

"And your enemy, Señor?" he questioned at last. "Where lieth he now to your knowledge?"

"At Nombre de Dios, in the dungeons of the Inquisition, 'tis said."

"The Inquisition!" quoth Don Federigo in a whisper, and crossed himself. "Sir," said he, and with a strange look. "Oh, young sir, if this be so indeed, rest you content, for God hath surely avenged you—aye, to the very uttermost!"

CHAPTER VIII

How the Days of My Watching Were
Accomplished

Our fresh meat being nearly all gone, I set out next morning with my bow and arrows (in the management of which I had made myself extreme dexterous); I set out, I say, minded to shoot me a young goat or, failing this, one of those great birds whose flesh I had found ere now to be very tender and delicate eating.

Hardly had I waved adieu to the Don (him sitting in the shade propped in one of my great elbow chairs) than I started a goat and immediately gave chase, not troubling to use my bow, for what with my open-air life and constant exercise I had become so long-winded and fleet of foot that I would frequently run these wild creatures down.

Away sped the goat and I after it, along perilous tracks and leaping from rock to rock, joying in the chase, since of late I had been abroad very little by reason of Don Federigo's sickness; on I ran after my quarry, the animal making ever for higher ground and more difficult ways until we were come to a rocky height whence I might behold a wide expanse of ocean.

Now, as had become my wont, I cast a look around about this vast horizon and stopped all at once, clean forgetting my goat and all else in the world excepting that which had caught my lonely glance, that for which I had looked and waited and prayed for so long. For there, dim-seen 'twixt the immensity of sea and sky, was a speck I knew for the topsails of a ship. Long stood

I staring as one entranced, my hands tight clasped,
and all a-sweat with fear lest this glimmering speck
should fade and vanish utterly away. At last, dreading this be but my fancy or a trick of the light, I summoned enough resolution to close my eyes and, bowing
my head between my hands, remained thus as long as
I might endure. Then, opening my eyes, I uttered a
cry of joy to see this speck loom more distinct and
plainer than before. Thereupon I turned and began
to hasten back with some wild notion of putting off in
Don Federigo's boat (the which lay securely afloat in
the lagoon) and of standing away for this ship lest
peradventure she miss the island. Full of this dreadful
possibility I took to running like any madman, staying
for nothing, leaping, scrambling, slipping and stumbling down sheer declivities, breasting precipitous cliffs
until I reached and began to descend Skeleton Cove.

I was half-way down the cliff when I heard the clash
of steel, and presently coming where I might look down
into the cove I saw this: with his back to a rock and
a smear of blood on his cheek stood Don Federigo,
armed with my cut-and-thrust, defending himself
against Joanna; and as I watched the flash of their
whirling, clashing blades, it did not take me long to see
that the Don was no match for her devilish skill and
cunning, and beholding her swift play of foot and wrist,
her lightning volts and passes, I read death in every
supple line of her. Even as I hasted towards them, I
saw the dart of her long blade, followed by a vivid,
ever-widening stain on the shoulder of the Don's tattered shirt.

"Ha-ha!" cried she and with a gasconading flourish
of her blade. "There's for Pierre Valdaigne you
hanged six months agone! There's for Jeremy Price!
And this for Tonio Moretti! And now for John Davis,
sa-ha!" With every name she uttered, her cruel steel,
flashing within his weakening guard, bit into him, arm

or leg, and I saw she meant to cut him to pieces. The sword was beaten from his failing grasp and her point menaced his throat, his breast, his eyes, whiles he, leaning feebly against the rock, fronted her unflinching and waited death calm and undismayed. But, staying for no more, I leapt down into the cove and fell, rolling upon the soft sand, whereupon she flashed a look at me over her shoulder and in that moment Don Federigo had grappled her sword-arm; then came I running and she, letting fall her sword, laughed to see me catch it up.

"Ha, my brave English clod," cried she. "There be two swords and two men against one defenceless woman! Come, end me, Martino, end me and be done— or will you suffer the Don to show you, yes?" And folding her arms she faced me mighty high and scornful. But now, whiles I stared at her insolent beauty and no word ready, Don Federigo made her one of his grand bows and staggered into the cave, spattering blood as he went.

And in a little (staying only to take up the other sword) I followed him, leaving her to stand and mock me with her laughter. Reaching the Don I found him a-swoon and straightway set myself to bare his wounds and staunch their bleeding as well as I might, in the doing of which I must needs marvel anew at Joanna's devilish skill, since each and every of these hurts came near no vital spot and were of little account in themselves, so that a man might be stabbed thus very many times ere death ended his torment.

After awhile, recovering himself somewhat, Don Federigo must needs strive to speak me his gratitude, but I cut him short to tell of the ship I had seen.

"I pray what manner of ship?"

"Nay, she is yet too far to determine," said I, glancing eagerly seawards. "But since ship she is, what matter for aught beside?"

"True, Señor Martino! I am selfish."

"How so?"

"Unless she be ship of Spain, here is no friend to me. But you will be yearning for sight of this vessel whiles I keep you. Go, young sir, go forth—make you a fire, a smoke plain to be seen and may this ship bring you to freedom and a surcease of all your tribulations!"

"A smoke!" cried I, leaping up. "Ha, yes—yes!" And off went I, running; but reaching Deliverance I saw there was no need for signal of mine, since on the cliff above a fire burned already, sending up huge columns of thick smoke very plain to be seen from afar, and beside this fire Joanna staring seaward beneath her hand. And looking whither she looked, I saw the ship so much nearer that I might distinguish her lower courses. Thus I stood, watching the vessel grow upon my sight, very slowly and by degrees, until it was evident she had seen the smoke and was standing in for the island. Once assured of this, I was seized of a passion of joy; and bethinking me of all she might mean to me and of the possibility that one might be aboard her whose sweet eyes even now gazed from her decks upon this lonely island, my heart leapt whiles ship and sea swam on my sight and I grew blinded by stinging tears. And now I paced to and fro upon the sand in a fever of longing and with my hungry gaze turned ever in the one direction.

As the time dragged by, my impatience grew almost beyond enduring; but on came the ship, slow but sure, nearer and nearer until I could discern shroud and spar and rope, the guns that yawned from her high, weather-beaten side, the people who crowded her decks. She seemed a great ship, heavily armed and manned, and high upon her towering poop lolled one in a vivid scarlet jacket.

I was gazing upon her in an ecstacy, straining my

eyes for the flutter of a petticoat upon her lofty quarter-deck, when I heard Don Federigo hail me faintly, and glancing about, espied him leaning against an adjacent rock.

"Alas, Señor," says he, "I know yon ship by her looks—aye, and so doth the Señorita—see yonder!" Now glancing whither he pointed, I beheld Joanna pacing daintily along the reef, pausing ever and anon to signal with her arm; then, as the ship went about to bear up towards the reef, from her crowded decks rose a great shouting and halloo, a hoarse clamour drowned all at once in the roar of great guns, and up to the main fluttered a black ancient; and beholding this accursed flag, its grisly skull and bones, I cast me down on the sands, my high hopes and fond expectations 'whelmed in a great despair.

But as I lay thus was a gentle touch on my bowed head and in my ear Don Federigo's voice:

"Alas, good my friend, and doth Hope die for you likewise? Then do I grieve indeed. But despair not, for in the cave yonder be two swords; go fetch them, I pray, for I am over-weak."

"Of what avail," cried I bitterly, looking up into the pale serenity of his face, "of what avail two swords 'gainst a ship's company?"

"We can die, Señor!" said he, with his gentle smile. "To die on our own steel, by our own hands—here— is clean death and honourable."

"True!" said I.

"Then I pray go fetch the swords, my friend; 'tis time methinks—look!" Glancing towards the ship, I saw she was already come to an anchor and a boatful of men pulling briskly for the reef where stood Joanna, and as they rowed they cheered her amain:

"La Culebra!" they roared. "Ahoy, Joanna! Give a rouse for Fighting Jo! Cap'n Jo—ha, Joanna!"

The boat being near enough, many eager hands were

reached out to her and with Joanna on board they paddled into the lagoon. Now as they drew in to Deliverance Beach they fell silent all, hearkening to her words, and I saw her point them suddenly to Skeleton Cove, whereupon they rowed amain towards that spit of sand where we stood screened among the rocks, shouting in fierce exultation as they came. Don Federigo sank upon his knees with head bowed reverently above his little crucifix, and when at last he looked up his face showed placid as ever.

"Señor," quoth he gently, "you do hear them howling for my blood? Well, you bear a knife in your girdle—I pray you lend it to me." For a moment I hesitated, then, drawing the weapon forth, I sent it spinning far out to sea.

"Sir," said I, "we English do hold that whiles life is—so is hope. Howbeit, if you die you shall not die alone, this I swear."

Then I sprang forth of the rocks and strode down where these lawless fellows were beaching their boat.

CHAPTER IX

We Fall Among Pirates

At my sudden coming they fell silent, one and all, staring from me to Joanna, where she stood beside a buxom, swaggering ruffling fellow whose moustachios and beard were cut after the Spanish mode but with a monstrous great periwig on his head surmounted by a gold-braided, looped hat. His coat was of scarlet velvet, brave with much adornment of gold lace; his legs were thrust into a pair of rough sea-boots; and on his hip a long, curved hanger very broad in the blade.

"'S fish!" said he, looking me over with his sleepy eyes. "Is this your Englishman, Jo? And what must we do wi' him—shall he hang?"

"Mayhap yes—when 'tis so my whim," answered she, 'twixt smiling lips and staring me in the eyes.

But now, and all at once, from the wild company rose a sudden hoarse murmur that swelled again to that fierce, exultant uproar as down towards us paced Don Federigo.

"Aha, 'tis the Marquis!" they cried. "'Tis the bloody Marquis! Shoot the dog! Nay, hang him up! Aye, by his thumbs. Nay, burn him—to the fire wi' the bloody rogue!"

Unheeding their vengeful outcry he advanced upon the men (and these ravening for his blood), viewing their lowering faces and brandished steel with his calm, dispassionate gaze and very proud and upright for all his bodily weakness; pausing beside me, he threw up his hand with haughty gesture and before the command of this ragged arm they abated their clamour somewhat.

"Of a surety," said he in his precise English, "it is the Capitan Belvedere. You captured my daughter—my son—in the *Margarita* carrack three years agone. 'Tis said he died at your hands, Señor Capitan——"

"Not mine, Don, not mine," answered this Belvedere, smiling sleepily. "We gave him to Black Pompey to carbonado." I felt Don Federigo's hand against me as if suddenly faint, but his wide-eyed gaze never left the Captain's handsome face, who, aware of this look, shifted his own gaze, cocked his hat and swaggered. "Stare your fill, now," quoth he with an oath, " 'tis little enough you'll be seeing presently. Aye, you'll be blind enough soon——"

"Blind is it, Cap'n—ha, good!" cried a squat, ill-looking fellow, whipping out a long knife. "Hung my comrade Jem, a did, so here's a knife shall blind him when ye will, Cap'n, by hookey!" And now he and his fellows began to crowd upon us with evil looks; but they halted suddenly, fumbling with their weapons and eyeing Joanna uncertainly where she stood, hand on hip, viewing them with her fleering smile.

"Die he shall, yes!" said she at last. "Die he must, but in proper fashion and time, not by such vermin as you—so put up that knife! You hear me, yes?"

"Hanged my comrade Jem, a did, along o' many others o' the Fellowship!" growled the squat man, flourishing his knife. "Moreover the Cap'n says 'blind' says he, so blind it is, says I, and this the knife to——" The growling voice was drowned in the roar of a pistol and, dropping his knife, the fellow screamed and caught at his hurt.

"And there's for you, yes!" said Joanna, smiling into the man's agonised face. "Be thankful I spared your worthless life. Crawl into the boat, worm, and wait till I'm minded to patch up your hurt—Go!"

For a moment was silence, then came a great gust of laughter, and men clapped and pummelled each other.

"La Culebra!" they roared. " 'Tis our Jo, 'tis Fighting Jo, sure and sartain; 'tis our luck, the luck o' the Brotherhood—ha, Joanna!"

But, tossing aside the smoking pistol, Joanna scowled from them to their captain.

"Hola, Belvedere," said she. "Your dogs do grow out of hand; 'tis well I'm back again. Now for these my prisoners, seize 'em up, bind 'em fast and heave 'em aboard ship."

"Aye, but," said Belvedere, fingering his beard, "why aboard, Jo, when we may do their business here and prettily. Yon's a tree shall make notable good gallows or—look now, here's right plenty o' kindling, and driftwood shall burn 'em merrily and 'twill better please the lads——"

"But then I do pleasure myself, yes. So aboard ship they go!"

"Why, look now, Jo," said Belvedere, biting at his thumb, " 'tis ever my rule to keep no prisoners——"

"Save women, Cap'n!" cried a voice, drowned in sudden evil laughter.

"So, as I say, Joanna, these prisoners cannot go aboard my ship."

"Your ship?" said she, mighty scornful. "Ah, ah, but 'twas I made you captain of your ship and 'tis I can unmake you——"

"Why look ye, Jo," said Belvedere, gnawing at his thumb more savagely and glancing towards his chafing company, "the good lads be growing impatient, being all heartily for ending these prisoners according to custom——"

"Aye, aye, Cap'n!" cried divers of the men, begin-

ning to crowd upon us again. "To the fire with 'em!
Nay, send aboard for Black Pompey! Aye, Pompey's
the lad to set 'em dancing Indian fashion——"

"You hear, Jo, you hear?" cried Belvedere. "The
lads are for ending of 'em sportive fashion—especially
the Don; he must die slow and quaint for sake o' the
good lads as do hang a-rotting on his cursed gibbets
e'en now—quaint and slow; the lads think so and so
think I——"

"But you were ever a dull fool, my pretty man,
yes!" said Joanna, showing her teeth. "And as for
these rogues, they do laugh at you—see!" But as
Belvedere turned to scowl upon and curse his ribalds,
Joanna deftly whisked the pistols from his belt and
every face was smitten to sudden anxious gravity as
she faced them.

"I am Joanna!" quoth she, her red lips curving to
the smile I ever found so hateful. "Oh, Madre de Dios,
where now are your tongues? And never a smile among
ye! Is there a man here that will not obey Joanna—no?
Joanna that could kill any of ye single-handed as she
killed Cestiforo!" At this was an uneasy stir and
muttering among them, and Belvedere's sleepy eyes
widened suddenly. "Apes!" cried she, beslavering them
with all manner of abuse, French, Spanish and English.
"Monkeys, cease your chattering and list to Joanna.
And mark—my prisoners go aboard this very hour, yes.
And to-day we sail for Nombre de Dios. Being before
the town we send in a boat under flag of truce to say
we hold captive their governor, Don Federigo de
Cosalva y Maldonada, demanding for him a sufficient
ransom. The money paid, then will we fire a broadside
into the city and the folk shall see their proud Governor
swung aloft to dangle and kick at our mainyard; so
do we achieve vengeance and money both——"

From every throat burst a yell of wild acclaim,
shout on shout:

"Hey, lads, for Cap'n Jo! 'Tis she hath the wise head, mates! Money and vengeance, says Jo! Shout, lads, for Fighting Jo—shout!"

"And what o' your big rogue, Jo?" demanded Belvedere, scowling on me.

"He?" said Joanna, curling her lip at me. Oh, la-la, he shall be our slave—'til he weary me. So—bring them along!"

But now (and all too late) perceiving death to be the nobler part, even as Don Federigo had said, I determined to end matters then and there; thus, turning from Joanna's baleful smile, I leapt suddenly upon the nearest of the pirates and felling him with a buffet, came to grips with another; this man I swung full-armed, hurling him among his fellows, and all before a shot might be fired. But as I stood fronting them, awaiting the stab or bullet should end me, I heard Joanna's voice shrill and imperious:

"Hold, lads! You are twelve and he but one and unarmed. So down with your weapons—down, I say! You shall take me this man with your naked hands—ha, fists—yes! Smite then—bruise him, fists shall never kill him! To it, with your hands then; the first man that draweth weapon I shoot! To it, lads, sa-ha —at him then, good bullies!"

For a moment they hesitated but seeing Joanna, her cheeks aglow, her pistols grasped in·ready hands, they laughed and cursed and, loosing off such things as incommoded them, prepared to come at me. Then, perceiving she had fathomed my design and that here was small chance of finding sudden quietus, I folded my arms, minded to let them use me as they would. But this fine resolution was brought to none account by a small piece of driftwood that one of these fellows hove at me, thereby setting my mouth a-bleeding. Stung by the blow and forgetting all but my anger, I leapt and smote with my fist, and then he and his

fellows were upon me.   But they being so many their
very numbers hampered them, so that as they leapt
upon me many a man was staggered by kick or buffet
aimed at me; moreover these passed their days cooped
up on shipboard whiles I was a man hardened by constant exercise.   Scarce conscious of the hurts I took as
we reeled to and fro, locked in furious grapple, I fought
them very joyously, making right good play with my
fists; but ever as I smote one down, another leapt to
smite, so that presently my breath began to labour.
How long I endured, I know not.   Only I remember
marvelling to find myself so strong and the keen joy of
it was succeeded by sudden weariness, a growing sickness: I remember a sound of groaning breaths all about
me, of thudding blows, hoarse shouts, these, waxing ever
fainter, until smiting with failing arms and ever-waning
strength, they dragged me down at last and I lay
vanquished and unresisting.   As I sprawled there, drawing my breath in painful gasps, the hands that smote,
the merciless feet that kicked and trampled me were
suddenly stilled and staring up with dimming eyes I
saw Joanna looking down on me.

"Oh, Martino," said she in my ear, "Oh, fool Englishman, could you but love as you do fight——"

But groaning, I turned my face to the trampled
sand and knew no more.

CHAPTER X

How I Came Aboard the *Happy Despatch* and of My Sufferings There

I awoke gasping to the shock of cold water and was dimly aware of divers people crowding about me.

" 'Tis a fine, bull-bodied boy, Job, all brawn and beef—witness your eye, Lord love me!" exclaimed a jovial voice. "Aha, Job, a lusty lad—heave t'other bucket over him!" There came another torrent of water, whereupon I strove to sit up, but finding this vain by reason of strict bonds, I cursed them all and sundry instead.

"A sturdy soul, Job, and of a comfortable conversation!" quoth the voice. "Moreover a man o' mark, as witnesseth your peeper."

"Rot him!" growled the man Job, a beastly-seeming fellow, very slovenly and foul of person, who glared down at me out of one eye, the other being so bruised and swollen as to serve him no whit.

"He should be overside wi' his guts full o' shot for this same heye of mine if 'twas my say——"

"But then it ain't your say, Job, nor yet Belvedere's—'tis hern, Job—hern—Cap'n Jo's. 'He's to be took care of,' says she, 'treated kind and gentle,' says she. And, mark me, here's Belvedere's nose out o' joint, d'ye see? And, talkin' o' noses, there's your eye, Job; sink me but he wiped your eye for you, my lad——"

"Plague and perish him!" snarled Job, kicking me viciously. "Burn him, 'tis keelhaul 'im I would first

and then give 'im to Pompey to carve up what
remained——"

"Pompey?" exclaimed this fellow Diccon, a merry-
seeming fellow but with a truculent eye. "Look 'ee,
Job, here's a match for Pompey at last, as I do think,
man to man, bare fists or knives, a match and I'll lay
to't."

"Pshaw!" growled Job. "Pompey could eat 'im—
bones and all, curse 'im! Pompey would break 'is back
as 'e did the big Spaniard's last week."

"Nay, Job, this fellow should make better fight for't
than did the Spanisher. Look 'ee now, match 'em, and
I'll lay all my share o' the voyage on this fellow, come
now!"

"A match? Why so I would, but what o' Belvedere?"

"He sulketh, Job, and yonde~ he cometh, a-sucking
of his thumb and all along o' this fellow and our Jo.
Joanna's cocked her eye on this fellow and Belvedere's
cake's dough—see him yonder!"

Now following the speaker's look, I perceived Captain Belvedere descending the quarter-ladder, his handsome face very evil and scowling; spying me where I
lay, he came striding up and folding his arms, stood
looking over me silently awhile.

"Lord love me!" he exclaimed at last in huge disgust
and spat upon me. "Aft with him—to the coach——"

"Coach, Cap'n?" questioned Job, staring. "And
why theer?"

"Because I say so!" roared Belvedere.

"And because," quoth Diccon, his eye more truculent than ever, "because women will be women, eh, Captain?" At this Belvedere's face grew suffused, his eyes
glared and he turned on the speaker with clenched fist;
then laughing grimly, he spurned me savagely with his
foot.

"Joanna hath her whimsies, and here's one of 'em!"

quoth he and spat on me again, whereat I raged and strove, despite my bonds, to come at him.

"I were a-saying to Job," quoth the man Diccon, thrusting me roughly beyond reach of Belvedere's heavy foot, "that here was a fellow to match Pompey at last."

"Tush!" said Belvedere, with an oath. "Pompey would quarter him wi' naked hands."

"I was a-saying to Job I would wager my share in the voyage on this fellow, Belvedere!"

"Aye, Cap'n," growled Job, " 'tis well enough keeping the Don to hang afore Nombre but why must this dog live aft and cosseted? He should walk overboard wi' slit weasand, or better—he's meat for Pompey, and wherefore no? I asks why, Cap'n?"

"Aye—why!" cried Belvedere, gnashing his teeth. "Ask her—go ask Joanna, the curst jade."

"She be only a woman, when all's said, Cap'n——"

"Nay, Job," quoth Belvedere, shaking his head. "She's Joanna and behind her do lie Tressady and Sol and Rory and Abnegation Mings—and all the Fellowship. So if she says he lives, lives it is, to lie soft and feed dainty, curse him. Let me die if I don't wish I'd left her on the island to end him her own way—wi' steel or kindness——"

"Kindness!" said Diccon, with an ugly leer. "Why, there it is, Cap'n; she's off wi' the old and on wi' the new, like——"

"Not yet, by God!" snarled Belvedere 'twixt shut teeth and scowling down on me while his hand clawed at the pistol in his belt; then his gaze wandered from me towards the poop and back again. "Curse him!" said he, stamping in his impotent fury. "I'd give a handful o' gold pieces to see him dead and be damned!" And here he fell a-biting savagely at his thumb again.

"Why, then, here's a lad to earn 'em," quoth Job, "an' that's me. I've a score agin him for this lick o' the eye he give me ashore—nigh blinded me, 'e did, burn an' blast his bones!"

"Aye, but what o' Joanna, what o' that she-snake, ha?"

" 'Tis no matter for her. I've a plan."

"What is't, Job lad? Speak fair and the money's good as yourn——"

"Aye, but it ain't mine yet, Cap'n, so mum it is—but I've a plan."

"Belay, Job!" exclaimed Diccon. "Easy all. Yonder she cometh."

Sure enough, I saw Joanna descend the ladder from the poop and come mincing across the deck towards us.

"Hola, Belvedere, mon Capitan!" said she, glancing about her quick-eyed. "You keep your ship very foul, yes. Dirt to dirt!—ah? But I am aboard and this shall be amended—look to it. And your mizzen yard is sprung; down with it and sway up another——"

"Aye, aye, Jo," said Belvedere, nodding. "It shall be done——"

"*Mañana!*" quoth she, frowning. "This doth not suit when I am aboard, no! The new yard must be rigged now, at once, for we sail with the flood—*voilà!*"

"Sail, Jo?" said Belvedere, staring. "Can't be, Jo!"

"And wherefore?"

"Why—we be short o' water, for one thing."

"Ah—bah, we shall take all we want from other ships!"

"And the lads be set, heart and soul, on a few days ashore."

"But then—I am set, my heart, my soul, on heaving anchor so soon as the tide serves. We will sail with the flood. Now see the new yard set up and have this slave Martin o' mine to my cabin." So saying, she turned on her heel and minced away, while Belvedere stood looking after her and biting at his thumb, Job scowled and Diccon smiled.

"So—ho!" quoth he. "Captain Jo says we sail, and sail it is, hey?"

"Blind you!" cried Belvedere, turning on him in a fury. "Go forward and turn out two o' the lads to draw this carcass aft!" Here bestowing a final kick on me, he swaggered away.

"Sail wi' the flood, is it?" growled Job. "And us wi' scarce any water and half on us rotten wi' scurvy or calenture, an' no luck this cruise, neither! 'Sail wi' the flood,' says she—'be damned,' says I. By hookey, but I marvel she lives; I wonder no one don't snuff her out for good an' all—aye, burn me but I do!"

"Because you're a fool, Job, and don't know her like we do. She's 'La Culebra,' and why? Because she's quick as any snake and as deadly. Besides, she's our luck and luck she'll bring us; she always do. Whatever ship she's aboard of has all the luck, wind, weather, and—what's better, rich prizes, Job. I know it and the lads forrad know it, and Belvedere he knows it and is mighty feared of her and small blame either— aye, and mayhap you'll be afeard of her when you know her better. 'She's only a woman,' says you. 'True,' says I. But in all this here world there ain't her match, woman or man, and you can lay to that, my lad."

Now the ropes that secured me being very tight, began to cause me no little pain, insomuch that I besought the man Diccon to loose me a little, where-upon he made as to comply, but Job, who it seemed was quartermaster, and new in the office, would have none of it but cursed me vehemently instead, and hail-ing two men had me forthwith dragged aft to a small cabin under the poop and there (having abused and cuffed me to his heart's content) left me.

And in right woful plight was I, with clothes nigh torn off and myself direly bruised from head to foot,

and what with this and the cramping strictness of my
bonds I could come by no easement, turn and twist me
how I might. After some while, as I lay thus miserable
and pain in every joint of me, the door opened, closed
and Joanna stood above me.

"Ah, ah—you are very foul o' blood!" said she in
bitter mockery. " 'Twas thus you spake me once,
Martino, you'll mind! 'Very foul o' blood,' said you,
and I famishing with hunger! Art hungry, Martino?"
she questioned, bending over me; but meeting her look,
I scowled and held my peace. "Ha, won't ye talk?
Is the sullen fit on you?" said she, scowling also. "Then
shall you hear me! And first, know this: you are mine
henceforth, aye—mine!" So saying, she seated herself on the cushioned locker whereby I lay and, setting
her foot upon my breast and elbow on knee, leaned
above me, dimpled chin on fist, staring down on me with
her sombre gaze. "You are mine," said she again, "to
use as I will, to exalt or cast down. I can bestow on
ye life or very evil death. By my will ye are alive;
when I will you must surely die. Your wants, your
every need must you look to me for—so am I your
goddess and ruler of your destiny, yes! Ah, had you
been more of man and less of fish, I had made you
captain of this ship, and loved you, Martino, loved
you——!"

"Aye," cried I bitterly, "until you wearied of me
as you have wearied of this rogue Belvedere, it seems
—aye, and God knoweth how many more——"

"Oh, la-la, fool—these I never loved——"

"Why, then," said I, "the more your shame!"

As I uttered the words, she leaned down and smote
me lightly upon my swollen lips and so left me. But
presently back she came and with her three of the
crew, bearing chains, etc., which fellows at her command (albeit they were something gone in liquor) forthwith clapped me up in these fetters and thereafter cut

away the irksome cords that bound me. Whiles this was a-doing, she (quick to mark their condition) lashed them with her tongue, giving them "loathly sots," "drunken swine," "scum o' the world" and the like epithets, all of the which they took in mighty humble fashion, knuckling their foreheads, ducking their heads with never a word and mighty glad to stumble away and be gone at flick of her contemptuous finger.

"So here's you, Martino," said she, when we were alone, "here's you in chains that might have been free, and here's myself very determined you shall learn somewhat of shame and be slave at command of such beasts as yonder. D'ye hear, fool, d'ye hear?" But I heeding her none at all, she kicked me viciously so that I flinched (despite myself) for I was very sore; whereat she gave a little laugh:

"Ah, ah!" said she, nodding. "If I did not love you, now would I watch you die! But the time is not yet—no. When that hour is, then, if I am not your death, you shall be mine—death for one or other or both, for I——"

She sprang to her feet as from the deck above came the uproar of sudden brawl with drunken outcry.

"Ah, Madre de Dios!" said she, stamping in her anger. "Oh, these bestial things called men!" which said, she whipped a pistol from her belt, cocked it and was gone with a quick, light patter of feet. Suddenly I heard the growing tumult overhead split and smitten to silence by a pistol-shot, followed by a wailing cry that was drowned in the tramp of feet away forward.

As for me, my poor body, freed of its bonds, found great easement thereby (and despite my irons) so that I presently laid myself down on one of these cushioned lockers (and indeed, though small, this cabin was rarely luxurious and fine) but scarce had I stretched my aching limbs than the door opened and a man entered.

And surely never in all this world was stranger creature to be seen. Gaunt and very lean was he of person and very well bedight from heel to head, but the face that peered out 'twixt the curls of his great periwig lacked for an eye and was seamed and seared with scars in horrid fashion; moreover the figure beneath his rich, wide-skirted coat seemed warped and twisted beyond nature; yet as he stood viewing me with his solitary eye (this grey and very quick and bright) there was that in his appearance that somehow took my fancy.

"What, messmate," quoth he, in full, hearty voice, advancing with a shambling limp, "here cometh one to lay alongside you awhile, old Resolution Day, friend, mate o' this here noble ship *Happy Despatch*, comrade, and that same myself, look'ee!"

But having no mind to truck with him or any of this evil company, I bid him leave me be and cursed him roundly for the pirate-rogue he was.

"Pirate," said he, no whit abashed at my outburst. "Why, pirate it is. But look'ee, there never was pirate the like o' me for holiness—'specially o' Sundays! Lord love you, there's never a parson or divine, high church or low, a patch on me for real holiness—'specially o' Sundays. So do I pray when cometh my time to die, be it in bed or boots, by sickness, bullet or noose, it may chance of a Sunday. And then again, why not a pirate? What o' yourself, friend? There's a regular fire-and-blood, skull-and-bones look about ye as liketh me very well. And there be many worse things than a mere pirate, brother. And what? You'll go for to ask. Answer I—Spanishers, Papishers, the Pope o' Rome and his bloody Inquisition, of which last I have lasting experience, *camarado*—aye, I have I!"

"Ah?" said I, sitting up. "You have suffered the torture?"

"Comrade, look at me! The fire, the pulley, the

rack, the wheel, the water—there's no devilment they ha'n't tried on this poor carcase o' mine and all by reason of a Spanish nun as bore away with my brother!"

"Your brother?"

"Aye, but 'twas me she loved, for I was younger then and something kinder to the eye. So him they burned, her they buried alive and me they tormented into the wrack ye see. But I escaped wi' my life, the Lord delivered me out o' their bloody hands, which was an ill thing for them, d'ye see, for though I lack my starboard blinker and am somewhat crank i' my spars alow and aloft, I can yet ply whinger and pull trigger rare and apt enough for the rooting out of evil. And where a fairer field for the aforesaid rooting out o' Papishers, Portingales, and the like evil men than this good ship, the *Happy Despatch?* Aha, messmate, there's many such as I've despatched hot-foot to their master Sathanas, 'twixt then and now. And so 'tis I'm a pirate and so being so do I sing along o' David: 'Blessed be the Lord my strength that teacheth my hands to war and my fingers to fight.' A rare gift o' words had Davy and for curses none may compare." Hereupon, seating himself on the locker over against me, he thrust a hand into his great side pocket and brought thence a hank of small-cord, a silver-mounted pistol and lastly a small, much battered volume.

"Look'ee, comrade," said he, tapping the worn covers with bony finger, "the Bible is a mighty fine book to fight by; to stir up a man for battle, murder or sudden death it hath no equal and for keeping his hate agin his enemies ever a-burning, there is no book written or ever will be——"

"You talk blasphemy!" quoth I.

"Avast, avast!" cried he. "Here's no blasphemy, thought or word. I love this little Bible o' mine; 'tis meat and drink to me, the friend o' my solitude,

my solace in pain, my joy for ever and alway. Some
men, being crossed in fortune, hopes, ambition or love,
take 'em to drink and the like vanities. I, that suffered
all this, took to the Bible and found all my needs
betwixt the covers o' this little book. For where shall
a wronged man find such a comfortable assurance as
this? Hark ye what saith our Psalmist!" Turning
over a page or so and lifting one knotted fist aloft,
Resolution Day read this:

"'I shall bathe my footsteps in the blood of mine
enemies and the tongues of the dogs shall be red with
the same!' The which," said he, rolling his bright
eye at me, "the which is a sweet, pretty fancy for the
solace of one hath endured as much as I. Aye, a noble
book is Psalms. I know it by heart. List ye to this,
now! 'The wicked shall perish and the enemies of the
Lord be as the fat of rams, as smoke shall they consume away.' Brother, I've watched 'em so consume
many's the time and been the better for't. Hark'ee
again: 'They shall be as chaff before the wind. As a
snail that melteth they shall every one pass away.
Break their teeth in their mouth, O God!' saith Davy,
aye and belike did it too, and so have I ere now with
a pistol butt. I mind once when we stormed Santa
Catalina and the women and children a-screaming in
the church which chanced to be afire, I took out my
Bible here and read these comfortable words: 'The
righteous shall rejoice when he seeth the vengeance,
he shall wash his feet in the blood of the wicked so
that a man shall say: Verily there is a reward for the
righteous.' Aha, brother, for filling a man wi' a gust
of hate and battle, there's nought like the Bible. And
when a curse is wanted, give me David. Davy was a
man of his hands, moreover, and so are you, friend.
I watched ye fight on the sand-spit yonder; twelve to
one is long enough odds for any man, and yet here's
five o' the twelve wi' bones broke and never a one but wi'

some mark o' your handiwork to show, which is vastly well, comrade. Joanna's choice is mine, messmate——"

"How d'ye mean?" I demanded, scowling, whereupon he beamed on me friendly-wise and blinked his solitary eye.

"There is no man aboard this ship," quoth he, nodding again, "no, not one as could keep twelve in play so long, friend, saving only Black Pompey——"

"I've heard his name already," said I, "what like is he and who?"

"A poor heathen, comrade, a blackamoor, friend, a child of Beelzebub abounding in blood, brother—being torturer, executioner and cook and notable in each several office. A man small of soul yet great of body, being nought but a poor, black heathen, as I say. And ashore yonder you shall hear our Christian messmates a-quarrelling over their rum as is the way o' your Christians hereabouts—hark to 'em!"

The *Happy Despatch* lay anchored hard by the reef and rode so near the island that, glancing from one of her stern-gallery windows I might behold Deliverance Beach shining under the moon and a great fire blazing, round which danced divers of the crew, filling the night with lewd, unholy riot of drunken singing and shouts that grew ever more fierce and threatening. I was gazing upon this scene and Resolution Day beside me, when the door was flung open and Job the quartermaster appeared.

"Cap'n Jo wants ye ashore wi' her!" said he, beckoning to Resolution, who nodded and thrusting Bible into pocket, took thence the silver-mounted pistol, examined flint and priming and thrusting it into his belt, followed Job out of the cabin, locking the door upon me. Thereafter I was presently aware of a boat putting off from the ship and craning my neck, saw it was rowed by Resolution with Joanna in the stern sheets, a naked sword across her knees; and my gaze held by the glimmer of this steel, I watched them row into the lagoon and so to that spit of sand opposite Skeleton Cove. I saw the hateful glitter of this deadly steel as Joanna leapt lightly ashore, followed more slowly by Resolution. But suddenly divers of the rogues about the fire, beholding Joanna as she advanced against them thus, sword in hand, cried out a warning to their fellows, who, ceasing from their strife, immediately betook them to their heels, fleeing before her like so many mischievous lads; marvelling, I watched until she had pursued them out of my view.

Hereupon I took to an examination of my fetters, link by link, but finding them mighty secure, laid me down as comfortably as they would allow and fell to pondering my desperate situation, and seeing no way out herefrom (and study how I might) I began to despond; but presently, bethinking me of Don Federigo and judging his case more hopeless than mine (if this could well be), and further, remembering how, but for me, he would by death have delivered himself, I (that had not prayed this many a long month) now petitioned the God to whom nothing is impossible that He would save alive this noble gentleman of Spain, and thus, in his sorrows, forgot mine own awhile.

All at once I started up, full of sudden great and joyful content in all that was, or might be, beholding in my fetters the very Providence of God (as it were) and in my captivity His answer to my so oft-repeated prayer; for now I remembered that with the flood this ship was to sail for Nombre de Dios, where, safedungeoned and secure against my coming lay my hated foe and deadly enemy, Richard Brandon. And now, in my vain and self-deluding pride (my heart firm-set on this miserable man, his undoing and destruction) I cast me down on my knees and babbled forth my passionate gratitude to Him that is from everlasting to everlasting the God of Mercy, Love and Forgiveness.

CHAPTER XI

How I Fought in the Dark With One Pompey, a Great Blackamoor

I was yet upon my knees when came Job the quarter-master with two men who, at his command, dragged me to my feet and out upon deck; cursing my hampering fetters, they tumbled me down the quarter-ladder and so down into the waist of the ship.

Now as I went I kept my eyes upraised to the serene majesty of the heavens; the moon rode high amid a glory of stars, and as I looked it seemed I had never seen them so bright and wonderful, never felt the air so good and sweet upon my lips.

Being come to the fore-hatchway I checked there, despite my captors' buffets and curses, to cast a final, long look up, above and round about me, for I had a sudden uneasy feeling, a dreadful suspicion that once I descended into the gloom below I never should come forth alive. So I stared eagerly upon these ever-restless waters, so bright beneath the moon, upon the white sands of Deliverance Beach, on lofty palmetto and bush-girt cliff and then, shivering despite all my resolution, I suffered them to drag me down into that place of shadows.

I remember a sharp, acrid smell, the reek of bilge and thick, mephitic air as I stumbled on betwixt my captors through this foul-breathing dimness until a door creaked, yawning suddenly upon a denser blackness, into which I was thrust so suddenly that I fell, clashing my fetters, and lying thus, heard the door slammed and bolted.

So here lay I in sweating, breathless expectation of I knew not what, my ears on the stretch, my manacled hands tight-clenched and every nerve a-tingle with this dreadful uncertainty. For a great while it seemed I lay thus, my ears full of strange noises, faint sighings, unchancy rustlings and a thousand sly, unaccountable sounds that at first caused me direful apprehensions but which, as I grew more calm, I knew for no more than the flow of the tide and the working of the vessel's timbers as she strained at her anchors. All at once I sat up, crouching in the dark, as from somewhere about me, soft yet plain to hear, came a sound that told me some one was stealthily drawing the bolts of the door. Rising to my feet I stood, shackled fists clenched, ready to leap and smite so soon as chance should offer. Then came a hissing whisper:

"Easy all, brother! Soft it is, comrade! 'Tis me, messmate, old Resolution, friend, come to loose thy bilboes, for fair is fair. Ha, 'tis plaguey dark, the pit o' Acheron ain't blacker, where d'ye lay—speak soft for there's ears a-hearkening very nigh us."

In the dark a hand touched me and then I felt the muzzle of a pistol at my throat.

"No tricks, lad—no running for't if I loose ye— you'll bide here—come life, come death? Is't agreed?"

"It is!" I whispered. Whereupon and with no more ado, he freed me from my gyves, making scarcely any sound, despite the dark.

"I'll take these wi' me, friend and—my finger's on trigger."

"Resolution, how am I to die?"

"Black Pompey!" came the hissing whisper.

"Hath Joanna ordered this?"

"Never think it, mate—she's ashore and I swam aboard, having my suspicions."

"Resolution, a dying man thanks you heartily. Surely never, after all, was there pirate the like o' you for holiness. Could I but find some weapon to. my defence now—a knife, say." In the dark came a groping hand that found mine and was gone again, but in my grasp was a stout, broad-bladed knife.

" 'Let the heathen rage,' saith Holy Writ, so rage it is, says I, only smite first, brother and smite—hard. And 'ware the starboard scuttle!" Hereafter was the rustle of his stealthy departure, the soft noise of bolts, and silence.

And now in this pitchy gloom, wondering what and where this scuttle might be, I crouched, a very wild and desperate creature, peering into the gloom and starting at every sound; thus presently I heard the scrape of a viol somewhere beyond the bulkheads that shut me in and therewith a voice that sang, the words very clear and distinct:

> "Oh, Moll she lives in Deptford town,
> In Deptford town lives she;
> Let maid be white or black or brown,
> Still Moll's the lass for me;
> Sweet Moll as lives in Deptford town,
> Yo-ho, shipmates, for Deptford town,
> 'Tis there as I would be."

Mingled with this singing I thought to hear the heavy thud of an unshod foot on the planking above my head, and setting my teeth I gripped my knife in sweating palm.

But now (and to my despair) came the singing again to drown all else, hearken how I would:

> "Come whistle, messmates all,
> For a breeze, for a breeze
> Come pipe up, messmates all,
> For a breeze.
> When to Deptford town we've rolled
> Wi' our pockets full o' gold;
> Then our lasses we will hold
> On our knees, on our knees."

Somewhere in the dark was the sudden, thin complaint of a rusty and unwilling bolt, though if this were to my right or left, above or below me, I could not discover and my passionate listening was once more vain by reason of this accursed rant:

"Who will not drink a glass,
Let him drown, let him drown;
Who will not drink a glass,
Let him drown.
Who will not drink a glass
For to toast a pretty lass,
Is no more than fool and ass;
So let him drown, let him drown!"

A sudden glow upon the gloom overhead, a thin line of light that widened suddenly to a square of blinding radiance and down through the trap came a lanthorn grasped in a hugeous, black fist and, beyond this, an arm, a mighty shoulder, two rows of flashing teeth, two eyes that glared here and there, rolling in horrid fashion; thus much I made out as I sprang and, grappling this arm, smote upwards with my knife. The lanthorn fell, clattering, and was extinguished, but beyond the writhing, shapeless thing that blocked the scuttle, I might, ever and anon, behold a star twinkling down upon me where I wrestled with this mighty arm that whirled me from my feet, and swung me, staggering, to and fro as I strove to get home with my knife at the vast bulk that loomed above me. Once and twice I stabbed vainly, but my third stroke seemed more successful, for the animal-like howl he uttered nigh deafened me; then (whether by my efforts or his own, I know not) down he came upon me headlong, dashing the good knife from my grasp and whirling me half-stunned against the bulkhead, and as I leaned there, sick and faint, a hand clapped-to the scuttle. And now in this dreadful dark I heard a deep and gusty breathing, like that of some monstrous beast, heard this breathing checked while he listened for me and a stealthy rustling as he felt here and there to discover my whereabouts. But I stood utterly still, breathless and sweating, with a horror of death at this great blackamoor's hands, since, what with the palsy of fear by reason of the loss of my knife, I did not doubt but that this monster would soon make an end of me and in horrid fashion.

Presently I heard him move again and (judging by the sound) creeping on hands and knees, therefore as he approached I edged myself silently along the bulkhead and thus (as I do think) we made the complete circuit of the place; once it seemed he came upon the lanthorn and dashing it fiercely aside, paused awhile to listen again, and my heart pounding within me so that I sweated afresh lest he catch the sound of it. And sometimes I would hear the soft, slurring whisper his fingers made against deck or bulkhead where he groped for me, and once a snorting gasp and the crunch of his murderous knife-point biting into wood and thereafter a hoarse and outlandish muttering. And ever as I crept thus, moving but when he moved, I felt before me with my foot, praying that I might discover my knife and, this in hand, face him and end matters one way or another and be done with the horror. And whiles we crawled thus round and round within this narrow space, ever and anon above the stealthy rustle of his movements, above his stertorous breathing and evil muttering, above the wild throbbing of my heart rose the wail of the fiddle and the singing:

> "Who will not kiss a maid,
> Let him hang, let him hang;
> Who fears to kiss a maid,
> Let him hang.
> Who will not kiss a maid
> Who of woman is afraid,
> Is no better than a shade;
> So let him hang, let him hang!"

until this foolish, ranting ditty seemed to mock me,

my breath came and went to it, my heart beat to it;
yet even so, I was praying passionately and this my
prayer, viz: That whoso was waiting above us for my
death-cry should not again lift the scuttle lest I be
discovered to this man-thing that crept and crept upon
me in the dark. Even as I prayed thus, the scuttle
was raised and, blinded by the sudden glare of a lanthorn, I heard Job's hoarse voice:

"Below there! Pompey, ahoy! Ha'n't ye done yet
an' be curst?"

And suddenly I found in this thing I had so much
dreaded the one chance to my preservation, for I espied
the great blackamoor huddled on his knees, shading
his eyes with both hands from the dazzling light and
lying on the deck before him a long knife.

"Oh, marse mate," he cried, "me done fin' no curs'
man here'bouts——"

Then I leaped and kicking the knife out of reach,
had him in my grip, my right hand fast about his
throat. I remember his roar, the crash of the trap
as it closed, and after this a grim and desperate scuf-
fling in the dark; now he had me down, rolling and
struggling and now we were up, locked breast to breast,
swaying and staggering, stumbling and slipping,
crashing into bulkheads, panting and groaning; and
ever he beat and buffeted me with mighty fists, but my
head bowed low betwixt my arms, took small hurt,
while ever my two hands squeezed and wrenched and
twisted at his great, fleshy throat. I remember an
awful gasping that changed to a strangling whistle,
choked to a feeble, hissing whine; his great body grew
all suddenly lax, swaying weakly in my grasp, and
then, as I momentarily eased my grip, with a sudden,
mighty effort he broke free. I heard a crash of splin-
tering wood, felt a rush of sweet, pure air, saw him
reel out through the shattered door and sink upon
his knees; but as I sprang towards him he was up and

fleeing along the deck amidships, screaming as he ran.

All about me was a babel of shouts and cries, a rush and trampling of feet, but I sped all unheeding, my gaze ever upon the loathed, fleeing shape of this vile blackamoor. I was hard on his heels as he scrambled up the quarter-ladder and within a yard of him as he gained the deck, while behind us in the waist were men who ran pell-mell, filling the night with raving clamour and drunken halloo. Now as I reached the quarter-deck, some one of these hurled after me a belaying pin and this, catching me on the thigh, staggered me so that I should have fallen but for the rail; so there clung I in a smother of sweat and blood while great moon and glittering stars span dizzily; but crouched before me on his hams, almost within arm's reach, was this accursed negro who gaped upon me with grinning teeth and rolled starting eyeballs, his breath coming in great, hoarse gasps. And I knew great joy to see him in no better case than I, his clothes hanging in blood-stained tatters so that I might see all the monstrous bulk of him. Now, as he caught his breath and glared upon me, I suffered my aching body to droop lower and lower over the rail like one nigh to swooning, yet very watchful of his every move. Suddenly as we faced each other thus, from the deck below rose a chorus of confused cries:

"At him, Pompey! Now's ye time, boy! Lay 'im aboard, lad, 'e be a-swounding! Ha—out wi' his liver, Pompey—at him, he's yourn!"

Heartened by these shouts and moreover seeing how feebly I clutched at the quarter-rail, the great negro uttered a shrill cry of triumph and leapt at me; but as he came I sprang to meet his rush and stooping swiftly, caught him below the knees and in that same moment, straining every nerve, every muscle and sinew to the uttermost, I rose up and hove him whirling over my shoulder.

I heard a scream, a scurry of feet, and then the thudding crash of his fall on the deck below and coming to the rail I leaned down and saw him lie, his mighty limbs hideously twisted and all about him men who peered and whispered.   But suddenly they found their voices to rage against me, shaking their fists and brandishing their steel; a pistol flashed and roared and the bullet hummed by my ear, but standing above them I laughed as a madman might, jibing at them and daring them to come on how they would, since indeed death had no terrors for me now.   And doubtless steel or shot would have ended me there and then but for the man Diccon who quelled their clamour and held them from me by voice and fist:

"Arrest, ye fools—stand by!" he roared.   "Yon man be the property o' Captain Jo—'tis Joanna's man and whoso harms him swings——"

"Aye, but he've murdered Pompey, ain't 'e?" demanded Job.

"Aye, aye—an' so 'e have, for sure!" cried a voice.

"Well an' good—murder's an 'anging matter, ain't it?"

"An' so it be, Job—up wi' him—hang him—hang him!"

"Well an' good!" cried Job again.   "'Ang 'im we will, lads, all on us, every man's fist to the rope—she can't hang us all, d'ye see.   You, Diccon, where be Belvedere; he shall be in it——"

"Safe fuddled wi' rum, surely.   Lord, Job, you do be takin' uncommon risks for a hatful o' guineas——"

So they took me and, all unresisting, I was dragged amidships beneath the main yard where a noose was for my destruction; and though hanging had seemed a clean death by contrast with that I had so lately escaped at the obscene hands of this loathly blackamoor, yet none the less a sick trembling took me as

I felt the rope about my neck, insomuch that I sank to my knees and closed my eyes.

Kneeling thus and nigh to fainting, I heard a sudden, quick patter of light-running feet, a gasping sigh and, glancing up, beheld Job before me, also upon his knees and staring down with wide and awful eyes at an ever-spreading stain that fouled the bosom of his shirt; and as he knelt thus, I saw above his stooping head the blue glitter of a long blade that lightly tapped his brawny neck.

"The noose—here, Diccon, here, yes!"

As one in a dream I felt the rope lifted from me and saw it set about the neck of Job.

"So! Ready there? Now—heave all!"

I heard the creak of the block, the quick tramp of feet, a strangling cry, and Job the quartermaster was snatched aloft to kick and writhe and dangle against the moon.

"Diccon, we have lost our quartermaster and we sail on the flood; you are quartermaster henceforth, yes. Ha—look—see, my Englishman is sick! Dowse a bucket o' water over him, then let him be ironed and take him forward to the fo'castle; he shall serve you all for sport—but no killing, mind." Thus lay I to . be kicked and buffeted and half-drowned; yet when they had shackled me, cometh the man Diccon to clap me heartily on the shoulder and after him Resolution to nod at me and blink with his single, twinkling eye:

"Oh, friend," quoth he, "Oh, brother, saw ye ever the like of our Captain Jo? Had Davy been here to-day he might perchance ha' wrote a psalm to her."

That morning with the flood tide we hove anchor and the *Happy Despatch* stood out to sea and, as she heeled to the freshening wind, Job's stiffening body lurched and swayed and twisted from the main yard. And thus it was I saw the last of my island.

CHAPTER XII

OF BATTLE, MURDER AND RESOLUTION DAY, HIS POINT OF VIEW

AND now, nothing heeding my defenceless situation and the further horrors that might be mine aboard this accursed pirate ship, I nevertheless knew great content for that, with every plunge and roll of the vessel, I was so much the nearer Nombre de Dios town where lay prisoned my enemy, Richard Brandon; thus I made of my sinful lust for vengeance a comfort to my present miseries, and plotting my enemy's destruction, found therein much solace and consolation.

I had crept into a sheltered corner and here, my knees drawn up, my back against one of the weather guns, presently fell a-dozing. I was roused by a kick to find the ship rolling prodigiously, the air full of spray and a piping wind, and Captain Belvedere scowling down on me, supporting himself by grasping a backstay in one hand and flourishing a case-bottle in the other.

"Ha, 's fish, d'ye live yet?" roared he in drunken frenzy. "Ha'n't Black Pompey done your business? Why, then—here's for ye!" And uttering a great oath, he whirled up the bottle to smite; but, rolling in beneath his arm, I staggered him with a blow of my fettered hands, then (or ever I might avoid him) he had crushed me beneath his foot: and then Joanna stood fronting him. Pallid, bare-headed, wild of eye,

she glared on him and before this look he cowered and
shrank away.

"Drunken sot!" cried she. "Begone lest I send ye
aloft to join yon carrion!" And she pointed where
Job's stiff body plunged and swung and twisted at
the reeling yard-arm.

"Nay, Jo, I—I meant him no harm!" he muttered,
and turning obedient to her gesture, slunk away.

"Ah, Martino," said Joanna, stooping above me,
" 'twould seem I must be for ever saving your life to
you, yes. Are you not grateful, no?"

"Aye, I am grateful!" quoth I, remembering my
enemy.

"Then prove me it!"

"As how?"

"Speak me gently, look kindly on me, for I am sick,
Martino, and shall be worse. I never can abide a rolling ship—'tis this cursed woman's body o' mine. So
to-day am I all woman and yearn for tenderness—and
we shall have more bad weather by the look o' things!
Have you enough knowledge to handle this ship in a
storm?"

"Not I!"

" 'Tis pity," she sighed, " 'tis pity! I would hang
Belvedere and make you captain in his room—he
wearies me, and would kill me were he man enough—ah,
Mother of Heaven, what a sea!" she cried, clinging to
me as a great wave broke forward, filling the air with
hissing spray. "Aid me aft, Martino!"

Hereupon, seeing her so haggard and faint, and the
decks deserted save for the watch, I did as she bade me
as well as I might by reason of my fetters and the
uneasy motion of the ship, and at last (and no small
labour) I brought her into the great cabin or roundhouse under the poop. And now she would have me
bide and talk with her awhile, but this I would by no
means do.

"And why not, Martino?" she questioned in soft, wheedling fashion. "Am I so hateful to you yet? Wherefore go?"

"Because I had rather lie in my fetters out yonder at the mercy o' wind and wave!" said I.

Now at this she fell to sudden weeping and, as suddenly, to reviling me with bitter curses.

"Go then!" cried she, striking me in her fury. "Keep your chains—aye, I will give ye to the mercy of this rabble crew . . . leave me!" The which I did forthwith and, finding me a sheltered corner, cast myself down there and fell to hearkening to the rush of the wind and to watching the awful might of the racing, foam-capped billows. And, beholding these manifestations of God's majesty and infinite power, of what must I be thinking but my own small desires and unworthy schemes of vengeance! And bethinking me of Don Federigo (and him governor of Nombre de Dios) I began planning how I might use him to my purpose. My mind full of this, I presently espied the mate, Resolution Day, his laced hat and noble periwig replaced by a close-fitting seaman's bonnet, making his way across the heaving deck as only a seaman might (and despite his limp) and as he drew nearer I hailed and beckoned him.

"Aha, and are ye there, camarado!" said he. " 'Tis well, for I am a-seeking ye."

"Tell me, Resolution, when shall we sight Nombre de Dios?"

"Why look now, if this wind holdeth fair, we should fetch up wi' it in some five days or thereabouts."

"Don Federigo is governor of the town, I think?"

"Verily and so he is. And what then?"

"Where lieth he now?"

"Safe, friend, and secure. You may lay to that, brother!"

"Could you but get me speech with him——"

"Not by no manner o' means whatsoever, *amigo!*
And the reason why? It being agin her orders."

"Is he well?"

"Well-ish, brother—fairly bobbish, all things con-
sidered, mate—though not such a hell-fire, roaring lad
o' mettle as yourself, comrade. David slew Goliath o'
Gath wi' a pebble and you broke Black Pompey's back
wi' your naked hands! Here's a thing as liketh me
mighty well! Wherefore I grieve to find ye such an
everlasting fool, brother."

"How so, Resolution?"

"When eyes look sweetness—why scowl? When lips
woo kisses—wherefore take a blow instead? When
comfort and all manner o' delights be offered—why
choose misery forrard and the bloody rogues o' her
fo'castle? For 'tis there as you be going, mate—aye,
verily!" Here he set a silver whistle to his mouth and
blew a shrill blast at which signal came two fellows
who, at his command, dragged me to my feet and so
away forward.

Thus true to her word, Joanna banished me from
the gilded luxury of cabin and roundhouse and gave
me up to the rogues forward, a wild and lawless company of divers races and conditions so that they
seemed the very scum of the world, and yet here, in
this reeking forecastle, each and every of them my master.

Nor can any words of mine justly paint the wild riot
and brutal licence of this crowded 'tween-deck, foul
with the reek of tobacco and a thousand worse savours,
its tiers on tiers of dark and noisome berths where men
snored or thrust forth shaggy heads to rave at and
curse each other; its blotched and narrow table amidships, its rows of battered sea chests, its loathsome
floor; a place of never-ceasing stir and tumult, dim-
lighted by sputtering lamps.

My advent was hailed by an exultant·roar and

they were all about me, an evil company in their rage
and draggled finery; here were faces scarred by battles and brutalised by their own misdeeds, this unlovely
company now thrust upon me with pointing fingers,
nudging elbows, scowls and mocking laughter.

"What now—is he to us, then?" cried one. "Hath
Jo sent us her plaything?"

"Aye, lads, and verily!" answered Resolution.
"Here's him as she calleth Martin O; here's him as
out-fought Pompey——"

"Aye, aye—remember Pompey!" cried a bedizened
rogue pushing towards me, hand on knife.

"Why, truly, Thomas Ford, remember Pompey, but
forget not Job as died so sudden—in the midst o' life
he were in death, were Job! So hands off your knife,
Thomas Ford; Captain Jo sendeth Martin for your
sport and what not, d'ye see, but when he dieth 'tis
herself will do the killing!"

Left alone and helpless in my fetters, I stood with
bowed head, nothing heeding them for all their bait-
ing of me, whereupon the man Ford, catching up a
pipkin that chanced handy, cast upon me some vileness
or other the which was the signal for others to do likewise so that I was soon miserably wet from head to
foot and this I endured without complaint. But now
they betook them to tormenting me with all manner
of missiles, joying to see me blench and stagger until,
stung to a frenzy of rage and being within reach of
the man Ford (my chiefest tormentor) I sprang upon
him and fell to belabouring him heartily with the chain
that swung betwixt my wrists, but an unseen foot
tripped me heavily and ere I could struggle free they
were upon me. But now as they kicked and trampled
and buffeted me, I once again called upon God with
a loud voice, and this was the manner of my supplication:

"Oh, God of Justice, for the pains I now endure,

give to me vengeance—vengeance, Oh, God, upon mine enemy!"

And hearing this passionate outcry, my tormentors presently drew away from me, staring on me where I lay and muttering together like men greatly amazed, and left me in peace awhile.

Very much might I tell of all I underwent at this time, of the shameful indignities, tricks and deviltries of which I was victim, so that there were times when I cursed my Maker and all in this world save only my miserable self—I, that by reason of my hate and vengeful pursuit of my enemy, had surely brought all these evils on my own head. Yet every shame I endured, every pain I suffered did but nerve me anew to this long-sought vengeance on him that (in my blind folly) I cursed as the author of these my sufferings.

But indeed little gust have I to write of these things; moreover I began to fear that my narrative grow to inordinate length, so will I incontinent pass on to that time when came the quartermaster Diccon with Resolution Day to deliver me from my hateful prison.

And joy unspeakable was it to breathe the sweet, clean air, to hear the piping song of the wind and the hiss of the tumbling billows, to feel the lift and roll of the great ship as she ploughed her course through seas blue as any sapphire; though indeed small leisure had I for the glory of it all, as they hurried me aft.

"What now?" I enquired hopelessly. "What new deviltries have ye in store?"

"'Tis Jo!" answered Diccon. "'Tis Joanna, my bully!" and here he leered and nodded. "Joanna is sick and groweth womanish——"

"And look'ee now, friend," quoth Resolution, clapping me on the back, "you'll mind 'twas old Resolution as was your stay and comfort by means of a

knife i' the matter o' the heathen Pompey, comrade?
You'll not forget old Resolution, shipmate?"

"And me," quoth Diccon, patting my other shoulder. "I stood your friend so much as I might—aye,
did I!"

Thus talked they, first in one ear then in the other,
picturing to my imagination favours done me, real or
imagined, until, to hear them, they might have been
my guardian angels; while I went between them silent
and mighty sullen, casting about in my mind as to
what all this should portend.

So they brought me aft to that gilded cabin the
which gave upon the stern-gallery; and here, outstretched on downy cushions and covered by a rich
embroidery, lay Joanna.

Perceiving me, she raised herself languidly and
motioned the others to be gone, whereupon they went
out, closing the door; whereupon she spake, quick and
passionate:

"I have sent for you because I am weak with my
sickness, Martino, faint and very solitary!"

"And must I weep therefore?" said I, and glancing
from her haggard face I beheld a small, ivory-hilted
dagger on the table at her elbow.

"Ah, mercy of God—how the ship rolls!" she
moaned feebly and then burst forth into cursings and
passionate revilings of ship and wind and sea until
these futile ravings were hushed for lack of breath;
anon she fell to sighing and with many wistful looks,
but finding me all unheeding, fell foul of me therefore:

"Ha, scowl, beast—scowl—this becomes thy surly
visage. I shall not know thee else! Didst ever smile
in all thy sullen days or speak me gentle word or
kindly? Never to me, oh, never to me! Will ye not
spare a look? Will ye not speak—have ye no word
to my comfort?"

"Why seek such of me?" I demanded bitterly. "I have endured much of shame and evil at your will——"

"Ah, fool," sighed she, "had you but sent to me—one word—and I had freed you ere this! And I have delivered you at last because I am sick and weak—a woman and lonely——"

"Why, there be rogues for you a-plenty hereabouts shall fit ye better than I——"

"Oh, 'tis a foul tongue yours, Martino!"

"Why, then, give me a boat, cast me adrift and be done with me."

"Ah, no, I would not you should die yet——"

"Mayhap you will torture me a little more first."

" 'Tis for you to choose! Oh, Martino," she cried; "will you not be my friend, rather?"

"Never in this world!"

At this, and all at once, she was weeping.

"Ah, but you are cruel!" she sobbed, looking up at me through her tears. "Have you no pity for one hath never known aught of true love or gentleness? Wilt not forget past scores and strive to love me —some little—Martino?"

Now hearkening to her piteous accents, beholding her thus transfigured, her tear-wet eyes, the pitiful tremor of her vivid lips and all the pleading humility of her, I was beyond all thought amazed.

"Surely," said I, "surely you are the strangest woman God ever made——"

"Why then," said she, smiling through her tears, "since God made me, then surely—ah, surely is there something in me worthy your love?"

"Love?" quoth I, frowning and clenching my shackled hands. " 'Tis an emptiness—I am done with the folly henceforth——"

"Ah—ah . . . and what of your Joan—your Damaris?" she questioned eagerly. "Do you not love her—no?"

"No!" said I fiercely. "My life holdeth but one purpose———"

"What purpose, Martino, what?"

"Vengeance!"

"On whom?"

" 'Tis no matter!" said I, and question me how she might I would say no more, whereupon she importuned me with more talk of love and the like folly until, finding me heedless alike of her tears and pleadings, she turned on me in sudden fury, vowing she would have me dragged back to the hell of the forecastle there and then.

"I'll shame your cursed pride," cried she. "You shall be rove to a gun and flayed with whips———" But here, reaching forward or ever she might stay me, I caught up the ivory-hilted dagger:

"Ah!" said she softly, staring where it glittered in my shackled hand. "Would you kill me! Come then, death have I never feared—strike, *Martino mio!*" and she proffered her white bosom to the blow; but I laughed in fierce derision.

"Silly wench," said I, "this steel is not for you! Call in your rogues and watch me blood a few———"

"Ah, damned coward," she cried, "ye dare not slay me lest Belvedere torment ye to death—'tis your own vile carcase you do think of!"

At this I did but laugh anew, whereat, falling to pallid fury, she sprang upon me, smiting with passionate, small fists, besetting me so close that I cowered and shrank back lest she impale herself on the dagger I grasped. But presently being wearied she turned away, then staggered as the ship rolled to a great sea, and would have fallen but for me. Suddenly, as she leaned upon me thus, her dark head pillowed on my breast, she reached up and clasped her hands about my neck and with head yet hid against me burst into a storm of fierce sobbing. Staring down at this bowed head, feeling the pleading passion of these vital, soft-clasping hands and shaken by her heart-bursting sobs, I grew swiftly abashed and discomfited and let the dagger fall and lie unheeded.

"Ah, Martino," said she at last, her voice muffled in my breast. "Surely nought is there in all this wretched world so desolate as a loveless woman! Can you not—pity me—a little, yes?"

"Aye, I do pity you!" quoth I, on impulse.

"And pity is kin to love, Martino! And I can be patient, patient, yes!"

" 'Twere vain!" said I. At this she loosed me and uttering a desolate cry, cast herself face down upon her couch.

"Be yourself," said I, spurning the dagger into a corner; "rather would I have your scorn and hate than tears——"

"You have," said she, never stirring. "I do scorn you greatly, hate you mightily, despise you infinitely —yet is my love greater than all——"

Suddenly she started to an elbow, dashing away her tears, fierce-eyed, grim-lipped, all womanly tenderness gone, as from the deck above rose the hoarse roar of a speaking trumpet and the running of feet; and now was loud rapping on the door that, opening, disclosed Diccon, the quartermaster.

"By your leave, Captain Jo," cried he, "but your luck's wi' us—aye, is it! A fine large ship a-plying to wind'ard of us——"

In a moment Joanna was on her feet and casting a boat-cloak about herself hasted out of the cabin, bidding Diccon bring me along.

The wind had fallen light though the seas yet ran high; and now being come to the lofty poop, I might behold our crowded decks where was mighty bustle and to-do, casting loose the guns, getting up shot and powder, a-setting out of half-pikes, swords, pistols and

the like with a prodigious coming and going; a heaving
and yo-ho-ing with shouts and boisterous laughter,
whiles ever and anon grimy hands pointed and all
heads were turned in the one direction where, far away
across the foam-flecked billows, was a speck that I
knew for a vessel.

And beholding these pirate rogues, how joyously
they laboured, with what lusty cheers they greeted
Joanna and clambered aloft upon swaying yards to get
more sail on the ship obedient to her shrill commands,
I knew a great pity for this ship we were pursuing and
a passionate desire that she might yet escape us. I
was yet straining my eyes towards the chase and
grieving for the poor souls aboard her, when, at word
from Joanna, I was seized and fast bound to a ring-
bolt.

Scarce was this done than Joanna uttered a groan
and, clapping her hand to her head, called out for
Resolution, and with his assistance got her down to
the quarter-deck.

By afternoon the sea was well-nigh calm and the
chase so close that we might behold her plainly enough
and the people on her decks. Her topmasts were gone,
doubtless in the great storm, and indeed a poor, battered thing she looked as she rolled to the long, oily
swell. All at once, out from her main broke the
golden banner of Spain, whereupon rose fierce outcries
from our rogues; then above the clamour rose the
voice of Diccon:

"Shout, lads—shout for Roger, give tongue to Jolly
Roger!" and looking where he pointed with glittering
cutlass, I beheld that hideous flag that is hated by all
honest mariners.

And now began a fight that yet indeed was no fight,
for seeing we had the range of them whereas their shot
fell pitifully short, Belvedere kept away and presently
let fly at them with every heavy gun that bore, and,

as the smoke thinned, I saw her foremast totter and fall, and her high, weather-beaten side sorely splintered by our shot. Having emptied her great guns to larboard the *Happy Despatch* went about and thundered death and destruction against them with her starboard broadside and they powerless to annoy us any way in return. And thus did we batter them with our great pieces, keeping ever out of their reach, so that none of all their missiles came aboard us, until they, poor souls, seeing their case altogether hopeless, were fain to cry us quarter. Hereupon, we stood towards them, and as we approached I could behold the havoc our great shot had wrought aboard them.

The enemy having yielded to our mercy and struck their flag, we ceased our fire, and thinking the worst over and done, I watched where Belvedere conned the ship with voice and gesture and the crew, mighty quick and dexterous in obedience, proved themselves prime sailor-men, despite their loose and riotous ways, so that, coming down upon the enemy, we presently fell aboard of them by the fore-chains; whereupon up scrambled old Resolution, sword in hand, first of any man (despite his lameness) and with a cry of "Boarders away!" sprang down upon the Spaniard's blood-spattered deck and his powder-blackened rogues leaping and hallooing on his heels.

And now from these poor, deluded souls who had cast themselves upon our mercy rose sudden awful shrieks and cries hateful to be heard as they fled hither and thither about their littered decks before the pitiless steel that hacked and thrust and smote. Shivering and sweating, I must needs watch this thing done until, grown faint and sick, I bowed my face that I might see no more. Gradually these distressful sounds grew weaker and weaker, and dying away at last, were lost in the fierce laughter and jubilant shouting of their murderers, where they fell to the work of pillage.

But hearing sudden roar of alarm, I looked up to see the Spanish ship was going down rapidly by the head, whereupon was wild uproar and panic, some of our rogues cutting away at the grapples even before their comrades had scrambled back to safety; so was strife amongst them and confusion worse confounded. The last man was barely aboard than our yards were braced round and we stood away clear of this sinking ship. Now presently uproar broke out anew and looking whence it proceeded, I beheld four Spaniards (who it seemed had leapt aboard us unnoticed in the press), and these miserable wretches methought would be torn in pieces. But thither swaggered Belvedere, flourishing his pistols and ordering his rogues back, and falls to questioning these prisoners and though I could not hear, I saw how they cast themselves upon their knees, with hands upraised to heaven, supplicating his mercy. He stood with arms folded, nodding his head now and then as he listened, so that I began to have some hopes that he would spare them; but all at once he gestured with his arms, whereon was a great gust of laughter and cheering, and divers men began rigging a wide plank out-board from the gangway amidships, whiles others hasted to pinion these still supplicating wretches. This done, they seized upon one, and hoisting him up on the plank with his face to the sea, betook them to pricking him with sword and pike, thus goading him to walk to his death. So this miserable, doomed man crept out along the plank, whimpering pleas for mercy to the murderers behind him and prayers for mercy to the God above him, until he was come to the plank's end and cowered there, raising and lowering his bound hands in his agony while he gazed down into the merciless sea that was to engulf him. All at once he stood erect, his fettered hands upraised to heaven, and then with a piteous, wailing cry he plunged down to his death and vanished 'mid the surge; once he came up, struggling and gasping, ere he was swept away in the race of the tide.

Now hereupon I cast myself on my knees and hiding my face in my fettered hands, fell to a passion o' prayer for the soul of this unknown man. And as I prayed, I heard yet other lamentable outcries, followed in due season by the hollow plunge of falling bodies; and so perished these four miserable captives.

I was yet upon my knees when I felt a hand upon my shoulder and the touch (for a wonder) was kindly, and raising my head I found Resolution Day looking down on me with his solitary, bright eye and his grim lips up-curling to friendly smile.

"So perish all Papishers, Romanists, Inquisitioners, and especially Spanishers, friend!"

" 'Twas cruel and bloody murder!" quoth I, scowling up at him.

"Why, perceive me now, *umigo*, let us reason together, *camarado*—thus now it all dependeth upon the point o' view; these were Papishers and evil men, regarding which Davy sayeth i' the Psalms, 'I will root 'em out,' says he; why, root it is! says I—and look'ee, brother, I have done a lot o' rooting hitherto and shall do more yet, as I pray. As to the fight now, mate, as to the fight, 'twas noble fight—pretty work, and the ship well handled, as you must allow, *camarado!*"

"Call it rather brutal butchery!" said I fiercely.

"Aye, there it is again," quoth he; "it all lieth in the point o' view! Now in my view was my brother screaming amid crackling flames and a fair young woman in her living tomb, who screamed for mercy and found none. 'Tis all in the point o' view!" he repeated, smiling down at a great gout of blood that blotched the skirt of his laced coat.

"And I say 'tis foul murder in the sight of God and man!" I cried.

"Ha, will ye squeak, rat!" quoth Belvedere, towering over me, where I crouched upon my knees. "'S fish, will ye yap, then, puppy-dog?"

"Aye—and bite!" quoth I, aiming a futile blow at him with my shackled fists. "Give me one hand free and I'd choke the beastly soul out o' ye and heave your foul carcase to the fishes——"

Now at this he swore a great oath and whipped pistol from belt, but as he did so Resolution stepped betwixt us.

"Put up, Belvedere, put up!" said he in soothing tone. "No shooting, stabbing nor maiming till *she* gives the word, Captain——"

"Curse her for a——" Resolution's long arm shot out and his knotted fingers plunged and buried themselves in Belvedere's bull-throat, choking the word on his lips.

"Belay, Captain! Avast, Belvedere! I am one as knew her when she was innocent child, so easy all's the word, Belvedere." Having said which, Resolution relaxed his grip and Belvedere staggered back, gasping, and with murder glaring in his eyes. But the left hand of Resolution Day was hidden in his great side pocket whose suspicious bulge betrayed the weapon there, perceiving which Belvedere, speaking no word, turned and swaggered away.

Now seating himself upon the gun beside me, Resolution drew forth from that same pocket his small Bible that fell open on his knee at an oft-studied chapter.

"Now regarding the point o' view, friend," quoth he, "touching upon the death o' the evil-doers, of the blood of a righteous man's enemies—hearken now to the words o' Davy."

CHAPTER XIII

How We Fought an English Ship

For the days immediately following I saw nothing of Joanna but learned from Resolution and Diccon that her sickness had increased upon her.

" 'Tis her soul, I doubt!" quoth Diccon, shaking his head. " 'Tis too great for her body—'tis giant soul and her but a woman—so doth strong soul overcome weak body, and small wonder, say I?"

"Nay, Diccon," said Resolution, his bright eye sweeping the hazy distance, " 'tis but that she refuseth her vittles, and since 'man cannot live by bread alone' neither may woman, and 'tis more than bread she needeth and so she rageth and thus, like unto Peter's wife's mother, lieth sick of a fever." Here for a brief moment his bright eye rested on me and he scowled as he turned to limp the narrow deck.

Much might I narrate of the divers hazards of battle and storm that befell us at this time, and more of the goodly ships pillaged and scuttled and their miserable crews with them, by Belvedere and his bloody rogues; of prayers for mercy mocked at, of the agonised screams of dying men, of flame and destruction and death in many hideous shapes. All of the which nameless evils I must perforce behold since this Belvedere that shrank at Joanna's mere look, freed of her presence, took joyous advantage to torment me with the sight of such horrors, such devil's work as shrieked to heaven for vengeance; insomuch that Diccon and divers others could ill-stomach it at last and even grim Resolution would have no more.

Now although Belvedere and his rogues had taken great store of treasure with small hurt to themselves, yet must they growl and curse their fortune, since in none of the captured vessels had they taken any women, and never was the cry of "Sail, ho!" than all men grew eager for chase and attack; and thus this accursed ship *Happy Despatch* stood on, day after day.

Much will I leave untold by reason of the horror of it, and moreover my space is short for all I have set myself to narrate, viz: how and in what manner I came at last to my vengeance and what profit I had therein. So will I pass on to that day when, being in the latitude of the great and fair island of Hispaniola, we descried a ship bearing westerly.

Hereupon (since greed is never satisfied) all men were vociferous for chase and attack, and Belvedere agreeing, we hauled our wind accordingly and stood after her with every sail we could carry.

The *Happy Despatch* was a great ship of some forty guns besides such smaller pieces as minions, patereros and the like; she was moreover a notable good sailer and as the hours passed it was manifest we were fast overhauling our quarry. And very pitiful was it to see her crowding sail away from us, to behold her (as it were) straining every nerve to escape the horrors in store. Twice she altered her course and twice we did the like, fetching ever nearer until it seemed she was doomed to share the bloody fate of so many others. By noon we were so close that she was plain to see, a middling-size ship, her paint blistered, her gilding tarnished as by a long voyage, and though very taut and trim as to spars and rigging, a heavy-sailing ship and sluggish. A poor thing indeed to cope with such powerful vessel as this *Happy Despatch*, for as we

closed in I could count no more than six guns in the
whole length of her. As to crew she might have been
deserted for all I saw of them, save one man who
paced her lofty poop, a smallish man in great wig and
befeathered hat and in his fist a sword prodigiously
long in the blade, which sword he flourished whereat
(as it were a signal) out from her mizzen wafted the
banner of Portugal, and immediately she opened fire
on us from her stern-chase guns. But their shooting
was so indifferent and artillery so pitiful that their
shot fell far short of us. Thus my heart grieved
mightily for her as with our guns run out and
crew roaring and eager we bore down to her destruction.

Now all at once, as I watched this unhappy ship,
I caught my breath and sank weakly to my knees as,
despite the distance and plain to see, upon her high
poop came a woman, hooded and cloaked, who stood
gazing earnestly towards us. Other eyes had noticed
her also, for up from our crowded decks rose a hum,
an evil murmur that swelled to a cry fierce, inarticulate, bestial, whiles all eyes glared upon that slender,
shapely form; presently amid this ravening clamour I
distinguished words:

"Oh, a woman! Aha—women! Hold your fire, lads
—no shooting; we want 'em all alive! Easy all, bullies
—nary a gun, mates—we'll lay 'em 'longside and board
—Aye, aye—board it is!"

Now being on my knees, I began to whisper in passionate prayer until, roused by a shambling step, I
glanced up to find Resolution Day beside me.

"What, d'ye pray, brother? 'Tis excellent well!"
said he, setting a musquetoon ready to hand and
glancing at the primings of his pistols. "Pray unceasing, friend, plague the Throne wi' petitions, comrade,
and a word or so on behalf of old Resolution ere the
battle joins, for there's——"

"I pray God utterly destroy this accursed ship and all aboard her!" I cried.

"And do ye so?" said he, setting the pistols in his belt. "Why, then, 'tis as well you're safe i' your bilboes, *amigo*, and as to your blasphemous praying, I will offset it wi' prayerful counterblast—Ha, by my deathless soul—what's doing yonder?" he cried, and leant to peer across at the chase, and well he might. For suddenly (and marvellous to behold) this ship that had sailed so heavily seemed to throw off her sluggishness and, taking on new life, to bound forward; her decks, hitherto deserted, grew alive with men who leapt to loose and haul at brace and rope and, coming about, she stood towards us and right athwart our course. So sudden had been this manœuvre and so wholly unexpected that all men it seemed could but stare in stupefied amaze.

"Ha!" cried Resolution, smiting fist on the rail before him. "Tricked, by hookey! She's been towing a sea anchor! Below there!" he hailed. "Belvedere, ahoy—go about, or she'll rake us——"

And now came Belvedere's voice in fierce and shrill alarm:

"Down wi' your helm—down! Let go weather braces, jump, ye dogs, jump!"

I heard the answering tramp of feet, the rattle and creak of the yards as they swung and a great flapping of canvas as the *Happy Despatch* came up into the wind; but watching where our adversary bore down upon us, I beheld her six guns suddenly multiplied and (or ever we might bring our broadside to bear) from these gaping muzzles leapt smoke and roaring flame, and we were smitten with a hurricane of shot that swept us from stem to stern.

Dazed, deafened, half-stunned, I crouched in the shelter of the mizzen mast, aware of shrieks and cries and the crash of falling spars, nor moved I for a space;

lifting my head at last, I beheld on the littered decks
below huddled figures that lay strangely twisted, that
writhed or crawled. Then came the hoarse roar of a
speaking trumpet and I saw Resolution, his face a
smother of blood, where he leaned hard by across the
quarter-rail.

"Stand to't, my bullies!" he roared, and his voice
had never sounded so jovial. "Clear the guns, baw-
cocky boys; 'tis our turn next—but stand by till she
comes about——"

From the companion below came one running, eyes
wild, mouth agape, and I recognised the man Ford
who had been my chief persecutor in the forecastle.

"What now, lad—what now?" demanded Resolution,
mopping at his bloody face.

"Death!" gasped Ford. "There be dead men a-laying forward—dead, look'ee——"

"Likely enough, John Ford, and there'll be dead
men a-laying aft if ye're not back to your gun and
lively, d'ye see?" But the fellow, gasping again, fell
to his knees, whereupon Resolution smote him over the
head with his speaking trumpet and tumbled him down
the ladder.

"Look'ee here," quoth he, scowling on me, "this all
cometh along o' your ill-praying us, for prayer is potent, as I know, which was not brotherly in you, Martin O, not brotherly nor yet friendly!" So saying, he
squatted on the gun beside me and sought to staunch
the splinter-gash in his brow; but seeing how ill he set
about it, I proffered to do it for him (and despite my
shackles), whereupon he gave me the scarf and knelt
that I might come at his hurt the better; and being
thus on his knees, he began to pray in a loud, strong
voice:

"Lord God o' battles, close up Thine ear, hearken
to and regard not the unseemly praying of this man
Martin that hath not the just point o' view, seeing

through a glass darkly. Yonder lieth the enemy, Lord,
Thine and mine, wherefore let 'em be rooted out and
utterly destroyed; for if these be Portingales and
Papishers—if—ha—if——?" Resolution ceased his
prayer and glancing up, pointed with stabbing finger:
"Yon ship's no more Portingale than I am—look,
friend, look!"

Now glancing whither he would have me, I saw two
things: first, that the *Happy Despatch* had turned
tail and second that our pursuers bore at her main the
English flag; beholding which, a great joy welled up
within me so that I had much ado to keep from shouting outright.

"English!" quoth Resolution. "And a fighting ship
—so fight we must, unless we win clear!"

"Ha, will ye run then?" cried I in bitter scorn.

"With might and main, friend. We are a pirate,
d'ye see, w' all to lose and nought to gain, and then 'tis
but a fool as fighteth out o' season!"

Even as he spoke the English ship yawed and let fly
at us with her fore-chase and mingled with their roar
was the sharp crack of parting timbers and down came
our main-topmast.

"Why, so be it!" quoth Resolution, scowling up at
the flapping ruin where it hung. "Very well, 'tis a
smooth sea and a fighting wind, so shall you ha' your
bellyful o' battle now, friend, for yonder cometh Joanna at last!"

And great wonder was it to behold how the mere
sight of her heartened our sullen rogues, to hear with
what howls of joy they welcomed her as she paced
daintily across the littered deck with her quick glance
now aloft, now upon our determined foe.

"Ha, 'tis so—'tis our Jo—our luck! Shout for
Cap'n Jo and the luck o' the Brotherhood!"

And now at her rapid commands from chaos came
order, the decks were cleared, and, despite wrecked

topmast, round swung the *Happy Despatch* until her broadside bore upon the English ship. Even then Joanna waited, every eye fixed on her where she lolled, hand on hip, watching the approach of our adversary. Suddenly she gestured with her arm and immediately the whole fabric of the ship leapt and quivered to the deafening roar of her guns; then, as the smoke cleared, I saw the enemy's foreyard was gone and her sides streaked and splintered by our shot, and from our decks rose shouts of fierce exultation, drowned in the answering thunder of their starboard broadside, the hiss of their shot all round about us, the crackle of riven woodwork, the vicious whirr of flying splinters, wails and screams and wild cheering.

And thus began a battle surely as desperate as ever was fought and which indeed no poor words of mine may justly describe. The enemy lay to windward and little enough could I see by reason of the dense smoke that enveloped us, a stifling, sulphurous cloud that drifted aboard us ever more thick as the fight waxed, a choking mist full of blurred shapes, dim forms that flitted by and vanished spectre-like, a rolling mystery whence came all manner of cries, piercing screams and shrill wailings dreadful to hear, while the deck beneath me, the air about me reeled and quivered to the never-ceasing thunder of artillery. But ever and anon, through some rent in this smoky curtain, I might catch a glimpse of the English ship, her shot-scarred side and rent sails, or the grim havoc of our own decks. And amidst it all, and hard beside me where I crouched in the shelter of the mizzenmast, I beheld Resolution Day limping to and fro, jovial of voice, cheering his sweating, powder-grimed gun-crews with word and hand. Suddenly I was aware of Joanna beside me, gay and debonnaire but ghastly pale.

"Hola, Martino!" cried she. "D'ye live yet? 'Tis well. If we die to-day we die together, and where a properer death or one more fitting for such as you and I, for am I killed first, Resolution shall send you after me to bear me company, yes."

So saying, she smiled and nodded and turned to summon Resolution, who came in limping haste.

"What, are ye hurt, Jo?" cried he, peering. "Ha, Joanna lass, are ye hit indeed?"

"A little, yes!" said she, and staggering against the mast leaned there as if faint, yet casting a swift, furtive glance over her shoulder. "But death cometh behind me, Resolution, and my pistol's gone and yours both empty——"

Now glancing whither she looked, I saw Captain Belvedere come bounding up the ladder, cutlass in one hand and pistol in the other.

"Are ye there, Jo, are ye there?" he cried and stood to scowl on her.

"Resolution," said she, drooping against the mast, "fight me the ship——"

"And what o' me?" snarled Belvedere.

"You?" cried she. "Ah—bah!" and turning, she spat at him and, screaming, fell headlong as his pistol flashed. But over her prostrate form leapt Resolution and there, while the battle roared about them, I watched as, with steel that crashed unheard in that raging uproar, they smote and parried and thrust until an eddying smoke-cloud blotted them from my view. Now fain would I have come at Joanna where she lay, yet might not for my bonds, although she was so near; suddenly as I watched her (and struggling thus vainly to reach her) I saw she was watching me.

"And would you aid your poor Joanna, yes?" she questioned faintly.

" 'Twas so my thought——"

"Because I am dying, Martino? Doth this grieve you?"

"You are over-young to die!"

"And my life hath been very hard and cruel! Would you kiss a dying woman an' she might creep to your arms, Martino?"

Slowly and painfully she dragged herself within my reach and, beholding the twisted agony of her look, reading the piteous supplication in her eyes, I stooped to kiss the pale brow she lifted to my lips and—felt two arms about me vigorous and strong and under mine the quivering passion of her mouth; then she had loosed me and was before me on her knees, flushed and tremulous as any simple maid.

I was yet gazing on her in dumb and stark amaze, when from somewhere hard by a man cried out in wild and awful fashion, and as this agonised screaming swelled upon the air, Joanna rose up to her feet and stood transfigured, her eyes fierce and wild, her clenched teeth agleam 'twixt curling lips; and presently through the swirling smoke limped Resolution Day, a dreadful, bedabbled figure, who, beholding Joanna on her feet, flourished a dripping blade and panted exultant.

"He is dead?" she questioned.

"Verily and thoroughly!" said Resolution, wringing blood from his beruffled shirt sleeve. "And a moist end he made on't. But thee, Joanna, I grieved thee surely dead——"

"Nay, I screamed and dropped in time, but—hark, the Englishman's fire is ceasing and see, Resolution —look yonder!" and she pointed where our antagonist, sore battered in hull and spars, was staggering out of the fight.

And now in place of roaring battle was sudden hush, yet a quietude this, troubled by thin cryings, wailings and the like distressful sounds; and the smoke lifting showed something of the havoc about us, viz: our riven bulwarks, the tangled confusion of shattered spars, ropes and fallen gear, the still and awful shapes that cumbered the spattered decks, more especially about the smoking guns where leaned their wearied crews, a blood-stained, powder-grimed company, cheering fitfully as they watched the English ship creeping away from us.

To us presently cometh Diccon, his blackened face streaked with sweat, hoarse-voiced but hearty:

"Aha, Captain Jo—your luck's wi' us as ever! Yon curst craft hath her bellyful at last, aye; has she!"

"I doubt!" quoth Resolution, shaking his head, whiles Joanna, leaning against the mast, pointed feebly and I noticed her sleeve was soaked with blood and her speech dull and indistinct:

"Resolution is i' the—right—see!"

And sure enough the English ship, having fetched ahead of us and beyond range of our broadside guns, had hauled her wind and now lay to, her people mighty busy making good their damage alow and aloft, stopping shot-holes, knotting and splicing their gear, etc. Hereupon Diccon falls to a passion of vain oaths, Resolution to quoting Psalms and Joanna, sighing, slips suddenly to the deck and lies a-swoon. In a moment Resolution was on his knees beside her.

"Water, Diccon, water!" said he. "The lads must never see her thus!" So Diccon fetched the water and between them they contrived to get Joanna to her feet, and standing thus supported by their arms, she must needs use her first breath to curse her weak woman's body:

"And our mainmast is shot through at the cap— we must wear ship or 'twill go! Veer, Resolution, wear ship and man the larboard guns . . . they are cool . . . I must go tend my hurt—a curst on't! Wear ship and fight, Resolution, fight—to the last!"

So saying, she put by their hold and (albeit she stumbled for very weakness) nevertheless contrived to descend the quarter-ladder and wave cheery greeting to the roar of acclaim that welcomed her.

"And there's for ye!" quoth Resolution. "Never was such hugeous great spirit in man's body or woman's body afore, neither in this world or any other—no, not even Davy at Adullam, by hookey! Down to your guns, Diccon lad, and cheerily, for it looks as we shall have some pretty fighting, after all!"

But at the hoarse roar of Resolution's speaking trumpet was stir and clamorous outcry from the battle-wearied crew who came aft in a body.

"Oho, Belvedere!" they shouted. "Us ha' fought as long as men may, and now what?"

"Fight again, bullies, and cheerily!" roared Resolution. At this the uproar grew; pistols and muskets were brandished.

"We ha' fought enough! 'Tis time to square away and run for't—aye, aye—what saith Belvedere, Belvedere be our Cap'n—we want Belvedere!"

"Why then, take him, bullies, take him and willing!" cried Resolution; then stooping (and with incredible strength) up to the quarter-railing he hoisted that awful, mutilated thing that had once been Captain Belvedere and hove it over to thud down among them on the deck below. "Eye him over, lads!" quoth Resolution. "View him well, bawcock boys! I made sure work, d'ye see, though scarce so complete as the heathen Pompey might ha' done, but 'tis a very thoroughly dead rogue, you'll allow. And I killed him because he would ha' murdered our Joanna, our luck—and because he was for yielding us up, you and me, to yon ship that is death for us—for look'ee, there is never a ship on the Main will grant quarter or show mercy for we; 'tis noose and tar and gibbet for every one on us, d'ye see? So fight, bully boys, fight for a chance o' life and happy days—here stand I to fight wi' you and Diccon 'twixt decks and Captain Jo everywhere.

We beat off yon Englishman once and so we will again.
So fight it is, comrades all, and a cheer for Captain
Jo—ha, Joanna!"

Cheer they did and (like the desperate rogues they
were) back they went, some to their reeking guns,
others to splice running and standing rigging, to secure our tottering mainmast and to clear the littered
decks; overboard alike went broken gear and dead comrade.   Then, with every man at his quarters, with port
fires burning, drums beating, black flag flaunting aloft,
round swung the *Happy Despatch* to face once more
her indomitable foe (since she might not fly) and to
fight for her very life.

So once again was smoke and flame and roaring battle; broadside for broadside we fought them until night
fell, a night of horror lit by the quivering red glare
of the guns, the vivid flash of pistol and musket and
the pale flicker of the battle lanthorns.   And presently the moon was casting her placid beam upon this
hell of destruction and death, whereas I lay, famished
with hunger and thirst, staring up at her pale serenity
with weary, swooning eyes, scarce heeding the raving
tumult about me.

I remember a sudden, rending crash, a stunning
shock and all things were blotted out awhile.

CHAPTER XIV

TELLETH HOW THE FIGHT ENDED

WHEN sight returned to me at last, I was yet staring up at the moon, but now she had climbed the zenith and looked down on me through a dense maze, a thicket of close-twining branches (as it were) whose density troubled me mightily. But in a little I saw that these twining branches were verily a mass of ropes and cordage, a twisted tangle that hung above me yet crushed me not by reason of a squat column that rose nearby, and staring on this column I presently knew it for the shattered stump of the mizzenmast. For a great while I lay staring on this (being yet much dazed) and thus gradually became aware that the guns had fallen silent; instead of their thunderous roar was a faint clamour, hoarse, inarticulate, and very far away. I was yet wondering dreamily and pondering this when I made the further discovery that by some miraculous chance the chain which had joined my fettered wrists was broken in sunder and I was free. Nevertheless I lay awhile blinking drowsily up at the moon until at last, impelled by my raging thirst, I got to my knees (though with strange reluctance) and strove to win clear from the tangle of ropes that encompassed me; in the which labour I came upon the body of a dead man and beyond this, yet another. Howbeit I was out of this maze at last and rising to my feet, found the deck to heave oddly 'neath my tread, and so (like one walking in a dream) came stumbling to the quar-

ter-ladder and paused there awhile to lean against
the splintered rail and to clasp my aching head, for
I was still greatly bemused and my body mighty stiff
and painful.

Looking up after some while I saw the *Happy Despatch* lay a helpless wreck, her main and mizzenmasts
shot away and her shattered hull fast locked in close
conflict with her indomitable foe. The English ship
had run us aboard at the fore-chains and as the two
vessels, fast grappled together, swung to the gentle
swell, the moon glinted on the play of vicious steel
where the fight raged upon our forecastle. Mightily
heartened by this, I strove to shake off this strange
lethargy that enthralled me and looked about for some
weapon, but finding none, got me down the ladder
(and marvellous clumsy about it) and reaching the
deck stumbled more than once over stiffening forms
that sprawled across my way. Here and there a battle lanthorn yet glimmered, casting its uncertain beam
on writhen legs, on wide-tossed arms and shapes that
seemed to stir in the gloom; and beholding so many
dead, I marvelled to find myself thus unharmed, though,
as I traversed this littered deck, its ghastliness dim-
lit by these flickering lanthorns and the moon's unearthly radiance, it seemed more than ever that I
walked within a dream, whiles the battle clamoured ever
more loud. Once I paused to twist a boarding-axe
from stiffening fingers, and, being come into the waist
of the ship, found myself beside the main hatchway
and leaned there to stare up at the reeling fray on the
forecastle where pike darted, axe whirled, sword smote
and the battle roared amain in angry summons. But
as I turned obedient to get me into this desperate fray,
I heard a low and feverish muttering and following
this evil sound came upon one who lay amid the wreck-
age of a gun, and bending above the man knew him
for Diccon the quartermaster.

"How now, Diccon?" I questioned, and wondered to hear my voice so strange and muffled.

"Dying!" said he. "Dying—aye, am I! And wi' two thousand doubloons hid away as I shall ne'er ha' the spending on—oh, for a mouthful o' water—two thousand—a pike-thrust i' the midriff is an—ill thing yet—'tis better than—noose and tar and gibbet—yet 'tis hard to die wi' two thousand doubloons unspent —oh, lad, I parch—I burn already—water—a mouthful for a dying man——"

So came I to the water-butt that stood abaft the hatchway, and filling a pannikin that chanced there with some of the little water that remained, hastened back to Diccon, but ere I could reach him he struggled to his knees and flinging arms aloft uttered a great cry and sank upon his face. Then, finding him verily dead, I drank the water myself and, though lukewarm and none too sweet, felt myself much refreshed and strengthened thereby and the numbness of mind and body abated somewhat.

And yet, as I knelt thus, chancing to lift my eyes from the dead man before me, it seemed that verily I must be dreaming after all, for there, all daintily bedight in purple gown, I beheld a fine lady tripping lightly among these mangled dead; crouched in the shadow of the bulwark I watched this approaching figure; then I saw it was Joanna, saw the moon glint evilly on the pistol she bore ere she vanished down the hatchway. And now, reading her fell purpose, I rose to my feet and stole after her down into the 'tween-decks.

An evil place this, crowded with forms that moaned and writhed fitfully in the light of the lanthorns that burned dimly here and there, a place foul with blood and reeking with the fumes of burnt powder, but I heeded only the graceful shape that flitted on before; once she paused to reach down a lanthorn and to open the slide, and when she went on again, flames smouldered behind her and as often as she stayed to set these fires a-going, I stayed to extinguish them as well as I might ere I hasted after her. At last she paused to unlock a door and presently her voice reached me, high and imperious as ever:

"Greeting, Don Federigo! The ship's afire and 'tis an ill thing to burn, so do I bring you kinder death!"

Creeping to the door óf this lock-up, I saw she had set down the lanthorn and stood above the poor fettered captive, the pistol in her hand.

"The Señorita is infinitely generous," said Don Federigo in his courtly fashion; then, or ever she might level the weapon, I had seized and wrested it from her grasp. Crying out in passionate fury, she turned and leapt at me.

"Off, murderess!" I cried, and whirling her from me, heard her fall and lie moaning. "Come, sir," said I, aiding the Don to his feet, "let us be gone!" But what with weakness and his fetters Don Federigo could scarce stand, so I stooped and taking him across my shoulder, bore him from the place. But as I went an acrid smoke met me and with here and there a glimmer of flame, so that it seemed Joanna had fired the ship, my efforts notwithstanding. So reeled I, panting, to the upper air and, loosing Don Federigo, sank to the deck and stared dreamily at a dim.moon.

And now I was aware of a voice in my ear, yet nothing heeded until, shaken by an importunate hand, I roused and sat up, marvelling to find myself so weak.

"Loose me, Señor Martino, loose off my bonds; the fire grows apace and I must go seek the Señorita— burning is an evil death as she said. Loose off my bonds—the Señorita must not burn——"

"No, she must not—burn!" said I dully, and struggling to my feet I saw a thin column of smoke that curled up the hatchway. Gasping and choking, I fought my way down where flames crackled and smoke grew ever denser. Suddenly amid this swirling vapour I heard a glad cry:

"Ah, *Martino mio*—you could not leave me then to die alone!" And I saw Joanna, with arms stretched out to me, swaying against the angry glow behind her. So I caught her up in my embrace and slipping, stumbling, blind and half-choked, struggled up and up until at last I reeled out upon deck, and with Joanna thus clasped upon my breast, stood staring with dazed and unbelieving eyes at the vision that had risen up to confront me. For there before me, hedged about by wild figures and brandished steel, with slender hands tight-clasped together, with vivid lips apart and eyes wide, I thought to behold at last my beloved Damaris, my Joan, my dear, dear lady; but knowing this false, I laughed and shook my head.

"Deluding vision," said I, "blest sight long-hoped and prayed for—why plague me now?"

I was on my knees, staring up at this beloved shape through blinding tears and babbling I know not what. And then arms were about me, tender yet strong and compelling, a soft cheek was pressed to mine and in my ear Joan's voice:

"Oh, my beloved—fret not thyself—here is no vision, my Martin——"

"Joan!" I panted. "Oh, Damaris—beloved!" And shaking off these fettering arms, I rose to my feet. "Joan, is it thou thyself in very truth, or do I see thee in heaven——"

And now it seemed I was sinking within an engulfing darkness and nought to see save only the pale oval of this so loved, oft-visioned face that held for me the beauty of all beauteous things. At last her voice reached me, soft and low, yet full of that sweet, vital ring that was beyond all forgetting.

"Martin—Oh, Martin!"

Out towards me in the growing dark I saw her hands reach down to me: and then these eager, welcoming hands were seized and Joanna was between us on her knees.

"Spare him—Oh, lady, in mercy spare my beloved—kill me an you will, but spare this man of mine—these arms have cradled him ere now, this bosom been his pillow——"

"Joan!" I muttered, "Oh, Damaris, beloved——" But seeing the stricken agony of her look and how she shrank from my touch, I uttered a great cry and turning, sped blindly away and stumbling, fell and was engulfed in choking blackness.

CHAPTER XV

It was the pommel of the long rapier dangling from
the chair-back that first drew and held my eye, for this
pommel was extremely bright and polished and
gleamed on me like a very keen and watchful eye as I
watched, though conscious also of the luxury of panelled walls, of rich floor coverings and tapestried hangings, and the man who sat writing so studiously at the
carven table. And presently, roused by the scratch of
his industrious quill, I fell to watching him, his bowed
head, the curve of his back as he stooped. A small,
lean man but very magnificent, for his coat of rich
purple velvet sat on him with scarce a wrinkle, his
great peruke fell in such ample profusion of curls
that I could see nought but the tip of his nose as he
bent to his writing, and I wondered idly at his so great
industry. Now presently he paused to read over what
he had written and doing so, began to push and pull
at his cumbrous wig and finally, lifting it off, laid it
on the table. Thus I saw the man was white-haired and
that his ears were mighty strange, being cut and
trimmed to points like a dog's ears; and beholding the
jut of brow and nose and resolute chin, I fell to sudden trembling, and striving to lift myself on the bed,
wondered to find this such a business.

"Adam!" said I, my voice strangely thin and far
away, "Adam Penfeather!"

In one movement, as it seemed to me, he was out of

the chair and leaning above me. "Why, Martin," said
he. "Why, comrade! Lord love you, Martin, are ye
awake at last? Here you've lain these twelve hours
like a dead man and small wonder, what with your
wound——"

"So you have come—at last, Adam?"

"And in good time, shipmate!"

"Where am I?"

"Safe aboard my ship, the *Deliverance*."

" 'Twas you fought the *Happy Despatch*?"

"Aye, Martin, and should have very properly destroyed every rogue aboard but for my lady——"

"My lady?" said I, sitting up. "My lady—Joan?"

"Aye, verily——"

"Then 'tis true—all true!" said I, and fell a-trembling. "My lady's here?"

"She is, Martin, and more's the pity. For look'ee,
having boarded yon devil's craft and cut down such
as resisted, I was very properly for hanging such as
remained, when down on me comes my lady and is for
carrying the rogues to trial, the which is but vain
labour and loss o' time, since each and all of my twenty
and three prisoners is bound to swing soon or late, as
I told her, but, 'No matter, Sir Adam,' says she. 'Law
is law, Sir Adam,' quo' she. When cometh Godby,
running, to say the cursed ship was afire, and coming
to the main hatchway, I beheld, half-strangled in the
smoke, yourself, shipmate, and a woman in your
arms——"

"Ha—'twas Joanna!" said I, leaping in the bed.
"What of her, Adam—what of her, man?"

"A fine woman, I'll allow, Martin, and by her looks
a lady of quality——"

"Say a demon rather—a very she-devil!"

"Why, as you will, Martin, as you will!" said he.
"Only rest you, lest the fever take you again."

"How was I wounded, then?"

"A flying splinter in the head, Martin, so Surgeon Penruddock says. But then you have a marvellous stout skull, as I do know, shipmate."

"What ha', you done with Joanna—where is she?"

"Content you, Martin, she is safe enough and well cared for; you shall see her anon," said he, stroking his long chin and viewing me with his quick, keen eyes. "But first you shall eat!" And he rang the small silver bell that stood upon the table, whereon in came a soft-footed serving-man in handsome livery, who, receiving Adam's commands, presently bowed himself out again.

Hereupon Adam set on his periwig and fell to pacing slowly to and fro, his feet soundless upon the rich carpet, viewing me now and then like one that ponders some problem. Now, beholding his air of latent power and indomitable mastery, the richness of his habit, the luxury that surrounded him, it seemed in very truth that he was the great gentleman and I the merest poor suppliant for his bounty; whereupon I must needs contrast his case with mine and perceiving myself no better than I had been three weary years since, to wit: the same poor, destitute wretch, I fell into a black and sullen humour:

"You go vastly fine these days!" quoth I, scowling (like the surly dog I was).

"Aye, Martin—I am so vastly rich!" he sighed. "I am a baronet, shipmate!" he nodded dolefully. "And what is worse, I own many rich manors and countless broad acres besides divers castles, mansions, houses and the like. Thus all men do protest friendship for me, and at this moment there be many noble ladies do sigh for me or the manors and castles aforesaid. And there was a duchess, Martin, was set upon wedding my riches (and me along of 'em) but I have no leaning to duchesses, though this one was young and comely enough. So went I to the King, who by his grace suf-

fered me to fit out, provision, arm and man this ship
at my own expense, Martin, and square away for the
Spanish Main to sink, burn and utterly destroy such
pirate vessels as I can bring to action. So here am
I, shipmate, since I had rather fight rogues when and
where I may than marry a duchess once. And here
cometh what shall do you a world o' good, Martin—
broth with a dash o' rum—which is good for a man,
soul and body!" said he, as the serving-fellow appeared,
bearing a silver tray whereon stood broth in a silver
bowl of most delectable odour. And indeed, very good
broth I found it.

So whiles I ate, Adam, sitting near, told me much
of his doings since he left me solitary on Bartlemy's
Island, but of my lady Joan Brandon he spoke no
word.

"'Tis but three short years since we parted, shipmate, three short years——"

"Three long, empty years!" said I bitterly.

"Aye, truth!" quoth he. "You had a mind to
nought but vengeance, which is an empty thing, as belike you'll allow, Martin, you being now three long,
empty years the wiser?"

Here, what with the hot broth and my hotter anger,
I came nigh to choking, whereupon he rose and, seeing
the bowl empty, took it from me and thereafter set
another pillow to my back, the while I reviled him im-
potently.

"There, there, Martin!" said he, patting my shoulder as I had been a petulant child. "Never miscall
Adam that is your friend, for if you have wasted yourself in a vanity, so have I, for here you see me full of
honours, Martin, a justice, a member o' Parliament, a
power at Court with great lords eager for my friendship and great ladies eager to wed me. Yet here am
I safe at sea and fighting rogues as often as I may,
for great riches is a plague that tainteth love and

friendship alike—*vanitas vanitatum, omnium vanitas!*"

"Yet your three years have been turned to better account than mine!" said I, grown suddenly humble.

"In the matter of houses and land, Martin?"

"Aye!" I nodded. "For my three years I've nought to show but scars and rags."

"Not so, Martin, for your fortune marched with mine. Lord love you, I never bought stick or stone or acre of land but I bought one for you, comrade, share and share, shipmate. So, if I am a man o' great possessions, so are you, Martin; there be lands and houses in old England waiting their master as you sit there." Now at this I lay silent awhile, but at last I reached out a fumbling hand, the which he took and wrung in his vital clasp.

"God help me, Adam!" said I. "What have these years made of me?"

"That same scowling, unlovely, honest-hearted self-deluder that is my sworn comrade and blood-brother and that I do love heartily for his own sake and the sake of my lady Joan. For look'ee, she hath oft told me of you and the life you lived together on Bartlemy's Island."

"And has she so indeed?" quoth I.

"Aye, verily. Lord, Martin, when she waked from her swoon aboard ship and found I had sailed without you, she was like one distraught and was for having me 'bout ship that she might stay to comfort you in your solitude. And so I did, Martin, but we were beset by storm and tempest and blown far out of our course and further beset by pirates and the like evils, and in the end came hardly to England with our lives. No sooner there than my lady fits out an expedition to your relief and I busied with divers weighty concerns, she sails without me and is wrecked in the Downs, whereby she lost her ship and therewith all she

possessed, save only Conisby Shene, the which she holdeth in your name, Martin."

"Adam," said I, "Oh, Adam, surely this world hath
not her like——"

"Assuredly not!" quoth he. "The which doth put
me to great wonder you should come to forget her a
while——"

"Forget her? I?"

"Aye, Martin—in the matter of the—the lady yonder—Madam Joanna——"

"Joanna!" I cried, clenching my fists. "That demon!"

"Ha—demon, is it?" quoth Adam, pinching his chin
and eyeing me askance. "Doth your love grow all
sudden cold——"

"Love?" cried I. "Nay—my hate waxeth for thing
so evil—she is a very devil——"

"Nay, Martin, she is a poor Spanish lady, exceeding comely and with a hand, a foot, an eye, a person
of birth and breeding, a dainty lady indeed, yet of a
marvellous sweet conversation and gentle deportment,
and worthy any man's love. I do allow——"

"Man," cried I, "you do speak arrant folly—she
is Joanna!"

"Why, true, Martin, true!" said Adam soothingly
and eyeing me anxious-eyed. "She is the lady Joanna
that you preserved from death and worse, it seems——"

"Says she so, Adam?"

"Aye! And, by her showing, some small—some few
small—kindnesses have passed betwixt you."

"Kindnesses?" I demanded.

"Aye, Martin, as is but natural, God knoweth.
Kisses, d'ye see, embraces——"

"She lies!" quoth I, starting up in bed, "she lies!"

"Why, very well, Martin——"

"Ha, d'ye doubt my word, Adam?"

"No, Martin, no—except—when first I clapped eyes

on you, she chanced to be lying in your arms, d'ye see?"

"Tush!" said I. "What o' that? 'Twas after she'd set the ship afire and sought to murder Don Federigo; we left her in the 'tween-decks and I found her nigh stifled by the smoke. Have you got her fast in the bilboes—safe under lock and key?"

"Lord love you—no, Martin!" said he, viewing me askance as I were raving. "So young, Martin! And a bullet wound i' the arm and mighty brave, despite her tenderness, so says Penruddock our surgeon."

"Why then, in God's name—where is she?"

"Where should she be, seeing she was wounded and solitary, but with my lady Joan!"

"God forbid!" cried I.

"Why, Martin, 'tis my lady's whim—they walk together, talk, eat, aye, and sleep together, for aught I know——"

"Adam," said I, grasping him by the arm. "You know Captain Tressady of old, and Mings and Red Rory, Sol Aiken and others of the Coast Brotherhood, but have you ever met the fiercest, bravest, greatest of these rogues; have you ever heard tell of Captain 'Jo'?"

"Aye, truly, Martin, some young springald that hath risen among 'em since my time, a bloody rogue by account and one I would fain come alongside of——"

"Captain Jo lies in your power, Adam; Captain Jo is aboard; Captain Jo is Joanna herself! 'Twas Joanna fought the *Happy Despatch* so desperately!"

Now hereupon Adam fell back a pace and stood staring down on me and pinching his chin, but with never a word. And seeing him thus incredulous still, I strove to get me out of bed.

"Easy, Martin!" said he, restraining me. "These be wild and whirling words and something hard to believe——"

"Why, then, if you doubt me still, summon hither Don Federigo an he be yet alive——"

"Look now, Martin," said he, seating himself on the bed beside me. "Since we left England I have burned or scuttled four rascally pirate craft and each and every a fighting ship, yet no one of them so mauled and battered us as this *Happy Despatch* (whereby I have lost fourteen good fellows dead besides thirty wounded) the which as I do know was captained by one calling himself Belvedere——"

"Tush!" cried I. "He was a man of straw and would have run or struck to you after your first broadside! 'Twas Joanna and Resolution Day fought the ship after Belvedere was dead——"

"Ah, dead, is he? Why, very good!" said Adam, rising and seating himself at the table. "Here is yet another name for my journal. You saw him dead, Martin?" he questioned, taking up his pen.

"Most horribly! He was killed by the mate, Resolution Day——"

"Ha!" says Adam, turning to his writing. " 'Tis a name sticks in my memory—a man I took out o' prison and saved from burning along with divers others, when we took Margarita—a tall, one-eyed man and scarred by the torment——?"

" 'Tis the same! But, God forgive you, Adam, why must you be wasting time over your curst journal and idle talk——"

"I think, Martin! I meditate! For, if this be true indeed, we must go like Agog—delicately—Martin—delicately!"

"Folly—oh, folly!" cried I. "Joanna may be firing the ship as you sit scribbling there, or contriving some harm to my dear lady—act, man—act!"

"As how, Martin?" he questioned, carefully sanding what he had writ.

"Seize her ere she can strike, set her fast under

lock and key, have her watched continually——"

"Hum!" said Adam, pinching his chin and viewing me with his keen gaze. "If she be so dangerous as you say, why not slay her out of hand——"

"No!" said I. "No!"

"But she is a pirate, you tell me?"

"She is! And I do know her for murderess beside!"

"How came you in her company, Martin?"

Hereupon in feverish haste I recounted much of what I have already set down concerning this strange, wild creature, to all of which he hearkened mighty attentive, pinching at his chin and a frown on his face.

"Verily!" said he, when I had done. "Never heard man stranger story!" But seeing how he regarded me in the same dubious manner, I leapt out of bed ere he might prevent and staggered with weakness. "Lord love you, Martin," said he, snatching me in his iron grip, "Lord love you, what would you be at? Here's Surgeon Penruddock and his two mates with their hands full enough, as it is, God knoweth, and you sick o' your wound——" So saying, Adam bundled me back into bed, willy-nilly.

"Why, then, question Don Federigo, who knoweth her better than I—summon him hither——"

"Impossible, Martin, he lieth very nigh to death."

"And what of Joanna? She is as swift as a snake and as deadly—she is a lurking danger—a constant menace, beyond thought subtle and crafty——"

"Hist!" quoth Adam, catching me by the arm and turning suddenly as came a soft rapping; then the door opened and Joanna herself stood before us, but indeed a Joanna such as I had never seen. Timid, abashed, great-eyed and wistful, she stood looking on me, her slender hands tight-clasped, her tremulous, parted lips more vivid by reason of the pallor of her cheeks, all shy and tender womanhood from the glossy ringlets at her white brow to the dainty shoe that peeped forth of her petticoat; as for me, I sank back among my pillows amazed beyond all speech by the infinite change in her, for here was a transformation that went beyond mere lace and velvets; the change was in her very self, her look, her voice, her every gesture.

"*Martino mio!*" said she at last, and sure this pen of mine may never tell all the languorous caress of these two words; and then, or ever I might speak or stir, she was beside me and had caught my hand to her lips. And then I saw Joan standing in the doorway, the Damaris of my dreams, and though her lips smiled upon us, there was that in her eyes that filled me with bitter shame and an agony beyond the telling.

"Damaris!" I groaned and freed my hand so suddenly that Joanna stumbled and would have fallen, but for Adam's ready arm. "Damaris!" I cried. "Ah, God—look not so! All these weary years I have lived and dreamed but of you—Joan, beloved, 'twas thy sweet memory made my solitude worth the living—without thee I had died——" Choking with my grief, I reached out my hands in passionate supplication to that loved shape that drooped in the doorway, one white hand against the carven panelling; and then Joanna was on her knees, her soft cheek pressed to my quivering fist, wetting it with her tears:

"Martino!" she sobbed. "Ah, *caro mio*, art so strange—dost not know thy Joanna—dost not know me, Martino?"

"Aye, I know you, Captain Jo," I cried. "Well I know you to my cost, as hath many another: I know you for 'La Culebra,' for Joanna that is worshipped, obeyed and followed by every pirate rogue along the Main. Oh, truly I know you to my bitter sorrow——"

Now at this she gave a little, pitiful, helpless gesture and looked from me to the others, her eyes a-swim with tears.

"Alas!" she sobbed. "And is he yet so direly sick?"

Then, bowing her head to the pillow beside me, "Oh, loved Martino," she sighed, "art so sick not to remember all that is betwixt us, that which doth make thee mine so long as life shall be to me—the wonder I have told to my lady Damaris——"

Now here I caught her in savage gripe.

"What," cried I, shaking her to and fro despite my weakness, "what ha' you told my lady?"

"Beloved Martino—I confessed our love—alas, was I wrong, Martino—I told her my joyous hope to be the mother of your child ere long——"

"Oh, shame!" cried I. "Oh, accursed liar!" And I hurled her from me; then, lying gasping amid my tumbled pillows, my aching head between my hands, I saw my beloved lady stoop to lift her, saw that lying head pillowed on Joan's pure bosom and uttering a great cry, I sank to a merciful unconsciousness.

CHAPTER XVI

How I Had Word With My Lady, Joan Brandon

"A MARVEL, Sir Adam (perceive me), a wonder! The constitution of a horse, an ox, nay an elephant, the which monstrous beast (you'll allow me!) hath a pachydermatous hide tolerably impervious to spears, axes, darts, javelins and the like puny offences, and a constitution whereby he liveth (you'll observe) whole centuries. Indeed, Sir Adam, 'tis a cure marvellous, being one I ha' wrought on my patient in spite of said patient. For look now (and heed me) here we have soul, mind and will, or what you will, pulling one way, and body hauling t'other, and body hath it, physics versus metaphysics—a pretty and notable case——"

"Why, he hath a notable hard head, Master Penruddock——"

"Head, Sir Adam, head—were his head as adamantine, as millstone or hard as one o' your cannon balls that shall not save him, if mind and body agreeably seek and desire death, and mind (pray understand, sir) is the more potent factor, thus (saving and excepting the abnormal vigour of his body) by all the rules of chirurgical science he should ha' died three days agone —when the seizure took him."

"Would to heaven I had!" said I, opening my eyes to scowl up at the little man who beamed down on me through monstrous horn-rimmed spectacles.

"Aha, and there we have it confessed, Sir Adam!" said he. "Yet we shall have him on his legs again in a day or so, thanks to my art——"

"And his lady's nursing!"

"What, hath she been with me in my sickness, Adam?" I questioned when the doctor had departed.

"Night and day, Martin, as sweet and patient with you as any angel in heaven, and you cursing and reviling her the while in your ravings——"

"Oh, God forgive me! Where is she now, Adam?"

"With my Lady Joan——"

"How?" I cried. "Was this Joanna nursed me?"

"Why, truly, Martin. Could she have better employ?" But hereupon I fell to such fury that Adam turned to stare at me, pen in hand.

"Lord love you, Martin," said he, pinching his chin, "I begin to think that skull o' yours is none so hard, after all——"

"And you," quoth I bitterly. "Your wits are none so keen as I had judged 'em. You are grown a very credulous fool, it seems!"

"Ha—'tis very well, shipmate!"

"For here you have Joanna—this evil creature stained by God knoweth how many shameful crimes —you have her beneath your hand and let her come and go as she lists, to work such new harms as her cunning may suggest—either you disbelieve my statements, or you've run mad, unless——"

"Unless what, Martin?"

"Unless she's bewitched you as she hath full many a man ere now."

Adam blenched and (for the first time in my remembrance) his keen eyes quailed before mine, and over his bronzed face, from aggressive chin to prominent brow, crept a slow and painful red.

"Martin," said he, his eyes steady again, "I will confess to you that is my blood-brother and comrade sworn, I have—thought better of—of her than any proud lady or duchess of 'em all——"

"Despite the foul and shameful lie you heard her utter?"

"Despite everything, Martin."

"Then God help you, Adam!"

"Amen," said he.

"You are surely crazed——"

"Why, very well, Martin, though you know me for a timid man——"

"Tush!" quoth I, turning my back on him.

"And a cautious, more especially in regard to women, having known but few and understanding none. Thus, Martin, though I seem crazed and foolish, 'tis very well, so long as I have eyes to see and ears to hear, and now I'll away and use 'em awhile. And here," said he, rising as a knock sounded on the door, "should be an old friend o' yours that got himself something scorched on your account." And opening the door he disclosed a squat, broad-shouldered fellow of a sober habit, his head swathed in a bandage, but the eyes of him very round and bright and his wide mouth up-curving in a smile.

"Godby!" said I, and reached out my hand to him.

"Why, Mart'n!" cried he. "Oh, pal—here's j'y, choke me wi' a rammer else! Lord, Mart'n—three years—how time doth gallop! And you no whit changed, save for your beard! But here's me wi' a fine stocked farm t'other side Lamberhurst—and, what's more, a wife in't as be sister to Cecily as you'll mind at the 'Hoppole'—and, what's more, a blessed infant, pal, as I've named Tom arter myself, by reason that my name is God-be-here, and Mart'n arter you, by reason you are my pal and brought me all the good fortun' as I ever had. Aha, 'twas a mortal good hour for me when we first struck hands, Mart'n."

"And you're more than quits, Godby, by saving me from the fire——"

"Why, pal, you fell all of a swound, d'ye see, and there's my Lady Brandon and t'other 'un a-running to fetch ye, flames or no—so what could I do——"

"My lady Joan?"

"Aye and t'other 'un—the Spanish dame as you come up a-cuddling of, Mart'n—and a notable fine piece she be, as I'm a gunner——"

"Is my lady on deck?"

"Which on 'em, pal?"

"Joan, man—my Lady Brandon!"

"Aye, and mighty downcast by her look. 'Godby,' says she to me a while back, 'if I find not my father now, I do think my poor heart will break!' And the sweet sad eyes of her, pal——"

"I'll get up!" said I, tossing off the bed clothes.

"Lord, Mart'n, what'll Cap'n Adam say——"

" 'Tis no matter!"

"Are ye strong enough, pal?"

"To be sure!" said I, and getting upon my feet, reeled for very weakness and should have fallen but that Godby propped me with his shoulder; supported thus and despite Godby's remonstrances, I staggered to and fro and gradually found my strength return in some small measure, whereupon I began to dress myself forthwith.

"Whither are we sailing, Godby?"

"To the nearest secure anchorage, Mart'n, for what wi' storm and battle we are so battered and sprung, alow and aloft—and small wonder, here's four ships we've destroyed since we left Old England, battle, murder and sudden death, pal!"

So with Godby's help I got me out upon the broad quarter-deck and saw the *Deliverance* for a fine, roomy ship, very clean and trim, her decks new-scoured, her brass-work gleaming in the sun; though here and there the carpenters were still repairing such damage as she had taken in the fight.

"A noble ship, pal," says Godby, as I sat me down on one of the guns, "and looks vasty different to what she did three days since, her foreyard and main-to'-

gallant mast shot away and her starboard bulwarks
shattered fore and aft and three shot-holes under water
as can't be come at till we careen."

" 'Twas hot fight—I marvel your damage was no
greater," says I, glancing hither and thither for
sight of my lady, and my heart throbbing with expectation.

"Nay, Mart'n, 'twas guile, 'twas craft, 'twas seamanship. Lord love your eyes, pal, Cap'n Adam
seized him the vantage point by means of a fore-course
towing under water, and kept it. For look'ee, 'tis
slip our floating anchor, up wi' our helm and down
on 'em 'thwart-hawse and let fly our larboard broadside, veer and pound 'em wi' our starboard guns, keeping the weather gauge, d'ye see, pal, till their fire slack-
ens and them blind wi' our smoke and theirs. Then
to close wi' 'em till our gun muzzles are nigh touching
and whiles we pound 'em below, 'tis grappling irons
and boarders away! Aha, a wonderful man is Cap'n
Adam—oh, 'tis beautiful sight to watch him take ship
into action; 'tis sight to warm a man's in'nards and
make archangels sing for j'y, pal. Aye, deafen, blind
and choke me. but a man o' men is Cap'n Adam Penfeather!"

"He is come to great repute, I hear!" said I, my
hungry gaze wandering.

"Verily he hath, Mart'n; the King do honour him
vastly especially since he pinked a strutting, quarrel-
some gentleman through the sword-arm in St. James's
Park, and him a nearl, pal!"

"At last!" says I.

"Anan, pal?" he questioned, but looking where I
looked. "Aye," he nodded, " 'tis my Lady Brandon,
and mighty despondent by her looks as I told ye,
Mart'n." All unconscious of me she crossed the deck
slow-footed and coming to the lee bulwark, paused
there, her lovely head down-bent upon her hands.

Now watching her as she stood thus, my eager gaze dwelling on every line of the beloved shape, I was filled with such overmastering emotion, an ecstasy so keen, that I fell a-trembling and my eyes filled with sudden, blinding tears; and bowing my face on my hand, I sat thus a while until I had composed myself. Then I arose and made my way towards her on stumbling feet.

Suddenly she turned and espying me, started and fell a-trembling, even as I.

"Martin," said she below her breath. "Oh, Martin!"

"Damaris!" I muttered. "Beloved——!"

Now at this she gave a little gasp and turned to gaze away across the placid waters, and I saw her slender hands clasp and wring each other.

"Have you no word of greeting for me?"

"I rejoice to—to see you well again, Martin!"

"Have you no word of—love for me, after all these years, Damaris?" At this she shrank away and, leaning 'gainst the bulwark, shook her head, and again I saw that hopeless gesture of her quivering hands.

"Is your love for me dead, then?" I questioned, coming a pace nearer.

"Ah, never that, Martin!" she whispered. "Only I have—buried it deep—within my heart—where it shall lie for ever hid for thy sake and her sake and—and that—which is to be—this poor Joanna hath told me——"

Now hereupon I laughed and caught her hands and kissed them and they, the pretty things, trembling 'neath my kisses.

"God love thee for sweet and noble woman, my Damaris," said I, sinking to my knees before her, "and now, thus kneeling in the sight of God and thee, hear me swear that hateful thing of which you speak never was and never shall be!" Here I clasped my arms

about her, felt her yield and sway to my embrace, saw
a dawning glory in her eyes.

"Martin," said she, quick-breathing, "if this be so
indeed——"

"Indeed and indeed, Joanna spake a shameful lie—
a woman prone to every evil, being a murderess
and——"

"A murderess, Martin?"

"Aye, by her own confession, and I do know her for
a pirate beside, more desperate and resolute than any,
known to every rogue along the Main as Captain Jo."

Now here my lady stirred in my embrace and looked
down on me with troubled gaze.

"And yet, dear Martin, you lived with her on——on
·our island?"

"Aye, I did—to my torment, and prayed God I
might not slay her." And here in breathless fashion
I told my lady of Joanna's coming and of the ills that
followed; but seeing the growing trouble in her look,
my arms fell from her and great bitterness filled me.
"Ah, God in heaven, Damaris!" I cried, "never say
you doubt my word——"

"Martin!"

I rose to my feet to behold Joanna within a yard
of us. For a long and breathless moment she looked
from me to other of us and then, shuddering, hid her
face in her two hands.

"Dear my lady," said she at last, "if by reason of
his wound my loved Martin hath grown strange to me
and all his love for me forgot—if indeed you do love
him—to you that have been more than sister and gentle friend to miserable Joanna, to you I do yield my
love henceforth, nor will I repine, since my love
for thee shall teach me how to bear my shame,
yes——"

"Ha, damned liar!" I cried, and turned on Joanna
with clenched fists; and then my lady's restraining

naked wines

Email: help@nakedwines.com
www.nakedwines.com/trynaked23

To claim go to **nakedwines.com/trynaked23**

Code **BD23**   Password **ASP32XYN**

£75

£75 WINE VOUCHER

For _Book Depository customers_

Get _£75 to spend on a case of_

delicious wine

JAMES
NAKED MD

★ Trustpilot ★★★★★ Rated 'Excellent'

Where the world's best independent winemakers make their best wine

We give the world's best independent winemakers the backing they need to make the best wines they've ever made... at the fairest prices you'll ever pay.

1. Claim
your **£75 voucher** at the website below

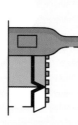

2. Choose
12 bottles of delicious wine

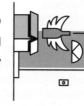

3. Enjoy
speedy delivery to your door or safe place

www.nakedwines.com/trynaked23

Please recycle me ♺

naked wines

Claim your **£75** today

❯ Get **£75 off** a case of wine priced £134.99 or more

❯ **SPEEDY DELIVERY** 1-2 days as standard

❯ Your **money back** on any bottle you don't love

Code	BD23
Password	ASP32XYN

▦ Claim within **30 days**

PROUDLY AWARDED ONLINE WINE RETAILER OF THE YEAR 2022

arms were about me and I sank half-swooning against the ship's side.

"Dear Martin," said she, viewing me tearful-eyed, "you are not yourself——"

"No!" cried I, burying my throbbing head betwixt my arms. "I am Fortune's Fool—the world is upside down—God help me, I shall run mad in very truth. Oh, damned Fortune—curst Fate!" and I brake out into futile raving awhile. When at last I raised my head it was to behold my lady clasping this vile creature in her arms and cherishing her with tender words and caresses, the which sight wrought me to a very frenzy of cold and bitter rage. Said I:

"My Lady Brandon, God knoweth I have greatly loved you, wherein I have wasted myself on a vain thing as is to me right manifest. So now, since you have buried your love, mine do I tear from me and cast utterly away; henceforth I am no more than an instrument of vengeance——"

"Martin!" cried she. "Oh, dear Martin, for the love of God——"

But (Oh, vain folly! Oh, detestable pride!) I heeded not this merciful appeal nor the crying of my own heart, but turning my back upon my noble lady, stumbled away and with never another word or look. And thus I (that was born to be my own undoer) once more barred myself out from all that life offered me of happiness, since pride is ever purblind.

Presently, espying Godby where divers of his fellows rove new tackle to a gun, I enquired for Adam.

"I' the gun room, Mart'n—nay, I'll stand along wi' you."

So he brought me down to the gun room where sat Adam, elbows on table, chin on hand, peering up at one who stood before him in fetters, a haggard, war-worn figure.

"What—Resolution?" said I.

"That same, friend, brought somewhat low, comrade, yet soon, it seems, to be exalted—on a gallows, d'ye see, yet constant in prayer, steadfast in faith and nowise repining—for where would be the use? And moreover, the way o' the Lord is my way—Amen, brother, and Amen."

"Adam," said I, turning where he yet gazed up at Resolution's scarred and bandaged face, "I would fain have you show mercy to this man. But for Resolution here I had died hideously at the hands of a vile blackamoor."

"Mercy?" said Adam, scowling up at Resolution.

"His life, Adam."

" 'Tis forfeit! Here standeth a notable pirate and one of authority among the rogues, so must he surely die along with Captain Jo——" I saw Resolution's shackled hands clench suddenly, then he laughed, harsh and strident.

"To hang Captain Jo you must needs catch him first!"

"Why then who—who and what is Joanna?" I demanded.

"Why, your light-o'-love, for sure, friend, as we found along o' you on a lonely island, *amigo.*"

"Resolution, you lie——"

"On a lonely island, *camarado,*" says he again.

"Wait!" I muttered, clasping my aching head. "Wait! Joanna is the daughter of the murdered Governor of Santa Catalina who was left behind in the burning town and rescued by Indians, who, being Indians, were kind to her. But these Indians were killed by white men who took her, and, being white men, they used her ill all save one who was to her father and mother, sister and brother and his name Resolution. So she grew up a pirate among pirates, dressed, spoke and acted as they and rose to be great among them by reason of her quick wit and resolute spirit, and because of her quickness and subtle wit is called 'La Culebra' and for her desperate courage is hailed as 'Captain Jo.' "

Resolution fell back a step, staring on me amazed, and I saw his shackled fists were quivering. Then suddenly Adam rose and leaned forward across the table.

"Resolution Day," said he, "have you a memory for faces?"

I saw Resolution's solitary eye widen and dilate as it took in the man before him, the spare form, the keen, aquiline face with its black brows, white hair and mutilated ears.

"Captain—Adam Penfeather—o' the Brotherhood!"

"Ha!" quoth Adam, nodding grimly. "I see you know me! So, Resolution Day, I warn you to prepare to make your final exodus with Captain Jo—at sunset!"

Resolution's scarred head sank, his maimed body seemed to shrink and there broke from him a groan:

"To hang—to die—she's so young—so young—all I ever had to love! Oh, Lord God o' battles——"

"Godby, summon the guard and see him safely bestowed—in the lock-up aft, and bring the key to my cabin." So at Godby's word, in came two armed fellows and marched out Resolution Day, his head still bowed and his fetters jangling dismally.

"You'll never hang her, Adam!" said I, when we were alone. "You cannot, man—you shall not!"

"Lord, Martin," said he, sitting on his great peruke and looking askance at me, "Lord, what a marvellous thick skull is thine!"

"Mayhap!" quoth I, "but you know my story for true at last—you know Joanna for Captain Jo."

Now here he answered never a word but falls to pacing back and forth, his hands clasped behind him; whereupon I seated myself at the table and leaned my aching head betwixt my hands.

"Adam," said I at last, "how far are we, do you reckon, from Nombre de Dios?"

"Some hundred and fifty miles, maybe a little less."

"Why, then, give me a boat."

"A boat?" said he, pausing in his walk to stare on me.

"Aye, a boat," I nodded. "You cast me adrift once, you'll mind—well—do so again!"

"And what o' my Lady Joan? Ha—will ye tell me you've quarrelled already in true lover-like fashion—is this it?"

" 'Tis no matter," quoth I, "only I do not stay on this ship another hour."

"Lord!" said he, "Lord love me, Martin! Here you've scarce found her and now eager to lose her again—heaven save me from love and lovers——"

"Give me a boat."

"A boat?" said he, pinching his chin. "A boat, is it? Why, very well, Martin—a boat! Ha, here methinks is the very hand o' Providence, and who am I to gainsay it? You shall have the longboat, Martin, well stored and armed; 'tis a goodly boat that I am loth to part with—but seeing 'tis you, comrade, why very well. Only you must bide till it be dark for reasons obvious——"

"So be it!" I nodded. "And if you could give me a chart and set me a course how to steer for Nombre de Dios, I should be grateful, Adam."

"Why, so I will, Martin. A course to Nombre—aye, verily! 'Tis said one Sir Richard Brandon lieth 'prisoned there. Ha—having quarrelled with daughter you speed away to sire——"

"And what then?" said I, scowling.

"Nought, Martin, nought in the world, only if in this world is a fool—art surely he, comrade. Nay, never rage against your true friend, comrade; give me your arm, let me aid you up to my cabin, for your legs are yet overly weak, I doubt."

CHAPTER XVII

Telleth the Outcome of My Prideful Folly

The moon had not yet risen when, in despite of Adam's warnings and remonstrances, I set the great boat-cloak about me and stepped forth into the stern-gallery of the ship, whence I might look down and behold the dark loom of the longboat, a gliding, glimmering shadow upon the white spume of the wake.

Now if there be any who, reading this my narrative, shall cry out against me for perverse fool (as I surely was) to all such I would but say that though indeed a man wild and headstrong by nature and given to passionate impulse, yet I was not wholly myself at this time by reason of my wound, so that the unlovely and gloomy spirit of selfishness that possessed me now had full sway to rule me how it listed; and I would have this plead such excuse as might be for this my so desperate and unreasonable determination, the which was to plunge me into further evils and miseries, as you shall hear.

"So you are determined on't, Martin?" said Adam, standing beside me where I prepared to descend the short rope ladder.

"I am!"

"Lord, Martin, there is so much to love in you 'tis pity you are so much of fool——"

"You said as much before——"

"Aye, so I did, comrade, so I did. But look'ee,

'tis a smooth sea, a fair wind—aha, it needeth no pistol butt to persuade you to it this time; you go of your own will and most express desire, comrade."

"I do, Adam."

"And who knoweth," said he, his gaze uplift to the Southern Cross that glimmered very bright and splendid above us, "who can say what lieth in wait for you, comrade,—hardship and suffering beyond doubt and —peradventure, death.   But by hardship and suffering man learneth the wisdom of mercy, or should do, and by death he is but translated to a greater living —so I do hope.   And thus, howsoever it be, all's well, Martin, all's well."

"Adam," said I, "give me your hand.   You have called me 'fool' and fool am I, mayhap, yet in my folly, wisdom have I enough for this—to know you for my good friend and true comrade now and always!"

"Hark'ee then," said he, grasping my hand and leaning to my ear in the gloom, "give up this desperate quest, stand by me, and I can promise ye that which is better than empty vengeance—wealth, Martin, rank, aye, and what is best of all, a noble woman's love——"

"Enough!" cried I, "I am no weathercock and my mind is set——"

"Why, very well, but so is mine, shipmate, and set upon two things—one to fulfil my duty to the King in the matter of exterminating these pirates and the like rogues, and t'other to redeem my promise to our lady Joan in the matter of her father—your enemy."

"How, are you for Nombre de Dios likewise, Adam?"

"Just as soon as I have this ship in staunch fighting trim, for, unless you and your vengeance are afore me, I will have Sir Richard Brandon out o' the Inquisition's bloody clutches either by battle or stratagem —aye, though it cost me all I possess, and God knoweth I am a vastly wealthy man, Martin."

"Why then, we are like to meet at Nombre de Dios?" said I.

"Mayhap, Martin, who can say? Meantime, here is the chart and your sailing directions with some few words for you to ponder at leisure, and so fortune attend you and farewell, comrade."

"One thing, Adam," said I, grasping the ladder of ropes, "you will save alive the man Resolution Day—for my sake——"

"Aha," quoth Adam, clapping me on the shoulder, "and there spake the man that is my friend! Never doubt it, comrade—he shall live. And look'ee, Martin, if I have been forced to play prank on ye now and then, think as kindly of me as ye can."

Hereupon, and with Adam's assistance, having hauled in the longboat until she was well under the gallery, I presently got me a-down the swaying rope ladder and safe aboard of her (though with no little to-do) and at my shout Adam cast off the towline, and I was adrift.

For some while I sat huddled in the bows, watching the lofty stern with its rows of lighted windows and three great lanthorns above topped by the loom of towering sails, until sails and ship merged into the night, and nought was to see save the yellow gleam of her lights that grew ever more dim, leaving me solitary upon that vast expanse of ocean that heaved all about me,—a dark and bodeful mystery.

At last, finding the wind, though very light, yet might serve me very well, I turned with intent to step the mast. And now I saw the sail was ill-stowed, the canvas lying all abroad and as I rose I beheld this canvas stirred as by a greater wind; then as I stared me this, it lifted, and from beneath it crept a shape that rose up very lithe and graceful and stood with hands reached out towards me, and then as I staggered back came a cry:

"Quick, Resolution—seize him!"

Two powerful arms clasped and dragged me down, and lying thus, dazed by the fall, I stared up to see bending above me the hated face of Joanna.

I waked to a blaze of sun, a young sun whose level beams made the bellying sail above me a thing of glory where it swung against an azure heaven, flecked with clouds pink and gold and flaming red; and stark against this splendour was the grim figure of Resolution Day, a bloody clout twisted about his head, where he sat, one sinewy hand upon the tiller, the other upon the worn Bible open upon his knees, his lips moving as he read, while hard beside me on the floor of the boat lay Joanna, fast asleep. At sight of her I started and shrank from her nearness, whereupon Resolution, lifting his head and closing the Bible on his finger, glared down on me with his solitary eye.

"Martin," said he below his breath, and tapping the brass butt of a pistol that protruded from the pocket of his coat, "there be times when I could joyfully make an end o' you—for her sake—her that do love you to her grief and sorrow, since her love is your hate—though what she can see in ye passes me! Howbeit, love you she doth, poor soul, and if so be you ha' no love for her, I would ha' you be a little kinder, Martin; 'twould comfort her and harm you no whit. Look at her now, so fair, so young, so tender——"

"Nay, here lies Captain Jo!" said I, scowling.

"Speak lower, man," he whispered fiercely. "I ha' given her a sleeping potion out o' the medicine chest Captain Penfeather provided for her; she is not yet cured of her wound, d'ye see, and I would not have her waked yet, so speak lower lest I quiet ye wi' a rap o' the tiller. Let her sleep,—'tis life to her. Saw ye ever a lovelier, sweeter soul?"

Now viewing her as she lay outstretched, the wild, passionate soul of her away on the wings of sleep, beholding the dark curtain of her lashes upon the pallor of her cheek, the wistful droop of her vivid lips and all the mute appeal of her tender womanhood, I could not but marvel within myself.

"And yet," said I at last, speaking my thoughts aloud, "I have seen her foully dabbled with a dead man's blood!"

"And why for not? Jehovah doth not always strike vile rogues dead, wherefore He hath given some women strength to do it for Him. And who are you to judge her; she was innocent once—a pearl before swine and if they—spattered her wi' their mud, they never trampled her i' their mire! She hath been at no man's bidding, and fearing no man, hath ruled all men, outdoing 'em word and deed—aha, two rogues have I seen her slay in duello. Howbeit, she is as God made her, and 'tis God only shall judge His own handiwork; she is one wi' the stars, the winds that go about the earth, blowing how they list, and these great waters that slumber or rage in dreadful tempest—she and they and we are all of God. So treat her a little kind, Martin, love or no—'tis little enough o' kindness she has known all her days; use her a little kinder, for 'tis in my mind you'll not regret it in after days! And talking o' tempest, I like not the look o' the sky—take you the tiller whiles I shorten sail and heed not to disturb Joanna."

"And so," said I, when he had shortened sail and was seated beside me again, "so Captain Penfeather gave you medicine for her?"

"Aye, did he!"

"And knew you were hid in the boat?"

" 'Twas himself set us there."

Now at this I fell to profound thought, and bethinking me of the letter and chart he had given me, I took it out of my pocket and breaking the seals, read as here followeth:

Dear Friend, Comrade and Brother,

Item: Thou art a fool! Yet is there (as it doth seem) an especial Providence for such fools, in particular fools of thy sort.   Thus do I bid thee farewell in the sure hope that (saving for shipwreck, fire, battle, pestilence and the like evils) I shall find thee again and perchance something wiser, since Folly plus Hardship shall mayhap work a miracle of Wisdom.

Herewith I have drawn you a chart, the parallels duly marked and course likewise, whereby you shall come (Providence aiding) unto Nombre de Dios.   And so to your vengeance, Martin, and when found much good may it do thee is the prayer of

Thy patient, hopeful, faithful friend,

ADAM.

NOTA BENE: Should we fail to meet at Nombre de Dios I give you for rendezvous the place which I have clearly marked on the chart (aforementioned) with a X.

"Look'ee, friend," said Resolution, when I had made an end of reading.   "You plead and spoke for my life of Captain Penfeather and he regarded your will, wherefore am I alive, wherefore are we quits in the matter o' the heathen Pompey and I your friend henceforth 'gainst all the world, saving only and excepting Joanna."

"Where do we make for, Resolution?"

"To a little island well beknown to the Fraternity, comrade—that is three islands close-set and called Foremast, Main and Mizzen islands, *amigo*, where we are apt to meet friends, as I say, and sure to find good store of food and the like, brother.   Though to be sure this boat is right well equipped, both for victuals and weapons."

"And when are we like to reach these islands?"

"We should raise 'em to-morrow about dawn, friend, if this wind hold."

"And what is to become of me, Resolution?"

" 'Tis for Joanna to say, *camarado.*"

Now hereupon, stretched out in such shadow as our scant sail afforded (the sun being very hot) I began to reflect upon this ill-chance Fate, in the person of Adam, had played me (cast again thus helpless at the mercy of Joanna) and instead of wasting myself in futile rages against Adam (and him so far out of my reach) I began instead to cast about in my mind how soonest I might escape from this hateful situation; to the which end I determined to follow Resolution's advice is so far as I might, viz: to preserve towards Joanna as kindly a seeming as might be, and here, chancing to look where she lay, I saw her awake and watching me.

"D'ye grieve for your Joan—Damaris—yes?" she demanded suddenly.

"Nay—of what avail?"

"Then I do—from my heart, Martino, from my heart! For she had faith in me, she was kind to me, oh, kind and very gentle! She is as I—might have been, perchance, had life but proved a little kinder."

After this she lay silent a great while and I thought her asleep until she questioned me again suddenly.

"She is a great lady in England—yes?"

"She is."

"And yourself?"

"An outcast."

"And you—loved each other—long since?"

"Long since."

"But I have you at the last!" cried Joanna, exultant. "And nought shall part us now save death and that but for a little while! Dost curse thyself, Martino—dost curse thyself for saving me from the·

fire? But for this I had been dead and thou safe with thy loved Joan—dost curse thyself?"

"Nay, of what avail?"

Now, at this, she falls to sudden rage and revilings, naming me "stock-fish," "clod," "worm," and the like and I (nothing heeding her), turning to behold the gathering clouds to windward, met the glare of Resolution's fierce eye.

"Tell me," cried Joanna, reaching out to nip my leg 'twixt petulant fingers, "why must you brave the fire to save me you do so hate—tell me?"

"Yonder, as I judge, is much wind, Resolution!" said I, nodding towards a threatening cloud bank. Hereupon she struck at me with passionate fist and thereafter turns from me with a great sob, whereat Resolution growled and tapped his pistol butt.

"You were fool to save me!" cried she. "For I, being dead, might now be in happy circumstance and you with your Joan! You were a fool——"

"Howbeit you have your life," said I.

"Life?" quoth she. "What is life to me but a pain, a grief I shall not fear to lose. Life hath ever brought me so much of evil, so little good, I were well rid of it that I might live again, to find perchance those joys but dim remembered that once were mine in better life than this. And now, if there be aught of food and drink aboard, Resolution, let us eat; then get you to sleep—you will be weary, yes."

And surely never was stranger meal than this, Joanna and Resolution, the compass betwixt them, discussing winds, tides and weather, parallels of latitude and longitude, the best course to steer, etc., and I watching the ever-rising billows and hearkening to the piping of the wind.

Evening found us running through a troubled sea beneath an angry sky and the wind so loud I might hear nothing of my companions where they crouched together in the stern sheets. But suddenly Joanna beckoned me with imperious gesture:

"Look, Martino!" cried she, with hand outflung towards the billows that foamed all about us. "Yonder is a death kinder than death by the fire and yet I do fear this more than the fire by reason of this my hateful woman's body. Now may you triumph over my weakness an you will, yet none can scorn it more than I——"

"God forbid!" said I and would have steadied her against the lurching of the boat, but Resolution, scowling at my effort, clasped her within his arm, shielding her as well as he might against the lashing spray, bidding me let be.

Thereafter and despite her sickness, she must needs stoop to cover me with the boat-cloak where I lay, and looking up at Resolution I saw his bronzed face glinted with moisture that was not of the sea.

CHAPTER XVIII

Of Roger Tressady and How the Silver Woman Claimed Her Own at Last

Starting from sleep, instead of gloomy heaven and a desolation of tempestuous waters, I saw this:

The sun, newly up, shed his waxing glory on troubled waters deeply blue and fringed with foam where the waves broke upon a narrow strip of golden sand backed by trees and dense-growing green boskages infinite pleasant to the sight; and beyond these greeny tangles rose a hill of no great altitude, deep-bowered in trees and brush and flowering vines. And viewing all this peaceful loveliness with sleep-filled eyes, I thought it at first no more than idle dream; but presently, knowing it for reality, I felt my hard nature touched and thrilled (as it were) with a great rush of tenderness, for what with this glory of sun and the thousand sweet and spicy odours that wafted to us from this fair island, I sudden felt as if, borne on this well-remembered fragrance, came the sweet and gentle soul of my lady Joan, a haunting presence, sad and very plaintive, for it seemed she knew at last that nought henceforth might stay me from my vengeance. And in my ears seemed the whisper of her desolate cry:

"Martin—Oh, blind and more than blind! Alas, dear Martin!"

Now at this, despite the joy of sun and the gladness of birds that shrilled 'mid the mazy thickets above, a great sadness took me and I bowed my head in gloomy thought.

"Forward there!"

Starting at this hoarse summons, I turned to behold Resolution crouched at the tiller, his great boat-cloak white with brine, his solitary eye scowling from me to the shore and back again.

"Ha, d'ye stir at last, sluggard? Here's Joanna been direly sick—speak low, she sleeps at last, poor lass—and me stiff o' my wounds, clemmed wi' hunger and parched wi' thirst, you a-snoring and a sea worse than Jonah's afore they hove him to the whale——"

"Why not wake me, then?" I demanded, creeping aft and beholding Joanna where she lay slumbering, pale and worn beneath weather-stained cloak. "Why not rouse me, Resolution?"

"Because she forbade me and her word is my law, d'ye see? Reach me a sup o' rum from the locker yonder."

"You have brought us safe through the tempest, then," said I, doing as he bade me.

"Aye, Joanna and I, and despite her qualms and sickness, poor lass, and you a-snoring!" Here, having drained the pannikin of rum, his eye lost something of its ferocity and he nodded. "Twice we came nigh swamping i' the dark but the Lord interposed to save His own yet a little, and you a-snoring, but here was Joanna's hand on the tiller and mine on the sail and plaguing the Almighty wi' prayers of a righteous, meek, long-suffering and God-fearing man and behold, comrade, here we are, safe in the lee of Mizzen Island, and yonder is creek very apt to our purpose. So stand by to let go the halyard and ship oars when I give word, *amigo*."

"She seems very worn with her sickness, Resolution!" said I, stooping to observe Joanna where she slumbered like one utterly exhausted.

"She is, friend!" he nodded. "She never could abide rough seas from a child, d'ye see, brother, and her wound troubleth her yet—but never a word o' complaint, comrade—aha, a great soul, a mighty spirit is hers, for all her woman's slenderness, Martin! Now, let fly your halyard, douse your sail—so! Now ship oars and pull, *camarado*, pull!"

Very soon, myself at the oars and Resolution steering, we crept in betwixt bush-girt rocks to a shelving, sandy beach. Hereupon, Resolution stooped to lift Joanna but finding his wounds irk him, beckoned to me:

"Come, friend," said he. "You are lusty and strong, I do know—bear her ashore and tenderly, brother, tenderly!"

So I stooped and raising Joanna in my arms, climbed out of the boat (though with no little to-do) and bore her ashore towards the pleasant shade of flowering trees adjacent to the sea. Now presently she stirred in my embrace, and looking down at her, I saw her regarding me, great-eyed.

"Here do I rest for the second time, Martino," she murmured. "I wonder—when the third shall be?"

"God knoweth!" said I; and being come to the trees, I laid her there as comfortably as I might and went to aid Resolution to secure the boat.

Having landed such things as we required and lighted a fire, while Resolution busied himself preparing a meal, I began to look about me and found this island marvellous fertile, for here on all sides flowers bloomed, together with divers fruits, as lemons, plantains, limes, grapes, a very wonder to behold. Now I chanced to reach a certain eminent place whence I might behold the general trend of the island; and now I saw that this was the smallest of three islands and remembered how Resolution had named them to me as Fore, Main and Mizzen islands. I was yet staring at these islands, each with its fringe of white surf to windward where the seas yet broke in foam, when my wandering gaze chanced to light on that which filled

me with sudden and strange foreboding, for, plain to
my view despite the distance, I saw the royal yards and
topgallant masts of a great ship (so far as I could
judge) betwixt Fore and Mainmast islands, and I very
full of question as to what manner of ship this should
be.

In my wanderings I chanced upon a little glen where
bubbled a limpid stream amid a very paradise of fruits
and flowers; here I sat me down well out of the sun's
heat, and having drunk my fill of the sweet water, fell
to munching grapes that grew to hand in great, purple clusters. And now, my bodily needs satisfied and
I stretched at mine ease within this greeny bower where
birds whistled and piped joyously amid flowery thickets and the little brook leapt and sang as (one and
all) vaunting the wondrous mercy of God, I, lying
thus ('as I say) surrounded by His goodly handiworks
(and yet blind to their message of mercy) must needs
set my wits to work and cast about in my mind how
I might the soonest win free of this goodly place and
set about the accomplishment of my vengeance. Once
or twice I thought to hear Resolution hallooing and
calling my name but, being drowsy, paid no heed and
thus, what with the peace and comfort of my sur-
roundings, I presently fell asleep.

But in my slumbers I had an evil dream, for I
thought to hear a voice, hoarse yet tuneful, upraised
in song, and voice, like the song, was one heard long
ago, the which in my dreaming troubled me mightily,
insomuch that I started up broad awake and infinitely
glad to know this no more than idle fancy. Sitting
up and looking about me, I saw the sun low and nigh
to setting, and great was my wonder that I should
have slept so long, yet I found myself vastly invig-
orated thereby and mightily hungered, therefore I
arose, minded to seek my companions.

But scarce was I gone a yard than I stopped all at

once, as from somewhere in the gathering shadows
about me, plain to be heard, came the sound of a voice
hoarse but tuneful, upraised in song, and these the
words:

> "Some by the knife did part wi' life
> And some the bullet took O.
> But three times three died plaguily
> A-wriggling on a hook O.
> A hook both long and sharp and strong
> They died by gash o' hook O."

For a long time (as it seemed) I stood motionless
with the words of this hateful chanty yet ringing in
my brain, until the sun flamed seawards, vanished, and
it was night. And here amid the gloom sat I, chin
on knees, my mind busied upon a thousand memories
conjured up by this evil song. At last, being come
to a determination, I arose and, stumbling in the dark,
made the best of my way towards that narrow, shelving beach where we had made our landing. In a little, through a tangle of leafy thickets, I espied the
glow of a fire and heard a sound of voices; and going
thitherwards, paused amid the leaves and hid thus,
saw this fire was built at the mouth of a small cave
where sat Joanna with Resolution at her elbow, while
opposite them were five wild-looking rogues with muskets in their hands grouped about a tall, great fellow
of a masterful, hectoring air, who stood staring down
on Joanna, his right hand upon the silver-hafted dagger in his girdle and tapping at his square chin with
the bright steel hook he bore in place of his left hand.
And as he stood thus, feet wide apart, tapping at his
chin with his glittering hook and looking down on
Joanna, she, leaning back against the side of the cave,
stared up at him eye to eye.

"So-ho!" quoth he at last. "So you are Captain
Jo, eh—Captain Jo of the Brotherhood?"

"And you," said she gently, "you are he that killed
my father!"

Now here ensued a silence wherein none moved, it seemed, only I saw Resolution's bony hand creep and bury itself in his capacious side pocket. Then, putting by the screening branches, I stepped forth into the firelight.

"What, Tressady," said I, "d'ye cheat the gallows yet?"

Almost as I spoke I saw the flash and glitter of his whirling hook as he turned, pinning me with it through the breast of my doublet (but with so just a nicety that the keen point never so much as touched my skin) and holding me at arm's length upon this hateful thing, he viewed me over, his pale eyes bright beneath their jut of shaggy brow. But knowing the man and feeling Joanna's gaze upon me, I folded my arms and scowled back at him.

"Who be you, bully, who and what?" he demanded, his fingers gripping at the dagger in his girdle whose silver hilt was wrought to the shape of a naked woman. "Speak, my hearty, discourse, or kiss this Silver Woman o' mine!"

"I am he that cut you down when you were choking your rogue's life out in Adam Penfeather's noose —along of Abnegation Mings yonder——"

As I spoke I saw Mings thrust away the pistol he had drawn and lean towards me, peering.

"Sink me!" cried he. "It's him, Roger; 'tis Martin sure as saved of us from Penfeather, curse him, on Bartlemy's Island three years agone—it's him, Roger, it's him!"

"Bleed me!" said Tressady, nodding. "But you're i' th' right on't, Abny. You ha' th' right on't, lad. 'Tis Marty, sure enough, Marty as was bonnet to me aboard the *Faithfull Friend* and since he stood friend to us in regard to Adam Penfeather (with a' curse!) it's us shall stand friends t' him. Here's luck and a fair wind t' ye, Marty!" So saying, he loosed me from his hook, and, clapping me on the shoulder, brought me to the circle about the fire.

"Oh, sink me!" cried Mings, flourishing a case-bottle under my nose. "Burn me, if this aren't pure joy! I know a man as don't forget past benefits and that's Abnegation! Sit down, Martin, and let us eat and, which is better, drink together!"

"Why, so we will, Abny, so we will," said Tressady, seating himself within reach of Joanna. " 'Twas pure luck us falling in wi' two old messmates like Marty and Resolution and us in need of a few hell-fire, roaring boys! 'Tis like a happy family, rot me, all love and good-fellowship and be damned! Come, we'll eat, drink and be merry, for to-morrow—we sail, all on us, aboard my ship *Vengeance*, as lieth 'twixt Fore and Main islands yonder, ready to slip her moorings!"

"Avast, friend!" said Resolution, blinking his solitary eye at Tressady. "The captain o' the Coast Brotherhood is Joanna here—Captain Jo, by the Brotherhood so ordained; 'tis Captain Jo commands here——"

"Say ye so, Resolution, say ye so, lad?" quoth Tressady, tapping at chin with glittering hook. "Now mark me—and keep both hands afore ye—so, my bully—hark'ee now—there's none commands where I am save Roger Tressady!" said he, looking round upon us and with a flourish of his hook. "Now if so be any man thinks different, let that man speak out!"

"And what o' Captain Jo?" demanded Resolution.

"That!" cried Tressady, snapping finger and thumb. "Captain Jo is not, henceforth—sit still, lad—so! Now lift his barkers, Abny—in his pockets. Still and patient, lad, still and patient!" So Resolution perforce suffered himself to be disarmed, while Joanna, pale and languid in the firelight, watched all with eyes that gleamed beneath drooping lashes.

"So now," quoth Tressady, "since I command here, none denying——"

"And what o' Captain Jo?" demanded Resolution.

"Why, I'll tell ye, bully, look'ee now! A man's a man and a woman's a woman, but from report here's one as playeth t'other and which, turn about. But 'tis as woman I judge her best, and as woman she sails along o' me, lad, along o' me!" So saying, he nodded and taking out a case-bottle, wrenched at the cork with his teeth.

"And how say you, Joanna?" questioned Abnegation.

"Tush!" said she, with a trill of laughter. "Here is one that talketh very loud and fool-like and flourisheth iron claw to no purpose, since I heed one no more than t'other——"

"Here's death!" cried he fiercely, stabbing the air with his hook. "Death, wench!"

"Tush!" said she again, "I fear death no more than I fear you, and as for your claw—go scratch where you will!"

Goaded to sudden fury, he raised his hook and would have smitten the slender foot of her that chanced within his reach, but I caught his arm and wrenched him round to face me.

"Hold off, Tressady!" said I. "Here's a man to fight an you're so minded. But as for Joanna, she's sick of her wounds and Resolution's little better; but give me a knife and I'm your man!" And I sprang to my feet. Here for a moment Joanna's eyes met mine full of that melting tenderness I had seen and wondered at before; then she laughed and turned to Tressady:

"Sick or no, I am Joanna and better than any man o' you all, yes. Here shall be no need for fight, for look now, Tressady, though you are fool, you are one I have yearned to meet—so here's to our better acquaintance." And speaking, she leaned forward, twitched the bottle from his hand, nodded and clapped it to her mouth all in a moment.

As for Tressady, he gaped, scowled, fumbled with the dagger in his girdle, loosed it, slapped his thigh and burst into a roar of laughter.

"Oh, burn me, here's a soul!" he cried. "'Tis a wench o' spirit, all hell-fire spirit and deviltry, rot me! Go to't, lass, drink hearty—here's you and me agin world and damn all, says I. Let me perish!" quoth he, when he had drunk the toast and viewing Joanna with something of respect. "Here's never a man, woman or child dared so much wi' Jolly Roger all his days—oh, sink me! Why ha' we never met afore—you and me might rule the Main——"

"I do!" said she.

"And how came ye here—in an open boat?"

"By reason of Adam Penfeather!"

"What, Adam again, curse him!"

"He sank the *Happy Despatch!*"

"Burn me! And there's a stout ship lost to us."

"But then—we stayed to fight, yes!"

"What then?" said Tressady, clenching his fist. "Will ye say I ran away—we beat him off!"

"Howbeit Adam sank and took us, and swears to hang you soon or late—unless you chance to die soon!"

"Blind him for a dog—a dog and murderous rogue as shall bite on this hook o' mine yet! A small, thieving rogue is Penfeather——"

"And the likest man to make an end o' the Brotherhood that ever sailed!" nodded Joanna.

"Where lays his course?"

"Who knows?"

"And what o' Belvedere?"

"Dead and damned for rogue and coward!"

"Why, then, drink, my bullies," cried Tressady, with a great oath. "Drink battle, murder, shipwreck and

hell-fire to Adam Penfeather, with a curse! Here's us
safe and snug in a good stout ship yonder, here's us
all love and good-fellowship, merry as grigs, happy
as piping birds, here's luck and long life to each and
all on us."

"Long life!" said Joanna, frowning. " 'Tis folly—
I weary of it already!"

So we ate and drank and sprawled about the fire
until the moon rose, and looking up at her as she sailed
serene, I shivered, for to-night it seemed that in her
pallid beam was something ominous and foreboding, and
casting my eyes round about on motionless tree and
shadowy thicket I felt my flesh stir again.

Now ever as the time passed, Tressady drew nearer
and nearer to Joanna, until they were sitting cheek
by jowl, he speaking quick and low, his pale eyes ever
upon her, she all careless languor, though once I saw
her take hold upon his gleaming hook and once she
pointed to the dagger in his girdle and laughed; whereupon he drew it forth (that evil thing) and holding it
up in her view fell suddenly a-singing:

"Oh, I've sought women everywhere
North, South and East and West;
And some were dark and some were fair
But here's what I love best!
Blow high, blow low, in weal or woe
My Silver Woman's best."

Thus sang Tressady, looking from the languorous
woman at his side to the languorous woman graven on
the dagger-hilt and so thrust it back into his girdle.

And in a while Joanna rose, drawing the heavy boat-
cloak about her shapeliness:

"There is a small bower I wot of down in the shadows
yonder shall be my chamber to-night," said she, staring
up at the moon. "And so good night! I'm a-weary!"
Then she turned, but doing so her foot touched Resolution's leg where he sat, whereat he did strange thing,
for at this soft touch he started, glanced up at her,

his eye very wide and bright, and I saw his two powerful hands become two quivering fists, yet when he spoke
his voice was calm and even.

"Good night, Joanna—fair dreams attend thee."
Then Joanna, eluding Tressady's clutching hand, went
her way, singing to herself very sweet and low.

Hereupon Tressady grew very boisterous and merry
and perceiving Mings and his fellows inclined for
slumber, roared them to wakefulness, bidding them
drink with him and damning them for sleepy dogs.
Yet in a while he fell silent also and presently takes
out his dagger and begins fondling it. Then all at
once he was on his feet, the dagger glittering evilly in
his hand the while he glared from me to Resolution and
back again.

"Good night, my bullies!" said he. "Good night—
and let him follow that dare!" And with a sound 'twixt
a growl and a laugh, he turned and strode away, singing as he went. Now hereupon, nothing doubting his
intent, I sprang to my feet and made to follow, but
felt myself caught in an iron grip and stared down
into the grim face of Resolution.

"Easy, friend—sit down, comrade—here beside me,
brother."

"Aye, truly, you were wiser, Martin!" said Mings,
winking and tapping the pistol in his belt.

Now Resolution sat in the mouth of the small cave
I have mentioned and I noticed he had slipped his right
hand behind him and sat thus, very still, his gaze on
the dying fire like one hearkening very eagerly for
distant sounds, wherefore I did the like and thus, from
somewhere amid the shadowy thickets, I heard Tressady
sing again that evil song of his:

> "Two by the knife did lose their life
> And three the bullet took O.
> But three times three died plaguily
> A-wriggling——"

The singing ended suddenly and indescribably in a sound that was neither cry nor groan nor choke, yet something of each and very ghastly to be heard.

"What was yon!" cried Mings, starting and blinking sleep from his eyes to peer towards those gloomy thickets.

"What should it be but Captain Jo!" said Resolution; and now I saw his right hand, hid no longer, grasped a pistol levelled across his knees. "Sit still, all on ye," he commanded. "Let a man move a leg and that man's dead! Mark now what saith Davy. 'He hath graven and digged a pit and is fallen himself into the destruction he made for others. For his travail shall come upon his own head and his wickedness fall on his own pate.' "

"Nay, look'ee," says Mings, wiping sweat from him, "nay, but I heard somewhat—aye, I did, an unchancy sound——"

"Peace, Abnegation, peace!" quoth Resolution. "Mew not and hark to the words o' Davy: 'The Lord is known to execute judgment, the ungodly is trapped in the work of his own hands'——"

"Nay, but," says Mings, pointing. "See—who comes yonder?"

And now we saw Joanna, a dark figure against the splendour of the moon, walking daintily, as was her wont, and as she came she falls a-singing that same evil song I had heard long ago:

> "There's a fine Spanish dame
> And Joanna's her name
> Shall follow wherever ye go
> Till your black heart shall feel
> Your own cursed steel——"

She stopped suddenly and stood in the light of the fire, looking from one to the other of us with that smile I ever found so hateful.

"I am Joanna," said she softly and nodding at Mings; "I am your Captain Jo and command here. Get you and your fellows aboard and wait my bidding."

"Aye, aye!" said Mings in strangled voice, his eyes fixed and glaring. "But what o' Cap'n Tressady? Where's my comrade, Roger?"

From behind her back Joanna drew forth a slender hand, awfully bedabbled and let fall a reeking thing at Abnegation's feet and I saw this for Tressady's silver-hilted dagger.

"Black Tressady is dead!" said she. "I have just killed him!"

"Dead!" gasped Mings, shrinking. "Roger dead! My comrade—murdered—I——" Uttering a wild, passionate cry he whipped forth his pistol, but in that moment Resolution fired, and rising to his feet, Abnegation Mings groaned and pitched upon his face and lay mute and still.

"Glory to God!" said Resolution, catching up the dead man's weapon and facing the others. "Come, my lads," quoth he; "if Tressady be as dead as Mings, he can't walk, wherefore he must be carried. And wherefore carried, you'll ask? Says I, you shall take 'em along wi' you. You shall bring 'em aboard ship, you shall tell your mates as Captain Jo sends these dead men aboard to show 'em she's alive. So come and bring away Tressady first—march it is for Roger, and lively, lads!"

Now when they were gone, Joanna came beside me where I sat and stood a while, looking down on me in silence.

"He forced me to it!" said she at last. "Oh, Martino, there—was none other way. And he killed my father."

But I not answering, she presently sighed and went away, leaving me staring where Mings lay huddled beyond the dying fire. And presently my gaze chanced

to light on Tressady's dagger of the Silver Woman
where it lay, stained by his life's blood, and leaping
to my feet, I caught it up and sent the evil thing whirling and glittering far out to sea.

CHAPTER XIX

How Joanna Changed Her Mind

"So there's an end o' Tressady and Mings and their fellows, comrade!" said Resolution, staring away into distant haze where showed the topsails of the *Vengeance* already hull down. "And God's will be done, says I, though here be we as must go solitary awhile and Joanna sick to death, comrade."

"Resolution," said I, staring up at his grim figure, "she schemed to lure Tressady to his death?"

"Aye, she did, brother. What other way was there? She hath wit womanish and nimble——"

"She smote him in the shadows——"

"Most true, friend! She hath a man's will and determination!"

"He had no chance——"

"Never a whit, Martin! She is swift as God's lightning and as infallible. Roger Tressady was an evil man and the evil within him she used to destroy him and all very right and proper! And now she lieth sick in the cave yonder and calls for you, brother."

So I arose and coming within the cave found Joanna outstretched upon a rough bed contrived of fern and the boat-cloaks.

"Alas, Martino, I cannot sleep," said she. "I am haunted by the man Tressady, which is surely very strange—oh, very strange. For he was evil like all other men save you and Resolution—and Adam Penfeather. Can you not say somewhat to my comfort? Did he not merit death?"

"Aye, most truly. Had you not killed him—I would."

"For my sake, Martino?"

"Aye," said I, "for yours."

"Why, then 'tis strange I should grieve thus—I have killed men ere this, as you do know, nor troubled; belike 'tis my sickness—or the memory of my lady Joan—Damaris, her gentleness. Howbeit I am sorry and sad and greatly afraid."

"Nay," said I. "What should fright you that do fear nothing?"

"Myself, Martino—I have been—minded to kill you —more than once?"

"Yet do I live."

"And yet do I fear!" said she, with a great sigh.

"And your wound pains you belike?"

"A little, Martino."

"Show me!"

Mutely she suffered me to uncover her arm and unwind the bandages and I saw the tender flesh was very angry and inflamed, whereupon I summoned Resolution from his cooking, who at my desire brought the chest of medicines with water, etc., and set myself to soothe and cherish this painful wound as gently as I might, and though she often blenched for the pain of it she uttered no complaint.

"Do I hurt you overmuch?" I questioned.

"Nay," said she, catching her breath for pain of it, "I am none so tender. D'ye mind how I burned the boat you had so laboured at?"

"Aye, I do!"

"And how I gave you an evil draught that was agony?"

"Aye, I do so!"

"And how I plagued you——"

"Nay, why remember all this, Joanna?"

"It helpeth me to endure this pain!"

When I had anointed and bound up her wound she must needs praise my skill and vow she was herself again and would be up and about, whereat Resolution reached down to aid her to rise, but this I would by no means suffer, telling her that she must rest and sleep the fever from her blood. At this she scowled, then all of a sudden laughed.

"Why, then, you shall stay and talk with me!"

"Rather shall Resolution mix you a sleeping draught."

"Verily, brother, two have I mixed, but she'll not take 'em!"

"Why, then, being two to one, we must force her to drink," said I.

"Force her to drink, comrade? Force Joanna—God's light——!"

"Mix the potion, man, or teach me!" So in the end Resolution did as I bade; then kneeling beside Joanna, I raised her upon my arm and set the pannikin to her lips, whereupon, though she frowned, she presently drank it off meekly enough, to Resolution's no small wonder and her own, it seemed.

"I grow marvellous obedient!" said she. "And 'tis hateful stuff!"

"Now sleep," quoth I. "'Tis life to you——"

"Wouldst have me live, to plague you again, may-hap?" she questioned.

"This is as God wills!"

"Nay, this is as you will, Martino. Wouldst have me live, indeed?"

Now seeing how she hung upon my answer, beholding the wistful pleading of her look, I nodded.

"Aye, I would indeed!" said I.

"Why, then I will, Martino, I will!" And smiling, she composed herself to slumber and smiling, she presently fell asleep, whereupon Resolution crept stealthily out of the little cave and I after him. Being outside, he turned and suddenly caught and wrung my hand.

"Friend," said he, his grim features relaxing to unwonted smile. "Brother, you are a man—the only man could ha' done it. I thought Death had her sure last night, she all of a fever and crying out for Death to take her."

"She'll do better out in the air!" said I, glancing about.

"The air, comrade?"

"Aye, I must contrive her a shelter of sorts to her comfort where she may sleep. 'Neath yonder tree should serve——"

"She'll live, Martino, she'll live and all by reason o' her love for you—the promise you made her——"

"I made no promise, man!"

"Why, 'twas good as promise, comrade."

"How so?"

" 'Wouldst ha' me live,' says she, 'to plague you again,' says she. 'Aye, that would I indeed,' says you! And what's that but a promise, Martin?"

"God forgive you!" quoth I. " 'Twas no promise I intended, as you very well know."

"Why, as to that, comrade, how if Joanna think as I think?"

" 'Twill be vain folly!" quoth I in petulant anger and strode away, leaving him to scowl after me, chin in hand.

Howbeit (and despite my anger) I presently took such tools as we had and set about making a small hut or rather bower, where an invalid might find such privacy as she wished and yet have benefit of the pure, sweet air rather than lie mewed in the stifling heat of the little cave. And presently, as I laboured, to me cometh Resolution full of praise for my handiwork and with proffer of aid. At this I turned to him face to face.

"Did I make Joanna any promise, aye or no?" I demanded.

"Aye, brother. You vowed Joanna must live to plague you, forsooth, how and when and where she would, comrade. In the which assured hope she lieth even now, sleeping herself to health and strength and all to pleasure you, Martin. And sure, oh, sure you are never one so vile to deceive the poor, sweet soul?"

Now perceiving all his specious sophistry and wilful misunderstanding of the matter, I came nigh choking with anger.

"Liar!" quoth I. "Liar!"

"Peace, brother, peace!" said he. "From any other man this were a fighting word, but as it is, let us reason together, brother! The Lord hath——"

"Enough!" cried I.

"Friend, the Lord hath set——"

"Leave Him out!" quoth I.

"What, Martin—will ye blaspheme now? Oh, shame on ye! 'The mouth o' the blasphemer is as an open sepulchre!' But as I say, the Lord hath set you here i' this flowery garden like Adam and her like Eve——"

"And yourself like the serpent!" said I.

"Ha' done, Martin, ha' done! 'The Lord shall root out deceitful lips and the tongue that speaks proud things!' mark that!"

"And mark you this, Resolution, an you fill Joanna's head with aught of such folly, whatsoever sorrow or evil befalls her is upon your head."

"Why, observe, friend and brother, for any man shall cause Joanna such, I have this, d'ye see!" And he showed me the butt of the pistol in his pocket; whereat I cursed him for meddlesome fool and turning my back went on with my labour, though my pleasure in it was gone. Howbeit I wrought this, rather than sit with idle hands, wasting myself in profitless repining. And presently, being intent on the business, I forgot all else and seeing this little bower was turning out much better than I had hoped, I fell a-whistling, until, hearing a step, I turned to find Joanna leaning upon Resolution's arm and in her eyes such a look of yearning tenderness as filled me with a mighty disquiet.

"And have you—made this for—me, Martino?" she questioned, a little breathlessly.

"Aye," I nodded, "because I do hate idleness——"

"Hark to him!" said Resolution. "And him picturing to me how snug you would lie here——"

"As to that, Resolution," said I, scowling, "you can lie anywhere."

"Why, true," said he, ignoring my meaning. "Since Jo sleeps here, I shall sleep 'neath the tree hard by, leaving you the cave yonder, friend."

That night Joanna lay in the bower and from this time she mended apace, but as for me, with every hour my impatience to be gone grew upon me beyond all measure, and as the time passed I waxed surly and morose, insomuch that upon a day as I sat frowning at the sea, Joanna stole upon me and stooping, kissed my hand or ever I might stay her.

"Do I offend?" she questioned with a strange, new humility. "Ah, prithee, why art grown so strange to me?"

"I am as I always was!"

"Nay, in my sickness thou wert kind and gentle——"

"So should I have been to any other!"

"You builded me my little house?"

"I had naught else to do."

"Martino," said she, sinking on her knees beside me. "Oh, *caro mio*, if—if you could kiss me in my sickness when I knew naught of it—wherefore not now when I am all awake and full of life——"

"I never did!" said I, speaking on rageful impulse.

"If Resolution told you this, he lies!" At this she shrank as I had struck her.

"And did you not—kiss me in my sickness—once, no?"

"Never once!"

Here, bowing her head upon her hands, she rested silent awhile.

"Nay, Joanna, wherefore seek the impossible. In these latter days I have learned to—to respect you——"

"Respect!" cried she, clenching her fists. "Rather give me hate; 'twere easier endured——"

"Why, then, this island is a rendezvous for the Brotherhood, soon will you have friends and comrades; give me then the boat and let me go——"

"To seek her? Nay, that you shall never do. I will kill you first, yes—for the cold, passionless thing you are!" So she left me and knowing that she wept, I felt greatly heartsick and ashamed.

Now the little cave wherein I slept gave upon that stretch of sandy beach where lay the boat and this night the weather being very hot and no wind stirring, I came without the cave and sat to watch the play of moonlight on the placid waters and hearken to their cool plash and ripple. Long time I sat thus, my mind full of foreboding, mightily cast down and hot with anger against Resolution, whose subtle lies had set Joanna on this vain folly of love, teaching her hopes for that which might never be; and guessing some of her pain therefor, I grieved for her and felt myself humbled that I (though all unwitting) should cause her this sorrow.

Sitting thus, full of heavy thoughts, my gaze by chance lighted upon the boat and, obeying sudden impulse, I arose and coming hither, fell to sudden temptation, for here she lay afloat; once aboard it needed but to slip her moorings and all these my present troubles would be resolved. And yet (thinks I) by so doing I should leave two people on this solitary island cut off from their kind. And yet again they run no chance of hardship or starvation, God knows, and this being a known meeting-place for their fellows, they shall not lack for company very long.

I was yet debating this in my mind when, roused by a sound behind me, I turned to find Resolution scowling on me and pistol in hand.

"Ha!" said he 'twixt shut teeth, "I ha' been expecting this and watched according. So you'll steal the boat, will ye—leave us marooned here, will ye?"

"I haven't decided yet!" quoth I.

"And what's to let me from shooting ye?"

"Nought in the world," said I, watching for a chance to close with him, "only bear witness I have not touched rope or timber yet——"

" 'Tis a rule o' the Coast to shoot or hang the like o' you!" quoth he, and I heard the sharp click of the pistol as he cocked it and then with a flutter of petticoats Joanna burst upon us.

"Resolution, what is't?" she questioned breathlessly, looking from one to other of us.

"He was for stealing the boat, Jo!"

"Is this true?" she demanded, her face set and very pale. But here, seeing speech was vain, I shook my head and turning my back on them came into my cave and cast myself down on my rough bed. Lying thus I heard the murmur of their talk a great while, yet I nothing heeded until Joanna spoke close without the cave.

"Bide you there, Resolution!" Then the moonlight was dimmed and I saw her form outlined in the mouth of the cave.

"What would you, Joanna?" said I, starting up.

"Talk with you a small while," said she and came where we might behold each other. "Nay, do not fear.

I will come no nearer, only I would speak to you now as I would speak if I lay a-dying, I would have you answer as you would if—if Death stood ready to strike these our bodies and bear our souls out to the infinite and a better life."

"Speak!" said I, wondering to see her shaken as by an ague-fit.

"You do not—love me, then? No?"

"No."

"You—never could love me, mind and heart and body? No?"

"No."

"You could not endure me beside you, to—to live—with me near you?"

"'Twould mean only pain, Joanna."

"Then go!" cried she. "I am not so base-souled to weep and wheedle, to scheme and pray for thing that can never be truly mine, or to keep you here in hated bondage—go! The boat lieth yonder; take her and what you will—only—get you gone!"

Now at this I rose and would have taken her hands but she snatched them behind her, and now I wondered at her deathly pallor,—her very lips were pale and set.

"Joanna," I stammered, "do you mean—am I——"

"Go!"

"Nay, first hear me say that wheresoever I go needs must I——"

"Respect me!" cried she with a strange, wild laugh. "Oh, begone!"

"Joanna," said I, "for any harsh word I have spoke you in the past, for any pain you have suffered because of me, I do most surely grieve and would most humbly crave your forgiveness and for this generous act I—I——"

"Respect me?" said she in a small voice. "Ah, cannot you see—how you—hurt me?" And now all suddenly I did strange thing for, scarce knowing what I did, I caught her in my arms and kissed her hair, her eyes, her cold lips and then, half ashamed, turned to leave her.

"Stay!" said she, but I never heeded. "Martino!" she called, but I never paused; and then, being come to the mouth of the cave, I heard the quick, light sound of her feet behind me and as I stepped into the moonlight felt two arms that swung me aside, saw Joanna leap before me as the night-silence was split by a ringing, deafening roar; and then I had her in my arms and she, smiling up at me with blood upon her lips, hid her face in my breast. "Here in thine arms do I lie for the third time—and last, Martino!" she sighed, and so Resolution found us.

"What!" he gasped. "Oh, God! What——?"

"Some one has shot Joanna!"

"Aye, Martin, 'twas I!" and I saw the pistol yet smoking in his hand—"I shot her thinking 'twas you —Oh, God!"

"Nay, Resolution," said Joanna, opening her eyes. "You did very right—'twas only that I—being a woman—changed my mind—at the last. 'Twas I bid him—kill you, Martino—if you came forth, but I— I dreamed you—you would not leave me. Nay, let be, Resolution, I'm a-dying—yes!"

"Ah, forbid it, God—Oh, God of Mercies, spare her!" he cried, his hands and eyes uplift to the radiant, starry heavens.

"Nay, grieve not, Resolution—dear friend!" she murmured painfully. "For oh, 'tis—a good thing to die—by your hand and with—such reason! Martino, when—you shall wed your Joan—Damaris, say I— gave you to her with—my life because I loved you— better than life—and Death had—no fears. I go back to life—a better life—where I shall find you one day, Martino, and learn what—happiness is like—mayhap. Resolution," she whispered, "when I—am dead, do not

let me lie a poor, pale thing to grieve over—bury me
—bury me so soon as I—am dead. Dig me a grave—
above the tide! Promise this!"

"I promise!"

"Now kiss me—you were ever true and kind—kiss
me? And you, Martino, wilt kiss me—not in gratitude
—this last time?" And so I kissed her and thereafter
she lay silent awhile, looking up at me great-eyed.

"Somewhere," she whispered, "some day—we shall
—meet again, beloved—but now is—farewell. Oh, 'tis
coming—'tis coming, Martino!" And then in stronger
voice, "Oh, Death!" she cried. "Oh, welcome Death—
I do not fear thee! Lift me, Martino—lift me—let me
die—upon my feet!"

Very tenderly we lifted her betwixt us and then suddenly with a soft, murmurous cry, she lifted her arms
to the glory of the wide firmament above us and with
shuddering sigh let them slowly fall, and with this sigh
the strange, wild soul of her sped away back to the
Infinite whence it had come.

And now Resolution, on his knees beside this slender
form that lay so mute and still, broke out into great
and awful sobs that were an agony to hear.

"Dead!" he gasped. "Oh, God—dead! And by my
hand! I that loved her all her days—that would ha'
died for her—Oh, smite me, merciful God—cast forth
Thy lightnings—shoot forth Thine arrows and consume me an Thou be merciful indeed." All at once he
arose and hasting away on stumbling feet, presently
came back again, bearing spade and mattock.

"Come, friend," said he in strange, piping tones.
"Come now, let us dig grave and bury her, according to
my promise. Come, brother!" Now looking on him as
he stood all bowed and shaking, I saw that he was suddenly become an old man; his twisted frame seemed
shrunken, while spade and mattock shook and rattled
in his palsied hands. "Come, lad, come!" cried he

querulously. "Why d'ye gape—bring along the body; 'tis nought else! Ah, God, how still now, she that was so full o' life! Bring her along to high water-mark and tenderly, friend, ah, tenderly, up wi' her to your heart!" So I did as he bade and followed Resolution's bowed and limping form till he paused well above where any sea might break and hard beside a great rock.

"She'll lie snug here, friend," quoth he, "snug against howling wind and raging tempest!" So together we dug the grave deep within that shelving, golden sand, and laying her tenderly therein, knelt together while the moon sank and shadows lengthened; and when Resolution had recited the prayers for the dead, he broke into a passion of prayer for himself, which done we rose and plied spade and mattock in silence; nor would Resolution pause or stay until we had raised mound sufficiently high to please him. When at last all was completed to his satisfaction, he dropped his spade and wiping sweat from him seated himself beside the grave, patting the mound very tenderly with his open palm.

"The moon is wondrous bright, friend," said he, staring up at it, "but so have I seen it many a night; but mark this, never in all our days shall we see again the like o' her that sleeps, Martino, that sleeps—below here!" And here he falls to soft mutterings and to patting that small mound of sand again.

"Come!" said I at last, touching his bowed shoulder. "Come!"

"Where away, *camarado?*" he questioned, looking up at me vacantly. "Nay, I'm best here—mayhap she'll be lonesome-like at first, so I'll bide here, lad, I'll bide here a while. Go your ways, brother, and leave old Resolution to pray a little, aye—and, mayhap weep a little, if God be kind."

So in the end I turned, miserably enough, and left him crouched there, his head bowed upon his breast. And in my mind was horror and grief and something beside these that filled me with a great wonder. Reaching the cave, I saw the sand there all trampled and stained with the blood she had shed to save mine own, and hard beside these, the print of her slender foot. And gazing thus, I was of a sudden blinded by scorching tears, and sinking upon my knees I wept as never before in all my days. And then sprang suddenly to my feet as, loud upon the air, rang out a shot that seemed to echo and re-echo in my brain ere, turning, I began to run back whence I had come.

And so I found Resolution face down across the mound that marked Joanna's grave, his arms clasped about it and on his dead face the marks of many tears.

CHAPTER XX

I Go to Seek My Vengeance

NEXT day, just as the sun rose, I buried Resolution 'twixt Joanna and the sea, yet over him I raised no mound, since I judged he would have it so. Thereafter I ate and drank and stored the boat with such things as I needed for my voyage and particularly with good supply of fruits. And now, though the wind and tide both served me, I yet lingered, for it seemed that the spirit of Joanna still tarried hereabouts. Moved by sudden desire, I began searching among the tumbled boulders that lay here and there and presently finding one to my purpose, urged it down the sloping beach and with infinite pains and labour contrived at last to set it up at the head of Joanna's resting-place. Then, taking hammer and chisel, I fell to work upon it, heedless of sun-glare, of thirst, fatigue or the lapse of time, staying not till my work was complete, and this no more than two words cut deep within the enduring stone; these:

JOANNA

VNFEARING

And now at last, the tide being on the turn, I unmoored the boat, and thrusting her off, clambered aboard and betook me to the oars, and ever as I rowed I kept my gaze upon that small, solitary heap of sand until it grew all blurred upon my sight. Having presently made sufficient headway, I unshipped oars and hoisting my sail, stood out into the immeasurable deep but with my eyes straining towards that stretch of golden sand where lay all that was mortal of Joanna.

And with my gaze thus fixed, I must needs wonder what was become of the fiery, passionate spirit of her, that tameless soul that was one with the winds and stars and ocean, even as Resolution had said. And thus I presently fell a-praying and my cheek wet with tears that I thought no shame. When I looked up, I saw that the narrow strip of beach was no longer in sight; Joanna had verily gone out of my life and was but a memory.

All afternoon I held on before a fair wind so that as the sun sank I saw the three islands no more than a faint speck on the horizon; wherefore, knowing I should see them no more in this life, I uncovered my head, and thus it was indeed I saw Joanna's resting-place for the last time.

And now as the sun slipped westward and vanished in glory, even now as night fell, I had a strange feeling that her spirit was all about me, tender and strong and protecting, and herein, as the darkness gathered, I found great comfort and was much strengthened in the desperate venture I was about.

Having close-reefed my sail and lashed the tiller, I rolled myself in a boat-cloak and, nothing fearing, presently fell asleep and dreamed Joanna sat above me at the helm, stooping to cover me from the weather as she had done once before.

Waking next morning to a glory of sun, I ate and drank (albeit sparingly) and fell to studying Adam's chart, whereby I saw I must steer due southwesterly and that by his calculation I should reach the mainland in some five or six days. Suffice it that instead of five days it was not until the tenth day (my water being nigh exhausted and I mightily downcast that I had sailed out of my proper course) that I discovered to

my inexpressible joy a faint, blue haze bearing westerly
that I knew must be the Main. And now the wind fell
so that it was not until the following morning that I
steered into a little, green bay where trees grew to the
very water's edge and so dense that, unstepping my
mast, I began paddling along this green barrier, looking for some likely opening, and thus presently came
on a narrow cleft 'mid the green where ran a small
creek roofed in with branches, vines and twining
boughs, into which I urged my boat forthwith (and
no little to-do) and passed immediately from the hot
glare of sun into the cool shade of trees and tangled
thickets. Having forced myself a passage so far as
I might by reason of these leafy tangles, my next
thought was to select such things as I should need and
this took me some time, I deeming so many things essen-
tial since I knew not how far I might have to tramp
through an unknown country, nor in what direction
Nombre de Dios lay. But in the end I narrowed down
my necessities to the following, viz:

> A compass
> A perspective-glass
> A sword
> Two pistols
> A gun with powder-horn and shot for same
> A light hatchet
> A tinder-box and store of buccaned meat

And now, having belted on sword and pistols and
wrapping the other things in one of the boat-cloaks,
I strapped the unwieldy bundle to my shoulders and
taking up the gun, scrambled ashore, and having found
my bearing, set off due southwesterly.

Hour after hour I struggled on, often having to hew
myself a passage with my axe, until towards evening I
came out upon a broad ride or thoroughfare amid the
green, the which greatly heartened me, since here was
evidence of man's handiwork and must soon or late

bring me to some town or village; forthwith, my weariness forgotten, I set off along this track, my face set
ever westwards; but presently my vaunting hopes were
dashed to find the track could be very little used nowadays, since here and there great trees had fallen and
lay athwart my going, and presently the way itself
narrowed to a mere path and this crossed here and
there by hanging vines which was sure proof that few,
if any, had passed this way these many months, mayhap
years. Hereupon I stopped to lean despondent on my
gun and looked about me; and with dejection of mind
came weariness of body and seeing night was at hand,
I determined to go no farther and turned in among
the trees, minded to sleep here, though the place was
wild and forbidding enough.

I had just loosed off my heavy pack when the per-
vading stillness was broken by a wailing cry, so sudden,
so shrill and evil to hear that my flesh crept and I
huddled against a tree, peering into the deepening
shadows that had begun to hem me in. At first I
judged this some wild beast and reached for my musket;
then, as the sound rose again, I knew this for human
cry, for I heard these words:

"Mercy, señors, mercy for the love o' God!"

Hereupon I began to run towards whence came this
dismal outcry and presently espied the glow of a fire,
and creeping thither discovered four men grouped
about a fifth and him fast bound to a tree, and this poor
wretch they were torturing with a ramrod heated in
the fire; even as I watched he writhed and screamed
for the intolerable pain of it. Staying for no more,
I burst upon them and levelling my piece at the chief
tormentor, pulled the trigger, whereupon was no more
than a flash of the flint; it seemed that in my hurry
to begone I had forgotten to load it. Howbeit, loaded
or not, it served me well enough, for, swinging it by
the barrel, I was upon them or ever they were aware

and smote down two of the rogues, whereupon their comrades betook them to their heels with the utmost precipitation. I therefore proceeded to cut the sufferer loose who, sinking to the earth, lay there, muttering and groaning.

"Are ye much hurt?" I questioned, stooping above him: whereupon he spat forth a string of curses by which I judged him English and very far from dying as I had feared. I now found myself master of four very good guns, a sword, a steel headpiece, two cloaks and other furniture, with food a-plenty and three flasks of wine. I was yet examining these and watching against the return of their late owners when, hearing a sound, I saw the late poor captive bending above the two men I had felled.

"Are they dead?" I questioned.

"Nay, not yet, master; give 'em six minutes or say ten and they'll be as dead as the pig you ate of last——"

"How so?" I demanded, staring at the wild, ragged figure of the speaker.

"By means o' this, master!" said he, and stooping towards the fire showed me a middling-sized black thorn upon his open palm. "Not much to look at, master—no, but 'tis death sure and sarten, howsomever. I've many more besides; I make 'em into darts and shoot 'em through a blowpipe—a trick I larned o' the Indians. Aye, I spits 'em through a pipe—which is better than your guns—no noise, no smoke, and sure death wherever it sticketh."

"Are you an Englishman?"

"I am that! Born within sound o' Bow Bells; 'tis all o' twenty years since I heard 'em but they ring in my dreams sometimes. I shipped on a venture to the Main twenty years ago and fought and rioted as a man may and by ill-luck fell into the hands o' the bloody Spaniards along o' six other good lads—all

dead long since, master. Then the Inquisition got me
and was going to burn me but not liking the thought
on't, I turned Roman. Then they made me a slave,
but I got away at last. Aha, all Spanishers are devils
for cruelty, but their Churchmen are worst and of all
their Churchmen the coldest, softest, bloodiest is Alexo
Valdez, Chief Inquisitor of Nombre de Dios yonder——"

"Ha, you know Nombre de Dios?"

"I ha' lived and suffered there, master, and 'tis
there I be a-going for to make an end o' Bloody
Valdez, if God be kind."

"Then," said I, "we will travel so far ,ogether——"

"And what doth an Englishman the like o' you want
with the accursed place; the Inquisition is strong
there——"

" 'Tis a matter of life and death," said I.

"Death!" said he, "Death—they should all be dead
and rotting, if I had my way." So saying, this strange
man, whose face I had scarce seen, laid him down
beyond the fire and composed himself to slumber.

"How then," I demanded, "will ye sleep here in the
wild and no watch?"

"I will that!" said he. "I know the wilderness and
I have endured much o' hardship o' late and as to
watching, there's small need. The rogues you fell
upon, being Spaniards, will doubtless be running yet
and nigh unto Nombre, by now."

"How far is it hence?"

"Twelve leagues by road, but less the ways I
travel."

"Good!" said I.

"Though 'tis hard going."

"No matter."

"Why, then, sleep, for we march at dawn. And my
name is John."

"And mine Martin."

"Why, then, Martin, good night."

"Good night, John."

Howbeit though (and despite his hurts) my companion presently slept and snored lustily, and though I kept myself awake and my weapons to hand, yet I fell a-nodding and at last, overcome with weariness, sank to sleep likewise.

I waked to find the sun up and the man John shaking me, a wild, unlovely, shaggy fellow, very furtive of eye and gesture, who cringed and cowered away as I started up.

"Lord, man," quoth I, "I am no enemy!"

"I know it!" said he, shaking tousled head. "But 'tis become nat'ral to me to slink and crawl and blench like any lashed cur, all along o' these accursed Spaniards; I've had more kicks and blows than I've lived days," he growled, munching away at the viands he had set forth.

"Have ye suffered so much then?"

"Suffered!" cried he with a snarl. "I've done little else. Aha, when I think o' what I've endured, I do love my little blowpipe——"

"Blowpipe?" I questioned.

"Aye—this!" And speaking, from somewhere among the pitiful rags that covered his lank carcase he drew forth a small wooden pipe scarce two foot long and having a bulbous mouthpiece at one end. "The Indians use 'em longer than this—aye, six foot I've seen 'em, but then, Lord! they'll blow ye a dart from eighty to a hundred paces sometimes, whereas I never risk shot farther away than ten or twenty at most; the nearer the surer, aha!" Hereupon he nodded, white teeth agleam through tangled beard, and with a swift, stealthy gesture hid the deadly tube in his rags again.

"What of the two Spaniards I struck down last night?" I questioned, looking vainly for them.

"In the bushes yonder," said he and with jerk of
thumb. "I hid 'em, master, they being a little
unsightly—black and swol—as is the natur' o' this
poison!" Hereupon I rose and going whither he
pointed, parted the undergrowth and saw this was
indeed so, insomuch that my stomach turned and I
had no more desire for food.

"You murdered those men!"

"Aye, that I did, master, an you call it murder.
Howbeit, there's more shall go the same road yet,
notably Alexo Valdez, a curse on him!"

"And you are an Englishman?"

"I was, but since then I've been slave to be whipped,
dog to be kicked, Lutheran dog to be spat upon, and
lastly Indian——"

"And what now?"

"A poor soul to be tormented, shot, hanged, or
burned as they will, once I'm taken."

"And yet you will adventure yourself to Nombre
de Dios?"

"Why, Alexo Valdez is lately come there and Alexo
Valdez burned my friend Dick Burbage, as was 'pren-
tice wi' me at Johnson's, the cutler's, in Friday Street
nigh St. Paul's, twenty odd years agone."

And in a while, being ready to start, I proffered this
wild fellow one of the Spaniard's guns, but he would
have none of it, nor sword, nor even cloak to cover his
rags, so in the end we left all things behind, and there
they be yet, for aught I know.

Now as we journeyed on together, in answer to my
questioning I learned from this man John something
of the illimitable pride and power of the Church of
Rome; more especially he told me of the Spanish
Inquisition, its cold mercilessness and passionless
ferocity, its unsleeping watchfulness, its undying ani-
mosity, its constant menace and the hopelessness of escape therefrom. He gave me particulars of burnings

and rackings, he described to me the torments of the
water, the wheel and the fire until my soul sickened.
He told me how it menaced alike the untrained savage,
the peasant in his hut and the noble in his hall. I
heard of parents who, by reason of this corroding fear,
had denounced their children to the torment and children their parents.

"Aye, and there was a Donna Bianca Vallambrosa,
a fine woman, I mind, was suspected of Lutheranism—
so they racked her and she in torment confessed whatsoever they would and accused her sister Donna Luisa
likewise. So they burned 'em both and made 'em pay
for stake and chain and faggots too, afore they died."

Many other horrors he recounted, but ever and
always he came back to the name of Alexo Valdez to
vomit curses upon until at last I questioned him as
to what manner of man this was to behold.

"Master," said John, turning to regard me, every
hair upon his sunburned face seeming to bristle,
"think o' the most sinful stench ever offended you,
the most loathly corruption you ever saw and there's
his soul; think o' the devil wi' eyes like dim glass, flesh
like dough and a sweet, soft voice, and you have Alexo
Valdez inside and out, and may every curse ever cursed
light on and blast him, says I!"

"Are there many English prisoners in the Inquisition at Nombre?"

"Why, I know of but one—though like enough
there's more—they are so cursed secret, master."

"Did ye ever hear of an English gentleman lost or
taken hereabouts some six years since and named Sir
Richard Brandon?"

"Nay, I was slaving down Panama way six years ago.
Is it him you come a-seeking of, master?"

"Aye," I nodded. "A very masterful man, hale and
florid and of a full habit."

"Nay, the only Englishman ever I see in Nombre was

old and bent wi' white hair, and went wi' a limp, so it can't be him."

"No!" said I, frowning. "No!" After this, small chance had we for talk by reason of the difficulty of our going, yet remembering all he had told, I had enough to think on, God knows.

We had now reached a broken, mountainous country very trying and perilous, what with torrents that foamed athwart our way, jagged boulders, shifting stones and the like, yet John strode on untiring; but as for me, what with all this, the heat of sun and the burden I carried, my breath began to labour painfully. The first thing I tossed away was my gun that fell, ringing and clattering, down the precipitous rocks below, and the next was my pack and thereafter my hatchet and pistols, so that by the time we reached the top of the ascent all I had to encumber me was my sword, and this I kept, since it was light and seemingly a good blade.

"Master," said John, with a flourish of his ragged arm, "here's freedom—here's God. A land o' milk and honey given over to devils—curse all Spanishers, say I!"

Now looking around me I stood mute in wonder, for from this height I might behold a vast stretch of country, towering mountains, deep, shady valleys, impenetrable woods, rushing rivers, wide-stretching plains and far beyond a vague haze that I knew was the sea.

"And yonder, master," said John, pointing with his blowpipe, "yonder lieth Nombre, though ye can't see it, the which we shall reach ere nightfall, wherefore it behoveth me to look to my artillery."

So saying, he squatted down upon his hams and from his rags produced a small gourd carefully wrapped about with leaves; unwinding these, I saw the gourd to contain a sticky, blackish substance.

"Aha!" said John, viewing this with gloating eyes. "Snake poison is mother's milk to this, master. Here's enough good stuff to make pocky corpses o' every cursed Spanisher in Nombre ere sunset. Here's that might end the sufferings o' the poor Indians, the hangings, burnings and mutilations. I've seen an Indian cut up alive to feed to the dogs afore now—but here's a cure for croolty, master!"

While speaking, he had laid on the ground before him some dozen or so little darts no longer than my finger, each armed with a needle-like point and feathered with a wad of silky fibres; the point of each of these darts he dipped into the poison one after the other and laid them in the sun to dry, which done he wrapped up the little gourd mighty carefully and thrust it back among his rags. And in a while, the poison on the darts or arrows being dried to his satisfaction, he took forth a small leathern quiver of native make and setting the missiles therein, shut down the lid securely and sprang to his feet.

"Here's sure death and sarten for some o' the dogs, master," quoth he, "and now if there truly be a God aloft there, all I ask is one chance at Alexo Valdez as burns women and maids, as tortures the innocent, as killed my friend and druv me into the wild—one chance, master, and I'm done!"

Thus he spake with eyes uplift and one hairy hand upraised to the serene heavens, then with a nod to me set off along the hazardous track before us.

Of this, the last stage of our journeying, I will make no mention save that footsore, bruised and weary I sank amid a place of trees and gloomy thickets as the sun went down and night came.

"Straight afore you about half a mile lieth Nombre, master!" said John in my ear. "Hearken! You may hear the dogs like bees in a hive and be cursed to 'em!"

And sure enough I heard an indistinct murmur of

sound that was made up of many; and presently came others more distinct; the faint baying of a hound, the distant roll of a drum, the soft, sweet tolling of a bell.

"So here y'are, master, and good luck t'ye!" said John and with scarce a rustle, swift and stealthy as an Indian, he was gone and I alone in the gloom. Hereupon I debated with myself whether I should get me into the city straight away or wait till the morrow, the which question was resolved by my falling into a sweet and dreamless slumber.

CHAPTER XXI

How I Came to Nombre de Dios

I awoke to the glare of a light and, starting up, was smitten to my knees and, lying half-stunned, was conscious of voices loud and excited, of hands that wrenched me here and there. And now (my hands securely trussed) I was hauled up and marched on stumbling feet amid shadowy captors, all of whom seemed to talk excitedly and none to listen, the which I little heeded being yet dazed by the blow. And presently I was aware of a dim street where lights gleamed, of tall buildings, an open square and a shadowy pile soaring upward into the dark. And presently from the surrounding gloom a darker figure stole, slow-moving and silent, at sight of which my captors halted to kneel, one and all, with bowed heads, whereupon the form raised a shadowy arm in salutation or blessing. And then a voice spake in sonorous Spanish, very soft and low and sweet, yet a voice that chilled me none the less:

"Whom bring ye?"

Here came voices five or six, speaking also in Spanish, and amid this babel I caught such words as:

"A stranger, holy father!"

"An Englishman!"

"A Lutheran dog!"

"Follow!" the sweet voice commanded, whereupon up sprang my captors and hauled me along and so presently into a spacious hall with a dais at one end where stood a table and great elbow-chair; but what drew

and held my gaze was the slender, dark-robed ecclesi-
astic that, moving on leisured, soundless feet, went on
before until, reaching the table, he seated himself there,
head bowed upon one hand; and thus he sat awhile
then beckoned with one imperious finger, whereupon my
captors led me forward to the dais.

"Begone!" spake the pleasant voice and immediately
my captors drew away and presently were gone, leaving
me staring upon the tonsured crown of the man at the
table who, with head still bowed upon his hand, struck
a silver bell that stood beside him. Scarce had the
sound died away than I heard a stealthy rustling and
beheld divers forms that closed silently about me,
figures shrouded from head to foot in black habits and
nought of them to see save their hands and the glitter
of eyes that gazed on me through the holes of their
black, enveloping hoods.

Now turning to him at the table, I saw that he had
raised his head at last and was viewing me also, and
as he stared on me so stared I on him and this is what
I saw: A lean and pallid face with eyes dim and slum-
berous, a high nose with nostrils thin and curling, a
wide, close-lipped mouth and long, pointed chin. When
we had stared thus a while, he leaned him back in the
great chair and spoke me in his soft, sweet voice:

"You are English, señor?"

"I am!" said I in Spanish.

"What do you here?"

"Seek another Englishman known to be prisoner to
the Inquisition of Nombre de Dios."

"His name?"

"Richard Brandon. Is he here?"

"Are you of the Faith?"

"Of all or any save that of Rome!" said I, staring
up into the pale, emotionless face. "But Rome I do
abominate and all its devil's work!" At this, from the
hooded figures about me rose a gasp of horror and

amaze, while into the dim eyes of my questioner came
a momentary glow.

"Oh, fleshly lips!" quoth he. "Oh, tongue of blasphemy damned. Since you by the flesh have sinned,
so by the flesh, its pains and travail, must your soul
win forgiveness and life hereafter. Oh, vain soul,
though your flesh hath uttered damnable sin and
heresy, yet Holy Church in its infinite mercy shall save
your soul in despite sinful flesh, to which end we must
lay on your evil flesh such castigation as shall, by its
very pain, purge your soul and win it to life hereafter——"

But now, and even as the black-robed familiars closed
upon me, I heard steps behind me, a clash of arms and
thereafter a voice whose calm tones I recognised.

"What is this, Father Alexo?"

"An Englishman and blasphemous Lutheran, captured and brought hither within the hour, Your Excellency." Now here the familiars, at sign of Fra Alexo,
moved aside, and thus I beheld to my surprise and inexpressible joy, Don Federigo, pale from his late sickness,
the which the sombre blackness of his rich velvet habit
did but offset; for a moment his eyes met mine and with
no sign of recognition, whereupon I checked the greeting on my lips.

"And am I of so little account as not to be warned
of this?" said he.

"Alas, Excellency, if I have something forgot the
respect due your high and noble office, let my zeal plead
my excuse. In your faithful charge do we leave this
miserable one until Holy Church shall require him of
you." So saying, Fra Alexo, crossing lean hands
meekly on his bosom, bowed himself in humble fashion,
and yet I thought to see his dull eyes lit by that stealthy
glow as Don Federigo, having duly acknowledged his
salutation, turned away.

Thence I was led into the soft night air to a noble

house, through goodly chambers richly furnished and
so at last to a small room; and ever as I went I had
an uneasy feeling that a long, black robe rustled
stealthily amid the shadows, and of dull eyes that
watched me unseen, nor could I altogether shake off
the feeling even when the door closed and I found
myself alone with Don Federigo.   Indeed it almost
seemed as he too felt something of this, for he stood
a while, his head bowed and very still, like one listening
intently; suddenly he was before me, had grasped my
two fettered hands, and when he spake it was in little
more than whisper.

"Alas, Don Martino—good my friend, Death creepeth all about you here——"

"Fra Alexo's spies!" I nodded.   Now at this he
gave me a troubled look and fell to pacing to and fro.

"A hard man and cunning!" quoth he, as to himself. "The Church—ah, the power of the Church!
Yet must I get you safe away, but how—how?"

"Nay, Don Federigo, never trouble."

"Trouble, Señor? Ah, think you I count that? My
life is yours, Don Martino, and joyfully do I risk
it——"

"Nay, sir," quoth I, grasping his hand, "well do I
know you for brave and noble gentleman whose friendship honoureth me, but here is no need you should
hazard your life for me, since I am here of my own
will.   I have delivered myself over to the Inquisition
to the fulfilment of a purpose."

"Sir," said he, his look of trouble deepening. "Alas,
young sir——"

"This only would I ask of your friendship—when
they take me hence, see to it that I am set in company
with one that lieth prisoned here, see that I am fettered
along with Sir Richard Brandon.   And this do I ask
of your friendship, sir!"

"Alas!" said he. "Alas, 'tis out of my jurisdiction;

when you go hence you are lost—you do pass from the eye of man—none knoweth whither."

"So long as I come unto mine enemy 'tis very well, sir. 'Tis this I have prayed for, lived for, hoped and suffered for. Wherefore now, Don Federigo, in memory of our friendship and all that hath passed betwixt us, I would ask you to contrive me this one thing howsoever you may."

At this he fell to his walking again and seemingly very full of anxious thought. Presently he sounded a whistle that hung about his neck, in answer to which summons came one I judged to be an Indian by his look, though he was dressed Christianly enough. And now, with a bow to me, Don Federigo speaks to him in tongue I had never heard before, a language very soft and pleasing:

"Your pardon, sir," said Don Federigo when we were alone, "but Hualipa is an Indian and hath but indifferent Spanish."

"An Indian?"

"An Aztec Cacique that I saved from an evil death. He is one of the few I can trust. And here another!" said he, as the door opened and a great blackamoor entered, bearing a roast with wine, etc., at sight whereof my mouth watered and I grew mightily hungered.

While I ate and drank and Don Federigo ministering to my wants, he told me of Adam Penfeather, praising his courtliness and seamanship; he spoke also of my lady and how she had cared for him in his sickness. He told me further how they had been attacked by a great ship and having beaten off this vessel were themselves so much further shattered and unseaworthy that 'twas wonder they kept afloat. None the less Adam had contrived to stand in as near to Nombre de Dios as possible and thus set him safely ashore. Suddenly the arras in the corner was lifted and Hualipa reappeared, who, lifting one hand, said somewhat in his soft speech, whereupon Don Federigo rose suddenly and I also.

"Señor Martino," said he, taking my hand, "good friend, the familiars of the Holy Office are come for you, so now is farewell, God go with you, and so long as I live, I am your friend to aid you whensoever I may. But now must I see you back in your bonds."

He now signed to Hualipa who forthwith bound my wrists, though looser than before, whereupon Don Federigo sighed and left me. Then the Indian brought me to a corner of the room and lifting the arras, showed me a small door and led me thence along many dim and winding passages into a lofty hall where I beheld Don Federigo in confabulation with divers of these black-robed ecclesiastics who, beholding me, ceased their talk and making him their several obeisances, carried me away whither they would. Thus very soon I found myself looking again into the pallid, dim-eyed face of the Chief Inquisitor who, lifting one white, bony finger, thus admonished me in his sweet, sad voice:

"Unworthy son, behold now! Holy Church, of its infinite mercy and great love to all such detestable sinners as thou manifestly art, doth study how to preserve thy soul from hell in despite of thyself. And because there is nought so purging as fire, to the fire art thou adjudged except, thy conscience teaching thee horror of thine apostacy, thou wilt abjure thy sin and live. And because nought may so awaken conscience as trouble of mind and pain of body, therefore to trouble and pain doth Holy Church adjudge thy sinful flesh, by water, by fire, by rack, pulley and the wheel." Here he paused and bowed his head upon his hands and thus remained a while; when at last he spoke, it was with face still hid and slowly, as if unwilling to give the words utterance: "Yet, first—thou art decreed—a space—for contemplation of thy heresy vile and abominable, having fellowship with one who, blasphemous as thyself and of a pride stubborn and hateful, long persisted in his sinfulness, yet at the last, by oft suffering, hath lately abjured his damnable heresy and is become of humble and contrite heart, and thus, being soon to die, shall, by pain of flesh and sorrow of mind, save his soul alive in Paradise everlasting. Go, miserable wretch, thy body is but corruption soon to perish, but the immortal soul of thee is in Holy Church her loving care henceforth, to save in thy despite."

Then, with face still bowed, he gestured with his hand, whereupon came two hooded familiars and led me forth of his presence. Now as I walked betwixt these shapeless forms that flitted on silent feet and spake no word, my flesh chilled in despite my reason, for they seemed rather spectres than truly men, yet phantoms of a grim and relentless purposefulness. Voiceless and silent they brought me down stone stairs and along echoing passages into a dim chamber where other cloaked forms moved on soundless feet and spake in hushed and sibilant whispers. Here my bonds were removed and in their place fetters were locked upon my wrists, which done, one came with a lanthorn, who presently led the way along other gloomy passageways where I beheld many narrow, evil-looking doorways. At last my silent guide halted, I heard the rattle of iron, the creak of bolts and a door opened suddenly before me upon a dank and noisome darkness. Into this evil place I was led, and the door clapped to upon me and locked and bolted forthwith. But to my wonder they had left me the lanthorn, and by its flickering beam I stared about me and saw I was in a large dungeon, its corners lost in gloom.

Suddenly as I stood thus, nigh choked with the foul air of the place and full of misgiving, I heard a groaning sigh, and from the shadow of a remote corner a figure reared itself upon its knees to peer under palsied hand with eyes that blinked as if dazzled by this poor light.

"So young—so young—oh, pity! God be merciful to thee—alas, what do you in this place of torment and living death—young sir?"

Now this voice was pitifully cracked and feeble, yet the words were English, wherefore I caught up the lanthorn and coming nearer, set it down where I might better behold the speaker.

"So young—so young! What dost thou among the living dead?"

"I come seeking Sir Richard Brandon!"

Now from the dim figure before me broke a sound that was neither scream nor laughter yet something of both. I saw wild hands upcast to the gloom above, a shrunken, pallid face, the gleam of snow-white hair.

"Oh, God of mercies—oh, God of Justice—at last, oh, God—at last!"

Stooping, I dragged him to the light and found myself suddenly a-trembling so violently that he shook in my gripe.

"What—what mean you?" I cried.

"That I—I am Richard Brandon."

"Liar!" I cried, shaking him. "Damned liar!"

And yet, looking down upon this old, withered creature who crouched before me on feeble knees, his shrivelled hands clasped and haggard face uplifted, I knew that he spoke truth, and uttering a great and bitter cry, I cast him from me, for here, in place of my proud and masterful enemy, the man I had hated for his fierce and arrogant spirit, God had given to my vengeance at last no more than this miserable thing, this poor, pale shadow. Wherefore now I cast myself down upon my face, beating the floor with my shackled fists and blaspheming my God like the very madman I was.

CHAPTER XXII

How at Last I Found My Enemy, Richard Brandon

Whether this paroxysm had wrought me to a swoon I know not, but I wondered to feel a hand upon my head, stroking my hair with touch marvellous gentle, and therewith a voice:

"Comfort thee, comfort thee, poor youth! These be rages and despairs that many do suffer at the first; in a little shall come back thy courage and with it hope—that hope, alas, that never dieth—even here. 'Lo, I am with thee,' saith the Lord—so be comforted, young sir. Let other thoughts distract thy mind—let us converse if thou wilt. Tell me, I pray, how didst know my unhappy name?"

"Because," said I, starting from his touch, "I am son to the man you foully murdered by false accusation. I am Martin Conisby, Lord Wendover of Shere and last of my line!"

Now at this he drew away and away, staring on me great-eyed and I heard the breath gasp between his pallid lips.

"What—do you here, my lord?"

"Seek my just vengeance!"

"The vengeance of a Conisby!" he murmured.

"Six years ago I broke from the hell of slavery you sold me into and ever since have sought you with intent to end the feud once and for ever."

"The feud?" he muttered. "Aye, we have shed each other's blood for generations—when your grandfather fought and slew my father on the highway beyond

Lamberhurst village I, a weeping boy, kissing the wound his rapier had made, vowed to end the Conisbys one day and came nigh doing it, God forgive me. So doth one sin beget others, and so here to-day, in the gloom of my dungeon, I yield myself to your vengeance, my lord, freely and humbly confessing the harms I did you and the base perfidy of my actions. So, an you will have my miserable life, take it and with my last breath I will beseech God pardon you my blood and bring you safe out of this place of torment and sorrow. God knoweth I have endured much of agony these latter years and yet have cherished my life in despite my sufferings hitherto, aye, cherished it so basely as to turn apostate that I might live yet a little longer—but now, my lord, freely—aye, joyfully will I give it for your vengeance, praying God of His abounding mercy to pardon my most grievous offences but, being grown weak in courage and body by reason of frequent and grievous torturings, this mayhap shall plead my excuse. Come then, Martin Conisby, your hand upon my throat, your fetter-chain about my neck——"

"Have done!" said I. "Have done!" And getting up, I crossed to the extremest corner of the dungeon and cast myself down there. But in a little he was beside me again, bearing the lanthorn and with straw from his bed for my pillow, whereupon I cursed and bade him begone, but he never stirred.

"Oh boy," said he, seeing me clench my fist, "I am inured to stripes and very fain to speech with thee, wherefore suffer me a little and answer me this question, I pray. You have sought me these many years, you have even followed me into this hell of suffering, and God at last hath given me to your vengeance—wherefore not take it?"

"Because he I sought was masterful, strong and arrogant!"

"Yet this my body, though sorely changed, is yet

the same; 'twill bleed if you prick it and I can die as well now as six years ago———"

But seeing I made no manner of answer, he left me at last and I watched him limp disconsolate to his corner, there to bow himself on feeble knees and with hands crossed on his bosom and white head bowed, fall to a passion of silent prayer yet with many woful sighings and moanings, and so got him to his miserable bed.

As for me, I lay outstretched upon my face, my head pillowed on my arm, with no desire of sleep, or to move, content only to lie thus staring into the yellow flame of the lanthorn as a child might, for it verily seemed that all emotions and desires were clean gone out of me; thus lay I, my mind a-swoon, staring at this glimmering flame until it flickered and vanished, leaving me in outer darkness. But within me was a darkness blacker still, wherein my soul groped vainly.

So the long night wore itself to an end, for presently, lifting heavy head, I was aware of a faint glow waxing ever brighter, till suddenly, athwart the gloom of my prison, shot a beam of radiant glory, like a very messenger of God, telling of a fair, green world, of tree and herb and flower, of the sweet, glad wind of morning and all the infinite mercies of God; so that, beholding this heavenly vision, I came nigh weeping for pure joy and thankfulness.

Now this thrice-blessed sunlight poured in through a small grating high up in the massy wall and showed me the form of my companion, the shining silver of his hair, his arms wide-tossed in slumber. Moved by sudden impulse I arose and (despite the ache and stiffness of my limbs) came softly to look upon him as he lay thus, his cares forgot awhile in blessed sleep; and thus, beneath his rags, I saw divers and many grievous scars of wounds old and new, the marks of hot and searing iron, of biting steel and cruel lash, and in joints,

swollen and inflamed, I read the oft-repeated torture
of the rack. And yet in these features, gaunt and
haggard by suffering, furrowed and lined by pain,
was a serene patience and nobility wholly unfamiliar.

Thus it seemed God had hearkened to my oft-repeated prayers, had given up to me mine enemy bound;
here at last, beneath my hand, lay the contriver of
my father's ruin and death and of my own evil for-
tunes. But it seemed the sufferings that had thus
whitened his hair, bowed his once stalwart frame and
chastened his fierce pride had left behind them something greater and more enduring, before which my
madness of hate and passionate desire of vengeance
shrank abashed. Now as I stood thus, lost in frowning contemplation of my enemy, he groaned of a sudden and starting to his elbow, stared up at me haggard-
eyed.

"Ah, my lord!" said he, meeting my threatening
look. "Is the hour of vengeance at hand—seek ye
my life indeed? Why, then, I am ready!"

But, nothing speaking, I got me back to my gloomy
corner and crouched there, my knees up-drawn, my
head bowed upon my arms; and now, my two hands
gripping upon the empty air, I prayed again these
words so often wrung from me by past agonies: "Oh,
God of Justice, give me now vengeance—vengeance
upon mine enemy. His life, Oh, God, his life!" But
even as I spake these words within myself I knew the
vengeance I had dreamed of and cherished so dearly
was but a dream indeed, a fire that had burned utterly
away, leaving nought but the dust and ashes of all
that might have been. And realising somewhat of the
bitter mockery of my situation, bethinking me of all
I had so wantonly cast away for this dream, and
remembering the vain labour and all the wasted years,
I fell to raging despair, insomuch that I groaned aloud

and casting myself down, smote upon the stone floor
of my prison with shackled fists. And thus I presently
felt a touch and glanced up to behold my enemy bending above me.

"My lord——" said he.

"Devil!" I cried, smiting the frail hand from me.
"I am no more than the poor outcast wretch you ha'
made of me!" Thus, with curses and revilings, I bade
him plague me no more and presently, wearied mind
and body by my long vigil, I fell a-nodding, until,
wakened by the opening of the door, I looked up to
behold one of the black-robed familiars, who, having
set down meat and drink, vanished again, silent and
speechless.

Roused by the delectable savours of this meat, which
was hot and well-seasoned, I felt myself ravenous and
ate with keen appetite, and taking up the drink, found
it to be wine, very rich and comforting. So I ate and
drank my fill, never heeding my companion, and thereafter, stretching myself as comfortably as I might,
I sank into a deep slumber. But my sleep was troubled
by all manner of dreams wherein was a nameless fear
that haunted me, a thing dim-seen and silent, save for
the stealthy rustling of a trailing robe. And even as
I strove to flee it grew upon me until I knew this was
Death in the shape of Fra Alexo. And now, as I
strove vainly to escape those white, cruel fingers,
Joanna was betwixt us; I heard her shrill, savage cry,
saw the glitter of her steel and, reeling back, Fra Alexo
stood clutching his throat in his two hands, staring
horribly ere he fell. But looking upon him as he lay
I saw this was not Fra Alexo, for gazing on the pale,
dead face, I recognised the beloved features of my
lady Joan. But, sudden and swift, Joanna stooped
to clasp that stilly form, to lay her ruddy mouth to
these pallid lips; and lo, she that was dead stirred, and
rose up quick and vivid with life and reached out

yearning arms to me, seeing nothing of Joanna where she lay, a pale, dead thing.

I started up, crying aloud, and blinked to the glare of a lanthorn; as I crouched thus, shielding my eyes from this dazzling beam, from the darkness beyond came a voice, very soft and tenderly sweet, the which set me shivering none the less.

"Most miserable man, forswear now the error of thy beliefs, or prepare thy unworthy flesh to chastisement. In this dead hour of night when all do sleep, save the God thou blasphemest and Holy Church, thou shall be brought to the question——"

"Hold, damned Churchman!" cried a voice, and turning I beheld my enemy, Sir Richard Brandon, his gaunt and fettered arms upraised, his eyes fierce and steadfast. "Heed not this bloody-minded man! And you, Fra Alexo and these cowled fiends that do your evil work, I take you to witness, one and all, that I, Richard Brandon, Knight banneret of Kent, do now, henceforth and for ever, renounce and abjure the oath you wrung from my coward flesh by your devilish tortures. Come, do to my body what ye will, but my soul —aye, my soul belongs to God—not to the Church of Rome! May God reckon up against you the innocent blood you have shed and in every groan and tear and cry you have wrung from tortured flesh may you find a curse in this world and hereafter!"

The loud, fierce voice ceased; instead I heard a long and gentle sigh, a murmured command, and Sir Richard was seized by dim forms and borne away, his irons clashing. Then I sprang, whirling up my fetter-chains to smite, was tripped heavily, felt my limbs close-pinioned and was dragged forth of the dungeon. And now, thus helpless at the mercy of these hideous, hooded forms that knew no mercy, my soul shrank for stark horror of what was to be, and my body shook and trembled in abject terror.

In this miserable state I was dragged along, until once again I heard the murmur of that sweet, soft voice, whereupon my captors halted, a door was unlocked, and I was cast into a place of outer darkness there to lie bruised and half-stunned yet agonised with fear, insomuch that for very shame I summoned up all my resolution, and mastering my fear, I clenched chattering teeth and sweating palms, determined to meet what was to be with what courage and fortitude I might. Slowly the shivering horror passed and in its place was a strange calm as I waited for them to bear me to the torture.

Suddenly my heart leapt to a shrill scream and thereafter I heard an awful voice, loud and hoarse and tremulous, and between each gasping cry, dreadful periods of silence:

"Oh, God. . . . Oh, God of pity, aid me . . . make me to endure. . . . Lord God, strengthen my coward soul . . . help me to be worthy . . . faithful at last . . . faithful to the end. . . ."

As for me, well knowing the wherefore of these outcries, the meaning of these ghastly silences, a frenzy of horror seized me so that I shouted and raved, rolling to and fro in my bonds. Yet even so I could hear them at their devil's work, until the hoarse screams sank to a piteous wailing, a dreadful inarticulate babble, until, wrought to a frenzy, I struggled to my feet (despite my bonds) and (like the madman I was) leapt towards whence these awful sounds came, and falling, knew no more.

From this blessed oblivion I was roused by a kindly warmth and opening my eyes, saw that I lay face down in a beam of sunshine that poured in through the small grille high in the wall like a blessing; being very weary and full of pain, and feeling this kindly ray mighty comforting, I lay where I was and no desire to move, minded to sleep again. But little by little I became conscious of a dull, low murmur of sound very distressful to hear and that set me vaguely a-wondering. Therefore, after some while, I troubled to lift my head and wondered no more.

A twisted heap of blood-stained rags, the pallid oval of a face, the dull gleam of a chain, this much I saw at a glance, but when I came beside Sir Richard's prostrate form and beheld the evils they had wrought on him, a cry of horror and passionate anger broke from me, whereupon he checked his groaning and opening swimming eyes, smiled wanly up at me.

"Glory—and thanks to God—I—endured!" he whispered. Now at this I sank on my knees beside him, and when I would have spoken, could not for a while; at last:

"Is there aught I may do?" I questioned.

"Water!" he murmured feebly. So I reached the water and setting my arm 'neath his neck (and despite my fetters) lifted him as gently as I might and held the jar to his cracked lips. When he had drank what he would I made a rough pillow for his head and rent strips from my shirt for bandages, and finding my pitcher full-charged with wine, mixed some with water and betook me to bathing his divers hurts (though greatly hampered by the chain of my fetters) and found him very patient to endure my awkward handling, in the midst of which, meeting my eye, he smiled faintly:

"Martin Conisby," he whispered. "Am I not—your —enemy?"

"Howbeit you endured!" quoth I.

"Thanks be to God!" said he humbly. "And is it for this. You will cherish thus—and comfort one— hath wronged you and yours—so bitterly?"

But at this I grew surly and having made an end of my rough surgery, I went and cast myself upon my bed of straw and, lying there, watching the sunbeam

creep upon the wall, I fell to pondering this problem,
viz: How came I thus striving to soothe the woes of
this man I had hunted all these years to his destruction; why must I pity his hurts and compassionate his
weakness—why?

And as I sat, my fists clenched, scowling at the sun-
ray, it verily seemed as he had read these my thoughts.

"Martin Conisby," said he, his voice grown stronger.
"Oh, Martin, think it not shame to pity thine enemy;
to cherish them that despitefully use you; this is God-
like. I was a proud man and merciless but I have
learned much by sufferings, and for the wrongs I did
you—bitterly have I repented. So would I humbly
sue forgiveness of you since I am to die so soon——"

"To die?"

"Aye, Martin, at the next auto-da-fé—by the
fire——"

"The fire!" said I, clenching my fists.

"They have left me my life that I may burn——"

"When?" I demanded 'twixt shut teeth. "When?"

"To-day—to-morrow—the day after—what matter?
But when the flames have done their work, I would fain
go to God bearing with me your forgiveness. But if
this be too much to hope—why, then, Martin, I will
beseech God to pluck you forth of this place of horror
and to give you back to England, to happiness, to
honour and all that I reft from you——"

"Nay, this were thing impossible!" I cried.

"There is nought impossible to God, Martin!" Here
fell silence awhile and then, "Oh, England—England!"
cried he. "D'ye mind how the road winds 'twixt the
hedgerows a-down hill into Lamberhurst, Martin; d'ye
mind the wonder of it all—the green meadows, the dim
woods full of bird song and fragrance—you shall see
it all again one day, but as for me—ah, to breathe
just once again the sweet smell of English earth! But
God's will be done!"

For a while I sat picturing to my fancy the visions
his words had conjured up; lifting my head at last,
I started up to see him so pale and still and bending
above him, saw him sleeping, placid as any child, yet
with the marks of tears upon his shrunken cheek.

CHAPTER XXIII

How I Found My Soul

THE torment by fire, torture by water, rack and thumbscrews, pulley and wheel, the weights, the press, the glove and the boot,—these the devices men hath schemed out for the plaguing of his neighbour, the hellish engines he hath troubled to invent and build for the crushing, twisting, tearing and maiming of his fellow-man, yet of all these devilish machines nought is there so constant, so pitiless and hard of endurance as the agony of suspense; there is a spectre mopping and mowing at our shoulder by day and haunting the misery of our nights; here is a disease slowly but surely sapping hope and courage and life itself.

Howbeit it was thus I found it in the time that followed, for little by little I became the prey of a terror that grew, until the opening of the door would bring me to my feet in sweating panic, or the mere rattle of my fellow-prisoner's chains fill me with shivering despair. And because of these sick fears I felt great scorn of myself, and knowing I was in this place of horror by my own will and contrivance, to despair and scorn was added a bitter self-hatred. And now, remembering how Adam had vowed to rescue Sir Richard, I prayed for his coming, at one moment full of hope, the next in an agony of despair lest he should come too late. Thus I fell to my black mood, speaking no word or answering my companion but by curses; and thus would I sit for hours, sullen and morose, gnawing my knuckles and staring on vacancy.

Or again, beholding my enemy so serene, so placid and unmoved (and his case no better than my own) I would fall to sudden bitter revilings of him, until, meeting the gentle patience of his look, I would fall silent for very shame.

At last, upon a night, tossing upon my wretched bed in dire torment of soul, I chanced to espy my enemy and him sleeping; whereat I fell to fierce anger.

"Ha, Brandon!" I cried. "Will ye sleep, man, will ye sleep and I in torment. Wake—wake and tell me, must we die soon? Wake, I say!" At this he raised himself to blink at me in the beam of the lanthorn. "Must we die soon, think ye?" I demanded fiercely.

"In God's time, Martin!" said he.

"Think ye they will—torture me first?" Now here, seeing his troubled look and how he groped for an answer, I cursed and bade him tell me, aye or no.

"Alas, I do fear it!" said he.

"We are beyond hope?" I demanded.

"Nay, there is always God," said he. "But we are beyond all human aid. This do I know by reason of this airy dungeon and the luxury of food and light. Fra Alexo doeth nought unreasonably; thus we have our lanthorn that we, haply waking from dreams of home and happiness, may behold our prison walls and know an added grief. Instead of the water-dungeon or the black terror of cell deep-hidden from the blessed day, he hath set us in this goodly place that we, beholding the sun, may yearn amain for the blessed freedom of God's green world——"

"Ha!" quoth I. "And for those he dooms to the torment he sendeth rich food and generous wine—aye, aye, I see it now—a man strong and full-blooded may endure more agony and longer. So they will torture me—as they did you—but when, ah, God—when?" And here I sank face down upon my bed and lay there shuddering. And presently I was aware of my companion kneeling beside me, his hand upon my shoulder, his gentle voice in my ear:

"Comfort ye, Martin, comfort ye, God shall give ye strength——"

"Nay, I am a coward!" I cried bitterly. "A shameful craven!"

"Yet you do not fear! You have endured! The fire hath no terrors for you!"

"Because I am old in suffering, and am done with fear, because, beyond smoke and flame, I shall find God at last."

"Think ye there is a God?"

"I know it, Martin!"

"Yet am I coward!" I groaned. "Though 'tis not death I fear, nor the torture so much, 'tis rather to be thus counting the hours——"

"I know," said he, sighing. "I know. 'Tis the waiting for what is to be, ah, the weary, weary waiting—'tis this doth shake the strongest; the hour of suffering may be now, or to-morrow, or a month hence."

"God send it be to-night!" said I fervently. "And to-night, and while I am yet the man I am, know this; I, that lived but for vengeance, dying, do renounce it once and for ever. I, that came hither seeking an enemy, find, in place of hated foe, a man ennobled by his sufferings and greater than myself. So, as long as life remains to us, let there be peace and good will betwixt us, Sir Richard. And as you once sued forgiveness of me, now do I sue your friendship ——"

"Martin!" said he in choking voice, and then again, "Oh, Martin Conisby, thus hath God answered my prayer and thus doth the feud betwixt Conisby and Brandon end——"

"Yes!" said I. "Yes—so do I know at last that I

have followed a vain thing and lost all the sweetness
life had to offer."

Now here, seeing me lie thus deject and forlorn, he
stooped and set his ragged arm about me.

"Grieve not, Martin," said he in strange, glad voice,
"grieve not, for in losing so much you have surely found
a greater thing. Here, in this dread place, you have
found your soul."

And presently, sheltered in the frail arm of the man
had been my bitter enemy, I took comfort and fell to
sweet and dreamless slumber.

Another day had dragged its weary length: Sir
Richard lay asleep, I think, and I, gloomy and sullen,
lay watching the light fade beyond the grating in the
wall when, catching my breath, I started and peered
up, misdoubting my eyes, for suddenly, 'twixt the bars
of this grating, furtive and silent crept a hand that
opening, let fall something white and shapeless that
struck the stone floor with a sharp, metallic sound,
and vanished stealthily as it had come. For a while
I stared up at this rusty grating, half-fearing I was
going mad at last, yet when I thought to look below,
there on the floor lay the shapeless something where
it had fallen. With every nerve a-thrill I rose and
creeping thither, took it up and saw it was Adam's
chart, the which had been taken from me, with all else
I possessed; this wrapped about a key and a small,
sharp knife; on the back of which, traced in a scrawl-
ing hand, I read these words, viz:

> "A key to your fetters. A knife to your release.
> Once free of your dungeon take every passage
> Bearing to the left; so shall you reach the postern.
> There one shall wait, wearing a white scarf.
> Follow him and God speed you.
> You will be visited at sunset."

To be lifted thus from blackest despair to hope's
very pinnacle wrought on me so that I was like one

entranced, staring down at knife and paper and key where they had fallen from my nerveless hold; then, catching up the knife, I stood ecstatic to thumb over point and edge and felt myself a man once more, calm and resolute, to defy every inquisitor in Spanish America, and this merely by reason of the touch of this good steel, since here was a means whereby (as a last resource) I might set myself safe beyond their devilish torments once and for all. And now my soul went out in passionate gratitude to Don Federigo since this (as I judged) must be of his contrivance.

But the shadows deepening warned me that the sun had set wherefore I slipped off my shoes as softly as possible not to disturb Sir Richard's slumbers, and made me ready to kill or be killed.

And presently I heard the creak of bolts and, creeping in my stockinged feet, posted myself behind the door as it opened to admit the silent, shrouded form of a familiar bearing a lanthorn. Now, seeing he came alone, I set the knife in my girdle and, crouched in the shadow of the door, watched my time; for a moment he stood, seeming to watch Sir Richard who, roused by the light, stirred and, waking, blinked fearfully at this silent shape.

"Ah, what now?" he questioned. "Is it me ye seek?" For answer the familiar set down the lanthorn and beckoned with his finger. Then, as Sir Richard struggled painfully to his feet, I sprang and grappled this hateful, muffled form ere he could cry out, had him fast by the throat, and dragging him backwards across my knee, I choked him thus, his hoarse whistling gasps muffled in his enveloping hood. And then Sir Richard was beside me.

"Will ye slay him, Martin?" cried he.

"Aye!" I nodded and tightened my grip.

"Nay, rather spare him because he is an enemy; thus shall your soul go lighter henceforth, Martin."

So in the end I loosed my hold, whereupon the familiar sank to the floor and lay, twitching feebly. Hereupon I rent off hood and robe and found him a poor, mean creature that wept and moaned, wherefore I incontinent gagged him with stuff from his own habit and thereafter locked him securely into my fetters. And now, trembling with haste, I donned his habit and, catching up the lanthorn, turned on Sir Richard:

"Come!" said I.

"Nay!" said he, wringing his fettered hands. "Nay —alas, I should but hamper you——"

"Come!" said I, my every nerve a-tingle to be gone. "Come—I will aid you—hurry, man—hurry!"

"Nay, 'twere vain, Martin, I can scarce walk—'twere selfish in me to let you run such needless risks. Go, Martin, go—God bless you and bring you safe out of this evil place."

Without more ado I tucked my shoes into my bosom, caught up the lanthorn and hasted away.

But as I went I must needs remember the pitiful eagerness of Sir Richard's look and the despairing gesture of those helpless, fettered hands.

Hereupon I cursed fiercely to myself and, turning about, came running back and, finding him upon his knees, hove him to his feet and, or ever he guessed my purpose, swung him across my shoulder and so away again, finding him no great burden (God knows) for all his fetters that clanked now and then despite his efforts. Presently espying a passage to my left, thither hurried I and so in a little to another; indeed it seemed the place was a very maze and with many evil-looking doors that shut in God only knew what of misery and horror. So I hasted on, while my breath laboured and the sweat ran from me; and with every clank of Sir Richard's fetters my heart leapt with dread lest any hear, though indeed these gloomy passageways seemed quite deserted. And ever as we went, nought was to see save these evil doors and gloomy walls, yet I struggled on until my strength began to fail and I reeled for very weariness, until at last I stopped and set Sir Richard on his feet since I could carry him no further, and leaned panting against the wall, my strength all gone and my heart full of despair, since it seemed I had missed my way.

Suddenly, as I leaned thus, I heard the tinkle of a lute and a voice singing, and though these sounds were dull and muffled, I judged them at no great distance; therefore I began to creep forward, the knife ready in one hand, the lanthorn in the other, and thus presently turning a sharp angle, I beheld a flight of steps surmounted by a door. Creeping up to this door, I hearkened and found the singing much nearer; trying the door, I found it yield readily and opening it an inch or so beheld a small chamber lighted by a hanging lamp and upon a table a pair of silver-mounted pistols; coming to the table I took them up and found them primed and loaded. I now beckoned Sir Richard who crept up the stairs with infinite caution lest his fetter-chains should rattle.

The chamber wherein we stood seemed the apartment of some officer, for across a small bed lay a cloak and plumed hat together with a silver-hilted rapier, which last I motioned Sir Richard to take. Beyond the bed was another door, and coming thither I heard a sound of voices and laughter, so that I judged here was a guard-room. As I stood listening, I saw Sir Richard standing calm and serene, the gleaming sword grasped in practised hand and such a look of resolution on his lined face as heartened me mightily. And now again came the tinkle of the lute and, giving a sign to Sir Richard, I softly raised the latch and, plucking open the door, stepped into the room behind, the pistols levelled in my hands.

Before me were five men—four at cards and a fifth fingering a lute, who turned to gape, one and all, at my sudden appearance.

"Hold!" said I in Spanish, through the muffling folds of my hood. "Let a man move and I shoot!" At this they sat still enough, save the man with the lute, a small, fat fellow who grovelled on his knees; to him I beckoned. "Bind me these fellows!" I commanded.

"No ropes here!" he stammered.

"With their belts, fool; their arms behind them—so!" Which done, I commanded him to free Sir Richard of his gyves; whereupon the little fellow obeyed me very expeditiously with one of the many keys that hung against the wall. Then I gave my pistols to Sir Richard and seizing on the little, fat man, bound him also. Hereupon I gagged them all five as well as I might and having further secured their legs with their scarves and neckerchiefs, I dragged them one by one into the inner chamber (the doors of which I locked) and left them there mightily secure. Then, catching up a good, stout sword and a cloak to cover Sir Richard's rags, I opened another door and, having traversed a sort of anteroom, presently stepped out into the free air.

It was a dark night; indeed I never saw Nombre de Dios any other than in the dark, yet the stars made a glory of the heavens and I walked awhile, my eyes upraised in a very ecstasy, clean forgetting my companion until he spoke.

"Whither now, Martin?"

"I am directed to a postern, and one bearing a white scarf."

"The postern?" quoth Sir Richard. "I know it well, as doth many another unhappy soul; 'tis the gate whereby suspects are conveyed secretly to the question!"

We kept to the smaller streets and lanes, the which,

being ill-lighted, we passed without observation; thus
at last, following the loom of a high wall, very grim
and forbidding, we came in sight of a small gateway
beneath a gloomy arch, where stood two shadowy figures as if on the lookout, whereupon I stopped to
reconnoitre them, loosening my sword in the scabbard.
But now one of these figures approached and, halting
to peer at us, spoke in strange, muffled tones.

"Seek ye the white scarf?" questioned the voice in
Spanish.

"We do!" said I. At this the man opened the long
cloak he wore and flourished to view a white scarf.

"Aye, but there were two of you," said I. "What
is come of your fellow?"

"He but goeth before, Señor." And true enough,
when I looked, the other dim form had vanished, the
which I liked so little that, drawing my sword, I clapped
it to the fellow's breast.

"Look now," quoth I, "play us false and you die!"

"The Señor may rest assured!" says he, never
flinching.

"Why, then, lead on!" I commanded.

Now as we followed this unknown, I had an uncanny
feeling that we were being dogged by something or some
one that flitted in the darkness, now behind us, now
before us, now upon our flank, wherefore I walked soft-
treading and with my ears on the stretch. And presently our guide brought us amid the denser gloom of
trees whose leaves rustled faintly above us and grass
whispered under foot; and thus (straining my ears,
as I say) I thought to catch the sound of stealthy
movement that was neither leaf nor grass, insomuch
that, shifting the sword to my left hand, I drew forth
and cocked one of the pistols. At last we came out
from among the trees and before us was the gleam
of water and I saw we were upon the bank of a stream.
Here our guide paused as if unsure; but suddenly was

the gleam of a lanthorn and I heard Don Federigo's welcome voice:

"Is that Hualipa?"

Our guide moved forward and, pausing in the glare of the lanthorn, let fall his cloak and I, beholding that pallid, impressive face, the dull eyes, small mouth, and high thin nose, knew him for Fra Alexo, Chief Inquisitor of Nombre de Dios. Then, lifting one hand to point slim finger at Don Federigo, he spoke in his soft, sweet voice:

"Don Federigo, long hath Holy Church suspected thee—and Holy Church hath many eyes—and hands. So is thy messenger dead and so I favoured the escape of these declared heretics that through them thou mightest be taken in thy shameful treachery. Even now come armed servants of the Church to take again these doomed heretics and with them—thee also. Now kill me an you will, but thine apostasy is uncovered; the Holy Inquisition hath thee safe at last. Thy good name, thy pride of birth and place shall not shelter thee from the avenging fire—oh, most treacherous one——"

Suddenly he choked, clapped his two hands to his throat, staring horribly; and betwixt his fingers I saw a small, tufted thing deep-buried in his throat. Then all at once there burst from his writhen lips an awful, gasping scream, dreadful to hear, and then he was down, writhing and gasping awhile, with Don Federigo and Sir Richard bending above him.

But I, well knowing what this was and remembering the unseen thing that had tracked us, turned to the shadow of a bush hard by and thus beheld a shaggy head that peered amid the leaves, a hairy face with wild, fierce eyes and teeth that gleamed.

So the man John stared down at his handiwork, flourished his deadly blowpipe and was gone.

"He is dead!" said Don Federigo. " 'Tis an Indian

poison I have met with ere this—very sudden and deadly. Fra Alexo stands at the tribunal of his God!" and baring his head, Don Federigo glanced down at the dark, contorted shape and thence to the gloomy trees beyond, and beckoning, brought me to a boat moored under the bank hard by.

"Señor Martino," said he, " 'tis time you were gone, for if Don Alexo hath turned out the guard——"

"Nay, sir," quoth I, "they must be some while a-coming," and I told him briefly how we had secured the watch.

"And Fra Alexo is dead!" said he.

Here I would fain have told him something of my gratitude for the dire risks and perils he had run on my behalf, but he caught my hands and silenced me.

"My friend Martino," said he in his careful English, "you adventured your life for me many times; if therefore I save yours, it is but just. And your vengeance —is it achieved?"

"Indeed, sir," quoth Sir Richard, "achieved to the very uttermost, for he hath carried that enemy out from the shadow of death, hath perilled his own chances of life that I might know the joys of freedom—I that was his bitter enemy."

"So may all enmity pass one day, I pray God," sighed Don Federigo. "And now, as for thee, Martino my friend, vengeance such as thine is thing so rare as maketh me to honour thy friendship and loath to lose thee, since we shall meet no more in this life. Thus I do grieve a little, for I am an old man, something solitary and weary, and my son, alas, is dead. This sword was my father's and should have been his; take you it, I pray, and wear it in memory of me." And speaking, he loosed off his sword and thrust it upon me.

"Noble sir," said I, "dear and good friend, it doth

not need this to mind me of all your high courage and steadfast friendship—and I have nought to offer in return——"

"I shall ever remember your strange method of vengeance!" said he. And when we had embraced each other, I got me into the boat and aided Sir Richard in beside me.

"Look now," warned Don Federigo as I loosed the mooring rope, "pull across the river and be wary, for in a little the whole town will be roused upon you. Get clear of the river as speedily as you may. And so, farewell, my friend, and God go with you!"

For answer I waved my hand, then, betaking me to the oars, I pulled out into the stream farther and farther, until the stately form of Don Federigo was merged and lost in the gloom.

Sure enough, scarcely had we come into the shadows of the opposite bank than the silence gave place to a distant clamour, lost all at once in a ringing of bells, a rolling of drums and a prodigious blowing of horns and trumpets, the which set me a-sweating in despite the cool night wind, as, chin on shoulder, I paddled slowly along, unsure of my going and very fearful lest I run aground. In the midst of which anxieties I heard Sir Richard's voice, calm and gentle and very comforting:

"With a will, Martin—pull! I know the river hereabouts; pull, Martin, and trust to me!" Hereupon I bent to the oars and with no fear of being heard above the din ashore, since every moment bells and drums and trumpets waxed louder. Thus presently we came opposite the town, a place of shadows where lights hovered; and seeing with what nicety Sir Richard steered, keeping ever within the denser shadow of the tree-clad bank, I rowed amain until we were past the raving town, and its twinkling lights were blotted out by a sudden bend of the river.

Suddenly I saw Sir Richard stand up, peering, heard his voice quick and commanding:

"Ship your oars!" Then came a chorus of hoarse shouts, a shock, and we were rocking, gunwale and gunwale, with a boat where dim figures moved, crying shrill curses. I remember letting drive at one fellow with an oar and thereafter laying about me until the stout timber shivered in my grasp. I remember the dull gleam of Sir Richard's darting blade and then the two boats had drifted apart. Tossing aside my shattered oar, I found me another and rowed until, gasping, I must needs pause awhile and so heard Sir Richard speaking:

"Easy, Martin, easy! There lieth the blessed ocean at last; but—see!"

Resting on my oars and glancing whither he pointed, I saw a light suspended high in air and knew this for the riding-lanthorn of a ship whose shadowy bulk grew upon me as I gazed, hull and towering masts outlined against the glimmer of stars and the vague light of a young moon. Hereupon I bowed my head, despairing, for this ship lay anchored in midstream, so that no boat might hope to pass unchallenged; thus I began to debate within me whether or no to row ashore and abandon our boat, when Sir Richard questioned me:

"Can you sing ever a Spanish boat song, Martin?"

"No," said I, miserably. "No——"

"Why, then, I must, though mine is a very indifferent voice and rusty from lack o' use; meantime do you get up the mast; the wind serves." Which said, Sir Richard forthwith began to sing a Spanish song very harsh and loud, whiles I sweated amain in panic fear; none the less I contrived to step mast and hoist sail and, crouched on the midship thwart, watched the great galleon as we bore down upon her.

And presently came a voice hailing us in Spanish

with demand as to who and what we were, whereat Sir Richard broke off his song to shout that we were fishermen, the which simple answer seemed to reassure our questioner, for we heard no more and soon the great ship was merely a vague shadow that, fading on our vision, merged into the night and was gone.

And thus in a while, having crossed the troubled waters of the bar, I felt the salt wind sweet and fresh on my brow like a caress, felt the free lift and roll of the seas; and now, beholding this illimitable expanse of sky and ocean, needs must I remember the strait prison and dire horrors whence God had so lately delivered me, and my soul swelled within me too full of gratitude for any words.

"Oh, give thanks unto the Lord, for He is good, for His mercy endureth for ever!"

Turning, I espied Sir Richard upon his knees, one hand grasping the tiller sailorly, the other upraised to the glimmering firmament; hereupon I knelt also, joining him in this prayer of thanksgiving. And thus we began our journey.

CHAPTER XXIV

OF OUR ADVENTURE AT SEA

DAWN found us standing easterly before a gentle wind with the land bearing away upon our right, a fair and constantly changing prospect of sandy bays, bold headlands and green uplands backed by lofty mountains blue with distance.

And what with all the varied beauties of earth, the blue heaven, the sparkle of sea, the soft, sweet wind, it verily seemed the late gloomy terrors of my dungeon were no more than a nightmare until, hearing a moan, I turned to see my companion stirring in uneasy slumber, his haggard features contorted as by some spasm, whereupon I touched him to wakefulness, bidding him see if we had aught aboard to eat or drink; but he crouched motionless as one rapt in an ecstasy, staring eager-eyed from cloudless heaven to sapphire sea and round about upon the glory of the dawn and fell suddenly a-laughing as from pure joy and as suddenly hid his face within his shrivelled hands.

"This—O, glory of God! This, instead of black despair!" said he in weeping voice. "This sweet, healing wind instead of searing flame—and you, Martin, 'tis you have given all this! I dreamed me back in the hell you brought me from! Sun and wind and sea—oh, God love thee—these be your gifts to me that was your enemy——"

"Nay, our enmity is dead and done with——"

"Martin Conisby," said he, looking on me through his tears, "through you, by God's grace, I know again the joy of living, and, God aiding me, you shall yet know the like happiness an I may compass it!"

Now seeing him thus deeply moved I grew abashed and, beckoning him to take the tiller, began to overhaul the contents of the boat's lockers and thus found that Don Federigo had furnished us to admiration with all things to our comfort and defence. Forthwith I set out breakfast, choosing such things as I judged the most perishable, and we ate and drank mighty cheerful.

But as Sir Richard sat thus in his rags, staring upon all things with ineffable content, the bright sun showed me the hideous marks of his many sufferings plain and manifest in his bent and twisted frame, the scars that disfigured him and the clumsy movements of his limbs misshapen by the torment, and moreover I noticed how, ever and anon, he would be seized of violent tremblings and shudderings like one in an ague, insomuch that I could scarce abide to look on him for very pity and marvelled within myself that any man could endure so much and yet live.

"Oh, friend!" said he suddenly, " 'tis a wondrous world you have given back to me; I almost grow a man again——"

Even as he uttered these brave words the shuddering took him once more, but when I would have aided him he smiled and spake 'twixt chattering teeth:

"Never heed me, Martin—this cometh of the water-dungeons—'twill soon pass——"

"God knoweth you have suffered over-much——"

"Yet He hath brought me forth a better man therefor, though my body is—something the worse, 'tis true. Indeed, I am a sorry companion for a voyage, I doubt——"

"Howbeit," said I, "last night, but for your ready wit, we had been taken——"

"Say you so, Martin? Here is kind thought and

comforting, for I began to dread lest I prove an encumbrance to you."

"Nay, sir, never think it!" said I. "For 'tis my earnest hope to bring you to the loving care of one who hath sought you long and patiently——"

"Is it Joan? Oh, mean you my daughter Joan? Is she in these latitudes?"

"Even so, sir. For you she hath braved a thousand horrors and evils."

And here, in answer to his eager questioning, I told him much of what I have writ here concerning the Lady Joan, her resolute spirit and numberless virtues, a theme whereof I never wearied. Thus, heedless of time, of thirst or hunger, I told of the many dire perils she had encountered in her quest, both aboard ship and on the island, to all of which Sir Richard hearkened, his haggard gaze now on my face, now fixed yearningly on the empty distances before us as he would fain conjure up the form of her whose noble qualities I was describing. When at last I had made an end, he sat silent a great while.

"I was a proud, harsh man of old," said he at last, "and a father most ungentle—and 'tis thus she doth repay me! You and she were children together—playfellows, Martin."

"Aye, sir, 'twas long ago."

"And in my prideful arrogance I parted you, because you were the son of my enemy, but God hath brought you together again and His will be done. But, Martin, if she be yet in these latitudes, where may we hope to find her?"

"At Darien, in the Gulf!"

"Darien?" said he. "Why there, Martin? 'Tis a wild country and full of hostile Indians. I landed there once——"

So I told him how Adam had appointed a place of meeting there, showing him also the chart Adam had drawn for my guidance, the which we fell to studying together, whereby we judged we had roughly but some eighty leagues to sail and a notable good sea-boat under us, and that by keeping in sight of the Main we could not fail of fetching up with the rendezvous, always suppose we lost not our bearings by being blown out to sea.

"Had I but quadrant and compass, Martin——"

"How, sir," said I, "can you navigate?"

"I could once," said he, with his faint smile. Hereupon I hasted to reach these instruments from one of the lockers (since it seemed Don Federigo had forgot nothing needful to our welfare, perceiving which, Sir Richard straightened his bowed shoulders somewhat and his sallow cheek flushed. "Here at last I may serve you somewhat, Martin," said he and, turning his back to the sun, he set the instrument to his eye and began moving the three vanes to and fro until he had the proper focus and might obtain the sun's altitude; whereby he had presently found our present position, the which he duly pricked upon the chart.

He now showed me how, by standing out on direct course instead of following the tortuous windings of the coast, we could shorten our passage by very many miles. Hereupon we shaped our course accordingly and, the wind freshening somewhat, by afternoon the high coast had faded to a faint blur of distant mountain peaks, and by sunset we had lost it altogether.

And so night came down on us, with a kindly wind, cool and refreshing after the heats of the day, a night full of a palpitant, starry splendour and lit by a young, horned moon that showed us this wide-rolling infinity of waters and these vast spaces filled, as it seemed, with the awful majesty of God, so that when we spake (which was seldom) it was in hushed voices. It being my turn to sleep, I lay down, yet could not close my eyes for a while for the wonder of the stars above, and with my gaze thus uplift, I must needs think of my lady and wonder where she might be, with passionate prayers for her safety; and beholding these heavenly splendours, I thought perchance she might be viewing them also and in this thought found me great solace and comfort. And now what must my companion do but speak of her that was thus in my thought.

"Martin," he questioned suddenly, "do you love her?"

"Aye, I do!" said I, "mightily!"

"And she you?"

"God grant it!"

"Here," said he after some while, "here were a noble ending to the feud, Martin?"

"Sir, 'tis ended already, once and for all."

"Aye, but," said he with a catch in his voice, "all my days I—have yearned—for a son. More especially now—when I am old and so feeble."

"Then, sir, you shall lack no longer, if I can thus make up in some small measure for all you have suffered——"

At this he fell silent again but in the dark his trembling hand stole down to touch me lightly as in blessing; and so I fell asleep.

From this slumber I was suddenly aroused by his calling on my name and, opening drowsy eyes, beheld (as it were) a luminous veil that blotted out moon and stars and ocean, and, looking about, saw we lay becalmed in a white mist.

"Martin," said Sir Richard, his face a pale oval in the dimness, "d'ye hear aught?"

"No more than the lapping of the waves," I answered, for indeed the sea was very calm and still.

"Nay, listen awhile, Martin, for either I'm mad or there's some one or something crying and wailing to larboard of us, an evil sound like one in torment. Three times the cry has reached me, yet here we lie far out to sea. So list ye, son, and tell me if my ears do play me false, for verily I——"

His speech died away as from somewhere amid the chill and ghostly vapour there stole a long-drawn, wailing cry, so woful, so desolate, and so unearthly here in this vasty solitude that I caught my breath and stared upon this eddying mist with gaze of fearful expectancy.

"You heard it, Martin; you heard it?"

"Aye!" I nodded.

" 'Tis like one cries upon the rack, Martin!"

" 'Tis belike from some ship hid in the fog yonder," said I, handing him a musket from the arms-locker.

"There was no ship to see before this fog came down on us," quoth Sir Richard uneasily; howbeit he took the weapon, handling it so purposefully as was great comfort to see, whereupon I took oars and began to row towards whence I judged this awful cry had come. And presently it rose again, dreadful to hear, a sound to freeze the blood. I heard Sir Richard cock his piece and glanced instinctively to make sure Don Federigo's sword lay within my reach. Three times the cry rose, ere, with weapon poised for action, Sir Richard motioned for me to stop rowing, and glancing over my shoulder, I saw that which loomed upon us through the mist, a dim shape that gradually resolved itself into a large ship's boat or pinnace. Sword in one hand and pistol in the other, I stood up and hailed lustily, yet got no sound in reply save a strange, dull whimpering.

Having shouted repeatedly to no better purpose, I took oars again and paddled cautiously nearer until at last, by standing on the thwart, I might look into this strange boat and (the fog being luminous) perceived three dark shapes dreadfully huddled and still; but as I gazed, one of these stirred slightly, and I heard a strange, dull, thumping sound and then I saw this for a great hound.   Hereupon I cast our boat-hook over their gunwale and while Sir Richard held the boats thus grappled, scrambled aboard them, pistol in hand, and so came upon two dead men and beside them this great dog.

And now I saw these men had died in fight and not so long since, for the blood that fouled them and the boat was still wet, and even as I bent over them the hound licked the face of him that lay uppermost and whined.   And men and dog alike seemed direly thin and emaciate.   Now it was in my mind to shoot the dog out of its misery, to which end I cocked my pistol, but seeing how piteously it looked on me and crawled to lick my hand, I resolved to carry it along with us and forthwith (and no little to-do) presently contrived to get the creature into our boat, thereby saving both our lives, as you shall hear.

So we cast off and I sat to watch the boat until like a phantom, it melted into the mist and vanished away. Turning, I beheld the hound, his great head on Sir Richard's knee, licking the hand that fondled him.

"He is pined of hunger and thirst, Martin; I will tend him whiles you sleep.   He shall be a notable good sentinel and these be very keen of scent—the Spaniards do use them to track down poor runaway slaves withal, but these dogs are faithful beasts and this hath been sent us, doubtless, to some good end."

CHAPTER XXV

We Are Driven Ashore

And now were days of stifling heat, of baffling airs and maddening calms, wherein we rolled helpless, until in my impatience I would betake me to the oars in a fever of desire to reach our destination and row until the sweat poured from me.

What with sea, wind and fierce sun we grew brown as any Indians, but Sir Richard seemed to mend apace and to my great joy, for as time passed my respect for him deepened and with it a kindlier feeling; for in these long days and nights of our fellowship I grew to know how, by suffering patiently borne, a man might come by a knowledge of himself and his fellows and a kindly sympathy for their sins and sorrows that is (as I do think) the truest of all wisdom.

Fain would I set down some of these heart-searching talks, but I fear lest my narration grows over-long; suffice it that few sons ever bore tenderer reverence and love to their father than I to this, my erstwhile enemy.

So will I now, passing over much that befell us on these treacherous seas, as scorching calms, torrential rains and rageful winds, and how in despite all these we held true on our course by reason of Sir Richard's sailorly skill, I will (I say) come to a certain grey dawn and myself at the tiller whiles Sir Richard slept and beside him the great hound that we had named Pluto, since he had come to us from the dead.

Now presently I saw the dog stir uneasily and lift his head to sniff the air to windward; thereafter, being on his legs, he growled in his throat, staring ever in the one direction, and uttered a loud, deep bay, whereupon up started Sir Richard, full of question.

"Sir, look at the dog!" said I, pointing where Pluto stood abaft the mast, snuffing and staring to windward; seeing which, Sir Richard took the perspective-glass and swept with it the hazy distance.

"There is wind yonder, Martin; we must reef!" said he, the glass at his eye. So presently, whiles he steered, I shortened sail but saw his gaze bent ever to windward. "Dogs have strange senses!" quoth he. "Take the glass, Martin; your eyes are very keen; tell me if you see aught yonder in the mist against the cloudbank bearing about three points." Looking whither he directed, I made out a dim shape that loomed amid the mist.

"You see it, Martin?"

"Aye, a ship!" said I, and even as I spoke, the wind freshening, the rain ceased, the mist thinned away, and I saw a large vessel ahead of us standing in for the land which bore some five miles to leeward, a high, rugged coast, very grim and forbidding.

"How is she heading, Martin?"

"Southwesterly, I make it, which should bring her close upon us mighty soon, if the wind hold." And passing Sir Richard the glass, I sat staring on this distant ship in no little apprehension, since I judged most vessels that plied hereabouts could be but one of two sorts, viz: pirates or Spaniards.

"She is a great ship, Martin, and by her cut I think Spanish."

"I had liefer she were a pirate!" said I, scowling.

"Your wish may be granted soon enough, for she is going free and much wind astern of her."

Now whiles Sir Richard watched this oncoming vessel, I took up Don Federigo's sword, and, struck by its beauty, began to examine it as I had not done hitherto. And indeed a very noble weapon it was, the

hilt of rare craftsmanship, being silver cunningly in-
laid with gold, long and narrow in the blade, whereon,
graven in old Spanish, I saw the legend:

TRUST IN GOD AND ME.

A most excellent weapon, quick in the hand by reason
of its marvellous poise and balance.   But looking upon
this, I must needs remember him that had given it and
bethinking me how he had plucked me forth from the
horror of death and worse, I raised my head to scowl
again upon the oncoming ship, and with teeth hard-set
vowed within myself that no power should drag me a
living man back to the terrors of dungeon and torment.
And now as I crouched thus, scowling on the ship, the
naked sword across my knees, Sir Richard called to me:

"She is Spanish-built beyond all doubting and who-
ever chance to be aboard, they've seen us," said he,
setting by the glass.   "Come now, let us take counsel
whether to go about, hold on, or adventure running
ashore, the which were desperate risk by the look of
things——"

"Let us stand on so long as we may," quoth I, "for
if the worst come, we have always this," and reaching
a pistol, I laid it on the thwart beside me.

"Nay, Martin," said he, his hand on my shoulder,
"first let us do all we may to live, trusting in God Who
hath saved and delivered us thus far.   We have arms
to our defence and I can still pull trigger at a pinch,
or at extremity we may run ashore and contrive to
land, though 'tis an evil coast as you may see and I,
alack! am a better traveller sitting thus than afoot.
As to dying, Martin, if it must be so, why then let us
choose our own fashion, for as Sir Richard Grenville
hath it, 'better fall into the hands of God than into
the claws of Spain!' "

Thus spake my companion mighty cheering, his serene blue eyes now on me, now on the distant ship, as

he held our heeling boat to the freshening wind; hereupon, greatly comforted I grasped his hand and together we vowed never to be taken alive.   Then, seeing
the ship come down on us apace, I busied myself laying
to hand such arsenal as Don Federigo had furnished
us withal, viz: four muskets with their bandoliers and
two brace of pistols; which done, I took to watching the
ship again until she was so close I might discern her
lofty, crowded decks.   And then, all at once, the wind
died utterly away, and left us becalmed, to my inexpressible joy.   For now, seeing the great ship roll
thus helpless, I seized the oars.

"Inshore!" I cried, and began to row might and
main, whereat those aboard ship fired a gun to windward and made a waft with their ensign as much as
to bid us aboard them.   But I heeding no whit, they
let fly a great shot at us that, falling short, plunged
astern in a whirl of spray.   Time and again they fired
such fore-chase guns as chanced to bear, but finding
us out of range, they gave over wasting more powder
and I rejoiced, until suddenly I espied that which made
me gloomy enough, for 'twixt the ship and us came a
boat full of men who rowed lustily; and they being
many and I one, they began to overhaul us rapidly
despite my efforts, till, panting in sweating despair, I
ceased my vain labour and made to reach for the nearest musket.

"Let be, my son!" quoth Sir Richard, on his knees
in the stern sheets.   "Row, Martin, the boat rides
steadier.   Ha!" said he, with a little chuckling laugh,
as a bullet hummed over us.   "So we must fight, after
all; well, on their own heads be it!"   And as he took
up and cocked a musket, I saw his eyes were shining
and his lips upcurled in grim smile.   "Alas, I was ever
too forward for fight in the old days, God forgive me,
but here, as I think, is just and sufficient cause for
bloodshed."

"They come on amain!" I gasped, as I swung to
the heavy oars, wondering to behold him so uncon-
cerned and deliberate.

"Let them come, Martin!" said he, crouching in the
stern sheets, "only keep you an even stroke—so, steady
it is! Aye, let them come, Martin, and God's will be
done!"

And now our pursuers began firing amain, though
for the most part their shooting was very wild; but
presently, finding we made no reply, they grew bolder,
hallooing and shouting blithely and taking better aim,
so that their shot hummed ever nearer and once or
twice the boat was struck. And as I hearkened to their
ribald shouting and the vicious hiss of their bullets,
fierce anger took me and I began to curse Sir Richard's delay; then came the roar of his piece and as
the smoke cleared I saw a man start up in the bows
of the pursuing boat and tossing up his arms, fall
backwards upon the rowers, thereby throwing them
into clamorous confusion so that their boat fell off
and lay rolling helplessly.

"Load, Martin!" quoth Sir Richard 'twixt shut
teeth. "Load as I fire—for now by God I have 'em
—see yonder!" And thrusting towards me his smoking weapon, he caught up the next, levelled and fired
again, whereupon their shouting and confusion were
redoubled.

Thus Sir Richard fired on them repeatedly and with
deadly effect, judging by their outcries, for I was too
busy loading and priming to afford them a glance, so
that Sir Richard maintained as rapid a fire as possible.
How long we fought them thus I know not; indeed I
remember little of the matter save smoke and noise,
Sir Richard's grim figure and the occasional hiss of a
bullet about us. Suddenly Sir Richard turned to stare
up at me, wild-eyed and trembling, as in one of his
ague-fits.

"Enough, Martin!" he gasped. "God forgive me, I ha' done enough—and here's the wind at last!"

Seeing this indeed was so, I sprang to loose out the reefs, which done, I saw the enemy's boat lie wallowing in the trough and never so much as an oar stirring. But beyond this was another boat hasting to their assistance and beyond this again the ship herself, so that I joyed to feel our little vessel bounding shorewards. But hearing a groan, I saw Sir Richard crouched at the tiller, his white head bowed upon his hand.

"God love me—are you hurt, sir?" I cried, scrambling towards him.

"No, Martin, no!" And then, "Ah, God forgive me," he groaned again, "I fear I have been the death of too many of them—more than was needful."

"Nay, sir," said I, wondering. "How should this be?"

"I killed—for the joy of it, Martin."

" 'Twas them or us, Sir Richard. And we may have to kill again—see yonder!" And I pointed where the ship was crowding sail after us with intent to cut us off ere we could make the shore—a desolation of shaggy rocks and tree-girt heights that looked ever the more formidable; yet thither we held our course, since it seemed the lesser of two evils.

Our boat, as I have said, was a good sailer; none the less the great ship overhauled us until she was near enough to open on us with her fore-chase guns again. But presently (being yet some distance from the shore) the water began to shoal, whereupon the ship bore up lest she run aground, and let fly her whole broadside, the which yet was short of us. In this comparative safety we would have brought to, but seeing the second boat had hoisted sail and was standing into these shallows after us, we perforce ran on for the shore. Soon we were among rocks and before us a line of breakers backed by frowning rocks, very dreadful to behold.

And now, at Sir Richard's command, I struck our sail and, taking to the oars, began to row, marvelling at the skill with which he steered amid these difficult waters, and both of us looking here and there for some opening amid the breakers whereby we might gain the land.

Presently, sure enough, we espied such a place, though one none would have attempted save poor souls in such desperate case. The air about us seemed full of spume and the noise of mighty waters, but Sir Richard never faltered; his eyes looked upon the death that roared about us, serene and untroubled. And now we were amid the breakers; over my shoulder, through whirling spray, I caught a glimpse of sandy foreshore where lay our salvation; then, with sudden, rending crash, we struck and a great wave engulfed us. Tossed and buffeted among this choking smother, I was whirled, half-stunned, into shoal water and stumbling to my knees, looked back for Sir Richard. And thus I saw the dog Pluto swimming valiantly and dragging at something that struggled feebly, and plunged back forthwith to the good beast's assistance, and thus together we brought Sir Richard ashore and lay there a while, panting and no strength to move.

At last, being recovered somewhat, I raised myself to behold my companion, his frail body shaking in an ague, his features blue and pinched. But beholding my look, he smiled and essayed a reassuring nod.

"Thanks to you and—the dog, I am very well, Martin!" said he, 'twixt chattering teeth. "But what of the boat; she should come ashore." Looking about, sure enough I espied our poor craft, rolling and tossing helplessly in the shallows hard by, and running thither, was seized of sudden despair, for I saw her bilged and shattered beyond repair. Now as she rolled thus, the sport of each incoming wave, I beheld something bright caught up in her tangled gear, whereupon I contrived to scramble aboard and so found this to be Don Federigo's rapier, the which was some small mitigation of my gloom and put me to great hopes that I might find more useful things, as compass or sextant, and so found a small barrico of water firm-wedged beneath a thwart; but save for this the boat was swept bare. So having secured the barrico (and with no small to-do) I hove it ashore and got myself after it, and so came mighty despondent where sat Sir Richard as one deep in thought, his gaze on the sea, his shrivelled hand upon the head of the dog Pluto crouched beside him.

"Truly we are in evil case, Martin!" quoth he, when I had told him the result of my search. "Aye, we are in woful plight! And this land of Darien is very mountainous and ill-travelling as I remember."

"Yet needs must we adventure it," said I gloomily.

"You must, Martin; but as for me, I bide here."

"Here?" said I, glancing around on the barren, unlovely spot. "Sir, you talk wildly, I think; to stay here is to die."

"Aye, Martin, so soon as God shall permit."

"Surely our case is not so hopeless you despair thus soon?"

"Sit down, here beside me," said he, smiling up at me. "Come and let us reason the matter, since 'tis reason lifteth man above the brutes."

So there, on the coast of this vast, unknown wilderness, sat we two poor castaways, the great hound at our feet, his bright eyes looking from one to other of us as we spake and reasoned together thus:

Sir Richard: First of all, we are destitute, Martin.

Myself: True.

Sir Richard: Therefore our food must be such game as we can contrive to take and kill empty-handed.

Myself: This shall be my duty.

Sir Richard: Second, 'tis a perilous country by reason of wild Indians, and we are scant of arms. Third, 'tis a country of vasty mountains, of torrents, swamps and thickets and I am a mighty poor walker, being weak of my leg-joints.

Myself: Then will I aid you.

Sir Richard: Fourthly, here is a journey where though one may succeed, two cannot: full of peril and hardship for such as have a resolute spirit and strong body, and I am very weak.

Myself: Yet shall your resolute spirit sustain you.

Sir Richard: Fifthly and lastly, I am a cripple, so will I stay here, Martin, praying God to bring you safe to your weary journey's end.

Myself: I had thought you much stronger of late.

Sir Richard: Indeed so I am, but my joints have been so oft stretched on the rack that I cannot go far and then but slowly, alas!

There was silence awhile, each of us gazing out across the troubled waters, yet I, for one, seeing nothing of them. Glancing presently at Sir Richard, I saw his eyes closed, but his mouth very resolute and grim.

"And what of Joan?" I demanded. "What of your daughter?"

Now at this he started and glancing at me, his mouth of a sudden lost its grimness and he averted his head when he answered:

"Why, Martin, 'tis for her sake I will not hamper you with my useless body."

"So is it for her sake I will never leave you here to perish!"

"Then here," says he in a little, "here is an end to reason, Martin?"

"Aye, indeed, sir!"

"God love thee, lad!' cried he, clasping my hand. "For if 'tis reason raiseth us 'bove the brutes 'tis unselfishness surely lifts us nigh to God!"

CHAPTER XXVI

.

Our Desperate Situation

"And now," quoth Sir Richard, "since you are bent on dragging this worn-out carcase along to be your careful burden (for the which may God bless you everlastingly, dear lad!) let us see what equipment Fortune hath left us beside your sword and the water."

Herewith, upon investigation we found our worldly possessions amount to the following:

In Sir Richard's Pockets:	In Mine:
1 ship's biscuit (somewhat spoiled by water).	A length of small cord.
A small clasp knife.	Adam's chart (and very limp).
A gunflint.	9 pistol balls.

These various objects we set together before us and I for one mighty disconsolate, for, excepting only the knife, a collection of more useless odds and ends could not be imagined. Sir Richard, on the contrary, having viewed each and every with his shrewd, kindly eyes, seemed in no wise cast down, for, said he,

"We might be richer, but then we might be poorer —for here we have in this biscuit one meal, though scant 'tis true and not over tasty. A sword and knife for weapons and tools, a flint to make us fires, three yards of small cord wherewith to contrive snares for small game, and though we ha' lost our compass, we have the coast to follow by day and the stars to guide us by night and furthermore——"

"Nine pistol balls!" quoth I gloomily.

"Hum!" said he, stroking his chin and eyeing me askance. "Having neither weapons nor powder to project them——"

"They shall arm me arrows!"

"Aye, but will they serve?" he questioned doubtfully.

"Well enough, supposing we find aught to shoot at——"

"Never fear, in Darien are beasts and fowls a-plenty."

"Well and good, sir!" said I, gathering up the bullets, and doing so, espied a piece of driftwood carrying many bent and rusty nails, the which (the wood being very dry and rotten) I presently broke out and to my nine bullets I added some dozen nails, pocketing them to the same purpose. And now having collected our possessions (of more value to us than all the treasures of Peru), we set forth upon our long and toilsome journey, our gaze bent ever upon the cliffs that frowned upon our right hand, looking for some place easy of ascent whereby we might come to the highlands above (where we judged it easier travelling) and with Pluto stalking on before like the dignified animal he was, looking back ever and anon as if bidding us to follow.

And as I watched this great beast, the thought occurred to me that here was what should save us from starvation should we come to such extremity; but I spake nothing of this to Sir Richard who had conceived a great affection for the dog from the first. And after some while we came to a place where the cliff had fallen and made a sloping causeway of earth and rocks, topped by shady trees. This we began to mount forthwith and, finding it none so steep, I (lost in my thoughts) climbed apace, forgetful of Sir Richard in my eagerness, until, missing him beside me, I turned to see him on hands and knees, dragging himself painfully after me thus, whereon I hasted back to him full of self-reproaches.

" 'Tis only my legs!" he gasped, lifting agonised face. "My spirit is willing, Martin, but alas, my poor flesh——"

"Nay—'tis I am selfish!" quoth I. "Aye, a selfish man ever, dreaming only of my own woes!" Saying which, I raised him and, setting an arm about his wasted form, aided him as well as I might until, seeing how he failed despite his brave struggles, I made him sit and rest awhile, unheeding his breathless protestations, and thus at last, by easy stages, we came to the top of the ascent amid a grove of very tall trees, in whose pleasant shade we paused awhile, it being now midday and very hot.

Behind us lay the ocean, before us a range of mighty mountains blue with distance that rose, jagged peak on peak, far as eye could see, and betwixt them and us a vast and rolling wilderness, a land of vivid sun and stark shadow, dazzling glare on the uplands, gloom in the valleys and above swamp and thicket and trackless forests a vapour that hung sullen and ominous like the brooding soul of this evil country.

"Fever!" quoth Sir Richard, stabbing at the sluggish mist with bony fingers. "Ague, the flux—death! We must travel ever by the higher levels, Martin— and I a cripple!"

"Why, then," said I, "you shall have a staff to aid you on one side and my arm on t'other, and shall attempt no great distance until you grow stronger." So having found and cut a staff to serve him, we set off together upon our long and arduous pilgrimage.

By mid-afternoon we reached a place of rocks whence bubbled a small rill mighty pleasant to behold and vastly refreshing to our parched throats and bodies. Here, though the day was still young and we had come (as I judged) scarce six miles, I proposed to camp for the night, whereon Sir Richard must needs earnestly protest he could go further an I would, but finding me determined, he heaved a prodigious sigh and stretching himself in the cool shadow, lay there silent awhile, yet mighty content, as I could see.

"Martin," quoth he at last, "by my reckoning we have some hundred and fifty miles to go."

"But, sir, they will be less to-morrow!" said I, busied with my knife on certain branches I had cut.

"And but half a ship's biscuit to our sustenance, and that spoiled."

"Why, then, throw it away; I will get us better fare!" said I, for as we came along I had spied several of those great birds the which I knew to be very excellent eating.

"As how, my son?" he questioned.

"With bow and arrows." At this he sat up to watch me at work and very eager to aid me therein. "So you shall, sir," said I, and having tapered my bow-stave sufficiently, I showed him how to trim the shafts as smooth and true as possible with a cleft or notch at one end into which I set one of my rusty nails, binding it there with strips from my tattered shirt; in place of feathers I used a tuft of grass and behold! my arrow was complete, and though a poor thing to look at yet it would answer well enough, as I knew by experience. So we fell to our arrow-making, wherein I found Sir Richard very quick and skilful, as I told him, the which seemed to please him mightily.

"For," said he miserably, "I feel myself such a burden to thee, Martin, that anything I can do to lighten thy travail be to me great comfort."

"Sir," said I, "these many years have I been a solitary man hungering for companionship, and, in place of enemy, God hath given me a friend and one I do love and honour. As to his crippled body, sir, it beareth no scar but is a badge of honour, and if he halt in his gait or fail by the way, this doth but remind me of his dauntless soul that, despite pain and torment, endured."

So saying, I caught up such arrows as were finished (four in all) and taking my bow, set forth in quest of supper, with Pluto at my heels. Nor had I far to seek, for presently I espied several of these monstrous birds among the trees and, stringing my bow with a length of cord, I crept forward until I was in easy range and, setting arrow to string, let fly. Away sang my shaft, a yard wide of the mark, soaring high into the air and far beyond all hope of recovery.

This put me in a fine rage, for not only had I lost my precious arrow, but the quarry also, for off flapped my bird, uttering a hoarse cackle as in derision of my ill aim. On I went, seeking for something should serve us for supper, yet look where I would, saw nothing, no, not so much as parrot or macaw that might stay us for lack of better fare. On I went, and mightily hungry, wandering haphazard and nothing to reward me until, reaching an opening or glade shut in by dense thickets beyond, I sat me upon a fallen tree and in mighty ill humour, the dog Pluto at my feet. Suddenly I saw him start and prick his ears, and presently, sure enough, heard a distant stir and rustling in the thickets that grew rapidly nearer and louder to trampling rush; and out from the leaves broke some dozen or so young pigs; but espying the dog they swung about in squealing terror and plunged back again. But in that moment I let fly among them and was mighty glad to see one roll over and lie kicking, filling the air with shrill outcry; then Pluto was upon it and had quickly finished the poor beast, aye, and would have devoured it, too, had I not driven him off with my bow-stave.

It was a small pig and something lean, yet never in

this world hunter more pleased than I as, shouldering the carcase and with Pluto going before, I made my way back to our halting-place and found Sir Richard had contrived to light a fire and full of wonder to behold my pig.

"Though to be sure," said he, "I've heard there were such in Darien, yet I never saw any, Martin, more especially in these high lands."

"They were fleeing from some wild beast, as I judge, sir," quoth I.

"Why, then, 'twere as well to keep our fire going all night!" said he: to the which I agreed and forthwith set about cutting up the pig, first flaying it as well as I might, since I judged the skin should be very serviceable in divers ways. So this night we supped excellent well.

The meal over, Sir Richard cut up what remained of the carcase into strips and set me to gather certain small branches with which he built a sort of grating above some glowing embers and thus dried and smoked the meat after the manner of the buccaneers. "For look now, Martin," said he, "besides drying the meat, these twigs are aromatic and do lend a most excellent flavour, so that there is no better meat in the world— besides, it will keep."

Beyond the rocky cleft bright with the light of our fire the vasty wilderness hemmed us in, black and sullen, for the trees being thick hereabouts we could see no glimpse of moon or star. And amid this gloom were things that moved stealthily, shapes that rustled and flitted, and ever and anon would come the howl of some beast, the cry of some bird, hunting or hunted, whereat Pluto, crunching on a bone, would lift his head to growl. So with the fire and the dog's watchfulness we felt tolerably secure and presently fell asleep.

CHAPTER XXVII

We Commence Our Journey

DAY after day we held on, suffering much by reason of heat, thirst and fatigue, since, fearing lest we should lose sight of our guide, the sea, and go astray to perish miserably in the wild, we followed ever the trend of this mountainous coast.

By rocky ways we marched, by swamps and mazy thickets, down precipitous slopes, through tangled woods, across wide savannahs, along perilous tracks high above dim forests that stretched away like a leafy ocean, whence we might behold a wide prospect of all those weary miles before us.

And surely nowhere in all this world is to be seen a country more full of marvels and wonders than this land of Darien. For here rise vasty mountains whose jagged summits split the very heaven; here are mighty rivers and roaring cataracts, rolling plains, thirsty deserts and illimitable forests in whose grim shadow lurk all manner of beasts and reptiles strange beyond thought; here lie dense groves and tangled thickets where bloom great flowers of unearthly beauty yet rank of smell and poisonous to the touch; here are birds of every kind and hue and far beyond this poor pen to describe by reason of the beauty and brilliancy of their plumage, some of which would warble so sweet 'twas great joy to hear while the discordant croakings and shrill clamours of others might scarce be endured. Here, too, are trees (like the cocos) so beneficent to yield a man food and drink, aye, and garments to cover

him; or others (like the maria and balsam trees) that
besides their timber do distil medicinal oils, and yet
here also are trees so noxious their mere touch bring-
eth a painful disease of the skin and to sleep in their
shadow breedeth sickness and death; here, too, grow
all manner of luscious fruits as the ananas or pine-
apple, with oranges, grapes, medlars and dates, but
here again are other fruits as fair to the eye, yet
deadly as fang of snake or sting of *cientopies*.
Truly (as I do think), nowhere is there country of
such extremes of good and evil as this land of
Darien.

Thus day by day we held on and daily learned I
much of tree and fruit and flower, of beast, bird and
reptile from Sir Richard who, it seemed, was deeply
versed in the lore of such, both by reading and experience; but hourly I learned more of this man's many
and noble qualities, as his fortitude, his unflinching
courage and the cheerful spirit that could make light
of pain and thirst and weariness so that, misjudging
his strength, I would sometimes march him well-nigh
beyond his endurance, but knew nought of it since he
never complained but masked his suffering in brave
and smiling words. And there were times when, burning with impatience, I would quicken my pace (God
forgive me) until, missing his plodding figure, I would
look back to see him stumbling after me afar.

It was upon the fifth day of our journey that, missing him thus, I turned to wait for him to come up and
found him nowhere in sight. Hereupon I hasted back
the way I had come and after some while beheld him
prone in the dust; he lay outstretched upon his face
in the hot glare of the sun, the dog Pluto squatting
beside him, and as I approached the desolate figure
I knew that he was weeping. So came I running to
fall beside him on my knees and lifting that abased
head, saw indeed the agony of his tears.

"Oh, Martin—forgive me!" he gasped. "I can crawl no faster—better were I dead, dear lad, than hamper you thus——"

"Rather will I perish!" said I, lifting him in my arms to bear him out of the sun and much grieved to find him a burden so light; and now, sitting 'neath a great tree, I took his head upon my bosom and wiped the tears from his furrowed cheeks and set myself diligently to comfort him, but seeing him so faint and foredone, I began alternately to berate myself heartily and lament over him so that he must needs presently take to comforting me in turn, vowing himself very well, that it was nought but the heat, that he would be able to go and none the worse in a little, etc. "Besides," said he, " 'tis worth such small discomfort to find you so tender of me, Martin. Yet indeed I am stronger than I seem and shall be ready to go on as soon as you will——"

"Nay, sir," said I, mighty determined, "here we bide till the sun moderates; 'tis too hot for the dog even," and I nodded where Pluto lay outstretched and panting, hard by. But now, even as I spoke, the dog lifted his head to snuff the air and, getting up, bolted off among the adjacent undergrowth. I was yet idly wondering at this when suddenly, from somewhere afar in the woods below, came a sound there was no mistaking—the faint, sharp crack of a firearm. In a moment I was on my feet and, with Sir Richard beside me, came where we might look into the green depths below us.

And sure enough, amid this leafy wilderness I saw a glitter that came and went, the which I knew must be armour, and presently made out the forms of men and horses with divers hooded litters and long files of tramping figures.

"Ah!" quoth Sir Richard. "Yon should be the gold-train for Panama or Carthagena, or mayhap Indians being marched to slavery in the mines, poor souls!"

As he spake, came a puff of white smoke plain to see and thereafter divers others, and presently the reports of this firing smote upon our ears in rapid succession.

"What now?" said I, straining my eyes. "Is there a battle toward——"

"Nay, Martin, 'tis more like some poor wretch hath broke his bonds and fled into the woods; if so, God send him safe out of their hands, for I have endured slavery and——" here his voice broke, and casting himself on his knees he clasped his arms about me, and I all amazed to see him so moved.

"Oh, Martin!" he wept, in voice of agony, "oh, dear and gentle lad, 'twas to such slavery, such shame and misery I sent thee once—thou—that I do so love—my son——"

"Sir," said I, stooping to lift him. "Sir, this is all forgot and out of mind."

"Yet, dear lad, you do bear the marks yet, scars o' the whip, marks o' the shackles. I have seen them when you slept—and never a one but set there by my hand—and now—now you must cherish me if I fail by the way—must bear me in your arms—grieve for my weakness—— Oh, dear lad, I would you were a little harsher—less kind."

Now seeing how it was with him, I sat me down and, folding him within my arm, sought to comfort him in my blundering way, reminding him of all he had endured and that my sufferings could nowise compare with his own and that in many ways I was no whit the worse: "Indeed," said I, "in many ways I am the better man, for solitude hath but taught me to think beyond myself, though 'tis true I am something slow of speech and rude of manner, and hardship hath but made me stronger of body than most men I have met."

"Oh, God love you, lad!" cried he of a sudden, 'twixt laughing and weeping. "You will be calling me your benefactor next!"

"And wherefore not?" quoth I. "For indeed, being made wise by suffering, you have taught me many things and most of all to love you in despite of myself!"

Now at this he looks at me all radiant-eyed, yet when he would have spoken, could not, and so was silence awhile. Now turning to look down into the valley I saw it all deserted and marking how the forest road ran due east, I spoke that which was in my thought.

"Sir, yonder, as I think, must be a highway; at least, where others go, so may we, and 'twill be easier travelling than these rocky highlands; how think you?"

"Why, truly, if road there be, it must bring us again to the sea soon or late; so come, let us go!"

So saying, he got him to his legs, whereupon Pluto leapt and fawned upon him for very joy; and thus finding him something recovered and very earnest to be gone, we set out again (maugre the sun) looking for some place whereby we might get us down into the valley, and after some while came upon a fissure in the cliff face which, though easy going for an able man, was a different matter I thought for my companion; but as I hesitated, the matter was put beyond despite by Sir Richard forthwith cheerily beginning the descent, whereupon I followed him and after me the dog. As we descended, the way grew easier until we reached at last a small plateau pleasantly shaded by palm trees; here (and despite his hardihood), Sir Richard sank down, sweating with the painful effort and gasping for breath, yet needs must he smile up at me triumphant, so that I admired anew the indomitable spirit of him.

"Oh, for a drink!" quoth he, as I set an armful of fern beneath his head.

"Alas!" said I, " 'tis far down to the river——"

"Nay—above, lad, look above—yonder is drink for a whole ship's company!" and he pointed feebly to the foliage of the tree 'neath which he lay:

"What! Is this a cocos palm?" said I, rejoicing; and forthwith doffing my sword belt, I clambered up this tree hand over fist and had soon plucked and tossed down a sufficiency of great, green nuts about the bigness of my two fists. Now sitting beside him, Sir Richard showed me how I must cut two holes in the green rind and we drank blissfully of this kindly juice that to our parched tongues was very nectar, for verily never in all my days have I tasted drink so delectable and invigorating. As for Pluto, when I offered him of this he merely sniffed and yawned contemptuous. Thus refreshed we went on again, the way growing ever easier until we entered the shade of those vast woods we had seen from above.

But scarce were we here than rose such a chattering, whistling and croaking from the leafy mysteries above and around us, such a screaming and wailing as was most distressful to hear, for all about us was a great multitude of birds; the forest seemed full of them, and very wonderful to see by reason of their plumage, its radiant and divers hues, so that as they flitted to and fro in their glowing splendour they seemed like so many flying jewels, while clustering high in the trees or swinging nimbly among the branches were troops of monkeys that screamed and chattered and grimaced down at us for all the world as they had been very fiends of the pit.

"Heard ye ever such unholy hubbub, Martin?" said Sir Richard, halting to glance about us. "This portendeth a storm, I judge, for these creatures possess gifts denied to us humans. See how they do begin to

cower and seek what shelter they may! We were wise
to do the like, my son. I marked a cave back yonder;
let us go there, for these woods be an evil place at
such times.".

So back we went accordingly and saw the sunlight
suddenly quenched and the sky lower above us ever
darker and more threatening, so that by the time we
had reached the little cave in question, it almost seemed
night was upon us. And now, crouching in this secure haven, I marvelled at the sudden, unearthly stillness of all things; not a leaf stirred and never a sound
to hear, for beast and bird alike had fallen mute.

Then all at once was a blinding glare followed by
roaring thunder-clap that echoed and re-echoed from
rugged cliff to mountain summit near and far until
this was whelmed and lost in the rush of a booming,
mighty wind and this howling riot full of whirling
leaves and twigs and riven branches. And now came
the rain, a hissing downpour that seemed it would
drown the world, while ever the lightning flared and
crackled and thunder roared ever more loud until I
shrank, blinded and half-stunned. After some while,
these awful sounds hushing a little, in their stead was
the lash and beat of rain, the rush and trickle of water
where it gushed and spouted down from the cliff above
in foaming cascades until I began to dread lest this
deluge overwhelm us and we be drowned miserably in
our little cave. But, all at once, sudden as it had come,
the storm was passed, rain and wind and thunder
ceased, the sombre clouds rolled away and down
beamed the sun to show us a new and radiant world
of vivid greens spangled as it were with a myriad
shimmering gems, a very glory to behold.

" 'Tis a passionate country this, Martin," as we
stepped forth of our refuge, "but its desperate rages
be soon over."

By late afternoon we came out upon a broad green

track that split the forest east and west, and where,
despite the rain, we might yet discern faint traces here
and there of the hoofs and feet had trampled it earlier
in the day, so that it seemed we must march behind
them. On we went, very grateful for the trees that
shaded us and the springy grass underfoot, Sir Richard swinging his staff and striding out right cheerily.
Suddenly Pluto, uttering a single joyous bark, sprang
off among the brush that grew very thick, and looking
thither, we espied a small stream and the day being
far spent we decided to pass the night hereabouts,
so we turned aside forthwith and having gone but a
few yards, found ourselves quite hidden from the highway, so thick grew the trees and so dense and tangled
the thickets that shut us in; and here ran this purling
brook, making sweet, soft noises in the shallows mighty
soothing to be heard. And here I would have stayed
but Sir Richard shook wise head and was for pushing
farther into the wild. "For," said he, "there may be
other travellers behind us to spy some gleam of our
fire and who shall these be but enemies?" So, following the rill that, it seemed, took its rise from the cliffs
to our left, we went on until Sir Richard paused in
the shade of a great tree that soared high above its
fellows and hard beside the stream.

But scarce were we come hither than Pluto uttered
a savage growl and turned, snuffing the air, whereupon
Sir Richard, grasping the battered collar about his
massy throat, bade him sternly to silence.

"What saw I, Martin? Some one comes—let us go
see, and softly!"

So, following whither Pluto led, we presently heard
voices speaking the Spanish tongue, and one cursed,
and one mocked and one sang. Hereupon I drew
sword, and moving with infinite caution, we came where,
screened 'mid the leaves, we might behold the highway. And thus we beheld six men approaching and

one a horseman; nearer they came until we could see
them sweating beneath their armour and the weapons
they bore, and driving before them a poor, blood-
stained wretch tied to the horseman's stirrup, yet who,
despite wounds and blows, strode with head proudly
erect, heeding them no whit. Yet suddenly he stumbled and fell, whereupon the horseman swore again
and the captive was kicked to his feet and so was
dragged on again, reeling for very weariness; and I
saw this poor creature was an Indian.

"Martin," said Sir Richard, when this sorry caval-
cade was gone by, "it would, I think, be action commendable to endeavour rescue of this poor soul."

"It would, sir!" quoth I. "And a foolhardy."

"Mayhap," said he, "yet am I minded to adventure it."

"How, sir—with one sword and a knife?"

"Nay, Martin, by God's aid, strategy and a dog.
Come then, let us follow; they cannot go far, and
I heard them talk of camping hereabouts. Softly,
lad!"

"But, sir," said I, amazed at this audacity, "will
you outface five lusty men well-armed?"

"And wherefore not, Martin? Is the outfacing of
five rogues any greater matter than outfacing this
God's wilderness? Nay, I am not mad," said he, meeting my glance with a smile, "there were times when
I adventured greater odds than this and to worse end,
God forgive me! Alas, I have wrought so much of
evil in the past I would fain offset it with a little good,
so bear with me, dear lad——"

"Yet this man you risk your life for is but a stranger
and an Indian at that!"

"And what then, Martin? Cannot an Indian suffer
—cannot he die?" Here, finding me silent, he continued. "Moreover, there be very cogent reasons do
urge a little risk, for look now, these rogues do go

well shod—and see our poor shoes! They bear equipment very necessary to us that have so far to go and
their horse should be useful to us.   Nor dream I would
lightly hazard your life, Martin, for these men have
been drinking, will drink more and should therefore
sleep sound, and I have a plan whereby Pluto and
I——"

"Sir Richard," said I, "where you go, I go!"

"Why, very well, Martin, 'twere like you—but you
shall be subject to my guidance and do nought without
my word."

As he spoke, his eyes quick and alert, his face grimly
purposeful, there was about him that indefinable air
of authority I had noticed more than once.   Thus,
with no better weapons than his staff and knife, and
my sword, bow and poor arrows, we held on after
these five Spanish soldiers, Sir Richard nothing
daunted by this disparity of power but rather the more
determined and mighty cheerful by his looks, but myself full of doubts and misgiving.   Perceiving which,
he presently stopped to slap me on the shoulder:

"Martin," said he, "if things go as I think, we shall
this night be very well off for equipment and all without a blow, which is good, and save a life, which is
better!"

"Aye, but, sir, how if things go contrary-wise?"

"Why, then, sure a quick death is better than to
perish miserably by the way, for we have cruel going
before us, thirsty deserts and barren wilds where game
is scarce; better steel or bullet than to die raving with
thirst or slow starvation—how say ye, lad?"

"Lead on!" quoth I and tightened my belt.

"Ha!" said he, halting suddenly as arose a sudden
crack of twigs and underbrush some distance on our
front.   "They have turned in to the water—let us
sit here and watch for their camp fire."   And presently, sure enough, we saw a red glow through the un-

derbrush ahead that grew ever brighter as the shadows deepened; and so came the night.

How long we waited thus, our eyes turned ever towards this red fire-glow, I know not, but at last I felt Sir Richard touch me and heard his voice in my ear:

"Let us advance until we have 'em in better view!" Forthwith we stole forward, Sir Richard's grasp on Pluto's collar and hushing him to silence, until we were nigh enough to catch the sound of their voices very loud and distinct. Here we paused again and so passed another period of patient waiting wherein we heard them begin to grow merry, to judge by their laughter and singing, a lewd clamour very strange and out of place in these wild solitudes, under cover of which uproar we crept upon them nearer and nearer until we might see them sprawled about the fire, their muskets piled against a tree, their miserable captive lashed fast to another and drooping in his bonds like one sleeping or a-swoon. So lay we watching and waiting while their carouse waxed to a riot and waned anon to sleepy talk and drowsy murmurs and at last to a lusty snoring. And after some wait, Sir Richard's hand ever upon Pluto's collar, we crept forward again until we were drawn close upon that tree where stood the muskets. Then up rose Sir Richard, letting slip the dog and we were upon them, all three of us, our roars and shouts mingled with the fierce raving of the great hound. At the which hellish clamour, these poor rogues waked in sudden panic to behold the dog snapping and snarling about them and ourselves covering them with their own weapons, and never a thought among them but to supplicate our mercy; the which they did forthwith upon their knees and with upraised hands. Hereupon Sir Richard, scowling mighty fierce, bid such of them as loved life to be gone, whereat in the utmost haste and as one man, up started they all five and took themselves off with such impetuous celerity that we stood alone and masters of all their gear in less time than it taketh me to write down.

"Well, Martin," said Sir Richard, grim-smiling, " 'twas none so desperate a business after all! Come now, let us minister to this poor prisoner."

` .We found him in sorry plight and having freed him of his bonds I fetched water from the brook near by and together we did what we might to his comfort, all of the which he suffered and never a word: which done, we supped heartily all three on the spoil we had taken. Only once did the Indian speak, and in broken Spanish, to know who we were.

"Content you, we are no Spaniards!" answered Sir Richard, setting a cloak about him as he lay.

"Truly this do I see, my father!" he murmured, and so fell asleep, the which so excellent example I bade Sir Richard follow and this after some demur, he agreed to (though first he must needs help me collect sticks for the fire), then commanding me wake him in two hours without fail, he rolled himself in one of the cloaks and very presently fell soundly asleep like the hardy old campaigner he was.

And now, the fire blazing cheerily, Pluto outstretched beside me, one bright eye opening ever and anon, and a pistol in my belt, I took careful stock of our new-come-by possessions and found them to comprise the following, viz:

3 muskets with powder and shot a-plenty.
2 brace of pistols.
3 swords, with belts, hangers, etc.
3 steel backs and breasts.
4 morions.
1 beaver hat excellent wide in the brim, should do for Sir Richard; he suffering much by the sun despite the hat of leaves I had made him.
1 axe heavy and something blunted.
2 excellent knives.
2 wine skins, both empty.

3 flasks, the same.
Good store of meat with cakes of very excellent bread of cassava.
1 horse with furniture for same.
5 cloaks, something worn.
3 pair of boots, very serviceable.
1 tinder box.
1 coat.

One brass compass in the pocket of same and of more value to us, I thought, than all the rest, the which pleased me mightily; so that for a long time I sat moving it to and fro to watch the swing of the needle and so at last, what with the crackle of the fire and the brooding stillness beyond and around us, I presently fell a-nodding and in a little (faithless sentinel that I was) to heavy slumber.

CHAPTER XXVIII

We Fall in With One Atlamatzin, an Indian Chief

I waked to a scream, a fierce trampling, an awful snarling, this drowned in the roar of a gun, and started up to see a glitter of darting steel that Sir Richard sought to parry with his smoking weapon. Then I was up, and, sword in hand, leapt towards his assailant, a tall, bearded man whose corselet flashed red in the fire-glow and who turned to meet my onset, shouting fiercely. And so we fell to it point and point; pushing desperately at each other in the half-light and raving pandemonium about us until more by good fortune than skill I ran him in the arm and shoulder, whereupon, gasping out hoarse maledictions, he incontinent made off into the dark. Then turned I to find myself alone; even the Indian had vanished, though from the darkness near at hand was a sound of fierce strife and a ringing shot. Catching up a musket I turned thitherward, but scarce had I gone a step than into the light of the fire limped Sir Richard and Pluto beside him, who licked and licked at his great muzzle as he came.

"Oh, Martin!" gasped Sir Richard, leaning on his musket and bowing his head, "oh, Martin—but for Pluto here——" And now, as he paused, I saw the dog's fangs and tongue horribly discoloured.

"'Tis all my fault!" said I bitterly. "I fell asleep at my post!"

"Aye!" he groaned, "whereby are two men dead and one by my hand, God forgive me!"

"Nay, but these were enemies bent on our murder!"

"Had they seen you wakeful and vigilant they had never dared attack us. As it is, I have another life on my conscience and I am an old man and soul-weary of strife and bloodshed, yet this it seems is my destiny!"

So saying he sat him down by the fire exceeding dejected, and when I would have comforted him I found no word. Suddenly I heard Pluto growl in his throat, saw the hair on neck and shoulders bristle, and looking where he looked, cocked my musket and raised it to my shoulder, then lowered it, as, with no sound of footstep, the Indian stepped into the firelight. In one hand he grasped the axe and as he came nearer I saw axe and hand and arm dripped red. At Sir Richard's word and gesture Pluto cowered down and suffered the Indian to approach, a tall, stately figure, who, coming close beside the fire, held out to us his left hand open and upon the palm three human ears, the which he let fall to stamp upon with his moccasined foot.

"Dead, my brothers!" said he in his broken Spanish and holding up three fingers. "So be all enemies of Atlamatzin and his good friends." Saying which he stooped to cleanse himself and the axe in the stream and with the same grave serenity he came back to the fire and stretching himself thereby, composed himself to slumber.

But as for Sir Richard and myself no thought had we of sleep but sat there very silent for the most part, staring into the fire until it paled to the day and the woods around us shrilled and echoed to the chatter and cries, the piping and sweet carol of new-waked birds.

Then, having broken our fast, we prepared to set out in the early freshness of the morning, when to us came the Indian Atlamatzin and taking my hand, touched it to his breast and forehead and having done as much by Sir Richard, crossed his arms, and looking from one to other of us, spake in his halting Spanish as much as to say, "My father and brother, whither go ye?" At this Sir Richard, who it seemed knew something of the Indian tongue, gave him to understand we went eastwards towards the Gulf. Whereupon the Indian bowed gravely, answering:

"Ye be lonely, even as I, and thitherward go I many moons to what little of good, war and evil have left to me. Therefore will I company with ye an ye would have me." To the which we presently agreeing, he forthwith took his share of our burden, and with the axe at his side and our spare musket on his shoulder, went on before, threading his way by brake and thicket with such sureness of direction that we were soon out upon the open thoroughfare.

And now seeing how stoutly Sir Richard stepped out (despite the gear he bore as gun, powder horn, water bottle, etc.) what with the sweet freshness here among the trees and seeing us so well provided against circumstances, I came nigh singing for pure lightness of heart. But scarce had we gone a mile than my gaiety was damped and in this fashion.

"Here is a land of death, Martin—see yonder!" said Sir Richard and pointed to divers great birds that flapped up heavily from the way before us. Coming nearer, I saw others of the breed that quarrelled and fought and screamed and, upon our nearer approach, hopped along in a kind of torpor ere they rose on lazy wings and flew away; and coming nearer yet I saw the wherefore of their gathering and Sir Richard's words and grew sick within me. It was an Indian woman who lay where she had fallen, a dead babe clasped to dead bosom with one arm, the other shorn off at the elbow.

"A Spanish sword-stroke, Martin!" said Sir Richard, pointing to this. "God pity this poor outraged people!" And with this prayer we left these poor remains, and hasting away, heard again the heavy beat

of wings and the carrion cry of these monstrous birds.
And now I bethought me that the Indian, striding
before us, had never so much as turned and scarce
deigned a glance at this pitiful sight, as I noted to
Sir Richard.

"And yet, Martin, he brought in three Spanish ears
last night! Moreover, he is an Indian and one of the
Maya tribe that at one time were a noble people and
notable good fighters, but now slaves, alas, all save a
sorry few that do live out of the white man's reach
'mid the ruin of noble cities high up in the Cordilleras
—sic transit gloria mundi, alas!"

For three days we tramped this highway in the wake
of the Spanish treasure-convoy and came on the
remains of many of these miserable slaves who, overcome with fatigue, had fallen in their chains and being
cut free, had been left thus to perish miserably.

On this, the fourth day, we turned off from this
forest road (the which began to trend southerly); we
struck off, I say, following our Indian, into a narrow
track bearing east and by north which heartened me
much since, according to Adam's chart, this should
bring us directly towards that spot he had marked as
our rendezvous. And as we advanced, the country
changed, the woods thinned away to a rolling hill-
country, and this to rocky ways that grew ever steeper
and more difficult, and though we had no lack of water,
we suffered much by reason of the heat. And now on
our right we beheld great mountains towering high
above us, peak on peak, soaring aloft to the cloudless
heaven where blazed a pitiless sun. Indeed, so unen-
durable was this heat that we would lie panting in
some shade until the day languished and instead of
glaring sun was radiant moon to light us on our pilgrimage. And here we were often beset by dreadful
tempests where mighty winds shouted and thunder
cracked and roared most awful to be heard among these

solitary mountains. So we skirted these great mountains, by frowning precipice and dark defile, past foaming cataracts and waters that roared unseen below us.

And very thankful we were for such a guide as this Indian Atlamatzin who, grave, solemn and seldom-speaking, was never at a loss and very wise as to this wilderness and all things in it,—beast and bird, tree and herb and flower. And stoutly did Sir Richard bear himself during this weary time, plodding on hour after hour until for very shame I would call a halt, and he, albeit ready to swoon for weariness, would find breath to berate me for a laggard and protest himself able to go on, until, taking him in my arms, I would lay him in some sheltered nook and find him sound asleep before ever I could prepare our meal.

Thus held we on until towering mountain and scowling cliff sank behind and we came into a gentle country of placid streams, grassy tracts, with herb and tree and flower a very joy to the eyes.

"Martin," said Sir Richard, as we sat at breakfast beside a crystal pool, "Martin," said he, pulling at Pluto's nearest ear with sunburned fingers, "I do begin to think that all these days I have been harbouring a shadow."

"How so, sir?"

"It hath seemed to me from the first that I should leave this poor body here in Darien——"

"God forbid!" quoth I fervently.

" 'Twould be but my body, Martin; my soul would go along with you, dear lad; aye, 'twould be close by to comfort and aid and bring you safe to—her—my sweet Joan—and mayhap—with you twain—to England."

"Nay, dear sir, I had liefer you bear your body along with it. Thank God, you do grow more hearty every day. And the ague scarce troubles you——"

"Truly, God hath been very kind. I am thrice the man I was, though I limp wofully, which grieves me since it shortens the day's journey, lad. We have been already these many days and yet, as I compute, we have fully eighty miles yet to go. Alas, dear lad, how my crawling must fret you."

"Sir Richard," said I, clapping my hand on his, "no man could have endured more courageously nor with stouter heart than you—no, not even Adam Penfeather himself, so grieve not for your lameness. Adam will wait us, of this I am assured."

"What manner of man is this Adam of yours, Martin?"

"He is himself, sir, and none other like him: a little, great man, a man of cunning plots and contrivances, very bold and determined and crafty beyond words. He is moreover a notable good seaman and commander, quick of hand and eye. Dangers and difficulty are but a whetstone to set a keener edge to his abilities. He was once a chief of buccaneers and is now a baronet of England and justice of the peace, aye, and I think a member of His Majesty's Parliament beside."

"Lord, Martin, you do paint me a very Proteus; fain would I meet such a man."

"Why, so you shall, sir, and judge for yourself."

Here Sir Richard sighed and turned to gaze where Atlamatzin was busied upon a small fire he had lighted some distance away. Now, as to this Indian, if I have not been particular in his description hitherto, it is because I know not how to do so, seeing he was (to my mind) rather as one of another world, a sombre figure proud and solitary and mostly beyond my ken, though I came to know him something better towards the end and but for him should have perished miserably. Thus then, I will try to show him to you in as few words as I may.

Neither young nor old, tall and slender yet of incred-

ible strength; his features pleasing and no darker than
my own sunburned skin, his voice soft and deep, his
bearing proud and stately and of a most grave courtesy.   Marvellous quick was he and nimble save for his
tongue, he being less given to talk even than I, so that
I have known us march by the hour together and
never a word betwixt us.   Yet was he a notable good
friend, true and steadfast and loyal, as you shall
hear.

Just now (as I say) he was busy with a fire whereon
he cast an armful of wet leaves so that he had presently
a thick column of smoke ascending into the stilly air;
and now he took him one of the cloaks and covered this
smoke, stifling and fanning it aside so that it was no
more than a mist, and anon looses it into a column
again; and thus he checked or broke his smoky pillar
at irregular intervals, so that at last I needs must call
to ask him what he did.

"Brother," answered he in his grave fashion, "I talk
with my people.   In a little you shall see them answer
me."   Hereupon Sir Richard told me how in some
parts these Indians will converse long distances apart
by means of drums, by which they will send you mes-
sages quicker than any relay of post horses may go.
And presently, sure enough, from a woody upland afar
rose an answering smoke that came and went and was
answered by our fire, as in question and answer, until
at last Atlamatzin, having extinguished his fire, came
and sat him down beside us.

"Father and my brother," said he, folding his arms,
"I read a tale of blood, fire and battle at sea and along
the coast.   White men slaying white men, which is good
—so they slay enough!"

"A battle at sea?   Do you mean ships?" I questioned
uneasily.

"And on land, brother.   Spanish soldiers have been
espied wounded and yet shouting with singing and

laughing. Galleons have sailed from Porto Bello and Carthagena."

"God send Adam is not beset!" said I.

"Amen!" quoth Sir Richard. "Nay, never despond, Martin, for if he be the man you say he shall not easily be outwitted."

"Ah, sir, I think on my dear lady."

"And I also, Martin. But she is in the hands of God Who hath cherished her thus far."

"Moreover, oh, father and my brother, yonder my people do send you greeting and will entertain you for so long as you will."

"Wherefore we thank you, Atlamatzin, good friend, you and them, but if fire and battle are abroad we must on so soon as we may." So saying, Sir Richard got to his feet and we did the like and, taking up our gear, set off with what speed we might.

CHAPTER XXIX

Telleth Somewhat of a Strange City

By midday we were come in sight of this Indian city, a place strange beyond thought, it being builded in vast terraces that rose one upon another up the face of a great cliff, and embattled by divers many towers. And the nearer I came the more grew my wonder by reason of the hugeness of this structure, for these outer defences were builded of wrought stones, but of such monstrous bulk and might as seemed rather the work of sweating Titans than the labour of puny man; as indeed I told Sir Richard.

"Aye, truly, Martin," said he, "this is the abiding wonder! Here standeth the noble monument of a once great and mighty people."

In a little Atlamatzin brought us to a stair or causeway that mounted up from terrace to terrace, and behold, this stair was lined with warriors grasping shield and lance, and brave in feathered cloaks and headdresses and betwixt their ordered ranks one advancing,—an old man of a reverend bearing, clad in a black robe and on whose bosom shone and glittered a golden emblem that I took for the sun. Upon the lowest platform he halted and lifted up his hands as in greeting, whereon up went painted shield and glittering spear and from the stalwart warriors rose a lusty shout, a word thrice repeated.

And now, to my wonder, forth stepped Atlamatzin, a proud and stately figure for all his rags, and lifting one hand aloft, spake to them in voice very loud and clear, pointing to us from time to time. When he had done they shouted amain and, descending from the platform, the priest (as he proved to be) knelt before Atlamatzin to touch his heart and brow. And now came divers Indians bearing litters, the which, at Atlamatzin's word, Sir Richard and I entered and so, Pluto trotting beside us, were borne up from terrace to terrace unto the town. And I saw this had once been a goodly city though its glory was departed, its noble buildings decayed or ruinated and cheek by jowl with primitive dwellings of clay. And these greater houses were of a noble simplicity, flat-roofed and builded of a red, porous stone, in some cases coated with white cement, whiles here and there, towering high among these, rose huge structures that I took for palaces or temples, yet one and all timeworn and crumbling to decay. Before one of such, standing in a goodly square, we alighted and here found a crowd of people —men, women and children—who stood to behold us: a mild, well-featured people, orderly and of a courteous bearing, yet who stared and pointed, chattering, at sight of the dog. And if this were all of them, a pitiful few I thought them in contrast to this great square, whence opened divers wide thoroughfares, and this mighty building that soared above us, its great walls most wonderful to sight by reason of all manner of decorations and carvings wrought into the semblance of writhing serpents cunningly intertwined.

Betwixt a kind of gatehouse to right and left we entered an enclosure where stood the temple itself, reared upon terraces. Here Atlamatzin giving us to know we must leave the dog, Sir Richard tied him up, whereon Pluto, seeing us leave him, howled in remonstrance, but, obedient to Sir Richard's word, cowered to silence, yet mighty dismal to behold. And now, Atlamatzin and the High Priest leading the way, we began to climb numberless steps, and though Sir

Richard found this no small labour despite my aid,
at last we stood before the massy portal of the temple
that seemed to scowl upon us. And from the dim
interior rose a sound of voices chanting, drowned all
at once in the roll of drums and blare of trumpets as
Atlamatzin and the Priest entered, signing on us to
follow.

"Have your weapons ready, Martin!" gasped Sir
Richard. "For I have heard evil tales of blood and
sacrifice in such places as this!"

And thus side by side we stepped into the cool dimness of this strange building. Once my eyes were
accustomed to the gloom, I stood amazed by the vast
extent of this mighty building and awed by the wonder
of it. Midway burned a dim fire whose small flame
flickered palely; all round us, huge and mountainous,
rose the shapes of strange deities wonderfully wrought;
round about the altar fire were grouped many black-
robed priests and hard by this fire stood a thing that
brought back memory of Adam Penfeather his words
—of how he had fought for his life on the death-stone;
and now, beholding this grim thing, I shifted round
my sword and felt if my pistols were to hand. And
now rose Atlamatzin's voice, rumbling in the dimness
high overhead, and coming to us, he took us each by
the hand and, leading us forward, spake awhile to the
motionless priests, who, when he had done, came about
us with hands uplifted in greeting. And now
Atlamatzin spake us on this wise:

"Father and my brother, well do I know ye have
clean hearts despite your pale skins, so do I make ye
welcome and free of this city that once was overruled
by my forefathers. And because ye are white men,
loving all such foolish things as all white men do love,
follow me!"

Saying which, he brought us before one of those
great idols that glared down on us. I saw him lift

one hand, then started back from the square of darkness that yawned suddenly as to engulf us.   Taking a torch, Atlamatzin led us down steps and along a broad passage beneath the temple and so into a vasty chamber where lay that which gave back the light he bore; everywhere about us was the sheen of gold.   In ordered piles, in great heaps, in scattered pieces it lay, wrought into a thousand fantastic shapes, as idols, serpents, basins, pots and the like,—a treasure beyond the telling.

"Behold the white man's God, the cause of my people's woes, the ruin of our cities, of blood and battle!"

And here he gives us to understand this wealth was ours if we would; all or such of it as we might bear away with us.   Whereupon I shook my head and Sir Richard told him that of more use to him than all this treasure would be pen, inkhorn and paper, and a compass.   Nothing speaking, Atlamatzin turned, and by a very maze of winding passageways brought us up the steps and so to a great and lofty chamber or hall where lay a vast medley of things: arms and armour, horse furniture and Spanish gear of every sort, and in one corner a small brass cannon, mounted on wheels. Amongst all of which Sir Richard began searching and had his patience rewarded, for presently he came on that he desired; viz: a travelling writing case with pens, paper, and a sealed bottle of ink, though why he should want such was beyond me, as I told him, whereat he did but smile, nothing speaking.

So back we came and unloosed our dog (and he mighty rejoiced to see us) whereafter, by Atlamatzin's command, we were lodged in a chamber very sumptuous and with servants observant to our every want; for our meals were dishes a-plenty, savoury and excellent well cooked and seasoned, and for our drink was milk, or water cunningly flavoured with fruits, as good as any wine, to my thinking. And cups and platters, nay, the very pots, were all of pure gold.

This night, having bathed me in a small bathhouse adjacent and very luxurious, I get me to bed early (which was no more than a mat) but Sir Richard, seated upon the floor hard by (for of chairs there were none), Sir Richard, I say, must needs fall to with pen and ink, the great hound drowsing beside him, so that, lulled by the soft scratching of his busy quill, I presently slumbered also.

Next morning I awoke late to find Sir Richard squatted where he had sat last night, but this time, instead of writing case, across his knees lay a musket, and he was busied in setting a flint to the lock.

"Why, sir—what now?" I questioned.

"A musket, lad, and fifty-and-five others in the corner yonder and all serviceable, which is well."

Now as I stared at him, his bowed figure and long white hair, there was about him (despite his benevolent expression) a certain grim, fighting look that set me wondering; moreover, upon the air I heard a stir that seemed all about us, a faint yet ominous clamour.

"Sir," quoth I, getting to my feet, "what's to do?"

"Battle, Martin!" said he, testing the musket's action.

"Ha!" cried I, catching up my sword. "Are we beset?"

"By an army of Spaniards and hostile Indians, Martin. In the night came Atlamatzin to say news had come of Indians from the West, ancient enemies of this people, led on by Spanish soldiers, cavalry and arquebuseros, and bidding us fly and save ourselves before the battle joined. But you were asleep, Martin, and besides, it seemed ill in us, that had eaten their bread, to fly and leave this poor folk to death—and worse——"

"True enough, sir," said I, buckling my weapons

about me, "but do you dream that we, you and I, can hinder such?"

" 'Twere at least commendable in us to so endeavour, Martin. Nor is it thing so impossible, having regard to these fifty-and-five muskets and the brass cannon, seeing there is powder and shot abundant."

"How then—must we stay and fight?" I demanded. And beholding the grim set of his mouth and chin, at such odds with his white hair and gentle eyes, I knew that it must be so indeed.

" 'Twas so I thought, Martin," said he a little humbly, and laying his hands upon my shoulders, "but only for myself, dear lad, I fight better than I walk, so will I stay and make this my cumbersome body of some little use, perchance; but as for thee, dear and loved lad, I would have you haste on——"

"Enough, sir," quoth I, catching his hands in mine, "if you must stay to fight, so do I."

"Tush, Martin!" said he, mighty earnest. "Be reasonable! Atlamatzin hath vowed, supposing we beat off our assailants, to provide me bearers and a litter, so shall I travel at mine ease and over-take you very soon; wherefore, I bid you go—for her sake!"

But finding me no whit moved by this or any other reason he could invent, he alternate frowned and sighed, and thereafter, slipping his arm in mine, brought me forth to show me such dispositions as he had caused to be made for the defence. Thus came we out upon the highest terrace, Pluto at our heels, and found divers of the Indians labouring amain to fill and set up baskets of loose earth after the manner of fascines, and showed me where he had caused them to plant our cannon where it might sweep that stair I have mentioned, and well screened from the enemy's observation and shel-tered from his fire. And hard beside the gun stood barrels of musket balls, and round-shot piled very orderly, and beyond these, powder a-plenty in covered kegs.

And now he showed me pieces of armour, that is, a vizored headpiece or armet, with cuirass, backplates, pauldrons and vambraces, all very richly gilded, the which it seemed he had chosen for my defence.

"So, then, sir, you knew I should stay?"

"Indeed, Martin," he confessed, a little discountenanced, "I guessed you might." But I (misliking to be so confined) would have none of this gilded armour until, seeing his distress, I agreed thereto if he would do the like; so we presently armed each other and I for one mighty hot and uncomfortable.

Posted upon this, the highest terrace, at every vantage point were Indians armed with bows and arrows —men and women, aye and children—and all gazing ever and anon towards that belt of forest to the West where it seemed Atlamatzin, with ten chosen warriors, was gone to watch the approach of the invading host. Presently, from these greeny depths came a distant shot followed by others in rapid succession, and after some while, forth of the woods broke six figures that we knew for Atlamatzin and five of the ten, at sight of whom spear-points glittered and a lusty shout went up.

"See now, Martin," quoth Sir Richard, speaking quick and incisive, a grim and warlike figure in his armour, for all his stoop and limping gait, "here's the way on't: let the Indians shoot their arrows as they may (poor souls!) but we wait until the enemy be a-throng upon the stair yonder, then we open on them with our cannon here,—'tis crammed to the muzzle with musket balls; then whiles you reload, I will to my fifty-and-five muskets yonder and let fly one after t'other, by which time you, having our brass piece ready, will reload so many o' the muskets as you may and so, God aiding, we will so batter these merciless

Dons they shall be glad to give over their bloody
attempt and leave these poor folk in peace."

As he ended, came Atlamatzin, telling us he had
fallen suddenly on the enemy's van and slain divers of
them, showing us his axe bloody, and so away to hearten
his people.

At last, forth of the forest marched the enemy, rank
on rank, a seemingly prodigious company. First rode
horsemen a score, and behind these I counted some
sixty musketeers and pikemen as many, marching very
orderly and flashing back the sun from their armour,
while behind these again came plumed Indians beyond
count, fierce, wild figures that leapt and shouted high
and shrill very dreadful to hear. On they came, leaping and dancing from the forest, until it seemed they
would never end, nearer and nearer until we might see
their faces and thus behold how these Spaniards talked
and laughed with each other as about a matter of little
moment. Indeed, it angered me to see with what careless assurance these steel-clad Spaniards advanced
against us in their insolent might, and bold in the
thought that they had nought to fear save Indian
arrows and lances and they secure in their armour.
Halting below the first terrace, they forthwith began
assault, for whiles divers of the pikemen began to
ascend the stairway, followed by their Indian allies,
the musketeers let fly up at us with their pieces to
cover their comrades' advance and all contemptuous of
the arrows discharged against them. But hard beside
the cannon stood Sir Richard, watching keen-eyed, and
ever and anon blowing on the slow-match he had made,
waiting until the stairway was choked with the glittering helmets and tossing feathers of the assailants.

A deafening roar, a belch of flame and smoke that
passing, showed a sight I will not seek to describe;
nor did I look twice, but fell to work with sponge and
rammer, loading this death-dealing piece as quickly

as I might, while louder than the awful wailing that
came from that gory shambles rose a wild hubbub from
their comrades,—shouts and cries telling their sudden
panic and consternation. But as they stood thus in
huddled amaze, Sir Richard opened on them with his
muskets, firing in rapid succession and with aim so
deadly that they forthwith turned and ran for it, nor
did they check or turn until they were out of range.
Then back limped Sir Richard, his cheek flushed, his
eyes bright and fierce in the shade of his helmet, his
voice loud and vibrant with the joy of battle, and seeing how far the gun was recoiled, summoned divers of
the Indians to urge it back into position; while this
was doing, down upon this awful stair leapt Atlamatzin
and his fellows and had soon made an end of such
wounded as lay there.

"I pray God," cried Sir Richard, harsh-voiced, as
he struck flint and steel to relight his match, "I pray
God this may suffice them!"

And beholding the wild disorder of our assailants,
I had great hopes this was so indeed, but as I watched,
they reformed their ranks and advanced again, but
with their Indians in the van, who suddenly found
themselves with death before them and behind, for the
Spanish musketeers had turned their pieces against
them to force them on to the attacks. So, having no
choice, these poor wretches came on again, leaping and
screaming their battle cries until the stair was a-throng
with them; on and up they rushed until Death met
them in roaring flame and smoke. But now all about
us was the hum of bullets, most of which whined harmlessly overhead, though some few smote the wall behind
us. But small chance had I to heed such, being hard-
set to prime and load as, time after time, these poor
Indians, driven on by their cruel masters, rushed, and
time after time were swept away; and thus we fought
the gun until the sweat ran from me and I panted and

cursed my stifling armour, stripping it from me piece
by piece as occasion offered. And thus I took a scathe
from bullet or splinter of stone, yet heeded not until
I sank down sick and spent and roused to find Pluto
licking my face and thereafter to see Sir Richard kneeling over me, his goodly armour dinted and scarred by
more than one chance bullet.

"Drink!" he commanded, and set water to my lips,
the which mightily refreshed me.

"Sir, what o' the fight?" I questioned.

"Done, lad, so far as we are concerned," said he.
"Atlamatzin fell upon 'em with all his powers and
routed them—hark!"

Sure enough, I heard the battle roar away into the
forest and beyond until, little by little, it sank to a
murmurous hum and died utterly away. But all about
us were other sounds, and getting unsteadily to my
legs, I saw the plain 'twixt town and forest thick-strewn
with the fallen.

"So then the town is saved, sir?"

"God be praised, Martin!"

"Why, then, let us on—to meet my dear lady!"
But now came an Indian to bathe my hurt, an ugly
tear in my upper arm, whereto he set a certain balsam
and a dressing of leaves and so bound it up very deftly
and to my comfort.

And now was I seized of a fierce desire to be gone;
I burned in a fever to tramp those weary miles that
lay 'twixt me and my lady Joan; wherefore, heedless
alike of my own weakness, of Sir Richard's remonstrances and weariness, or aught beside in my own
fevered desire, I set out forthwith, seeing, as in a
dream, the forms of Indians, men, women and children,
who knelt and cried to us as in gratitude or farewell;
fast I strode, all unmindful of the old man who plodded
so patiently, limping as fast as he might to keep pace
with me, heeding but dimly his appeals, his cries, hast-

ing on and on until, stumbling at last, I sank upon my
knees and, looking about, found myself alone and night
coming down upon me apace. Then was I seized of
pity for him and myself and a great yearning for my
lady, and sinking upon my face I wept myself to sleep.

CHAPTER XXX

We Resume Our Journey

I waked in a place of trees, very still and quiet save for the crackle of the fire that blazed near by. Close beside me lay my musket; pendant from a branch within reach dangled my sword. Hereupon, finding myself thus solitary, I began to call on Sir Richard and wondered to hear my voice so weak; yet I persisted in my shouting and after some while heard a joyous bark, and to me bounded Pluto to rub himself against me and butt at me with his great head. While I was caressing this good friend, cometh Sir Richard himself and in his hand a goodly fish much like to a trout.

"Lord, Martin!" said he, sitting beside me, " 'tis well art thyself again, lad. Last evening you must set out, and night upon us, must stride away like a madman and leave me alone; but for this good dog I should ha' lost you quite. See now, lad, what I have caught for our breakfast. I was a notable good angler in the old days and have not lost my cunning, it seems."

Now as he showed me his fish and set about gutting and preparing it, I could not but mark his drawn and haggard look, despite his brave bearing, and my heart smote me.

"Sir, you are sick!" quoth I.

"Nay, Martin, I am well enough and able to go on as soon as you will. But for the present, rest awhile, lest the fever take you again, this cloak 'neath your head—so!"

"What o'clock is it?"

"Scarce noon and the sun very hot."

"How came I here in the shade?"

"I dragged you, Martin. Now sleep, lad, and I'll to my cooking."

At this I protested I had no mind for sleep, yet presently slumbered amain, only to dream vilely of fire and of Adam and his fellows in desperate battle, and above the din of fight heard my lady calling on my name as one in mortal extremity and waking in sweating panic, my throbbing head full of this evil vision, was for setting out instantly to her succour. But at Sir Richard's desire I stayed to gulp down such food as he had prepared, telling him meanwhile of my vision and something comforted by his assurance that dreams went by contrary. Howbeit, the meal done, we set out once more, bearing due northeast by the compass Sir Richard had brought from the Maya city. So we journeyed through this tangled wilderness, my head full of strange and evil fancies, cursing the wound that sapped my strength so that I must stumble for very weakness, yet dreaming ever of my lady's danger, struggling up and on until I sank to lie and curse or weep because of my helplessness.

Very evil times were these, wherein I moved in a vague world, sometimes aware of Sir Richard's patient, plodding form, of the dog trotting before, of misty mountains, of rushing streams that must be crossed, of glaring heats and grateful shadow; sometimes I lay dazzled by a blazing sun, sometimes it was the fire and Sir Richard's travel-worn figure beyond, sometimes the calm serenity of stars, but ever and always in my mind was a growing fear, a soul-blasting dread lest our journey be vain, lest the peril that methought threatened Joan be before us and we find her dead. And this cruel thought was like a whip that lashed me to a frenzy, so that despite wound and weakness I would drive my fainting body on, pursuing the phantom of her I sought and oft calling miserably upon her name like the madman I was; all of the which I learned after from Sir Richard. For, of an early morning I waked to find myself alone, but a fire of sticks burned brightly and against an adjacent rock stood our two muskets, orderly and to hand.

Now as I gazed about, I was aware of frequent sighings hard by and going thitherward, beheld Sir Richard upon his knees, absorbed in a passion of prayer, his furrowed cheeks wet with tears. But beyond this I was struck with the change in him, his haggard face burned nigh black with fierce suns, his garments rent and tattered, his poor body more bent and shrunken than I had thought. Before him sat Pluto, wagging his tail responsive to every passionate gesture of those reverently clasped hands, but who, espying me, uttered his deep bark and came leaping to welcome me; whereupon, seeing I was discovered, I went to Sir Richard and, his prayer ended, lifted him in my arms.

"Ah, Martin, dear lad," said he, embracing me likewise, "surely God hath answered my prayer. You are yourself again." And now, he sitting beside the fire whiles I prepared such food as we had, he told me how for five days I had been as one distraught, wandering haphazard and running like any madman, calling upon my lady's name, and that he should have lost me but for the dog.

"Alas, dear sir," quoth I, abashed by this recital, "I fear in my fool's madness I have worn you out and nigh beyond endurance."

"Nay, Martin," said he, "it doth but teach me what I knew, that lusty youth and feeble age are ill travelling companions, for needs must you go, your soul ever ahead of you, yet schooling your pace to mine, and for this I do love you so that I would I were dead and you free to speed on your strength——"

"Never say so, dear father," quoth I, folding my arm about his drooping form, "my strength shall be yours henceforth."

And presently he grew eager to be gone, but seeing me unwilling, grew the more insistent to travel so far as we might before the scorching heats should overtake us. So we started, I carrying his musket beside my own and despite his remonstrances.

An evil country this, destitute of trees and all vegetation save small bushes few and prickly cactus a-many, a desolation of grim and jagged rocks and barren, sandy wastes full of sun-glare and intolerable heat. And now, our water being gone, we began to be plagued with thirst and a great host of flies so bold as to settle on our mouths, nostrils and eyes, so that we must be for ever slapping and brushing them away. Night found us faint and spent and ravenous for water and none to be found, and to add further to our agonies, these accursed flies were all about us still, singing and humming, and whose bite set up a tickling itch, so that what with these and our thirst we got little or no rest.

"Martin," said Sir Richard, hearing me groan, "we should be scarce four days from the sea by my reckoning——"

"Aye," said I, staring up at the glory of stars, "but how if we come on no water? Our journey shall end the sooner, methinks."

"True, Martin," said he, "but we are sure to find water soon or late——"

"God send it be soon!" I groaned. Here he sets himself to comfort Pluto who lay betwixt us, panting miserably, with lolling tongue or snapping fiercely at these pestilent flies.

And thus we lay agonising until the moon rose and then, by common consent, we stumbled on, seeking our great desire. And now as I went, my mouth parched, my tongue thickening to the roof of my mouth, I must

needs think of plashing brooks, of bubbling rills, of
sweet and pellucid streams, so that my torment was
redoubled, yet we dared not stop, even when day came.

Then forth of a pitiless heaven blazed a cruel sun
to scorch us, thereby adding to this agony of thirst
that parched us where we crawled with fainting steps,
our sunken eyes seeking vainly for the kindly shade of
some tree in this arid desolation. And always was
my mind obsessed by that dream of gurgling brooks
and bubbling rills; and now I would imagine I was
drinking long, cool draughts, and thrusting leathern
tongue 'twixt cracking lips, groaned in sharper agony.
So crept we on, mile after mile, hoping the next would
show us some blessed glimpse of water, and always dis-
appointed until at last it seemed that here was our
miserable end.

"Martin," gasped Sir Richard, sinking in my failing
clasp, his words scarce articulate, "I can go no farther—leave me, sweet son—'tis better I die here—go
you on———"

"No!" groaned I, and seeing Sir Richard nigh to
swooning, I took him in my arms. Reeling and staggering I bore him on, my gaze upon a few scattered
rocks ahead of us where we might at least find shade
from this murderous sun. Thus I struggled on until
my strength failed and I sank to this burning sand
where it seemed we were doomed to perish after all, here
in this pitiless wild where even the dog had deserted us.
And seeing Death so near, I clasped Sir Richard ever
closer and strove to tell him something of my love for
him, whereupon he raised one feeble hand to touch my
drooping head.

Now as I babbled thus, I heard a lazy flap of wings
and lifting weary eyes, beheld divers of these great birds
that, settling about, hopped languidly towards us and
so stood to watch us, raffling their feathers and croaking hoarsely. So I watched them, and well-knowing

what they portended, drew forth a pistol and, cocking
it, had it ready to hand.   But as I did so they broke
into shrill clamour and, rising on heavy wings, soared
away as came Pluto to leap about us, uttering joyous
barks and butting at us with his head.   And then I
saw him all wet, nay, as I gazed on him, disbelieving
my eyes, he shook himself, sprinkling us with blessed
water.   Somehow I was upon my feet and, taking Sir
Richard's swooning body across my shoulder, I stumbled on towards that place of rocks, Pluto running on
before and turning ever and anon to bark, as bidding
me hasten.   So at last, panting and all foredone, came
I among these rocks and saw them open to a narrow
cleft that gave upon a gorge a-bloom with flowers,
a very paradise; and here, close to hand, a little pool
fed by a rill or spring that bubbled up amid these
mossy rocks.

So took I this life-giving water in my two hands
and dashed it in Sir Richard's face, and he, opening
his eyes, uttered a hoarse cry of rapture.   And so we
drank, kneeling side by side.   Yet our throats and
tongues so swollen we could scarce swallow at the first,
and yet these scant drops a very ecstasy.   But when
I would have drunk my fill, Sir Richard stayed me lest
I do myself an injury and I, minding how poor souls
had killed themselves thus, drank but moderately as he
bade me, yet together we plunged our heads and arms
into this watery delight, praising God and laughing
for pure joy and thankfulness.   Then, the rage of our
thirst something appeased, we lay down within this
shadow side by side and presently fell into a most
blessed slumber.

I waked suddenly to a piteous whining and, starting
up, beheld Pluto crawling towards me, his flank trans-
fixed with an Indian arrow.   Up I sprang to wake Sir
Richard and peer down into the shadowy gorge below,
but saw no more than flowering thickets and bush-girt

rock. But as I gazed thus, musket in hand, Sir Richard gave fire and while the report yet rang and echoed, I saw an Indian spring up from amid these bushes and go rolling down into the thickets below.

"One, Martin!" quoth Sir Richard and, giving me his piece to reload, turned to minister to Pluto's hurt, where he lay whining and whimpering. Suddenly an arrow struck the rock hard beside me and then came a whizzing shower, whereupon we took such shelter as offered and whence we might retort upon them with our shot. And after some while, as we lay thus, staring down into the gorge, came the report of a musket and a bullet whipped betwixt us.

"Lord, Martin!" quoth Sir Richard cheerily, his eyes kindling. "It was vastly unwise to fall asleep by this well in so thirsty a country; 'tis a known place and much frequented, doubtless. Wisdom doth urge a retreat so soon as you have filled our water bottles; meantime I will do all I may to dissuade our assailants from approaching too near."

So saying, he levelled his piece and, dwelling on his aim, fired, whiles I, screened from bullets and arrows alike, filled our flasks and doing so, espied a small cave, excellent suited to our defence and where two determined men might hold in check a whole army.

Hereupon I summoned Sir Richard who, seeing this cave commanded the gorge and might only be carried in front, approved it heartily, so thither we repaired, taking Pluto with us and him very woful. And lying thus in our little fort we laid out our armament, that is, our two muskets and four pistols, and took stock of our ammunition, I somewhat dashed to find we had but thirty charges betwixt us, the pistols included. Sir Richard, on the other hand, seemed but the more resolute and cheery therefor.

"For look now, Martin," said he, cocking his musket and levelling it betwixt the boulders we had piled to our better defence, "here we have fifteen lives, or say twenty, though you are better with sword than musket I take it; should these not suffice, then we have two excellent swords and lastly our legs, indifferent bad as regards mine own, but in a little 'twill be black dark, the moon doth not rise till near dawn. So here are we snug for the moment and very able to our defence these many hours, God be thanked!" And thus he of his own indomitable spirit cheered me. Suddenly he pulled trigger and as the smoke cleared I saw his bullet had sped true, for amid certain rocks below us a man rose up, clad in Spanish half-armour, and sinking forward, lay there motionless, plain to our view.

"Two!" quoth Sir Richard, and fell to reloading his piece, wadding the charge with strips from his ragged garments.

The fall of this Spaniard caused no little stir among our unseen assailants, for the air rang with fierce outcries and the shrill battle hootings of the Indians, and a shower of arrows rattled among the rocks about us and thereafter a volley of shot, and no scathe to us.

"War is a hateful thing!" quoth Sir Richard suddenly. "See yon Spaniard I shot, God forgive me—hark how he groaneth, poor soul!" And he showed me the Spaniard, who writhed ever and anon where he lay across the rock and wailed feebly for water. "Methinks 'twere merciful to end his sufferings, Martin!"

"Mayhap, sir, though we have few enough charges to spare!"

"Thus speaketh cold prudence and common sense, Martin, and yet——"

But here the matter was put beyond dispute for, even as Sir Richard levelled his musket, the wounded Spaniard slipped and rolled behind the rock and lay quite hid save for a hand and arm that twitched feebly ever and anon.

"And he was crying for water!" sighed Sir Richard. "Thirst is an agony, as we do know. Hark, he crieth yet! 'Twere act commendable to give drink to a dying man, enemy though he be."

"Most true, sir, but—nay, what would you?" I said, grasping his arm as he made to rise.

"Endeavour as much good as I may in the little of life left to me, Martin. The poor soul lieth none so far and——"

"Sir—sir!" quoth I, tightening my hold. "You would be shot ere you had gone a yard—are ye mad indeed or—do you seek death?" Now at this he was silent, and I felt him trembling.

"This is as God willeth, Martin!" said he at last. "Howbeit I must go; prithee loose me, dear lad!"

"Nay!" cried I harshly. "If you will have our enemy drink, I shall bear it myself——"

"No, no!" cried he, grappling me in turn as I rose. "What I may do you cannot—be reasonable, Martin —you bulk so much greater than I, they cannot fail of such a mark——"

Now as we argued the matter thus, each mighty determined, Pluto set up a joyous barking and, rising on three legs, stood with ears cocked and tail wagging, the which put me in no small perplexity until, all at once, certain bushes that grew hard by swayed gently and forth of the leaves stepped an Indian clad for battle, like a great chief or cacique (as 'tis called) for on arm and breast and forehead gold glittered, and immediately we knew him for Atlamatzin.

"Greeting to ye, father and brother!" said he, saluting us in his grave and stately fashion. "Atlamatzin and his people are full of gratitude to ye and because ye are great and notable warriors, scornful of the white man's God, Atlamatzin and his warriors have followed to do ye homage and bring ye safe to your journey's end, and finding ye, lo! we find

also our enemies, whose eyes seeing nought but ye two,
behold nought of the death that creepeth about them;
so now, when the shadow shall kiss the small rock
yonder, do you make your thunder and in that
moment shall Atlamatzin smite them to their destruction and, if the gods spare him, shall surely find ye
again that are his father and brother!"

Something thus spake he below his breath in his
halting Spanish, very grave and placid, then saluting
us, was gone swift and silent as he came.

"An inch!" quoth Sir Richard, pointing to the
creeping shadow and so we watched this fateful shade
until it was come upon the rock, whereupon I let off
my piece and Sir Richard a moment after, and like an
echo to these shots rose sudden dreadful clamour,
shouts, the rapid discharge of firearms; but wilder,
fiercer, and louder than all the shrill and awful Indian
battle cry.   And now, on bush-girt slopes to right and
left was bitter strife, a close-locked fray that burst
suddenly asunder and swirled down till pursued and
pursuer were lost amid that tangle of blooming thickets where it seemed the battle clamoured awhile, then
roared away as the enemy broke and fled before the
sudden furious onset of Atlamatzin's warriors.

As for us, we lay within our refuge, nor stirred
until this din of conflict was but a vague murmur, for
though we might see divers of the fallen where they
lay, these neither stirred nor made any outcry since
it seemed their business was done effectually.

"And now, Martin," said Sir Richard, rising, " 'tis
time we got hence lest any of our assailants come
a-seeking us."

So being out of the cave, I set myself to see that
we had all our gear to hand, to empty and refill my
flask with this good water and the like until, missing
Sir Richard, I turned to behold him already hard
upon that rock where lay the wounded Spaniard, Pluto

limping at his heels. Being come to the rock, Sir Richard unslung his water bottle and stopped, was blotted out in sudden smoke-cloud, and, even as the report reached me, I began to run, raving like any madman; and thus, panting out prayers and curses, I came where stood Sir Richard leaning against this rock, one hand clasped to his side, and the fingers of this hand horribly red. And now I was aware of a shrill screaming that, ending suddenly, gave place to dreadful snarling and worrying sound, but heedless of aught but Sir Richard's wound, I ran to bear him in my arms as he fell.

"Oh, Martin," said he faintly, looking up at me with his old brave smile, " 'tis come at last—my journeying is done——"

Scarce knowing what I did, I gathered him to my bosom and bore him back to the cave; and now, when I would have staunched his hurt, he shook feeble head.

"Let be, dear lad," said he, "nought shall avail— not all your care and love—for here is friend Death at last come to lift me up to a merciful God!"

None the less I did all that I might for his hurt save to probe for the pistol ball that was gone too deep. And presently, as I knelt beside him in a very agony of helplessness, cometh Pluto, fouled with blood other than his own, and limping hither, cast himself down, his great paw across Sir Richard's legs, licking at those weary feet that should tramp beside us no farther. And thus night found us.

"Martin," said Sir Richard suddenly, his voice strong, "bear me out where I may behold the stars, for I—ever loved them and the wonder of them—even in my—unregenerate days." So I bore him without, and indeed the heavens were a glory.

"Dear lad," said he, clasping my hand, "grieve not that I die, for Death is my friend—hath marched beside me these many weary miles, yet spared me long enough to know and love you ever better for the man you are.—Now as to Joan, my daughter, I—grieve not to see her—but—God's will be done, lad, Amen. And because I knew I must die here in Darien, I writ her a letter—'tis here in my bosom—give it her, saying I—ever loved her greatly more than I let her guess and that —by my sufferings I was a something better man, being —humbler, gentler, and of—a contrite heart. And now, Martin—thou that didst forgive and love thine enemy, saving him at thine own peril and using him as thy dear friend—my time is come—I go into the infinite— Death's hand is on me but—a kindly hand—lifting me —to my God—my love shall go with ye—all the way —you and her—alway. Into Thy hands, O·Lord!"

And thus died my enemy, like the brave and noble gentleman he was, his head pillowed upon my bosom, his great soul steadfast and unfearing to the last.

And I, a lost and desolate wretch, wept at my bitter loss and cried out against the God who had snatched from me this the only man I had ever truly loved and honoured. And bethinking me of his patient endurance, I thought I might have been kinder and more loving in many ways and to my grief was added bitter self-reproaches.

At last, the day appearing, I arose and, taking up my dead, bore him down to the gorge and presently came upon a quiet spot unsullied by the foulness of battle; and here, amid the glory of these blooming thickets, I laid him to his last rest, whiles Pluto watched me, whining ever and anon. And when I had made an end, I fell on my knees and would have prayed, yet could not.

So back went I at last, slow-footed, to the cave and thus came on Sir Richard's letter, it sealed and superscribed thus:

Unto my loved daughter, Joan Brandon.

And beholding this beloved name, a great heart-sickness came on me with a vision of a joy I scarce dared think on that had been mine but for my blind selfishness and stubborn will; and with this was a knowledge of all the wasted years and a loss unutterable. And thus my grief took me again, so that this letter was wetted with tears of bitter remorse.

At last I arose (the letter in my bosom) and girding my weapons about me (choosing that musket had been Sir Richard's) stood ready to begone. But now, missing the dog, I called to him, and though he howled in answer, he came not, wherefore following his outcries, they brought me to Sir Richard's grave and Pluto crouched thereby, whimpering. At my command he limped towards me a little way, then crawled back again, and this he did as often as I called, wherefore at last I turned away and, setting forth in my loneliness, left these two together.

CHAPTER XXXI

I Meet a Madman

Having taken my bearings, I set off at speed nor did I stay for rest or refreshment until I had traversed many miles and the sun's heat was grown nigh intolerable. So I halted in such shade as the place offered, and having eaten and drunk, I presently fell asleep and awoke to find the day far spent and to look around for Sir Richard as had become my wont. And finding him not, in rushed memory to smite me anew with his death, so that I must needs fall to thinking of his lonely grave so far behind me in these wilds; wherefore in my sorrow I bitterly cursed this land of cruel heat, of quenchless thirst and trackless, weary ways, and falling on my knees, I prayed as I had never prayed, humbly and with no thought of self, save that God would guide me henceforth and make me more worthy the great health and strength wherewith He had blessed me, and, if it so pleased Him, bring me safe at last to my dear lady's love. Thus after some while I arose and went my solitary way, and it seemed that I was in some ways a different and a better man, by reason of Sir Richard his death and my grief therefor.

And as the darkness of night deepened about me and I striding on, guided by the dim-seen needle of my compass, often I would fancy Sir Richard's loved form beside me or the sound of his limping step in my ear, so that in the solitude of this vasty wilderness I was not solitary, since verily his love seemed all about me yet, even as he had promised.

All this night I travelled apace nor stayed until I fell for very weariness and lying there, ate such food as I had, not troubling to light a fire, and fell asleep. Now as I lay, it seemed that Sir Richard stood above me, his arm reached out as to fend from me some evil thing, yet when he spoke, voice and words were those of Joanna:

"Hola, Martino fool, and must I be for ever saving your life?"

And now I saw it was Joanna indeed who stood there, clad in her male attire, hand on hip, all glowing, insolent beauty; but as I stared she changed, and I saw her as I had beheld her last, her gown and white bosom all dabbled with her blood, but on her lips was smile ineffably tender and in her eyes the radiance of a joy great beyond all telling.

"Lover Martino," said she, bending above me, "I went for you to death, unfearing, for only the dead do know the perfect love, since death is more than life, so is my love around you for ever—wake, beloved!"

Herewith she bent and touched me and, waking, I saw this that touched me was no more than the leafy end of a branch 'neath which I chanced to lie,—but pendant from this swaying branch I espied a monstrous shape that writhed toward me in the dimness; beholding which awful, silent thing I leapt up, crying out for very horror and staying but to snatch my gun, sped from this evil place, nigh sick with dread and loathing.

The moon was up, dappling these gloomy shades with her pure light and as I sped, staring fearfully about me, I espied divers of these great serpents twisted among the boughs overhead, and monstrous bat-like shapes that flitted hither and thither so that I ran in sweating panic until the leafage, above and

around me, thinning out, showed me the full splendour
of this tropic moon and a single great tree that soared
mightily aloft to thrust out spreading branches high
in air. Now as I approached this, I checked suddenly
and, cocking my musket, called out in fierce challenge,
for round the bole of this tree peeped the pallid oval
of a face; thrice I summoned, and getting no answer,
levelled and fired point-blank, the report of my piece
waking a thousand echoes and therewith a chattering
and screeching from the strange beasts that stirred
in the denser woods about me; and there (maugre my
shot), there, I say, was the face peering at me evilly
as before. But now something in its stark and utter
stillness clutched me with new dread as, slinging my
musket and drawing pistol, I crept towards this pallid,
motionless thing and saw it for a face indeed, with
mouth foolishly agape, and presently beheld this for
a man fast-bound to the tree and miserably dead by
torture. And coming near this awful, writhen form,
I apprehended something about it vaguely familiar,
and suddenly (being come close) saw this poor body
was clad as an English sailor; perceiving which, I
shivered in sudden dread and made haste to recharge
my musket, spilling some of my precious powder in
my hurry, and so hasting from this awful thing with
this new dread gnawing at my heart.

Presently before me rose steepy crags very wild
and desolate, but nowhere a tree to daunt me. Here
I halted and my first thought to light a fire, since the
gloomy thickets adjacent and the sombre forests
beyond were full of unchancy noises, stealthy rustlings, shrill cries and challengings very dismal to hear.
But in a while, my fire burning brightly, sword loose in
scabbard, musket across my knee and my back 'gainst
the rock, I fell to pondering my dream and the wonder
of it, of Joanna and her many noble qualities, of her
strange, tempestuous nature; and lifting my gaze to

the wonder of stars, it seemed indeed that she, though dead, yet lived and must do so for ever, even as these quenchless lights of heaven; and thus I revolved the mystery of life and death until sleep stole upon me.

I waked suddenly to snatch up my musket and peer at the dim figure sitting motionless beyond the dying fire, then, as a long arm rose in salutation, lowered my weapon, mighty relieved to recognise the Indian, Atlamatzin.

"Greeting, my brother," quoth he; "all yesterday I followed on thy track, but my brother is swift and Atlamatzin weary of battle."

"And what of the battle?"

"Death, my brother: as leaves of the forest lie the Maya warriors, but of our enemies none return. So am I solitary, my work done, and solitary go I to Pachacamac that lieth beside the Great Sea. But there is an empty place betwixt us, brother—what of the old cacique so cunning in battle—what of my father?"

Here, as well as I might, I told him of Sir Richard's cruel murder; at this he was silent a great while, staring sombrely into the fire. Suddenly he started and pointed upward at a great, flitting shape that hovered above us and sprang to his feet as one sore affrighted, whereupon I told him this was but a bat (though of monstrous size) and could nothing harm us.

"Nay, brother, here is Zotzilaha Chimalman that reigneth in the House of Bats, for though Atlamatzin was born without fear, yet doth he respect the gods, in especial Zotzilaha Chimalman!"

Now hereupon, seeing the dawn was at hand, I rose, nor waited a second bidding for, gods or no, this seemed to me a place abounding in terrors and strange evils, and I mighty glad of this Indian's fellowship. So up I rose, tightening my girdle, but scarce had I shouldered my musket than I stood motionless, my heart a-leaping, staring towards a certain part of the surrounding woods whence had sounded a sudden cry. And hearkening to this, back rushed that sick dread I had known already, for this was a human cry, very desolate and wistful, and the words English:

"Jeremy, ahoy—oho, Jeremy!"

Breaking the spell that numbed me, I made all haste to discover the wherefore of these dolorous sounds and plunged into the noxious gloom of the woods, Atlamatzin hard on my heels; and ever as we went, guided by these hoarse shouts, the dawn lightened about us.

Thus presently I espied a forlorn figure afar off, crouched beneath a tree, a strange, wild figure that tossed a knife from hand to hand and laughed and chattered 'twixt his shouting.

"Ahoy, Jerry, I'm all adrift—where be you? I'm out o' my soundings, lad—'tis me—'tis Dick—your old messmate as drank many a pint wi' you alongside Deptford Pool—Ahoy, Jeremy!"

Now espying us where we stood, he scrambled to his feet, peering at us, through his tangled hair; then, dropping his knife, comes running, his arms outstretched, then checks as suddenly and stares me over with a cunning leer.

"Avast, Dick!" said he, smiting himself on ragged breast. "This bean't poor Jerry—poor Jerry ain't half his size—a little man be Jeremy, not so big as Sir Adam——"

"Who!" cried I and, dropping my gun, I caught him by his ragged sleeve, whereupon he grinned foolishly, then as suddenly scowled and wrenched free. "Speak, man!" said I in passionate pleading. "Is it Sir Adam Penfeather you mean—Captain Penfeather?"

"Maybe I do an' maybe I don't, so all's one!" said he. "Howsomever, 'tis Jerry I'm arter—my mate

Jeremy as went adrift from me—my mate Jerry as could sing so true, but I was the lad to dance!" And here he must needs fall a-dancing in his rags, singing hoarsely:

> "Heave-ho, lads, and here's my ditty!
> Saw ye e'er in town or city
> A lass to kiss so sweet an' pretty
> As Bess o' Bednall Green.
>
> "Heave-ho, lads, she's one to please ye
> Bess will kiss an' Bess will——"

"Oho, Jerry—Jeremy-ahoy—haul your wind, lad; bear up, Jerry, an' let Dick come 'longside ye, lad——!" and here the poor wretch, from singing and dancing, falls to doleful wailing with gush of tears and bitter sobs.

"Tell me," said I as gently as I might and laying a hand on his hairy shoulder, "who are you—the name of your ship—who was your captain?"

But all I got was a scowl, a sudden buffet of his fist, and away he sped, raising again his hoarse and plaintive cry:

"Ahoy, Jerry—Jeremy, ho!"

And thus, my mind in a ferment, I must needs watch him go, torn at by briars, tripped by unseen obstacles, running and leaping like the poor, mad thing he was.

Long I stood thus in painful perplexity, when I heard a sudden dreadful screaming at no great distance:

"Oh, Jerry—Oh, Jerry, lad—what ha' they done to thee—Oh, Christ Jesus!"

Then came a ringing shot, and guessing what this was I turned away. "Atlamatzin," said I, taking up my musket, "you spake truth—verily this place is accursed—come, let us begone!"

For long hours I strode on, scarce heeding my silent companion or aught else, my mind pondering the men-

tion this poor, mad wretch had made of "Sir Adam,"
and ever my trouble grew, for if he and the dead man
Jeremy were indeed of Adam's company (the which
I suspected) how should they come thus lost in the wild,
except Adam had met with some disaster, and were this
truly so indeed, then what of my dear and gentle
lady? And now I must needs picture to myself Adam
slain, his men scattered and, for Joan, such horrors
that it was great wonder I did not run mad like this
poor, lost mariner. Tormented thus of my doubts and
most horrid speculations, I went at furious speed, yet
ever my fears grew the more passionate until it grew
beyond enduring and I sighed and groaned, insomuch that my Indian comrade stood off, eyeing me
askance where I had cast myself miserably beside the
way.

"My brother is haunted by the evil spirits sent
abroad for his destruction by Chimalman, so shall
he presently run mad and become sacred to Zotzilaha
Chimalman and suddenly die, except he obey me. For
I, Atlamatzin, that am without fear and wise in the
magic of my people, shall drive hence these devils an
ye will."

"Do aught you will," groaned I, "if you can but
rid me of evil fancies and imaginings."

Forthwith he kindled a fire and I, watching dull
and abstracted, being full of my trouble, was aware of
him cracking and bruising certain herbs or leaves he
had plucked, mingling these with brownish powder
from the deerskin pouch he bore at his girdle, which
mixture he cast upon the fire, whence came a smoke
very sweet and pungent that he fanned towards me.

"Behold my smoke, brother!" saith he, his voice
suddenly loud and commanding, "smell of it and watch
how it doth thicken and close about thee!" And verily
as I looked, I saw nought but a column of whirling

smoke that grew ever more dense and in it, this loud compelling voice.

"Hearken, my brother, to the voices of thy good angels; behold and see truth afar——" The loud voice died away and in its place came another, and I knew that Joanna spoke to me out of this whirling smoke cloud.

"Oh, Martino, hast thou so little faith to think my blood spilt in vain? Did I not give thee unto her that waiteth, living but for thee, yes? Look and behold!"

I saw a gleam of metal amid the green and four ship's culverins or demi-cannon mounted on rough, wheeled carriages and hauled at by wild-looking men, who toiled and sweated amain, for the way was difficult and their ordnance heavy; and amongst these men one very quick and active, very masterful of look and imperious of gesture, a small man in battered harness, and knowing him for Adam, I would have hailed him, but even then he was gone and nought to see but this writhing smoke cloud.

I beheld a great, orbed moon, very bright and clear, and slumbering in this calm radiance a goodly city with a harbour where rode many ships great and small, and beside this harbour, defending these ships and the city itself, a notable strong castle or fort, high-walled and embattled, with great ordnance mounted both landward and towards the sea. And nigh upon this fort I beheld the stealthy forms of men, toilworn and ragged, whose battered, rusty armour glinted ever and anon as they crept in two companies advancing to right and left. Behind these, masked in the brush on the edge of the forest, four demi-cannon with gunners to serve them, foremost of whom was a short, squat fellow who crept from gun to gun, and him I knew for Godby. And presently from these four guns leapt smoke and flame to batter and burst asunder the postern gate of the fort, and through this ruin I saw

Adam leap, sword in hand, his desperate company hard
on his heels.

I saw a great galleon spread her sails against the
moon, and the red glare of her broadside flame against
the town as, squaring her yards, she bore away for
the open sea.

I saw the deck of a ship, deserted save for one desolate figure that stood gazing ever in the one direction;
and as I watched, eager-eyed, this lonely figure knelt
suddenly and reached towards me yearning arms, and
I saw this was my beloved Joan. Now would I have
leapt to those empty arms, but the smoke blinded me
again, and in this smoke I heard the voice of Joanna.

"Oh, Martino, thou that love doth make coward,
be comforted and of good courage, for thy happiness
is hers—and mine, yes!"

So I presently waked and, staring about me, started
up amazed to see it was dawn and the sun rising
already, and beyond the fire the sombre form of
Atlamatzin.

"Are the evil spirits fled from my brother?" he
questioned.

"Indeed," said I, "I have dreamed wonderfully and
to my great comfort."

"Great is the magic of Atlamatzin!" quoth he.
" 'Tis secret that shall die with him and that soon,
for now must he begone to achieve his destiny. As
for thee—yonder, a day's journey, lieth the Great
Water. May Kukulcan have thee in his care, he that
is Father of Life—fare ye well."

But at this, seeing him on his feet, I rose also, to
grasp his hand, asking whither he went. For answer
he pointed to the trackless wild and then raised his
finger to the sun that was flooding the world with his
splendour.

"Brother," said Atlamatzin, pointing to this glory,
"I go back whence I came, back to Kukulcan that

some so call Quetzalcoatl, back to the Father of
Life!"

So saying, he lifted hand aloft in salutation and
turning, strode away due east, so that his form was
swallowed up (as it were) in this radiant glory.

CHAPTER XXXII

How I Found My Beloved at Last

LEFT alone, I broke my fast with such food as I had, meanwhile meditating upon the visions of last night, debating within myself if this were indeed a marvel conjured up of Atlamatzin his black magic, or no more than a dream of my own tortured mind, to the which I found no answer, ponder the matter how I might.

None the less I found myself much easier, the haunting fear clean lifted from me; nay, in my heart sang Hope, blithe as any bird, for the which comfort I did not fail humbly to thank God.

I now consulted my compass and decided to bear up more northerly lest I strike too far east and thus overshoot that bay Adam had marked on his chart. So having collected my gear, I took my musket in the crook of my arm and set out accordingly.

Before me was a wild, rolling country that rose, level on level, very thick of brush and thickets so tangled that I must oft win me a path by dint of mine axe. Yet I struggled on as speedily as I might (maugre this arduous labour and the sun's heat) for more than once amid the thousand heavy scents of flower and herb and tree, I thought to catch the sweet, keen tang of the sea.

All this day I strode resolutely forward, scarce pausing to eat or drink, nor will I say more of this day's journey except that the sun was setting as I reached the top of a wooded eminence and, halting suddenly, fell upon my knees and within me such a joy as I had seen the gates of paradise opening to receive me; for there, all glorious with the blaze of sunset, lay the ocean at last. And beholding thus my long and weary journey so nearly ended, and bethinking me how many times God had preserved me and brought me safe through so many dire perils of this most evil country, I bowed my head and strove to tell Him my heart's gratitude. My prayer ended (and most inadequate!) I began to run, my weariness all forgot, the breath of the sea sweet in my nostrils, nor stayed until I might look down on the foaming breakers far below and hear their distant roar.

Long stood I, like one entranced, for from this height I could make out the blue shapes of several islands and beyond these a faint blur upon the horizon, the which added greatly to my comfort and delight, since this I knew must be the opposite shore of Terra Firma or the Main, and this great body of water the Gulf of Darien itself. And so came night.

All next day I followed the coast, keeping the sea upon my left, looking for some such landlocked harbourage with its cliff shaped like a lion's head as Adam had described, yet though I was at great pains (and no small risk to my neck) to peer down into every bay I came upon, nowhere did I discover any such bay or cliff as bore out his description; thus night found me eager to push on, yet something despondent and very weary. So I lighted my fire and ate my supper, harassed by a growing dread lest I was come too far to the east, after all.

And presently up came the moon in glory; indeed, never do I remember seeing it so vivid bright, its radiance flashing back from the waters far below and showing tree and bush and precipitous cliff, very sharp and clear. Upon my left, as I sat, the jagged coast line curved away out to sea, forming thus the lofty headland I had traversed scarce an hour since, that rose

sheer from the moon-dappled waters, a huge, shapeless
bluff. Now after some while I arose, and seeing the
moon so glorious, shouldered my gun, minded to seek a
little further before I slept. I had gone thus but a few
yards, my gaze now on the difficult path before me,
now upon the sea, when, chancing to look towards the
bluff I have mentioned, I stopped to stare amazed,
for in this little distance, this formless headland, seen
from this angle, had suddenly taken a new shape and
there before me, plain and manifest, was the rough
semblance of a lion's head; and I knew that betwixt it
and the high cliff whereon I stood must be Adam's
excellent secure haven. This sudden discovery filled
me with such an ecstacy that I fell a-trembling, howbeit I began to quest here and there for some place
where I might get me down whence I might behold this
bay and see if Adam's ship lay therein. And in a
little, finding such a place, I began to descend and
found it so easy and secure it seemed like some natural
stair, and I did not doubt that Adam and his fellows
had belike used it as such ere now.

At last I came where I could look down into a narrow bay shut in by these high, bush-girt cliffs and
floored with gleaming, silver sand, whose waters, calm
and untroubled, mirrored the serene moon, and close
under the dense shadows of these cliffs I made out the
loom of a great ship. Hereupon I looked no more, but
gave all my attention to hands and feet, and so, slipping and stumbling in my eagerness, got me down at
last and began running across these silvery sands. But
as I approached the ship where she lay now plain in
my view, I saw her topmasts were gone, and beholding
the ruin of her gear and rigging, I grew cold with
sudden dread and came running.

She lay upon an even keel, her forefoot deep-buried
in the shifting sand that had silted about her with
the tide, and beholding her paint and gilding blackened

and scorched by fire, her timbers rent and scarred by shot, I knew this fire-blackened, shattered wreck would never sail again. And now as I viewed this dismal ruin, I prayed this might be some strange ship rather than that I had come so far a-seeking and, so praying, waded out beneath her lofty stern (the tide being low) and, gazing up, read as much of her name as the searing fire had left: viz:

D E L . . . . A N C E

And hereupon, knowing her indeed for Adam's ship, I took to wandering round about her, gazing idly up at this pitiful ruin, until there rushed upon me the realisation of what all this meant. Adam was dead or prisoner, and my dear lady lost to me after all; my coming was too late.

And now a great sickness took me, my strength deserted me and, groaning, I sank upon the sand and lying thus, yearned amain for death. Then I heard a sound, and lifting heavy head, beheld one who stood upon the bulwark above me, holding on by a backstay with one hand and pistol levelled down at me in the other. And beholding this slender, youthful figure thus outlined against the moon, the velvet coat brave with silver lace, the ruffles at throat and wrist, the silken stockings and buckled shoes, I knew myself surely mad, for this I saw was Joanna—alive and breathing.

"Shoot!" I cried. "Death has reft from me all I loved—shoot!"

"Martin!" cried she, and down came the pistol well-nigh upon me where I lay. "Oh, dear, kind God, 'tis Martin!"

"Joan?" said I, wondering. "Damaris—beloved!"

I was on my feet and, heaving myself up by means of the tangle of gear that hung from the ship's lofty side, I sprang upon the deck and fell on my knees to clasp this lovely, trembling youth in my hungry arms, my head bowed against this tender woman's body, lest she see how I wept out of pure joy and thankfulness. But now she raised my head, and thus I saw her weeping also, felt her tears upon my face; and now she was laughing albeit she wept still, her two hands clasping me to her.

"Such a great—fierce—wild man!" she sobbed; and then: "My man!" and stooping, she kissed me on the lips. But as for me, I could but gaze up at her in rapture and never a word to say. Then she was on her knees before me and thus we knelt in each other's fast clasping arms. "Oh, Martin!" said she. "Oh, loved Martin—God hath answered my ceaseless prayers!"

And now when she would have voiced to Him her gratitude, I must needs crush her upon my heart to look down into this flushed and tear-wet face that held for me the beauty of all the world and to kiss away her prayers and breath together, yet even so did she return my kisses.

At last we arose but had gone scarce a step when we were in each other's arms again, to stand thus fast clasped together, for I almost dreaded she might vanish again and feared to let her go.

"We have been parted so cruelly—so often!" said I.

"But never again, my Martin!"

"No, by God!" quoth I fervently. "Not even death——"

"Not even death!" said she.

And thus we remained a great while, wandering to and fro upon the weather-beaten deck, very silent for the most part, being content with each other's nearness and, for myself, merely to behold her loveliness was joy unutterable.

She brought me into Adam's great cabin under the poop, lighted by a great swinging silver lamp, its stern windows carefully shaded, lest any see this betraying beam; and standing amid all the luxury of tapestried hangings and soft carpets, I felt myself mighty strange and out of place; and presently, catching sight of myself in one of the mirrors, I stood all abashed to behold the unlovely object I was in my rough and weather-stained garments, my face burned nigh black by the sun and all set about in a tangle of wild hair and ragged beard.

"Is it so great wonder I should not know you at first, dear Martin, and you so wild and fierce-seeming?"

"Indeed I am an ill spectacle," quoth I; at this, beholding me thus rueful, she fell to kissing me, whereat I did but miscall myself the more, telling her 'twas great marvel she should love one so ill-matched with her; for, said I, "here are you beautiful beyond all women, and here stand I, of manners most uncouth, harsh-featured, slow of tongue, dull-witted, and one you have seldom seen but in sorry rags!"

"Oh, my dearest heart," said she, nestling but closer in my embrace, "here is long catalogue and 'tis for each and every I do love you infinitely more than you do guess, and for this beside—because you are Martin Conisby that I have loved, do love, and shall love always and ever!"

"And there's the marvel!" quoth I, kissing her bowed head.

"And you do think me—very beautiful, Martin?"

"Aye, I do."

"Even clad—in these—these things?" she questioned, not looking at me.

"Aye, truly!"

"I had not meant you to see me thus, Martin, but it was my custom to watch for your coming, and 'twas hard to climb the cliff in petticoats, and besides, since I have been alone, there was so much to do—and it didn't matter."

"Aye, but how came you alone, what of Adam and the rest?"

"Nay, 'tis long story."

"But why are you thus solitary, you that do so fear solitude, as I remember."

"When Adam marched away, I stayed to wait for you, Martin."

"For me?"

"Yes, Martin!"

"Were you not afraid?"

"Often," said she, clasping me tighter, "but you are come at last, so are my fears all past and done. And, more than the loneliness I feared lest you should come and find this poor ship all deserted, and lose hope and faith in God's mercy."

"Oh, my brave, sweet soul!" said I, falling on my knees to kiss her hands. "Oh, God love you for this— had I found you not, I should have dreamed you dead and died myself, cursing God."

"Ah hush," said she, closing my lips with her sweet fingers. "Rather will we bless Him all our days for giving us such a love!"

And now having no will or thought to sleep, she sets about preparing supper, while I with scissors, razors, etc. (that she had brought at my earnest entreaty), began to rid my face of its shaggy hair, and busied with my razor, must needs turn ever and anon for blessed sight of her where she flitted lightly to and fro, she bidding me take heed lest I cut myself. Cut myself I did forthwith, and she, beholding the blood, must come running to staunch it and it no more than a merest nick. And now, seeing her thus tender of me who had endured so many hurts and none to grieve or soothe, I came very near weeping for pure joy.

And now as she bustled to and fro, she fell silent and oft I caught her viewing me wistfully, and once or twice she made as to speak yet did not, and I,

guessing what she would say, would have told her,
yet could think of no gentle way of breaking the
matter, ponder how I might, and in the end blurted
out the bald truth, very sudden and fool-like, as you
shall hear. For, at last, supper being over (and we
having eaten very little and no eyes for our food or
aught in the world save each other) my lady questioned
me at last.

"Dear Martin, what of my father?"

"Why, first," said I, avoiding her eyes, "he is dead!"

"Yes!" said she faintly, "this I guessed."

"He died nobly like the brave gentleman he was.
I buried him in the wilderness, where flowers bloomed,
three days' march back."

"In the wilderness?" says she a little breathlessly.
"But he was in prison!"

"Aye, 'twas there I found him. But we escaped by
the unselfish bravery and kindness of Don Federigo.
So together we set out to find you."

"Together, Martin?"

"Yes, and he very cheery, despite his sufferings."

"Sufferings, Martin?"

"He—he halted somewhat in his walk——"

"Nay, he was strong, as I remember—ah, you mean
they—had tortured him——"

"Aye," said I, dreading to see her grief. "Yet
despite their devilish cruelties, he rose triumphant
above agony of body, thereby winning to a great and
noble manhood, wherefore I loved and honoured him
beyond all men——"

"He was—your enemy——"

"He was my friend, that comforted me when I was
greatly afraid; he was my companion amid the perils
of our cruel journey, calm and undismayed, uncom-
plaining, brave, and unselfish to his last breath, so
needs must I cherish his memory."

"Martin!" Lifting my head I saw she was looking

at me, her vivid lips quivering, her eyes all radiant
despite their tears, and then, or ever I might prevent,
she was kneeling to me, had caught my hand and kissed
it passionately.

"Oh, man that I love—you that learned to—love
your enemy!"

"Nay, my Damaris, 'twas he that taught me how to
love him, 'twas himself slew my hatred!"

And now, drawing her to my heart, I told her much
of Sir Richard's indomitable spirit and bravery, how
in my blind haste I would march him until he sank
swooning by the way, of our fightings and sufferings
and he ever serene and undismayed. I told of how we
had talked of her beside our camp fires and how, dying,
he had bid me tell her he had ever loved her better than
he had let her guess, and bethinking me of his letter
at last, I gave it to her. But instead of reading it,
she put this letter in her pocket.

"Come," said she, " 'tis near the dawn, and you
weary with your journey, 'tis time you were abed."
And when I vowed I was not sleepy, she took my hand
(as I had been a child) and bringing me into that had
been Adam's cabin, showed me his bed all prepared. "It hath waited for these many weeks, dear
Martin!" said she, smoothing the pillows with gentle
hand.

"But we have so much to tell each other——"

"To-morrow?"

Hereupon she slipped past me to the door and stood
there to shake admonishing finger:

"Sleep!" said she, nodding her lovely head might;
determined, "and scowl not, naughty child, I shall be
near you—to—to mother you—nay, come and see for
yourself." So saying, she took my hand again and
brought me into the next cabin, a fragrant nest, dainty-
sweet as herself, save that in the panelling above her
bed she had driven two nails where hung a brace of

pistols. Seeing my gaze on these, she shivered suddenly and nestled into my arm.

"Oh, Martin," said she, her face hid against me, "one night I seemed to hear a foot that crept on the deck above, and I thought I should have died with fear. So I kept these ever after, one for—them, and the other for myself."

"And all this you endured for my sake!" quoth I.

"And God hath sent you safe to me, dear Martin, to take care of me, so am I safe with nought to fright or harm me henceforth."

"Nothing under heaven," quoth I. Very gingerly she took down the pistols and gave them to me and, bringing me to the door, kissed me.

"Good night, dear heart!" said she softly. "God send you sweet dreams!"

Thus came I back to my cabin and laying by the pistols, got me to bed, and mighty luxurious, what with these sheets and pillows, and yet, or ever I had fully appreciated the unwonted comfort, I was asleep.

I waked to the sudden clasp of her soft arms and a tear-wet cheek against mine, and opening my eyes, saw her kneeling by my bed in the grey dawn.

"Oh, loved Martin," said she, "I love you more than I guessed because you are greater than I dreamed—my father's letter hath told me so much of you—your goodness to your enemy—how you wiped away his tears, ministered to his hurts, carried him in your arms. I have read it but now and—'tis tale so noble —so wonderful, that needs must I come to tell you I do love you so much—so much. And now——"

"You are mine!" said I, gathering her in my arms. "Mine for alway."

"Yes, dear Martin! But because I am yours so utterly, you will be gentle with me—patient a little and forbearing to a—very foolish maid——"

For answer I loosed her, whereupon she caught my

hand to press it to her tender cheek, her quivering lips.

"Oh, Martin!" she whispered. "For this needs must I worship thee!" And so was gone.

CHAPTER XXXIII

Of Dreams

I WAKED marvellous refreshed and full of a great joy to hear her sweet singing and the light tread of her foot going to and fro in the great cabin, where she was setting out a meal, as I guessed by the tinkle of platters, etc., the which homely sound reminded me that I was vastly hungry. Up I sprang to a glory of sun flooding in at shattered window and the jagged rent where a round-shot had pierced the stout timbering above; and having washed and bathed me as well as I might, found my lady had replaced my ragged, weather-stained garments by others chosen from the ship's stores. And so at last forth I stepped into the great cabin, eager for sight of my dear lady, albeit somewhat conscious of my new clothes and hampered by their tightness.

"Indeed," said she, holding me off, the better to examine me, "I do find you something better-looking than you were!"

"Nay, but I am burned browner than any Indian."

"This but maketh your eyes the bluer, Martin. And then you are changed besides—so much more gentle—kindlier—the man I dreamed you might become——" Here I kissed her.

"And you," said I, "my Damaris that I have ever loved and shall do, you are more beautiful than my dream of you——"

"Am I, Martin—in spite of these things?"

"Indeed," said I heartily, "they do but reveal to me so much of——"

Here she kissed me and brought me to the table. Now, seeing her as she sat thus beside me, I started and stared, well-nigh open-mouthed.

"What now?" she questioned.

"Your hair!"

" 'Twill grow again, Martin. But why must you stare?"

"Because when you look and turn so, and your hair short on your shoulders, you are marvellously like to Joanna." Now at this, seeing how my lady shrank and turned from me, I could have cursed my foolish tongue.

"What of her, Martin?"

"She is dead!" And here I described how bravely Joanna had met Death standing, and her arms outstretched to the infinite. When I had done, my lady was silent, as expecting more, and her head still averted.

"And is this—all?" she questioned at last.

"Yes!" said I. "Yes!"

"Yet you do not tell me of the cruel wrong she did you—and me! You do not say she lied of you."

"She is dead!" said I. "And very nobly, as I do think!"

Hereupon my lady rose and going into her cabin, was back all in a moment and unfolding a paper, set it before me. "This," said she, "I found after you were fled the ship!" Opening this paper, I saw there, very boldly writ:

"I lied about him and 'twas a notable lie, notably spoke. Martino is not like ordinary men and so it is I do most truly love him—yes—for always. So do I take him for mine now, so shall lie become truth, mayhap.　　　　　　　　　　"Joanna."

And even as I refolded this letter, my lady's arms were about me, her lovely head upon my shoulder:

"Dear," said she, " 'twas like you to speak no harsh thing of the dead. And she gave you back to me with her life—so needs must I love her memory for this."

And so we presently got to our breakfast,—sweet, white bread new-baked, with divers fish she had caught that morning whiles I slept. And surely never was meal more joyous, the sun twinkling on Adam's silver and cut glass, and my lady sweeter and more radiant than the morn in all the vigour of her glowing beauty.

Much we talked and much she said that I would fain set down, since there is nothing about her that is not a joy to me to dwell upon, yet lest I weary my readers with overmuch of lovers' talk, I will only set down all she now told me concerning Adam.

"For here were we, Martin," said my lady, "our poor ship much wounded with her many battles and beset by a storm so that we all gave ourselves up for lost; even Adam confessed he could do no more, and I very woful because I must die away from you, yet the storm drove us by good hap into these waters, and next day, the wind moderating, we began to hope we might make this anchorage, though the ship was dreadfully a-leak, and all night and all day I would hear the dreadful clank of the pumps always at work. And thus at last, to our great rejoicing, we saw this land ahead of us that was to be our salvation. But as we drew nearer our rejoicing changed to dismay to behold three ships betwixt us and this refuge. So Sir Adam decided to fight his way through and sailed down upon these three ships accordingly. And presently we were among them and the battle began, and very dreadful, what with the smoke and shouting and noise of guns——"

"Ah!" cried I. "And did not Adam see you safely below?"

"To be sure, Martin, but I stole up again and found him something hurt by a splinter yet very happy because Godby had shot away one of the enemy's masts and nobody hurt but himself, and so we won past these ships for all their shooting, and I bound up Adam's hurt where he stood conning the ship, shouting orders and bidding me below, all in a breath. But now cometh Amos Marsh, the carpenter, running, to say the enemy's shot had widened our leaks and the water gaining upon the pumps beyond recovery and that we were sinking. 'How long will she last?' said Adam, staring at the two ships that were close behind, and still shooting at us now and then. 'An hour, Captain, maybe less!' said the carpenter. ' 'Twill serve,' said Adam, in his quiet voice. 'Do you and your lads stand to the pumps, and we will be safe ashore within the hour. But mark me, if any man turn laggard or faint-hearted, shoot that man, but pump your best, Amos—away wi' you!' "

"Aye," quoth I, clasping tighter the hand I held, "that was like Adam; 'tis as I had heard him speak. And you in such dire peril of death, my beloved——"

"Why, Martin, I did not fear or grieve very much, for methought you were lost to me forever in this life perchance, but in the next——"

"This and the next I do pray God," quoth I, and kissed her till she bade me leave her breath for her story. The which she presently did something as followeth:

"And now, whiles Godby and his chosen gunners plied our stern cannons, firing very fast and furious, Adam calls for volunteers to set more sail and himself was first aloft for all his wounded arm——"

"And where were you?"

"Giving water to Godby and his men, for they were parched. And presently back cometh Adam, panting with his exertions. 'God send no spars carry away,' quoth he, 'and we must lay alongside the nearest Spaniard and board.' ' 'Tis desperate venture,' said Godby, 'they be great ships and full o' Dons.' 'Aye,' said Adam, 'but we are Englishmen and desperate.' And so we stood on, Martin, and these great ships after us, and even our own poor ship lying lower and lower in the water, until I looked to see it sink under us and go down altogether. But at last we reached this bay and none too soon, for to us cometh Amos Marsh, all wet and woebegone with labour, to say the ship was going. But nothing heeding, Adam took the helm, shouting to him to let fly braces, and with our sails all shivering we ran aground, just as she lies now, poor thing. While I lay half-stunned with the fall, for the shock of grounding had thrown me down, Adam commanded every one on shore with muskets and pistols, so I presently found myself running across the sands 'twixt Adam and Godby, nor stayed we till we reached the cliff yonder, where are many caves very wonderful, as I will show you, Martin. And then I saw the reason of this haste, for the greatest Spanish ship was turning to bring her whole broadside to bear, and so began to shoot off all their cannon, battering our poor ship as you see. Then came Spaniards in boats with fire to burn it, but our men shot so many of these that although they set the ship on fire, yet they did it so hastily because of our shooting that once they were gone, the fire was quickly put out. But the ship was beyond repair which greatly disheartened us all, save only Adam, who having walked around the wreck and examined her, chin in hand, summoned all men to a council on the beach. 'Look now, my comrades,' said he (as well as I remember, Martin), 'we have fought a sinking ship so long as we might, and here we lie driven ashore in a hostile country but we have only one killed and five injured, which is good;

but we are Englishmen, which is better and bad to beat.
Well, then, shall we stay here sucking our thumbs?
Shall we set about building another vessel and the
enemy come upon us before 'tis done? Shall we
despair? Not us! We stand a hundred and thirty
and two men, and every man a proved and seasoned
fighter; so will we, being smitten thus, forthwith smite
back, and smite where the enemy will least expect.
We'll march overland on Carthagena—I know it well
—fall on 'em in the dead hush o' night, surprise their
fort, spike their guns and down to the harbour for a
ship. Here's our vessel a wreck—we'll have one of
theirs in place. So, comrades all, who's for Carthagena along with me; who's for a Spanish ship and Old
England?' "

"Why, then," cried I, amazed, "my dream was true.
They have marched across country on Carthagena——"

"Yes, Martin, but what dream——?"

"With four guns mounted on wheels?"

"Yes, Martin; they built four gun-carriages to
Adam's design. But what of your dream?"

So I told her of Atlamatzin and the visions I had
beheld; "and I saw you also, my loved Joan; aye, as
I do remember, you knelt on the deck above, praying
and with your arms reached out——"

"Why, so I did often—one night in especial, I
remember, weeping and calling to you, for I was very
fearful and—lonely, dear Martin. And that night, I
remember, I dreamed I saw you, your back leaned to
a great rock as you were very weary, and staring into
a fire, sad-eyed and desolate. Across your knees was
your gun and all around you a dark and dismal forest,
and I yearned to come to you and could not, and so
watched and lay to weep anew.—Oh, dear, loved
Martin!"

Here she turned, her eyes dark with remembered

sorrow, wherefore I took and lifted her to my knee, holding her thus close upon my heart.

"Tell me," said I after some while, "when Adam marched on his desperate venture, did he name any day for his likely return?"

"Yes, Martin!"

"And when was that?"

" 'Twas the day you came."

"Then he is already late," quoth I. "And he was ever mighty careful and exact in his calculations. 'Tis an adventure so daring as few would have attempted, saving only our 'timid' Adam. And how if he never returns, my Damaris—how then?"

"Ah, then—we have each other!" said she.

"And therein is vast comfort and—for me great joy!" quoth I.

CHAPTER XXXIV

Of Love

My first care was to see how we stood in regard to stores, more especially powder and shot great and small, the which I found sufficient and to spare, as also divers weapons, as muskets, pistols, hangers, etc. The more I thought, the more I was determined to put the ship into as good a posture of defence as might be, since I judged it likely the Spaniards might pay us a visit soon or late, or mayhap some chance band of hostile Indians. To this end and with great exertion, by means of lever and tackle, I hauled inboard her four great stern-chase guns, at the which labour my lady chancing to find me, falls to work beside me right merrily.

"Why, Martin," said she, when the four pieces stood ready to hand, "I have seen five men strain hard to move one of these; indeed you must be marvellous strong."

At this I grew so foolishly pleased that I fell to charging these pieces amain, lest she should see aught of this.

"Strong, great men be usually the gentlest," said she.

"And generally thick-skulled and dull-witted!" quoth I.

"Are you so dull-witted, my Martin?"

"Ah, Damaris, my sweet Joan, when I think on all the wasted tears——"

"Not wasted, Martin, no, not one, since each hath but helped to make the man I do so love."

"That you should so love me is the abiding wonder. I am no man o' the world and with no fine-gentlemanly graces, alas! I am a simple fellow and nought to show for his years of life——"

"Wherefore so humble, poor man? You that were so proud and savage in England and must burst open gates and beat my servants and fright me in my chamber——"

"Aye, I was brute indeed!" said I, sitting down and clean forgetting my guns in sudden dejection.

"And so gloomy with me on the island at the first and then something harsh, and then very wild and masterful; do you remember you would kiss me and I would not—and struggled—so desperately—and vainly—and was compelled?"

"Oh, vile!" said I. "You so lonely and helpless, and I would have forced you to my base will."

"And did not, Martin! Because yours was a noble love. So is the memory of our dear island unutterably sweet."

"Indeed and is this so?" quoth I, lifting my head.

"Beyond all expression!" said she a little breathlessly and her eyes very bright. "Ah, did you not know —whatever you did, 'twas you—that I loved. And, dear Martin, at your fiercest, you were ever—so innocent!"

"Innocent!" quoth I, wondering. And now her clear gaze wavered, her cheek flushed, and all in a moment she was beside me on her knees, her face hid against me and speaking quick and low and passionate.

"I am a very woman—and had loved for all my life—and there were times—on the island when—I, too—oh, dear Martin, oft in the night the sound of your steps going to and fro without our cave—those restless feet—seemed to tread upon my heart! I loved these fierce, strong arms, even whilst I struggled in their hold! A man of the world would have known

—taken advantage. But you never guessed because
you regarded ever the highest in me. So would I have
you do still—honouring me with your patience—a little longer—until Adam be come again, or until we
be sure he hath perished and England beyond our
reach. Thus, dear, I have confessed my very secret
soul to thee and lie here in thy merciful care even more
than I did on our island, since I do love thee—greatly
better! Therefore, be not so—infinite humble!"

Here for a while I was silent, being greatly moved
and finding no word to say. At last, clasping her tender loveliness to me, and stooping to kiss this so loved
head:

"Dear, my lady," said I, "thou art to me the sweet-
est, holiest thing in all the world, and so shalt thou
ever be."

Some time after, having put all things in excellent
posture to our defence, viz: our four great pieces full-
charged astern, with four lighter guns and divers
pateraros ranged to sweep the quarter-deck, forecastle
and all approaches thereto, I felt my precious charge
more secure and myself (seconded by her brave spirit)
able to withstand well-nigh any chance attack, so long
as our powder and shot held.

This done, I brought hammer, nails, etc., from the
carpenter's stores and set myself to mend such shot-
holes, cracks, and rents in the panelling and the like
as I judged would incommode us in wind or rain, and
while I did this (and whistling cheerily) needs must
I stay ever and anon to watch my sweet soul busy at
her cookery (and mighty savoury dishes) and she
pause to look on me, until we must needs run to kiss
each other and so to our several labours again.

For now indeed came I to know a happiness so calm
and deep, so much greater than I had ventured to hope
that often I would be seized of panic dread lest aught
came to snatch it from me. Thus lived we, joying

in each hour, busied with such daily duties as came to hand, yet I for one finding these labours sweet by reason of her that shared them; yet ever our love grew and we ever more happy in each other's companionship.

And here I, that by mine own folly of stubborn pride had known so little of content and the deep and restful joy of it; here, I say, greatly tempted am I to dwell and enlarge upon these swift-flying, halcyon days whose memory Time cannot wither; I would paint you her changing moods, her sweet gravity, her tender seriousness, her pretty rogueries, her demureness, her thousand winsome tricks of gesture and expression, the vital ring of her sweet voice, her long-lashed eyes, the dimple in her chin, and all the constant charm and wonder of her. But what pen could do the sweet soul justice, what word describe her innumerable graces? Surely not mine, so would it be but vain labour and mayhap, to you who take up this book, great weariness to read.

So I will pass to a certain night, the moon flooding her radiance all about me and the world very hushed and still with nought to hear save the murmurous ripple and soft lapping of the incoming tide, and I upon my bed (very wakeful) and full of speculation and the problem I pondered this: Adam (and he so precise and exact in all things) had named to my lady a day for his return, which day was already long past, therefore it was but natural to suppose his desperate venture against this great fortified city a failure, his hardy fellows scattered, and his brave self either slain or a prisoner. What then of our situation, my dear lady's and mine, left thus solitary in a hostile country and little or no chance of ever reaching England, but doomed rather to seek some solitude where we might live secure from hostile Indians or the implacable persecution of the Spaniards. Thus we must live alone with Nature henceforth, she and I and God.

And this thought filled me alternately with intoxicating joy for my own sake, since all I sought of life was this loved woman, and despair for her sake, since secretly she must crave all those refinements of life and civilisation as had become of none account to myself. And if Adam were slain indeed and England thus beyond our reach, how long must we wait to be sure of this?

Here I started to hear my lady calling me softly:
"Art awake, dear Martin?"
"Yes, my Joan!"
"I dreamed myself alone again. Oh, 'tis good to hear your voice! Are you sleepy?"
"No whit."
"Then let us talk awhile as we used sometimes on our loved island."
"Loved you it—so greatly, Joan?"
"Beyond any place in the world, Martin."
"Why, then——" said I and stopped, lest my voice should betray the sudden joy that filled me.
"Go on, Martin."
" 'Twas nought."
"Aye, but it was! You said 'Why, then.' Prithee, dear sir, continue."
Myself (sitting up and blinking at the moon): Why, then, if you—we—are—if we should be so unfortunate as to be left solitary in these cruel wilds and no hope of winning back to England, should you grieve therefor?
She (after a moment): Should you, Martin?
Myself (mighty fervently): Aye, indeed!
She (quickly): Why, Martin—pray why?
Myself (clenching my fists): For that we should be miserable outcasts cut off from all the best of life.
She: The best? As what, Martin?
Myself: Civilisation and all its refinements, all neighbourliness, the comforts of friendship, all secur-

ity, all laws, and instead of these—dangers, hardship, and solitude.

She (softly): Aye, this methinks should break our hearts. Indeed, Martin, you do fright me.

Myself (bitterly): Why, 'tis a something desolate possibility!

She (dolefully): And alas, Adam cometh not!

Myself: Alas, no!

She: And is long overdue.

Myself: He marched on a perilous venture; aye, mighty hazardous and desperate.

She: Indeed, dear Martin, so desperate that I do almost pity the folk of Carthagena.

Myself (wondering): Then you do think he will succeed—will come sailing back one day?

She: Yes, Martin, if he hath to sail the ship back alone.

Myself: And wherefore believe this?

She: I know not, except that he is Adam and none like to him.

Myself: Yet is he only mortal, to be captured or slain one way or another. How if he cometh never back?

She: Why then, Martin—needs must I forego all thought of England, of home, of the comfortable joys of civilisation, of all laws, and instead of all these cleave to you—my beloved!

Myself: Damaris!

She: Oh, Martin, dear, foolish blunderer to dream you could fright me with tales of hardship, or dangers, or solitude when you were by, to think I must break my heart for home and England when you are both to me. England or home without you were a desert; with you the desert shall be my England, my home all my days, if God so will it.

Myself: Oh, loved woman, my brave, sweet Joan! And the laws—what of the laws?

She: God shall be our law, shall give us some sign.

Myself: Joan—come to me!

She (faintly): No! Ah, no!

Myself: Come!

She: Very well, Martin.

In a little I heard her light step, slow and something hesitant, and then she stood before me in her loveliness, wrapped about in my travel-stained boat-cloak; so came she to sink beside me on her knees.

"I am here, Martin," said she, "since I am yours and because I know my will, thine also. For sure am I that Adam will yet come and with him cometh law and England and all else; shall we not rest then for God's sign, be it soon or a little late, and I honour thee the more hereafter. If this indeed be foolish scruple to your mind, dear Martin, I am here; but if for this you shall one day reverence your wife the more —beloved, let me go!"

"Indeed—indeed, sign or no sign, thus do I love thee!" said I, and loosed her. And now, as she rose from my reluctant arms, even then, soft and faint with distance but plain and unmistakable came the boom of a gun.

CHAPTER XXXV

Of the Coming of Adam and Of Our Great Joy Therein

THE moon was paling to daybreak as, having climbed that rocky stair I have mentioned, we came upon the cliff and stood, hands tight-clasped, where we might behold the infinity of waters; and after some while, looming phantom-like upon the dawn, we descried the lofty sails of a great ship standing in towards the land and growing ever more distinct. And as we watched, and never a word, her towering canvas flushed rosy with coming day, a changing colour that grew ever brighter until it glowed all glorious, and up rose the sun.

Suddenly, as we watched the proud oncoming of this ship of glory, my lady uttered a little, soft cry and nestled to me.

"The sign, Martin!" cried she, "God hath sent us the sign, beloved; see what she beareth at the main!" And there, sure enough, stirring languid upon the gentle air was the Cross of St. George. And beholding this thing (that was no more than shred of bunting) and in these hostile seas, ship and sea swam upon my vision, and bowing my head lest my beloved behold this weakness, felt her warm lips on mine.

"Dear Martin," said she, "hide not your tears from me, for yonder is England, a noble future—home, at last."

"Home?" said I. "Aye, home and peace at last and, best of all—you!" Thus stood we, clean forgetting this great ship in each other until, roused by the thunder of another gun, we started and turned to see the ship so near that we could distinguish the glint of armour on her decks here and there, and presently up to us rose a cheer (though faint) and we saw them make a waft with the ensign, so that it seemed they had discovered us where we stood. Hereupon, seeing the ship already going about to fetch into the harbour, we descended the cliff and, reaching the sands below, stood there until the vesel hove into view round the headland that was like unto a lion's head, and, furling upper and lower courses, let go her anchor and brought up in fashion very seamanlike, and she indeed a great and noble vessel from whose lofty decks rose lusty shouts of welcome, drowned all at once in the silvery fanfare of trumpets and a prodigious rolling of drums. Presently, to this merry clamour, a boat was lowered and pulled towards us, and surely never was seen a wilder, more ragged company than this that manned her. In the stern-sheets sat Adam, one hand upon the tiller, the other slung about him by a scarf, his harness rusty and dinted, but his eyes very bright beneath the pent of his weather-beaten hat. Scarce had the boat touched shore than his legs (dight in prodigiously long Spanish boots) were over the side and he came wading ashore, first of any.

"Praise God!" said he, halting suddenly to flourish off his battered hat and glance from one to other of us with his old, whimsical look. "Praise God I do see again two souls, the most wilful and unruly in all this world, yet here stand ye that should be most thoroughly dead (what with the peril consequent upon wilfulness) but for a most especial Providence—there stand ye fuller of life and the joy o' living than ever."

"And you, Adam," reaching her hands to him in welcome, "you that must march 'gainst a mighty city with men so few! Death surely hath been very nigh you also, yet here are you come back to us unscathed save for your arm; surely God hath been to us infinitely kind and good!"

"Amen!" said Adam and stooping, raised these slender hands to his lips. "Howbeit, my Lady Wilfulness," quoth he, shaking his head, "I vow you ha' caused me more carking care than any unhanged pirate or Spaniard on the Main! You that must bide here all alone, contemning alike my prayers and commands, nor suffering any to stay for your comfort and protection and all for sake of this hare-brained, most obstinate comrade o' mine, that must go running his poor sconce into a thousand dangers (which was bad) and upsetting all my schemes and calculations (which was worse, mark you!) and all to chase a will-o'-the-wisp, a mare's-nest, a—oh, Lord love you, Martin——!" And so we clasped hands.

In a little, my dear lady betwixt us, and Adam discoursing of his adventures and particularly of his men's resolution, endurance and discipline, we got us aboard the *Deliverance* which the men were already stripping of such stores as remained, filling the air with cheery shouts, and yo-ho-ing as they hove at this or hauled at that. Climbing to the quarter-deck we came at last to the great cabin, where Adam was pleased to commend the means I had taken to our defence, though more than once I noticed his quick glance flash here and there as if seeking somewhat. At last, my lady having left us awhile, he turns his sharp eyes on me:

"Comrade, how goeth vengeance nowadays?" he questioned. "What of Sir Richard, your enemy?"

"Dead, Adam!"

"Aha!" said he, pinching his chin and eyeing me askance, "was it steel or did ye shoot him, comrade?"

"God forgive you for saying such thing, Adam!" quoth I, scowling into his lean, brown face.

"Aha," said he again, and viewing me with his furtive leer. "Do ye regret his murder then, Martin?"

"Aye, I do from my heart—now and always!"

"Hum!" said he, seating himself on my tumbled bed and glancing whimsically at me, "Martin," quoth he, "friend—brother—you that talked bloody murder and hell-fire with a heart inside you clean and gentle as a child's, thou'rt plaguey fool to think thy friend Adam be such fool as not to know thee better. Hark'ee now, here's your fashion: If you found the enemy you sought so long and him in a Spanish prison, first you cursed, then you comforted, then eased his pains, watched your chance, throttled your gaoler and away to freedom, bearing your enemy along wi' you—is't not something the way of it—come?"

"Truly, Adam!" said I, all amazed, "though how you chance to know this——"

"Tush!" said he. " 'Tis writ plain all over thee, Martin, and yonder cometh our lady, as peerless a maid as ever blessed man's sight—for all of the which I do love thee, Martin. Come, now, I will take ye aboard the prize and hey for England—this night we sail!" So we joined my lady and coming down to the boat were presently rowed to the Spanish ship, a great vessel, her towering stem brave with gilding and her massy timbers enriched by all manner of carved work.

"She had a name well-nigh long as herself, Martin," said Adam, "but Godby christened her *The Joyous Hope* instead, which shall serve well enough." So we came beneath her high, curving side, where leaned familiar figures—lean, bronzed fellows who welcomed us with cheer that waked many an echo. Upon the quarter-deck was Penruddock the surgeon, who bustled forward to greet us himself as loquacious as ever and very loud in praise of the cure he had once wrought in me; and here, too, was Godby, to make a leg to my lady and grasp my hand.

"Why, Mart'n—why, pal, here's j'y, scorch me wi' a port-fire else!" quoth he, then, hearing a hail from the beach, rolled away to look to his many duties.

"She's good enough vessel—to look at, Martin," said Adam, bringing us into the panelled splendour of the coach or roundhouse; "aye, she's roomy and handsome enough and rich-laden, though something heavy on her helm; of guns fifty and nine and well-found in all things save clothes, hence my scurvy rags; but we'll better 'em when our stores come aboard."

And now, my lady being retired, he showed me over this great galleon, so massy built for all her gilding and carved finery, and so stout-timbered as made her well-nigh shot-proof.

"She's a notable rich prize, Adam!" said I, as we came above deck again, where the crew were at work getting aboard us the stores from the *Deliverance* under Godby's watchful eye.

"Aye, we were fortunate, Martin," pausing to view this busy scene, "and all with scarce a blow and but five men lost, and they mostly by sunstroke or snake-bite; we could ha' taken the city also had I been so minded."

" 'Twas marvellous achievement for man so timid, Adam!" quoth I.

"Nay, comrade, I did but smite the enemy unbeknown and where least expected; 'twas simple enough. See now, Martin," said he, pinching his chin and averting his head, "I am very fain to learn more of —to hear your adventures—you shall tell me of—of 'em if you will, but later, for we sail on the flood and I have much to do in consequence."

So I presently fell to pacing the broad deck alone, dreaming on the future and in my heart a song of gratitude to God. Presently to me comes Godby:

"Lord, Mart'n!" said he, hitching fiercely at the broad belt of his galligaskins. "Here's been doin's o' late, pal, doin's as outdoes all other doin's as ever was done! Talk o' glory? Talk o' fame? There's enough on't aboard this here ship t' last every man on us all his days and longer. And what's more to the p'int, Mart'n, there's gold! And silver! In bars! Aye, pal, shoot me if 'tisn't a-laying in the hold like so much ballast! Cap'n Adam hath give his share to be divided atwixt us, which is noble in him and doeth us a power o' good!"

"Why, the men deserve it; 'twas a desperate business, Godby!"

"Aye, pal, good lads every one, though we had Cap'n Adam to lead 'em. 'Twas ever 'Come' wi' him! Ten minutes arter our first salvo the fort was ours, their guns spiked, an' we running for the harbour, Sir Adam showing the way. And, Lord! To hear the folk in the tower, you'd ha' thought 'twas the last trump—such shrieks and howls, Mart'n. So, hard in Cap'n Adam's wake we scrambled aboard this ship, she laying nighest to shore and well under the guns o' the fort as we'd just spiked so mighty careful, d'ye see, and here was some small disputation wi' steel and pistol, and her people was very presently swimming or rowing for it. So 'twas hoist sail, up anchor and away, and though this galleon is no duck, being something lubberly on a wind, she should bear us home well enough. 'Tis long since I last clapped eye on old England, and never a day I ha'n't blessed that hour I met wi' you at the 'Hop-pole,' for I'm rich, pal, rich, though I'd give a lot for a glimpse o' the child I left a babe and a kiss from his bonny mother."

Thus, walking the broad deck of this stout ship that was soon to bear us (and myself especially) to England and a new life, I hearkened to God-be-here Jenkins, who talked, his eyes now cocked aloft at spars or rigging, now observing the serene blue distances, now upon the boats plying busily to and fro, until one of the men came to say the last of our stores was aboard. And presently, being summoned, Adam appeared on the lofty poop in all the bravery of flowing periwig and 'broidered coat.

"Ha, Mart'n," sighed Godby, hitching at his belt as we went to meet him, "I love him best in buff and steel, though he'll ever be my cap'n, pal. There aren't what you'd call a lot of him, neither, but what there is goeth a prodigious long way in steel or velvet. Talk o' glory! Talk o' fame! Pal, glory's a goblin and fame's a phantom compared wi' Cap'n Sir Adam Penfeather, and you can keel haul, burn and hang me else!"

This night at moonrise we warped out from our anchorage and with drums beating and fifes sounding merrily, stood out into the great deep and never a heart that did not leap at thought of home and England. And now cometh my lady, dressed in gown I thought marvellous becoming, and herself beautiful beyond all women, as I told her, whereat she cast down her eyes and smoothed her dainty silks with her pretty hands. "Fie, Martin!" said she, mighty demure. "Is it well to be so extravagant in praise of your own?" Which last words put me to such ecstasy that I fell dumb forthwith; noting the which, she came a little nearer to slip her cool fingers into mine, "Though, indeed," quoth she, "I am glad to find you so observant! And my hair? Doth it please you, thus?" And now I saw her silky tresses (and for all their mutilation) right cunningly ordered, and amid their beauty that same wooden comb I had made for her on the island. "Well, dear sir?" said she, leaning nearer. At this, being ever a man scant of words (and the deck deserted hereabouts) I kissed her. And now, hand in hand, we stood silent awhile to watch this cruel land of Darien fade upon our sight. At last she turned and I also, to view that vast horizon that lay before us.

"What see you, yonder in the distance, dear Martin?" she questioned.

"Yourself!" said I. "You fill my world. God make me worthy! Aye, in the future—ever beside me henceforth, I do see you, my Damaris!"

"Why, to be sure, loved man! But what more?"

"I want for no more!"

"Nay, do but look!" said she, soft cheek to mine. "There I do see happiness, fortune, honours—and—mayhap, if God is kind to us——" She stopped, with sound like a little sob.

"What, my Joan?" I questioned, fool-like.

"Greater blessings——"

"But," said I, "what should be greater——"

"Ah, Martin—dear—cannot you guess?"

"Why, Joan—oh, my beloved!" But stepping out of my hold, she fled from me. "Nay," cried I, "do not leave me so soon."

"I must, dear Martin. You—you will be wanting to speak with Adam——"

"Not I—Lord, no!"

"Why, then—you shall!" said she and vanished into the roundhouse forthwith, leaving me wondering like the dull fellow I was until (and all at once) I understood and my wonder changed to joy so great I might scarce contain myself; wherefore, beholding Adam coming, I hasted to meet him and had clapped him in my arms or ever he was aware.

"Marry us, Adam!" said I. "Marry us, man!"

"What, ha' ye just thought on't at last, Martin?"

"Aye, I have!"

"Tush!" said he. "'Twas all arranged by my lady and me hours agone. Come into the coach."

And thus, upon the high seas, Adam (being both captain and magistrate) married us forthwith, and because I had no other, I wed my Damaris with my signet ring whereon was graven the motto of my house,

viz: a couchant leopard and the words, "Rouse me
not." And who so sweet and grave as my dear lady
as she made the responses and hearkened to Adam,
and he mighty impressive. For witnesses we had Master Penruddock the surgeon and Godby, and now, my
lady retiring, we must crack a bottle, all four, though
I know not what we drank.

And presently Adam drew me out upon the quarter-
deck, there to walk with me a while under a great
moon.

"Martin," said he suddenly, "you have come by
rough seas and mighty roundabout course to your happiness, but there be some do never make this blessed
haven all their days."

"God comfort them, poor souls!" quoth I.

"Amen!" said he; and then in changed voice, and
his keen gaze aloft amid the swelling sail, "What o'
the lady Joanna, shipmate?" So I told him all the
best I remembered of her and described how nobly she
had died; and he pacing beside me said never a word.

"Martin," said he, when I had made an end, "I am
a mighty rich man, yet for all this, I shall be something
solitary, I guess."

"Never in this world, Adam, so long as liveth my
dear lady——"

"Your wife, comrade—'tis a sweet word!"

"Aye—my wife. And then, am I not your sworn
brother? So like brothers will we live together in
England, and friends always!" And hereupon I
clasped an arm about him.

"This is well, Martin," said he, gripping my hand.
"Aye, 'tis mighty well, for nought under heaven is
there to compare with true friendship, except it be
the love of a noble woman. So now go, comrade, go
to her who hath believed in you so faithfully, hath
steadfastly endured so much for you—get you to your
wife!"

Ingram Content Group UK Ltd.
Milton Keynes UK
UKHW022037140323
418579UK00005B/117